Withdrawn

KIMIKO
AND THE
ACCIDENTAL PROPOSAL

BY FORTHRIGHT

FORTHWRITES.COM

Amaranthine Saga, Book 2
Kimiko and the Accidental Proposal

Copyright © 2018 by FORTHRIGHT
ISBN: 978-1-63123-064-6

TWINKLE PRESS

because I like to make you wonder

TABLE OF CONTENTS

KIMIKO

AND THE
ACCIDENTAL
PROPOSAL

1

RUNT

Eloquence's resolve wavered. Rumbles of rowdy good humor drifted across the ice-bitten garden, which meant Dad was busy. Too busy for a son's petty grievances and injured pride. But he had to *try*, for Ever's sake if not his own. And soon. Time was as short as the fading day. The winter solstice had slipped past, and the New Year was fast approaching. "Tonight, then," he promised himself. "Provided they don't crack a second cask of star wine."

He tested the air for telltale scents. Today's guests were a blend he knew well enough—wolf, cat, fox, and dragon. A meeting of the Five.

Over the past few decades, Eloquence had grown accustomed to the comings and goings of his father's assorted friends. Few Amaranthine mingled outside their clans except to establish an enclave or cooperative, but Harmonious Starmark wasn't one to

1

enforce boundary lines. Dad had never liked barriers.

Giving up, Eloquence turned toward the pavilion he shared with his younger brothers and all but ran into an elder one. Sly dog.

"What's with the glare, runt?" Prospect's perpetual grin widened. "You always used to like our little games."

"When I was *a pup*." Eloquence ducked out from under his brother's heavy arm. Quen was no longer the youngest Starmark, but that didn't stop his three older brothers from reminding him of his place within the pack. This amounted to a whole lot of tussling and teasing, with an ego-wrecking range of embarrassing stories thrown in for good measure.

"Not my fault you're too lazy to mark corners." Prospect mussed his hair, irreparably loosening Eloquence's heavy, auburn braid. "What would Uncle Laud say?"

"That a downwind approach is as rude inside the den as out."

"Granted." Prospect's copper eyes sparkled. "But seriously, Quen. You should make *some* effort. I'm not the only one on the prowl."

"Journalists wouldn't dare. Not after the last time."

"Don't say I didn't warn you. But speaking of pups, I'll loan you mine."

All this while, Prospect had been carelessly cradling a dozing newborn, his third child. Swaddled in a blanket lavishly embroidered with copper ribbon rosettes, she fit neatly in the crook of his arm.

"If your bondmate put you on baby duty, who am I to interfere?" But Eloquence was already reaching for the newest member of the Starmark clan. It wasn't little Clarion's fault that her dad couldn't tune his instrument with a little one hobbling

2

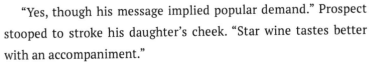

his hands. "Dad asked for you?"

"Yes, though his message implied popular demand." Prospect stooped to stroke his daughter's cheek. "Star wine tastes better with an accompaniment."

"I don't mind." This was both trust and a treat. "Lyric and Lavish are always so quick to carry her off, Ever and I barely get a turn. Rise even grumbles."

"Further proof she's my girl. We're *both* in high demand." Prospect's gloating smile faded, and his tone took a turn toward the serious. "I heard you're to be recognized soon. That's good. You've waited long enough."

Eloquence could feel embarrassment burn into the tips of his ears. There was a reason his brothers had nicknamed him *runt*.

On the day he was born, his mother had died. No one would give him any details, but according to the pack's songs and stories, Aurora Starmark had clung to life long enough to protect his passage into the world. She could no longer run with them, but her strength had not gone from the pack. Her influence lingered. Many of Quen's sisters had her daintier chin and fine brows. And there were subtler legacies—quick wits, quiet manners, and a fondness for stringed instruments.

For whatever reason, Eloquence had always been small for his age. Standing tall, he barely reached his brothers' shoulders, but his hands and feet were large enough to suggest that he hadn't yet reached his full growth. And so Dad kept putting off his attainment, waiting for him to grow into his paws.

"I've been old enough for a long time now," Eloquence said stiffly. He was nearly twice the age Valor had been when the pack recognized his next-older brother as an adult.

"Everyone knows it." For once, Prospect didn't tease. "You know, Anna's the one who put her foot down."

Eloquence had no doubt that had been a *lively* conversation. And his step-mother's bark was nothing compared to her bite. "I'll be sure to thank her."

With a final brush of knuckles across his daughter's fuzz of auburn hair, Prospect said, "I need to go."

"You know where to find us."

His brother stalled long enough to press a kiss to Clarion's forehead. A good sign that his heart was in the right place. But then he grinned and kissed Eloquence's forehead as if he were a half-weaned nuzzler again.

Quen felt fully justified in delivering a parting kick to Prospect's shin.

Fussing with Clarion's blanket, he meandered slowly toward his rooms, a sway to his steps.

Across the way, his brother was already tuning his instrument. Low notes quickly ascended in a glissade that led seamlessly into a sprightly tune more suited to dancing than drinking. Quen flowed through the steps of one of the walking dances that would be part of this little one's whelping feast.

Clarion opened her eyes, and he chuckled. "Do you hear your sire? He plays for you."

She squeaked and squirmed. Only then did Eloquence notice the source of her dismay, a figure standing quietly at the end of the porch. Watching him. And probably waiting on him.

With a soothing rumble, Eloquence strolled on. "Good nose,

little one. You found a stranger, but he's a friend to this pack. Trust your Uncle Quen."

Her answering gurgle put a smile on his face. And a pang in the secret places of his heart. Prospect was so lucky.

At the moment, all Eloquence could claim was a vague sense of being cornered. But he covered his surprise, tossing off a casual gesture of welcome and peace. "Good day, Spokesperson Twineshaft."

2

THE STARMARK TRIBUTE

r good evening, if you prefer," Eloquence continued. The deepening blue of the sky would soon be showing stars. He drew up before the spokesperson for the cat clans. "My brother may hold out hope that Clarion will inherit his talent for music, but I think she shows a tracker's instinct."

"My apologies for disturbing your dance partner. Whatever her path, I am sure she will be a credit to her den." Hisoka offered a finger, which Clarion promptly grasped and gummed. "I was hoping to meet you, Eloquence. Can you spare a few minutes?"

He dipped his head. It was only polite ... and probably a great honor. But Quen was a little wary of Hisoka's pleasantries. They often led to suggestions that were more like requests, which could be taken as commands, and always—*always*—demanded a great deal of effort to see through. Like the time the cat had suggested Harmonious learn Spanish. So of course Dad made

6

sure the *whole pack* was fluent.

"I wanted to personally thank you for agreeing to join the inaugural class at New Saga High School. I'll rest much easier knowing you're involved."

In point of fact, Eloquence *hadn't* agreed; Dad had volunteered him. And if his father had been able to spare the time this evening, Quen had planned to argue his way out of the commitment. Hisoka probably knew, or at least guessed as much. So Quen filed his grievance at the source. "I'm too old for this."

"But you look the part."

Hardly a compliment. "I've waited for attainment longer than anyone. That's embarrassing enough without being pushed into a group of human children." Bitterness sharpened his words. "They'll assume I'm like them."

"Yes, they will." Hisoka's hand settled on his shoulder. "I would have thought you'd appreciate the respite, given the usual round of social obligations triggered by a young male's advancement."

Eloquence's eyes stung. He couldn't tell if the cat was being coy or if he was truly ignorant. Since all of Quen's older sisters were bonded and building dens of their own, it was *possible* that Hisoka hadn't realized he had nine older siblings. "I will be spared. I am the Starmark clan's tribute."

"Yes."

So he *did* know. "Then why...?" Emotion cracked his voice in an embarrassingly adolescent manner, and his face burned. The more he insisted he was an adult, the more childish he sounded.

Hisoka eased even closer and carefully took Eloquence's hand, the one that wasn't supporting Clarion. "This has been an awkward season for you—not quite full-grown, yet full of years. I'm glad your father will finally acknowledge your maturity."

Eloquence nodded jerkily, but he kept his gaze fixed on his niece's face. She'd drifted back to sleep after Hisoka reclaimed his finger.

"I do believe you'll find common ground with the humans in your class. In one year, they'll graduate, but they don't really know what they want, let alone how to achieve it. And they're under a lot of pressure to make the right choice, to distinguish themselves, to succeed. Except most of them really only feel trapped and confused."

"Are you saying that's how I feel?"

"I am saying that this is the usual state of mind for those who stand between adolescence and adulthood."

Irritation flashed so hotly, it was a good thing Eloquence was holding a baby. He forced himself to stay calm lest his spoiling mood rouse her. But even the fact that he was shorter than Hisoka was becoming a source of frustration. Why did the cat know all his sore spots?

"While I want Dad's blessing, I don't need it to know that I left childhood behind long ago." His chin lifted. "What is the median age of your Amaranthine volunteers?"

Hisoka's gaze never wavered. "All of our student representatives have passed but are close to the two-century mark."

"And how many have reached their attainment?"

A slight hesitation, a wry smile. "Nearly all."

"Am I your only straggler?"

"Yes."

"I have three-hundred and eighty-three years," he said wearily. "Look to my nieces and nephews for a Starmark representative. I know my place, and it is here."

"None of your packmates have the qualities I require."

And suddenly, Eloquence noticed that Hisoka wasn't simply holding his hand, he was gently kneading his palm. A soothing gesture, to be sure, but focused on the calluses he'd developed through long years of training with Uncle Laud and with Uncle Karoo-ren.

"You *need* a tribute?" He'd overheard snatches of concerned conversations here and there, but maybe he shouldn't jump to conclusions. There were many tasks given to a tenth child. "Because you need someone to speak for our Kith?"

Hisoka gestured to the negative.

Which really only left one sobering possibility. "You expect trouble."

"Expectation and preparation are certainly part of my job description." His smile was bland. "Didn't I mention how much easier I'll rest knowing you're at New Saga? I'm sure I did."

Eloquence mounted the steps to the pavilion that had been his home ever since Dad had given him over to Uncle Laud for training. He eased through the door. In the corner, a large dog raised his head, copper eyes catching the light.

Rise's tail thumped against tatami. *Welcome back.*

He grunted an acknowledgment as he toed out of his boots and wriggled free of his socks. "How's Ever?"

Peaceful.

The Kith curled protectively around Quen's greatest responsibility. Sure, Ever still spent much of his day with Mum, but he slept here. And that made *this* his den. Because even before Ever was weaned, Dad had settled matters. Eloquence was Ever's big brother, babysitter, and bodyguard. They belonged to each other in much the way Eloquence belonged to Uncle Laud. A fosterling.

Did he change his mind?

Eloquence leaned into the big auburn dog's flank and slid to the floor. "It's no use. I have to go."

Rise whined sympathetically.

Stroking his baby brother's silky hair, Quen gently tugged at a pointed puppy ear. "Wake up, little brother. I brought you a baby."

The ear flickered, and Ever's head popped up, nose already twitching. "Clare!"

"Yes, Clarion is here." He patted a place at his side. "Uncle Prospect needs us to protect her while he plays music."

The boy crawled closer. "Baby," he crooned. "Ours?"

"Yes, she's our packmate." As the boy gave her blanket an experimental poke, Quen murmured, "Gently, Ever. Mind your claws."

"I mind," he promised.

Born the same year as the Emergence, Ever Starmark was the most famous hybrid on the planet. His mother, Dad's second bondmate, was human, and Ever's very existence was considered proof that peace wasn't just possible, it offered new possibilities for the human and inhuman races.

Eloquence slouched into Rise and smiled at Ever's shifting expression. He knew every quirk and dip of those auburn ears, the

10

swirl of emotion through shining eyes, and the eager thump of his stubby tail. If Quen was completely honest, Ever was the main reason he'd dragged his feet about enrollment. He couldn't exactly bring a three-year-old to class.

How was he supposed to explain high school to Ever?

"I don't have a choice," he whispered.

The Kith nosed the top of his head and licked his ear. *I will be here.*

"Thanks." Eloquence tangled his fingers in Rise's fur. "I'll be counting on you."

But Quen's frown deepened. Because Hisoka's subtle request had definitely carried the weight of a command. And although Eloquence had never attended any kind of school, he'd known students, seen textbooks, and heard enough grievances about homework to strongly suspect that his immediate future would require large amounts of *effort*.

And quite possibly danger.

3

MIDDLE SISTER

Kimiko joined the flow of people entering the subway's rear car and dropped gratefully onto an open seat. Her trek through the crowded shopping district had been worthwhile, but exhausting. Every housewife in Keishi must be doing last-minute errands before New Year's Eve.

Settling her bags between her feet, she draped her forearms over her knees and peered toward the back. At first, she couldn't see past the incoming passengers, but once they sorted into their seats, she had a clear view of the train's security post. Usually, these were manned by an officer and their Kith partner, and she loved catching the eye of these sentient animals.

Today was a little different. No, *a lot* different.

Her curious gaze locked with the alert yellow eyes of an Amaranthine male. Clan was obvious. Even with the concession he'd made by donning the starched shirt and pleated pants worn by

12

security officers, his long hair was held back by a furry headband, and the top two buttons of his shift were undone, revealing a colorful collection of beaded necklaces. Definitely a wolf. Maybe even an Elderbough tracker. She couldn't see which crest he wore on his armband.

His eyebrows lifted, and a faint smile touched his lips.

Whoops. Kimiko quickly offered a series of silent messages—embarrassed apology, one of the warmer greetings, the hope for peace, and sincere gratitude for the protection his presence offered. People around her probably didn't even notice. Amaranthine communication wasn't like human sign language, which depended heavily on hand gestures. Their expressions were often subtler, relying on nuances of posture.

Those yellow eyes took on an appreciative shine, and he responded in kind—surprised delight, acknowledgement of her reaver status, a promise of harmony. And after a moment's pause, a wholly unnecessary—and intensely personal—compliment on the sweetness of her soul.

Which was really very kind, but Kimiko didn't let it go to her head. It was practically the *only* nice thing he could have said, given her low rating. But it was still nice to hear, and she flashed him a smile.

A twittering giggle snagged her attention, and she tuned in to a whispered argument across the aisle.

"No, *you* ask him."

"*You're* the one who's curious."

"Shhh!"

Kimiko turned, and two high school girls were suddenly

fascinated by their phones. This again? She scratched the side of her face and glanced sheepishly back at the wolf.

He was laughing at her. Or them. Or maybe this whole silly situation. Any Amaranthine—with their keener senses—could detect something as basic as gender. With discreet gestures, the wolf called the human girls blind, he complimented Kimiko's skill as a trickster, and he declared the advantage hers.

Another kindness. But really, she didn't need cheering up. It happened *all the time*. If it had bothered her, she could have changed her appearance or behavior. But she'd come to enjoy making people wonder.

"*Ask* him."

"He must be a reaver. That tunic, for instance."

"Could be a knock-off. Besides, you can't tell a reaver by looking. They're human, but with *skills*."

"Would you date a reaver?"

"Depends on his skills."

"*Eee*, I can't believe you *said* that!"

Kimiko wondered what these girls would think if they knew how totally unromantic reaver marriages usually were. It was hard to get excited about pedigree reports, progeny projections, and the filing of a dozen or more spousal applications. Often for a person you'd never met.

As one of three unmatched daughters, she knew *more* than enough about the process.

Even though looks and personality were of secondary consideration, Kimiko's mother was forever comparing her to her older sister. Noriko was gentle and lovely and petite, just like

Mama had been, back when she caught their father's eye.

Fourteen-year-old Sakiko was promisingly pretty, if a bit taller than average. But Kimiko's younger sister would never be mistaken for a boy. Not when her straight black hair hung like a satin curtain almost to her knees.

Kimiko was tall and flat-chested, and she kept her hair cropped. Reaver attire was unisex, and the freedom it offered only encouraged an unladylike stride. Her boots, which were standard issue for the Ingress Academy uniform, made her big feet look even bigger. Having grown up in a very normal human community, Kimiko knew she held exactly zero feminine appeal. But as a slightly-too-pretty boy, she turned heads.

Most of the time, she ignored the whispers, giggles, and long looks. But once in a while, when the circumstances fit, she was silly in her own way. Kimiko understood the elation of being noticed. She so rarely was.

So as the train neared her stop, she tucked her chin, making it even harder for her admirers to catch on. The hum of the subway changed pitch, and an automated voice announced Kikusawa's station. Kimiko gathered up her shopping bags and, gazing up through the fringe of her bangs, caught the girls watching.

She smirked, then strode out, adding some swagger to her step. Her harmless little performance was rewarded by gasps, giggles, and bright smiles.

Curious if the wolf had seen, Kimiko continued along the side of the train to the back window. He was there, grinning now, all fang and fraternity. And he bid her farewell in a way that roughly translated *you've made me glad our paths crossed.*

Kimiko returned the gesture, waved goodbye in a completely human way, then mounted the stairs to street level with even more spring in her step than usual.

Home for Kimiko was Kikusawa, an aging neighborhood within Keishi, full of small shops and nosy neighbors. Faded paint, rusted metal, curling advertisements tacked to walls. She supposed Kikusawa was a little on the shabby side, but she preferred to focus on the good parts. Vivid bins of satsuma oranges at the grocers. The tempting sizzle of croquettes, served piping hot in paper sleeves. Sticky-sweet burned sugar smells coming from the tea shop that grilled their dango out front to lure in customers.

People lived over shops or behind businesses. Poky alleys hid the entrances to restaurants, the barber, a hardware store, and the candy shop Kimiko had frequented since she could walk. She hoped this part of the city—*her* part—would never change. Everyone bought their produce from the Nakamura's and their fish from Satoh and Sons. The Smiling Cat was famous for its western-style lunch menu, and The House of the Noble Chrysanthemum sold traditional sweets.

It was a matter of pride to shop locally, which made Kimiko self-conscious about her collection of bags. But some things couldn't be bought in Kikusawa.

"Kimi-chan," called Mrs. Miura, who was sprinkling salt on the public bath house's front step. Wrinkles might hide the little old woman's eyes, but she never missed a thing. "Adding to your collection?"

"Yes, Auntie." Kimiko hurried to her side and held out one of the bags. "I found these two stations over. Limited editions for the New Year."

Mrs. Miura pawed gently through the bag, humming and clucking. "I used to like these when I was a girl. My father worked for Junzi, you know."

She knew that, of course. Mrs. Miura had told her the story dozens of times. The local chocolate-maker was famous throughout Japan for the superior quality of their sweets and for the artistry in their packaging. "My grandfather used to buy them for me."

"I used to play with Miyabe-kun." She lifted one of the squat chocolate bars, foil wrapped, with a heavy paper sleeve adorned with plum blossoms. "He always had a sweet tooth."

"Me, too. Would you like that one, Auntie?"

"No, no, dear." Mrs. Miura returned the chocolate to her bag. "Didn't you go a long way for these? Only bring your book down sometime soon."

"As soon as I add these," Kimiko promised.

She'd been collecting labels from Junzi chocolate bars since grade school, when she'd first realized what *limited edition* meant. Her grandfather had helped her find them, buy them, and organize them. And he'd never left Keishi without bringing home Junzi chocolate bars exclusive to other prefectures.

Kimiko missed him terribly.

But her usual trick mostly worked. Focus on the good parts, like the tradition he had started and she would carry on. Not out of

17

duty, but for love.

With a parting wave for Mrs. Miura, Kimiko continued homeward. Theirs was a tight-knit community, mostly overlooked by outsiders and ruled by the Kikusawa Business Association and the Ladies Neighborhood Improvement Committee. They had their own schools—preschool through middle—and a community center where folks gathered to play shogi, mahjong, or table tennis. Kimiko passed the pharmacy, a twenty-four hour convenience store, and old Mr. Ryota's steamy oden cart.

"Miyabe-kun!"

Kimiko waved cheerily at Mr. Fujiwara, who owned the butcher shop. The deep-voiced man with his craggy features and bloody apron used to frighten her when she was small. But there was a good nature behind his gruff way of speaking.

He beckoned her over to the window at the front of his shop and its brightly-lit glass case. Making a big show of looking both ways, he passed her a steamed bun.

"Are you sure?" she asked. The glossy white bread was hot against her palm.

Mr. Fujiwara pointed knowingly at the bags looped over her arms. "Sweets aren't strength, and you'll be needing yours."

"Thank you!" Kimiko broke the bun in half, releasing a fragrant cloud of steam. "Will we see you up top tonight?"

The man, who had gone to school with her mother, patted his muscular bicep. "You can count on me and my boys! These are the times when friends and neighbors rally together!"

"Until later." Kimiko waved and called, "Thank you, again!"

Many of the shops had closed up early. No doubt they were

already hard at work, helping with the finishing touches for tomorrow's New Year's Eve festivities.

She'd polished off the last of the pork bun by the time she reached the pair of ancient cherry trees that marked the turning to the elementary school. Then a covered bus stop. Beyond was a steep, forested slope, thick with evergreens. Nestled beneath the overhanging boughs was a long, narrow stairway, its foot framed by a distinctive red arch and a pair of crouching stone dragons.

Home for Kimiko Miyabe was Kikusawa, but especially Kikusawa Shrine. Because the Miyabe family had always lived on the outermost edge of the In-between, serving the human community as shrinekeepers.

ʮ

KIKUSAWA SHRINE

re you waiting for me?" Kimiko called.

"Not particularly. But welcome home, anyhow."

Her younger sister was sitting on the third step from the bottom, a round cushion protecting her posterior from frigid stone. The full legs of her red hakama billowed above the neat set of her feet, and her long hair pooled artfully at her side. She made a lovely picture. And knew it.

It was Kimiko's private opinion that her sister only exerted herself if a minimum of three reasons hung in the balance. Like a strategy quota.

Sakiko took in her appearance with a sweeping gaze. "Your priorities are as baffling as ever."

Kimiko hunched her shoulders. "Daddy said I could go."

"I'm not sure we should be relying on *his* priorities, either." Her sister's chin lifted. "You need to make the best possible impression the day after tomorrow. Our future depends on it."

"One year at New Saga High School isn't going to add any polish to our pedigree."

"No, but you'll be meeting important people." Sakiko shook a finger at her. "Connections lead to contracts!"

While she didn't necessarily share her sister's ambitious brand of optimism, Kimiko couldn't deny that New Saga represented a unique chance. All members of the Kikusawa branch of the Miyabe family were reavers in good standing, but their numbers and ranking had diminished over the generations.

The only way to bring up the quality of their pedigree was through marriage. But reavers from the best families didn't apply for lackluster girls. And the daughters of Kikusawa Shrine had few chances to make the kinds of connections that might improve their circumstances.

That was mostly their mother's doing.

Although Sakiko had a point about their father's priorities.

Mama was a local girl—not a reaver—but Daddy had brought her into the family. His bride remained blissfully ignorant of the In-between until Noriko was of the usual age to enroll at Ingress. Then came an almighty falling out and an intensely awkward coming out. But Kikuko Miyabe flat-out refused to uphold reaver tradition and send her children away.

People would have *talked*.

So Noriko, Kimiko, and Sakiko had attended the neighborhood kindergarten, primary, and middle schools. On the condition that they forgo any extracurricular clubs in favor of reaver training at home.

Until her entrance exam for Ingress Academy two years ago, Kimiko's way of life was barely distinguishable from that of any other girl in Kikusawa. At least outwardly. Because those extra lessons at home had brought a covert stream of intriguing tutors. At the beginning, Kimiko hadn't understood that many of these people weren't human.

One of her earliest memories was of a smooth face and strange eyes, soft hands and a gentle smile. She could remember reaching up ... and the stranger reaching back. And being called *puppy*. Now, she understood that their special guest had been brought in to assess the girls' potential.

Grandma's crisp words cut across the good memory. "*This* is what comes of marrying for love."

But then her grandfather had said, "A star is a star, no matter how brightly it shines."

And that had made Kimiko so happy, because the Star Festival had already been her favorite, even back then.

She quickly learned to tell the difference between her human and inhuman instructors. The reavers were usually Daddy's old classmates, former teachers, or acquaintances from other temples and shrines. Amaranthine visitors were usually acquaintances of her grandfather, or more accurately, of her grandfather's grandfather. Their memories were as long as their lifespans, and they were willing to show kindness to the descendants of a friend.

Piecemeal. Secretive. Detached. Eclectic. It was like being stuck in the very middle of the middle. Her childhood had rung with constant warnings from Grandma about keeping the family secret from kids at school. She'd then enrolled at Ingress Academy a full decade behind other reavers her age—unknown and unremarkable.

New Saga really *might* help matters. And the only reason Kimiko would have this opportunity was because Sakiko had applied on her behalf.

"What are you even doing down here?" Kimiko asked.

Her sister patted a squat clay pot at her side. One grandpa used to use during certain ceremonies and rituals. "Checking for icy patches."

"No, really." Because the south-facing stairway needed salting about as often as it needed purifying. "What are you waiting for?"

"There might be a packet."

"Our mailbox is at the back gate."

Sakiko lifted her eyes to the sky as if asking for patience. "I'm waiting for a herald."

Kimiko followed her gaze, scanning the scattering of puffy clouds in the winter-blue sky. "Are we actually *expecting* one?"

"Why not? This week is the most popular for wedding feasts, betrothal announcements, apprenticeship postings, and class advancements. Any applications filed on Dichotomy Day could still arrive today. Or responses to applications."

"I suppose so." Kimiko's heart seized at a disturbing thought. "You didn't file any applications on my behalf, did you?"

"Would I do that?"

Kimiko groaned. "*Please* say you didn't."

Sakiko shook her head. "We need to get Noriko contracted first. And if nothing better turns up at New Saga, you can sift through her spares."

She nodded. That was pretty much what she'd expected. After all, they were searching for young men who were interested in transferring permanently to Kikusawa and serving as shrinekeepers. Far from a typical career path. Any reavers who applied for Noriko would fit the same profile Kimiko needed.

Grandma was adamant that the girls stay, and Mama showed a shockingly ambitious streak. Reavers were quite fashionable now, and she was all for securing the best for Noriko. Only Daddy seemed unhappy with the family's current obsession with genetic inheritances, and Kimiko wasn't entirely sure why. This is how matches were made in the In-between, with an eye to continuing—and ideally, strengthening—one's line.

Sakiko's lips pressed thin. "I filed thirty blind applications and added Noriko's name to a couple of circulating lists. We extended the search parameters."

Kimiko shuffled her feet. They'd searched locally at first, mostly focusing on graduates of Ingress Academy. "What's the extent now?"

"Worldwide."

A drastic change that smacked of desperation. "Hasn't anyone applied for her?"

"Yes, but none of those men can *improve* our situation." Sakiko pouted. "We can do better."

Kimiko started to say that they really couldn't do worse. Except ... they *could*. "I think Abe Fujiwara is interested in Noriko."

"The butcher's son. Yes, I'd noticed." Sakiko propped her chin on her fists. "Worse, Noriko's finally noticed."

"You don't think she would ...?"

"Based on the flush in her cheeks and the shine in her eyes, I'd say our big sister is perilously close to repeating a pattern that could doom us to ever-deepening mediocrity and eventual expulsion from the In-between." Sakiko's lips trembled for a moment, but her conviction was rock-steady. "You *need* to make the best possible impression at New Saga."

5

CLASS THREE C

In keeping with reaver tradition, New Saga High School began its inaugural term on the first day of the New Year. After opening assembly, Kimiko walked slowly through the halls, marveling at the sheer number of Amaranthine in attendance.

Yes, she'd had afternoon tutors from this or that clan. And sure, there were Amaranthine advisers, lecturers, and mentors among the staff at Ingress Academy. But there, most of the teachers and all of the students had been reavers. Here, at least a quarter of the student body wasn't human.

She'd been fascinated by the clans all her life, but from a distance. Everything she knew from stories and fables now felt secondhand and stale. Because *this* was vividly, dazzlingly *real*. Did reavers of the upper ranks get to mingle this freely with the Amaranthine? Envy pinched at her soul, but only for a moment.

Because she was intensely glad to be here.

She owed Sakiko *big time*.

Savor this. Never forget this. Kimiko slowed her steps even further, trying to prolong the minutes. She needed to collect every moment and keep it safe. They were limited editions in the truest, cruelest possible sense. This year might be the only time she'd ever have any lasting contact with the Amaranthine.

They were by far the most eye-catching students in the halls, since they were dressed for celebration. She recognized the colors and crests of a wide range of clans—bear, dove, horse, moth, deer. She'd even spotted a phoenix during the assembly.

Hisoka Twineshaft himself had delivered the opening address, reason enough for the news crews and paparazzi cordoned off in a sizeable section to one side of the auditorium. Spokesperson Twineshaft extolled New Saga students as the world's future, a generation committed to living in harmony. And he'd pressed home one surprising point: they *weren't* the same. And they didn't need to be. New Saga's students would be an example to the world—exploring their differences, finding their balance, forging the bonds of trust.

She guessed that this principle explained why New Saga had such an unusual dress code. In most schools in this part of the world, no matter what grade level, differences were banished by uniforms. New Saga's non-reavers held to this tradition with high-collared black uniforms with gold buttons for the boys, pleated skirts and wide collars with knotted scarves for the girls.

Kimiko herself was dressed in reaver garb—fitted breeches and plush winter tunics that came in a variety of muted colors depending on specialization. She wore the basic black of general studies. To her relief, most of the other reavers were the same. But several had already managed to distinguish themselves. Their tunics stood out. Willow and mulberry. Indigo and plum. Coffee and clay.

She jogged lightly up a few flights of stairs and paused at a window. The fourth floor view on this side of the building was impressive—snowy woods and a frozen lake. Property generously set aside for the school's use by Harmonious Starmark.

A rowdy group came up behind her, and someone clipped her shoulder in passing.

"Sorry! Didn't notice you there!" he exclaimed, hands upraised.

Wolves really *did* travel in packs, even here. And his remark stung more than it should have. As a reaver, she'd never had much presence.

"Oh, little sister. I'm as rude as I am clumsy." Light brown eyes wide, tail tucking, he reached for her hand. Then dropped it as if burned. He babbled to himself in another language, then switched back to Japanese. "I don't remember if I'm allowed to touch."

His accent was decidedly American.

Kimiko quickly signaled to reassure him and enunciated carefully. "Local citizens will shy away from the familiarity, but reavers will understand." Taking his hand between hers, she shyly added, "Brother wolf."

The Amaranthine's tail swayed, and Kimiko's heart swelled. He seemed like such a nice guy.

He glanced along the hall, where his two packmates waited. All three of the young wolves were quite tall, broad in the shoulder, with ebony skin and shaggy black hair. He called to them in English, and their posture shifted to indicate patience. And amusement.

With more confidence, he gathered both her hands into his own. "Ploom-ret Nightspangle, but everyone calls me Ploom."

"I'm Kimiko Miyabe, and I'm *fine*, Ploom. Go ahead with your packmates. We all need to get to class."

Bending until they were nose-to-nose, he softly repeated, "Kimiko Miyabe. I will remember."

"Find me anytime."

His fangs flashed in a grateful grin before he hurried away.

She followed more slowly, but not so far back that she didn't see which classroom the Nightspangle contingent entered. They were in Class 3-C.

The same as her.

Kimiko stepped through the classroom door and sized up the milling students. They looked like a bunch of middle schoolers at their first mixer. Only instead of boys on one end and girls on the other, their class had divided neatly into thirds.

All the Amaranthine stood at the front of the room; humans clustered at the back. And reavers fanned out between them, assuming their traditional role as gatekeepers, guardians, and go-betweens. Kimiko crossed to the long row of windows and, finding the sill wide enough, perched there to see what might happen next.

Moments later, a stocky, graying woman in a willow-green tunic strolled in and smiled sweetly. "Welcome again to New Saga! I'm Ms. Reeves, and I'll be your homeroom teacher. My reaver designation is diplomat, and it will be my pleasure to guide your learning this year."

Kimiko tried to place her accent, though it was faint. A lot of diplomats spent their internships in Belgium, so maybe French? She wondered if travel had contributed to the woman's air of confident competence. Must be nice.

Ms. Reeves surveyed them, blue eyes taking on a shine. "First things first, we must overcome all this shyness. We'll be sorting you into triads."

"What's a triad?" called one of the girls from the tight cluster at the back.

Their teacher acknowledged the question with a nod. "You'll be dividing into integrated groups of three. Those representing the general populace, please take a seat at one of the tables."

A few students moved to obey, spreading out.

Kimiko was used to classrooms with long rows of single desks, but this one almost looked like a restaurant, with comfortable seats arranged around three-sided tables. She was paying attention to other differences now. High ceilings, windows lining two walls, smooth wood underfoot, and an utter lack of light fixtures. Hanging baskets filled two corners of the room with greenery, and ... yes, she was quite sure she caught a brief flutter and flash of Ephemera hiding amidst the leaves.

"One each, please," Ms. Reeves called when two girls tried to stick together. "Since triads will remain together for the duration of the year, I will ask our Amaranthine students to decide who they would like as a partner."

"Do Rivven always get to pick first?"

Kimiko flinched at the popular—if improper—word choice, but the boy seemed more curious than anything.

"The correct term is *Amaranthine*," Ms. Reeves said firmly. "And yes. This is both a matter of courtesy and necessity. The Amaranthine will make their decision based on different criteria than you might expect. Things no human can sense or alter."

"Like scent," offered one of the reaver girls. "And the clarity and resonance of our souls."

"Yes." Ms. Reeves signaled to her inhuman students while she talked. "When you are chosen, it will be because your classmate thinks they can make lasting peace with you."

Another hand popped up. "What do we do after we find a match?"

Kimiko had to lean to one side to see the short boy. A male phoenix stood behind him, both arms wrapped securely around his slender shoulders. Even though he wore the standard human uniform, the boy didn't look remotely uneasy in the Amaranthine's embrace.

Ms. Reeves glanced at her class list. "And you are...?"

"Akira Hajime, and this is my best friend Suuzu Farroost. We've been rooming together since middle school, so we've already made peace."

"Do you want to broaden your experience by trading partners?"

Immediately, Suuzu's hold tightened, and his eyes narrowed.

Akira's grin was apologetic. "We'd rather stick together, sensei."

"So I see." The woman offered peaceable signs. "Relax, Suuzu.

Your friendship with Akira is *exactly* the sort of camaraderie we're trying to encourage. You may consider yourself the first pair. Once we have a few more, I'll ask that our students of reaver descent present themselves for consideration."

Kimiko watched in fascination as the Amaranthine considered their options. Some hung back, allowing the wolves, dog, and bear to have first choice. She knew this wasn't any kind of hierarchy. Rather their sense of smell was keenest, so their needs were more particular.

An uneasy titter came from one side of the room, where a wolf clansman slowly wove between tables. He nodded politely to a couple of girls before offering his hand to a wide-eyed boy.

Ms. Reeves kept right on talking, her voice a calm backdrop to these activities. "Reavers, let your potential partners know your designation. I see most of you are undecided. That's fine. Your classmates may be the key to uncovering your unique aptitudes."

A soft gasp came from a table near Kimiko's perch. A burly young male with a crest from one of the bear clans had cornered the smallest girl in the class. She seemed to be trembling, which surprised Kimiko. Hadn't these people applied *knowing* they'd be in close contact with Amaranthine?

"My name is Brev." He crouched, balancing on the balls of his feet, clawed hands hanging loosely across his knees. "Will you tell me your name?"

Kimiko couldn't hear what the girl mumbled, but the bear with his shock of golden-brown hair smiled softly and joined her at the table.

If only finding suitable marriage applicants were half so simple.

Kimiko glanced around to check on Ploom, but the short boy suddenly stepped up and thrust out his hand. "Are you the sort who likes to be picked instead of doing her own picking? Because if you wait much longer, you won't *have* a choice."

Sliding from the sill, she realized he was right. Only two or three other reavers had yet to join a pair. "I suppose I do tend to wait and see."

"Akira Hajime," he reminded.

And when she accepted his handclasp, he held on.

6

FORMING A TRIAD

What do you say? Want to be our reaver?" And without giving her a chance to respond, he launched into a list of reasons they didn't *need* an intermediary.

She looked him over while she heard him out.

Akira was several centimeters shorter than Kimiko. He'd been quick to make himself comfortable—top button undone, sleeves rolled up, hands in pockets. Not that they stayed there. He gestured a lot with them and tended to go up on tiptoe when making a point. It all gave him a buoyant, enthusiastic air.

Kimiko liked him. But this decision—like so many others—wasn't truly hers to make. Bracing herself for disappointment, she sought Suuzu's gaze.

Unlike his friend, the phoenix gave away very little. His reserve was imposing, and this close, Kimiko could actually sense a little of

34

the strength he held in check. Suuzu was only a shade taller than she was and very slender. Brown skin, a hooked nose, and black hair that showed signs of product and combing ... and a lack of cooperation. Kimiko hoped her smile wouldn't be misunderstood, but she couldn't help cheering on those rebel curls. They softened the intimidating young male's strict demeanor.

Akira rocked back and forth on his heels. "Do you have a name?"

"Kimiko Miyabe." She belatedly offered her palms. "Do you think we can get along, Suuzu Farroost?"

"You do not offend my eyes, nor do you offend my senses." His hands settled over hers, hot and dry. "In truth, I did not notice you."

"Suuzu!" Akira punched his friend's arm and hissed, "She's a girl! *And* she's a reaver. Even I know that's kinda rude."

Akira was worried about her feminine sensibilities? This was the first time any guy had ever tried to defend her honor. Hardly necessary, but kind of cute.

Bewilderment settled on Suuzu's features, his strikingly orange eyes widening. And for the first time, he looked young.

Akira folded his arms over his chest and gruffly muttered, "Apologize to Kimi."

An increasingly flustered phoenix angled his face away, assuming a posture of regret. "I have been thoughtless. Please forgive my words. They were unnecessarily sharp."

"It's okay." Kimiko managed a small smile. "I rank pretty low, so Amaranthine don't usually register my presence when there are brighter souls around."

"Really?" Akira looked to Suuzu for confirmation. "Is that how it works?"

The phoenix's gaze sharpened, and Kimiko consciously slowed her breathing and relaxed her posture. Trust. Because there was little else she could offer. She'd passed her certification for tending during her first year at Ingress Academy, but hers wasn't the sort of soul that attracted interest. No one ever came to her for tending. But reavers of low ranking were encouraged to learn their limitations so they could work safely within them.

Kimiko hadn't been tapped by any of the High Amaranthine on campus, so she'd presented herself to the many Kith fostered at Ingress. Retired from active service, these were aged beasts whose limbs had grown creaky and whose sight was dimming. But their minds were sharp, and their wordless guidance had strengthened Kimiko's self-possession.

Suuzu finally said, "Not the brightest soul in this room, but certainly the brightest in our group."

Akira blinked, then burst out laughing. "There you have it, Kimi! You're our one and only reaver."

The phoenix gestured toward their table. "I will accept Kimiko Miyabe for your sake."

"Mine?" Akira led the way across the room. "How come she's mine?"

"You are in need of information a reaver possesses."

"And you're not?"

Suuzu pulled out a chair for his friend. "If I have questions, I will pose them."

"Kimi's not just a resource, you know." Akira waved her over and made her sit in his chair. "We're friends now."

The phoenix quietly took a seat.

Although he hadn't said a word, Akira frowned. "Oh, come on. I'm not asking you to take her as a nestmate or anything."

Kimiko knew—in the textbook way of knowing—that Amaranthine of the bird clans were slow to trust. She wasn't about to rush Suuzu, but Akira wasn't half so reticent. He was already calling her *Kimi*.

"We're a triad." Akira glanced at the front of the room before flipping his chair around and straddling it backwards. "You heard Hisoka-sensei. We're supposed to be setting a good example for the whole world."

Suuzu sighed.

"We've talked about this." Akira flapped a hand. "We're still roommates—*nestmates*. That won't change just because we make other friends."

Now that was interesting. Kimiko asked, "You consider Akira to be a nestmate?"

"He is mine." Suuzu's voice lowered. "He understands it as a bond of brotherhood."

Intrigued, she turned to the boy. "Hajime-kun, are you familiar with the nuances of such a pledge? An honor like this isn't given lightly, nor is it ever revoked."

"Fine by me." Akira grinned. "I like knowing he'll stick around forever. I'm an orphan, you know. So this is a big deal for me, having someone to rely on. Suuzu will always be here for me."

For the first time, Kimiko thought she understood why the world still needed reavers. Because even two friends, with all kinds of trust and loyalty already established, could miss nuances of meaning. She turned to Suuzu and jumbled several signals—

37

confusion, sympathy, apology, and a willingness to mediate.

Even though she hardly knew what she meant, Suuzu seemed to understand. "Enough, reaver. It is enough."

And with that Kimiko decided that she liked this young phoenix. He'd given a human boy something rare and precious. Even if Akira didn't understand everything, he expected to remain friends with Suuzu his whole life. Over time, and with the learning he'd receive here at New Saga, maybe Akira would move past the limits of impressions and assumptions ... into the realm of true understanding.

"Partners?" Kimiko stretched across the table, offering them each a hand.

"*Friends.*" Akira went one better, locking his fingers around her wrist and reaching for Suuzu.

The phoenix completed the link, and although he offered no words, Kimiko felt the tentative brush of his presence against her soul. Feather-light and friendly.

The gentle intimacy filled her with the awe of discovery. Yet there was something hauntingly familiar about that fleeting connection. If only she could remember why.

7

PANIC ATTACK

Tenma had really only applied to the integration program because his father insisted. For the sake of the company. For the sake of the future. New Saga was supposed to be a good place for his lesser son to meet a whole new breed of influential families. Except Tenma didn't think Amaranthine priorities ran to market shares and mergers.

His father had been pleased when Tenma's letter of acceptance arrived, but the man barely looked beyond a few key words—elite, exclusive, unrivaled, unprecedented. Enrollment in the inaugural class would add gloss to Tenma Subaru's vitae. But it was left to Tenma to navigate the halls of a school teeming with strangeness.

There were plenty of normal things—uniforms, shoe lockers, stairwells, club posters, and homeroom assignments. He could tell that some effort had been made to put average humans on familiar footing.

This should be thrilling. Hadn't he been looking forward to meeting a wolf? Then why was his heart pounding, his skin prickling? Why were his palms slick and his nerves a quivering wreck?

Inhuman races. Tenma had been as thrilled as the next kid when the Emergence hit the news three years ago … almost four, now. He'd been in his last year of middle school. Impressionable. Idealistic. And clearly an idiot.

He'd never been bothered by the photos, the broadcasts, the documentaries. But seeing a Rivven on a screen was very different than sharing space with them. They were beautiful people, but wasn't that how it worked in all the stories? Danger lurking behind a pleasing veneer. And he knew that while they might look human, they were actually animals. Somehow.

Was it too late to transfer out?

All through school, Tenma had been that slouching, awkwardly tall boy with glasses. He'd shied away from the attention his height commanded, so it was *almost* a relief when he realized that the majority of Amaranthine students outstripped him. But it was unnerving to look directly into inhuman eyes; their wildness fed his uneasiness.

The Rivven greeted him with polite nods and peaceful expressions.

So graceful. Even gracious.

Still, his anxiety mounted as he climbed stairs.

Nerves made him hyper-sensitive to signs of danger. Many of the Rivven had fangs or claws, and some retained animalistic features. Like the wolves and their tails. And Tenma was sure he'd spotted a pair of antlers disappearing around a corner.

Maybe he should latch onto a reaver. They were supposed to be able to contain a Rivven, keep humanity safe, things like that. Once he started looking for them, he realized that there were just as many of these so-called guardians of humanity walking through the halls.

And reason finally asserted itself.

Equal parts. Evenly divided. Evenly matched?

Humans outnumbered the Rivven two-to-one.

Tenma calmed enough to scan room numbers, but he refrained from looking into any more sets of the strange eyes. Which worked all right, up until 3-C's homeroom teacher announced that they'd be dividing into three-person teams.

Suddenly, the whole mood in the room changed, and the Rivven began to prowl. Tenma was quite sure there was sniffing, and he felt a sudden, frantic need to run. Panic was building and boiling in his gut, and it looked to be even odds whether he would kick off the school year by passing out or vomiting.

And then someone stopped at his table. Tenma froze—head down, fists on knees, staring at the tabletop—as a clawed hand lifted the chair opposite and came around to set it beside his. Too close!

The person sat and said, "Now that I'm here, the others will stay away."

Male. Tenma stole a look and swallowed hard. He was shoulder-to-shoulder with a Rivven who was easily as tall as he was. Tanned skin and reddish-brown hair mostly gathered in a braid. His face was averted, and a thicket of framing waves hid his expression. But Tenma could see his hands just fine. They rested quietly on the table, tipped by claws that were probably as sharp as they looked.

41

Tenma may have been hyperventilating.

"You seem to be sensitive to our presence," the Rivven said softly. "In much the same way we are aware of reavers. That's what's triggering your flight instinct."

He couldn't get his voice to work right. Had he whimpered?

"You're safe," soothed his companion. "No one here would ever harm you."

It made sense. Of course it made sense. But Tenma felt trapped.

"I can help you. Do you know anything about sigils?"

Tenma shook his head.

"If you're willing, I can create a simple ward."

The Rivven spoke slowly, as if to a frightened child. But Tenma couldn't bring himself to protest the patronization. The concepts were so foreign. He risked a longer look, hanging on every word.

"I'm pretty good with defensive barriers, and I think you could use one." The Rivven turned his way, enough for Tenma to see his face, but he didn't raise his eyes. "May I borrow a piece of paper?"

Tenma reached for his bag. His hands were shaking, but he managed to locate a notebook.

"Set it on the table. And ... might I also borrow a writing implement?"

Not until Tenma had set a mechanical pencil beside his notebook did the Rivven move his hands. Slow and precise, he creased a page and tore out a wide strip. "So you don't know anything about sigils?"

"N-no."

"I've heard this sort of thing called *magic* by humans." He swiftly drew a pattern on the paper—detailed and delicate. Then he placed one finger at its center. "Perhaps it is."

The air seemed to shiver, and then it ... cleared. Tenma hadn't noticed the clamor until it was gone, like the sudden silencing of cicadas on a summer's day. He peered dazedly around the room.

"Better?" The Rivven was quietly folding that miraculous slip of paper.

Tenma mumbled, "Thank you."

He nodded, then slid the sigil his way. Returning his hands to their neutral position on the table, he said, "Keep it in your pocket. Or sew it into an omamori, if you'd rather carry a charm."

"How did you know what to do?"

"My uncle has been teaching me about wards. I adapted one that some Amaranthine use when they find a reaver's presence overwhelming."

"Oh." The pall of danger had vanished, to be replaced by deepening mortification. "I'm sorry."

His classmate turned, and Tenma was staring into inhuman eyes. Only instead of unsettling him, recognition slammed him upside the head. Copper. This guy's eyes really *did* shimmer like pools of liquid metal, a phrase that appeared so often in the newsfeeds, it was woefully hackneyed.

"You had everyone in here worried. The Amaranthine, anyhow." He still spoke in that slow, soft undertone. "I don't think Ms. Reeves noticed."

"How did *you* know?"

"Scent." He slouched a little in his seat, getting comfortable. "Fear is distinctive. And unwanted. The wolves all had their hackles up, but none of them knew how to help."

Tenma took a longer look around the classroom. The nearest wolf's tail was puffed out like a hissing cat's. Concern and relief showed on several faces. Removing his glasses, Tenma rubbed at his eyes, mostly to cover his face. "Sorry," he muttered.

"Will you permit my touch?"

"Huh?" He fumbled his glasses back into place.

"For my clan, touch and trust are closely woven. It would put me at ease if you'll allow contact." With a faint smile, he reminded, "The meeting of palms is a traditional greeting."

Muttering more apologies, Tenma held out his hands. Was it palm-up or palm-down? To his embarrassment, he saw that his hands were still shaking.

"Normally, the first to offer raises their palms." He gently took Tenma's hands, rotating them into position and covered them. "This is the simplest greeting, a basic courtesy that holds no great significance. Although the pressure and duration of the touch can lend certain nuances."

The Rivven's hands were larger than his. Although his touch was light, his hands lingered. And Tenma had a vague impression that this was a good thing. Like showing someone that you're glad to see them.

"Less common is this." He moved so his hands were cupped under Tenma's. The Rivven's thumbs curved around to brush lightly against Tenma's palms. "This is an offer of support. An invitation to ask for help or for a favor. Like saying, 'Whatever you need, it's yours.'"

Tenma had wanted to learn things like this. He managed a shaky smile.

Those famous eyes flashed with approval, and the Rivven's hands moved. Again their palms briefly touched, but then he shifted upward to wrap his fingers around Tenma's wrists. "This goes beyond courtesy to commitment. Once matched, this clasp shows that two people wish to forge a close bond."

"Like being part of a triad?"

"I offer my loyalty. And whatever else you need."

So Tenma eased his fingers around the Rivven's wrists and murmured, "Please."

8

ONE SHY

Despite his earlier reluctance, Eloquence was glad he'd come. This boy had needed him. "May I ask your name?"

"Tenma Subaru."

He was definitely calmer, but obviously embarrassed. Retaining his hold on his classmate's wrists, he lifted them until the boy's gaze jumped back to his. "Nice to meet you, Subaru-kun. I'm Eloquence Starmark."

"R-really?"

"Quite sure."

"Does that mean you're related to Harmonious Starmark?"

"Closely." Quen nodded to the embroidered crest on his shoulder—copper thread glinting against dark brown cloth. "Dad's the spokesperson for the dog clans."

"You're a dog."

"Yes."

46

"And your mother's human?"

Tenma's grip had tightened, but this wasn't fear. If anything, he seemed eager. His scent had brightened considerably. Eloquence smiled. "Yes, Mum is human. She's my stepmother."

"I saw that special. The one with all the interviews."

"Who hasn't?" Quen rolled his eyes. "They've aired 'Heart of a Dog' every year since my brother was born. It's becoming an international Christmas Eve tradition."

"You're a *dog*."

"Third generation. We covered that bit, remember?" Tenma's scent was all over the place. "Hey, are you okay, Subaru-kun?"

But before he could quiz the boy further, Ms. Reeves called for attention.

"We'll dedicate the rest of our morning to essentials. Let's address a few matters of cultural diversity. As I said before, like a third of you, I'm a reaver. We're an international community with no borders, and over many centuries, we've developed our own unique culture. Part of your curriculum at New Saga will involve learning about reaver history, traditions, and festivals."

Eloquence's attention strayed to his other classmates. Twelve groups, with Amaranthine representatives from seven clans. He'd fully expected the support of horses and wolves, but the phoenix was a surprise.

Ms. Reeves went on. "Although the extent varies by clan, the Amaranthine are generally known for expressing themselves in tactile ways. They seek contact. So let me remind the Amaranthine representatives that all of our human students are Japanese. Local culture will require you to exercise restraint."

Quen's gaze drifted between the phoenix and his boy. The pair must have attended the all-boys' school just down the road from the Starmark compound. It had been the first to welcome a small group of Amaranthine students. If they'd been roommates since then, they must have transferred together. That was interesting.

He dismissed their reaver partner at a glance. Hisoka Twineshaft must have cut a wide swath through the lower ranks of reavers at Ingress, choosing those with diplomatic leanings. These emissaries of the In-between were a far cry from the dazzling set still being groomed by the mentors and staff at the Academy. Was it a concession to the risk the clans were taking in yielding their young?

"Another potential source of discomfiture surrounds the use of names." Ms. Reeves began writing a series of honorifics on the board. "Please bear in mind that our human students are accustomed to being addressed by their surname. Only use a classmate's given name with their express permission, since it's intensely personal. Wolves, you might consider it the equivalent of being asked by a casual acquaintance if they can touch your tail."

Soft grunts and a quickly-stifled growl rippled from the three wolf clan representatives.

"Horse and gazelle clans, consider the presumption involved when someone asks you to transform so they can ride you."

Pained expressions and more murmurs. Eloquence had to admire the diplomat's use of examples that would serve as warnings to the human students. Those kinds of requests were as common as they were rude.

After a brief explanation of honorifics, Ms. Reeves moved on to Amaranthine forms of address. "Several clans do have titles that denote high rank or respect. You'll be familiar with *spokesperson*, which is given to those who speak for their clan. Some assign *lord* and *lady* to their members of the upper rank. And other titles inform about age, role, line, expertise, or familial attachments. But we shall proceed as a classroom of peers. Humans, simply tell your partners what name you wish your classmates to use. Your opportunity will come next, for when dealing with Amaranthine, the first courtesy is a proper introduction."

Tenma whispered, "That was in our registration packets. I forgot. I'm sorry."

"Our meeting was not lacking in any way." Eloquence withdrew a hand and placed it over Tenma's heart. "You carry my sigil. You know my name. You have my loyalty. If anything, I am remiss; all of my questions for you remain unasked."

"Is this important?" Tenma stared at Quen's hand. "What does this mean?"

He frowned thoughtfully. "I've never tried to put it into words before. I ... wanted to reassure you. To ask you to trust me."

"Oh." Tenma relaxed noticeably.

At the front of the room, Ms. Reeves said, "It's simplest to demonstrate. Then you can go through a round of introductions within your triads. Hanoo-fel, would you be willing to assist?"

One of the adolescent wolves seated near the front of the room stood.

Their teacher offered her hands to him, palms up. "I'm Reaver Adelaide Reeves, diplomat class and a teacher at New Saga High School in Keishi. Welcome to Class 3-C."

The wolf settled his hands atop hers. "I am called Hanoo-fel

Nightspangle. If you can't already tell by my garbling of the local language, I transferred here from America. I'm grateful for your mediation."

Ms. Reeves smiled. "Hanoo-fel is your given name?"

"Yes. Nightspangle is my pack, and Hanoo-fel is my given name. In the language of wolves, it means 'thundering moon,' since I was born during a summer storm."

"And how would you like your classmates to address you?"

"Hanoo is good," he said, turning to include all of them in his invitation. "Please feel free to call me Hanoo."

Their teacher nodded again and addressed the class. "At this point in any introduction, the way is made for other questions. Your curiosity and interest show your new Amaranthine acquaintance that you're interested in becoming friends. Do any of you have questions for Hanoo?"

One of the reavers led the way. "What part of America does the Nightspangle pack call home?"

"We helped found an urban enclave in the Midwest." He gave a little shrug. "I probably shouldn't say anything else since we're still in hiding."

Eloquence knew that their people were having a harder time finding acceptance in the United States. In many places, stigmas and suspicion kept whole Amaranthine communities from declaring themselves.

Akira's hand shot up. "How are you related to the other two guys wearing the Nightspangle crest?"

"First and foremost, we're packmates." At Hanoo's signal, the other two wolves stood. He said, "Yoota-soh is my cousin, the son of my mother's sister. I can tell him from Ploom by his scent and by the swing of his tail, but you might want to check for beads. Yoota's are blue."

The young wolf, whose tail swept wide in silent amusement, turned so everyone could see the collection of turquoise beads knotted into his long hair.

Hanoo continued, "Ploom-ret is also my cousin, the son of my father's sister. He's never gotten the hang of shoes, so he's usually barefoot. You can tell him apart because he has brown eyes. Yoota and I both have yellow, which is more common for our pack."

"And what's your distinguishing feature?" asked Ms. Reeves.

Hanoo's grin was all fang. "Rank. I'm acting alpha."

"Which just means he struts more," said Yoota. "But the way he spikes his hair is hard to ignore."

"Hey!" grumbled Hanoo, running one hand over his bristling shock. "I don't do nothing to my hair. This is natural."

Ploom chimed in. "And his baby sister made him swear never to take off that bracelet."

"And I won't." Without a trace of embarrassment, Hanoo raised his left arm, showing off a double-strand of pink plastic pearls. "Wolves *keep* their promises."

A couple of the human girls made soft *aww*-ing noises that put a little extra lift in Hanoo's tail.

Ms. Reeves seemed pleased with progress and set the groups to the task of formal introductions. "We have until mid-high before we need to move on, so take your time asking questions. I'll be available to mediate as needed."

"Mid-high?" asked Tenma.

All around the room, other students were asking the same thing. Ms. Reeves simply smiled and left the explanations to the group members.

Eloquence used a flat hand to describe the angle of the sun. "Halfway to the sun's zenith, so midmorning. Amaranthine don't rely on clocks, so we'll reference the position of the sun, moon, stars, or tides, as appropriate."

Tenma checked his watch, then glanced around the room. "Is it just me, or are we short a reaver?"

Quen slouched further in his chair. "Do we really need one?"

But a weedy, wide-eyed boy at the neighboring table had noticed the lone duo. "Reeves-sensei, those two don't have a reaver."

"What? Oh, my. Why didn't you speak up, Eloquence?"

A couple of titters came from the same girls who'd approved Hanoo's bracelet.

Ms. Reeves' posture begged for patience. "I suppose that *was* rather ironic. But *Eloquence* is his given name. You'll get used to the dog clans' naming sense as you meet more of them. For instance, Sentinel Skybellow is head of our school's security team."

Conscious of the whole class's interested scrutiny, Tenma turned and placed his hands on the table. Quen did the same, giving the boy some space.

"We should divide neatly." Scanning the class, then peering at her roster, Ms. Reeves murmured, "Who's missing?"

Every Amaranthine in the room turned their attention to the door.

Several moments later, the rest could hear the echo of running feet out in the hallway. Then the door slid open, and a girl entered.

"Sorry!" she gasped, doubling over as she tried to catch her breath.

Quen tested the air, then leaned forward. This reaver—*their* reaver—was pink-cheeked from her run, bright-eyed with eagerness, and closely-kept by no less than three levels of warding. She was a slender, leggy pre-adolescent with an abundance of dark blonde curls, and her eyes picked up the willow-green of her tunic.

The girl straightened, then bowed to their teacher. "I apologize for being so late, Reeves-sensei. There was a mix-up in the office, and they wouldn't let me through." With a mischievous little smile, she added, "They seemed to think I was too young, but my mentor sorted them out."

"I'm sure he did." Ms. Reeves made a note on her paper. "We've been chatting about proper introductions. Will you make yours for the class?"

"Of course, Sensei." And turning to the room with a warm smile, she said, "I'm Isla Ward of Stately House, apprentice to Hisoka Twineshaft. My designations are linguist, cultural liaison, and diplomat."

9

STRAGGLER

Eloquence noticed a small stir in the corner where the phoenix's triad sat. Suuzu's human friend waved furiously at Isla, mouthing something incomprehensible.

Ms. Reeves also caught his gyrations and peered at him bemusedly. "Did you have something to contribute, Hajime-kun?"

Akira bounced to his feet. "Mostly just saying *hey*. Me and Isla are practically family, so I knew she'd be here at New Saga. But she never mentioned we'd be in the *same class*."

Isla's posture pleaded ignorance and innocence.

The boy grumbled something about keeping denmates informed, and several facts shifted into sudden focus. Eloquence blurted, "Akira Hajime, are you the Mettlebright beacon's kin?"

"Yep, I'm her younger brother," he cheerfully replied.

That made direct ties to three of the Five. What was Hisoka Twineshaft *doing*? If there was a risk here, why endanger children

54

with such prominent connections? Or were Argent Mettlebright's bondmate's brother and the cat's own apprentice the reason the cat was relying on him? He dearly wished the feline spokesperson was less fond of subtleties.

"You guys be nice to Isla."

Akira's gruff demand was almost rude and wholly unnecessary, but it struck the right sort of chord with a dog. Eloquence stood to give his words the proper weight. "Her welcome is assured. Her place is secure. Rest easy, friend of phoenixes."

The boy's grin was grateful.

"Akira, I'll be *fine*." Isla bowed again to their teacher and strode purposefully to their table to offer her hands. "Will you accept my presence, Eloquence Starmark?"

"Gladly." Her hands were so small beneath his that he kept his touch light. "I am certain Tenma Subaru will have need of your expertise."

She turned to their human counterpart with an expectant smile. "You have questions?"

Tenma looked nearly as wary of Isla as he'd been of the Amaranthine. Leaning forward and lowering his voice, he asked, "How old *are* you?"

Isla drew herself up. "I'm twelve."

"But this is *third* year. High school, third year." He fidgeted in his seat. "Aren't you supposed to be eighteen?"

"I'll eventually be eighteen." After a brief assessment, she dragged their third chair around and placed it on the other side of Tenma. "I completed my coursework at Ingress Academy, but there aren't many jobs for a twelve-year-old diplomat. So I've been assigned to this class."

"Are you some kind of reaver prodigy?" Tenma asked.

"Let's just say I'm good at my job."

She favored them with a smile that Quen found achingly familiar. Ward. Of course. He'd known her father when Michael was this age. He'd been just as brilliant, just as sure of himself. Did Twineshaft know of their connection? Probably. Michael had been one of the cat's special favorites while he was teaching at Ingress Academy.

Fingers tugged at his sleeve, and he refocused on his companions. "Yes?"

"Please, call me Isla. Both of you. No honorifics."

"I'll try," said Tenma, who may have been blushing. "And you can use my given name, too."

They both turned to him, Isla expectant, Tenma tentative. So he reached for their hands and closed his fingers around their wrists. Their heartbeats leapt under his touch, a joyous beat. His touch was welcome. Their trust was his. "Isla. Tenma. You may call me Quen."

After lunch and a lengthy explanation of cleaning duties, upcoming club activities, and the following day's visit to the Kith shelter, Ms. Reeves called for everyone's attention. "Our final order of business will be the selection of our class representatives. This is a human custom, similar to the election a spokesperson. The position is voluntary. Three of you will serve as both leader and liaison for your peers. Let's begin with our Amaranthine representative."

As she outlined the role's responsibilities, Quen groaned inwardly. The last thing he needed were more duties that would keep him from home … and from Ever. A swift flicker of movement passed through the room, and Quen slouched gratefully in his chair.

Hanoo-fel stood. "We are agreed. I will represent the Amaranthine."

One of the human students raised his hand. "How did you decide? And so fast! Can you read each other's minds?"

"No." Hanoo plainly made the gesture for a negative answer. "Not at all."

"Sign language?"

Ms. Reeves said, "Some of our lessons will include nonverbal communication. Until then, have your partners teach you some basics. But we'd all benefit from a demonstration. May I ask the Amaranthine to show us how you reached your decision?"

Quen stifled a sigh and stood with the others, since he'd been part of the process.

Hanoo's posture shifted, and he flicked a finger. But this time, he also narrated the gesture. "What do you think we should do?"

The bear rolled his wrist and curled two fingers. "All choices are good. Which is best?"

Ploom's fingers darted. "Who has the years?"

"The years are mine," said Quen, slowly replaying his gestures. "But I defer."

One of the horses brought her hands together. "A stronger voice than mine."

Yoota's stance changed, and he indicated his packmates. "A wolf understands pack. One of us, surely."

"Hanoo-fel already has their trust," said Quen. "Let him thunder."

Laughter rippled through the room.

The young bear spoke again. "Our voices will be heard, our concerns will be his. Hanoo-fel Nightspangle watches over this den."

Suuzu made a graceful flourish which the others mimicked. "We are agreed. We will be your support."

Ms. Reeves said, "Although this classroom isn't a proper den, a wolf always thinks in terms of pack. Thank you, Hanoo. Now, do we have a volunteer from among the human students? My only request is that the representative be someone from a different triad than Hanoo."

During the intervening moments of silence, Eloquence tried to read the mood of the prospects. He half-expected the energetic Akira to rush into responsibility, but the phoenix seemed to be holding him back. Then a hand slashed upward.

"Sosuke Fujimoto," said the weedy boy who'd spoken up earlier. "I'm more than willing. If everyone's okay with it, I'll speak for those of us who are ordinary."

Softly, too softly for human ears, someone murmured, "We are each ordinary in our own way."

Hanoo turned in his seat, as did Ploom. The filly signaled approval, and then Quen found the speaker. The reaver sitting with Suuzu and Akira.

Ms. Reeves said, "Thank you Fujimoto-kun. That just leaves our reaver representative. And as is our custom, we'll defer to Hanoo-fel, since he'll be working closely with them."

Eloquence wasn't sure what reasoning might guide the wolf's choice. By sheer magnitude, Isla was superior, but she was also a child. Pack instinct was to protect their young, not follow them. But none of the others stood out.

Yet Hanoo didn't hesitate in his choice. He presented his palms to the phoenix's reaver. "Your name again?"

"Kimiko Miyabe." More quietly, she asked, "Are you sure?"

"Sure of foot, true of heart, and glad of your support, little sister."

The girl made deft use of several signals not normally taught to reavers, which piqued Quen's interest. Was she enclave-bred? And then the audacity of her messages hit home. Was she *actually* accusing Hanoo of coddling her in his sister's place? The teasing glint in her eye, the tilt of her head—reavers of her rank were usually much more ... awed.

Eloquence was obliged to take a longer look.

She was lean and long in the leg, and her shorn hair offered an unimpeded view of her neck, which had a pleasing line. To his amazement, he caught a few whispers from classmates who seemed at a loss to her gender. Had they missed her introduction? While some given names were neutral, *Kimiko* was obviously feminine. Perhaps her nose was too wide, her figure too spare, but that didn't confuse his nose. He was more puzzled by Hanoo's swiftness in singling her out.

Why her?

It wasn't caliber. The young woman's presence was felt more in that teasing smile than in the pale light she carried. He could barely catch a whisper of her soul with so many other reavers in the room. Even warded, Isla glinted more tantalizingly off the periphery of his awareness.

Eloquence had seen Kimiko's type a thousand times over, for reavers with low ratings filled many unassuming roles in the In-between—file clerks, receptionists, couriers, and the service staff for dozens of reaver facilities and Amaranthine enclaves. One reaver in a hundred gained the prestige Isla was born to. The rest were their support.

And it was as if Uncle Laud's voice was in Quen's ear, deep and disdainful. *And who are you to criticize, pup?*

Wasn't he here because he still passed for a whelp? He fared poorly in any comparison with his father and brothers. And he would *always* hold a supporting role within the Starmark pack. Baby-minder. Dog-brusher. Perimeter-prowler.

Uncle Laud insisted on the nobility of every effort made on the pack's behalf. Even the humblest tasks should be accomplished with pride. Maybe his classmates were destined to empty trash bins, mine crystals, till fields, and file paperwork, but they belonged to the In-between, and every part was needed.

But still, why her?

As he watched the Nightspangle pack's pleased posturing, he could only surmise that Kimiko had distinguished herself by calling out the fallacy in the Fujimoto boy's remark. He'd heard Dad say it often enough to know that the Five were challenging humanity to redefine personhood, and not just on the legislative level. *Ordinary* no longer existed in this world, not if there was to be anything resembling equality.

Perhaps that was Kimiko's charm. Hanoo hadn't wanted fear or formalities. A girl who teased instead of tucking her proverbial tail had already dismissed the very distinctions they were here to study.

A satisfactory explanation. One that didn't much concern him. And so Quen's thoughts strayed to more important things, like his den and its denizens. For his heart yearned for home.

10

BIRDS AND BROODING

After their first day's dismissal, Akira snooped around the school for more than an hour, course schedule and campus map in hand. "I think I'm going to like Integrated History of the Unknown World."

"Hmm."

"Not because of the topic, of course." Akira turned into a long, empty hallway. "I mean, even if you add in the Amaranthine parts, history is still just going to be history. Long lectures. Hand cramps from note taking. Memorizing facts. But I really liked Sedge-sensei."

"Hmm."

Akira tried a door and found it locked. Pressing his nose to the window, he squinted into the dim room beyond. "This hall must be for club rooms. I see shogi boards. Or maybe they're for go? I can't tell, the way they're stacked."

Moving along, Akira found evidence of a wide variety of

extracurricular opportunities. Clubs were supposed to begin rallying for members next week. He'd like to join one, but only if Suuzu was interested, too. His best friend trailed after him, not complaining—not that he ever *did*—but extra solemn in a way that Akira had decided was Suuzu's version of sulking. Change was hard for him, on a very basic level. But that's exactly why they needed to hurry up and familiarize themselves with their new home.

"Do you think I could be like him?"

Suuzu's head came up and angled sharply. "Who?"

"Sedge-sensei." Akira waved a hand. "He's short like me, but he holds his head high. And everyone treats him with so much respect."

His best friend absently rearranged Akira's hair. "You lack his dignity. And his posture is a practical necessity."

Sedge Daphollow was a member of one of the deer clans, as evidenced by the graceful set of antlers crowning his head. Akira supposed they did contribute to his bearing. They were probably heavy.

Suuzu's narrow gaze hadn't wavered. "I was not aware you craved respect."

Akira blinked. "I don't."

"What *do* you want?"

"Usually, I want to be taller."

His best friend's expression faltered into bafflement. "Then why would you aspire to be like the shortest teacher on campus?"

He wasn't sure how to explain. "If I can't be tall, I can still be ... well, I dunno. Since you say *dignity* is out."

Suuzu's soft trill was apologetic. Pulling Akira backward into his chest, the phoenix said, "Greater height will not win a greater portion of my regard."

"Hey, no one said I was trying to impress *you*."

"Impression was accomplished nearly four years ago, at a time when you were several inches shorter." Suuzu drooped against him. "Please, Akira. I want to go home."

"Dorms next, then. Maybe we can hang out with Kimi some more."

The phoenix's grip tightened.

Akira remained still, letting Suuzu have his way. "Just us and Kimi for now. But you'll see. Pretty soon, we'll be friends with the whole class."

"Hmm."

Gently pulling free, Akira grabbed his friend's hand and hauled him toward the closest stairwell. Because his nestmate needed him and home—two things that Akira had already learned were nearly synonymous.

Akira backtracked more slowly along the double-row of mailboxes, reading the neat labels. "Her name's not here."

"She may have found other, more private accommodations," Suuzu said.

"Isla's name's not here, either."

The phoenix patiently pointed out, "Isla is a child. She is undoubtedly quartered with her mentor."

64

"I wanted to talk more with Kimi."

"We are not allowed in the female section of the dormitory, nor they in ours."

"Yeah, I know." Akira shuffled out of the narrow mail room and into the building's spacious student center. "But there's plenty of places to meet down here."

"Hmm."

Akira knew full well that Suuzu would have preferred 'other, more private accommodations.' They could have afforded a large, quiet apartment nearby, but Akira had insisted that the dorm would be more convenient. And more fun. If he let Suuzu take him off campus every night, they'd miss out on mingling with their classmates after school. Or meeting students in the grades below theirs.

His phone warbled, and he pulled it from his jacket pocket. He'd sent out New Year's greetings in the form of text messages, and he'd been getting replies all day. "Timur this time," he said, holding the phone for Suuzu to see.

Timur was Isla's older brother. The photo he'd sent showed the young man—sixteen now—striking a pose on a snowy mountaintop.

"Where is he?" asked the phoenix.

"He can't tell us. I'm pretty sure it's some kind of family secret." The young battler had been away since the previous summer, training with relatives from his mother's side of the family. "But based on that hat, I'm guessing Russia."

"There is an excess of fur." Suuzu had always shown a marked preference for feathers.

They cut across the student center, aiming for the elevators, but Akira's steps slowed. "This is so unreal."

No expense had been spared on the housing for this brand new educational facility. The central lounge that served as a student center wasn't unnecessarily lavish, but Akira figured the extras had been pricey. Like the classrooms, every effort had been made to combine human expectations with Amaranthine requirements.

Elaborate skylights let in daylight, which bounced from polished metal disks and silvered mirrors into quiet corners and alcoves. A central fire pit crackled under a ventilation shaft, and tables and lampstands held fat candles or oil lamps. Natural materials dominated—rough stone, polished wood, woven mats—and sturdy couches and chairs clustered here and there throughout the space.

Most eye-catching were the living elements. Trees grew in tubs, and vines swung from planters along three levels of balconies. Akira could hear the steady trickle of water coming from one corner, and birds twittered. He even spotted a couple of really weird winged lizard thingies that had to be Ephemera.

"Wow. Is that an eagle?" he asked, pointing to a large bird whose perch looked to be cut from a good-sized cedar.

"Hawk," Suuzu replied, lifting a hand in greeting. "She is one of the dormitory's Kith guardians. Her partner is there."

Akira spun and located the second vantage point. A lofty platform had been set up, and he could see enough protruding sticks to recognize its purpose. "A nest?"

"Naturally." A shrilling call pierced the air, and the phoenix acknowledged the greeting with a dip of his head and demure trill. "The clans did not send their student representatives alone. We will see to the comfort of the Kith even as they see to our safety."

Kith were another kind of Amaranthine, sentient animals

66

that lived and worked in cooperation with their clans or sometimes with a reaver partner. Akira knew one personally since a large black feline lived at Stately House. Minx was partnered to Isla's battler mom.

"Hard to miss the ones at the entrances." Akira peered toward the east-facing door, which was flanked by deep alcoves. Today, the posts were filled by a pair of wire-haired wolfhounds the size of horses.

"Hmm." Suuzu's whole attitude begged for retreat.

Akira took the hint and headed for the elevator on the boys' side of the dormitory. A push of the button, and the doors glided open with a soft whoosh of air and a barely discernible *ding*. Suuzu crept into the corner and sagged against the railing. Akira jabbed the button for the top floor, but before the doors could slide all the way shut, a hand cut in and the doors parted.

Another passenger stepped in, looming in the close space and eyeing them narrowly. Utter silence reigned as the doors whispered shut, and then Akira shook free of his shock. Suuzu reacted at almost the same time as they threw themselves at the newcomer.

"Juuyu!" Akira's nose mashed against silk-draped strength as he was pulled firmly against their visitor's side. "I thought you were in Europe or something!"

His best friend was tucked under Juuyu's other arm, his cheek pressed against the lapel of a dark wool suit, his hair gently rearranged by a clawed hand.

An undercurrent of joy suffused Suuzu's greeting. "*Brother.*"

11

COPING MECHANISMS

Akira ran ahead to unlock their room, knowing the phoenixes would want to be away from public spaces before saying more. He'd met Suuzu's older brother during the two visits that the Farroost clan had allowed him to their island colony. A tropical paradise of birds and beaches.

There, Juuyu had always worn the flowing clothes common to the phoenix clan—draping layers, loose pantaloons, sunset hues. Today's only concession to his heritage was a silken shirt, obviously of Amaranthine crafting. The cloth was as dark as Juuyu's western-style suit, but when he moved, it glowed like embers, fire buried in a black opal.

"This is us." Akira fumbled a little with the key, then pushed the door wide, stepping aside. "Welcome."

Suuzu hurried in, but his older brother firmly steered Akira through next. "Allow me." Juuyu shut and locked the door, then silently set about adding sigils.

Akira emptied his pockets. Suuzu tidied everything away. Akira plunked down in the middle of the floor. Suuzu hesitated, as if torn between who he wanted closer, then joined Akira to wait.

Their room wasn't exactly furnished. All Amaranthine students had been allowed to specify their particular needs and preferences, and Suuzu needed space to transform at night. Akira didn't miss the bunk beds that came standard in most dormitories. He and Suuzu had barely used theirs at their last school. The phoenix preferred building a nest atop futons each evening, then folding away their bedding in the morning.

Suuzu kept fidgeting, so Akira casually messed up his own hair. His roommate's exasperated glance turned sheepish. Akira just grinned and tilted his head forward, inviting him to preen. That sort of thing usually calmed Suuzu down.

Phoenixes disliked clutter, so their room echoed slightly with the drastic minimalism of their belongings. They had a fold-away table to use for either snacks or studying, but that was currently stored in their futon cupboard. A low bookcase just inside the door held textbooks, student ID, spare change, and Akira's phone charger.

Few needs and fewer wants.

Akira had come to appreciate a life unburdened by extraneous stuff. Just as he'd learned what mattered most to Suuzu, because a phoenix's needs might be simple … but desperate. Air and light, a view of the sky and the ready means to reach it. Privacy, safety, orderliness, and stability. And closeness, but only in the presence of mutual trust.

He'd often wondered why the Farroost clan had sent Suuzu away from home. This whole ambassador thing didn't really seem to suit anyone from their colony. Yet Suuzu endured it. As did Juuyu, who worked for some unmentionable section of the In-between.

Akira suspected that Juuyu was an international spy. He certainly looked the part.

In their speaking form—as in their truest form—the brothers bore a strong family resemblance. But where Suuzu kept his hair short, Juuyu's riot of black curls was somewhat contained by a series of golden hoops descending to the base of his spine. The hooked nose was the same, but Juuyu's managed to be much more imposing. Unlike most Amaranthine Akira had met—and that included every one of the Five—this one actually felt dangerous. He couldn't have explained why. Juuyu just seemed capable of anything.

Juuyu finally turned to study them.

"You came," murmured Suuzu.

"You are mine. Of course I came. Are you well?"

"Well enough."

"Hmm." Juuyu's gaze swung to Akira. "How is he faring?"

Leaning supportively into his best friend's side, he said, "Pretty much what you'd expect."

With a grumbling huff, Juuyu sank to the floor. "While I appreciate your commitment to your duty, I would rather you showed me more than your brave face. Our circumstances are similar, brother mine."

"Are you homesick, too?" asked Akira.

"Not as such." Juuyu hunched his shoulders, then relaxed them with a purposeful shake, as if settling his feathers. "My superiors are well aware of my instinctual idiosyncrasies; indeed, they have reason to appreciate my sensitivity to minutia. So I have learned to cope with ... necessary disarray."

Suuzu shuffled forward on his knees. "How?"

Juuyu inclined his head. "Routines that can be maintained no matter where I may find myself."

"Like ... a morning jog? Or always packing your own pillow?" asked Akira.

The phoenix's lips twitched. "In my line of work, those are not always convenient, but that is the general idea."

"Okay, but what kinds of routines?" Akira pressed. "Can you be more specific?"

"By necessity, they are small things." Juuyu riffled through his pockets and withdrew an old-fashioned pocket watch, a slim packet of pistachios, two clementines, and a green glass bottle with a stopper. "I keep the basics of a nest about my person."

Akira tapped the timepiece. "I thought Amaranthine didn't use clocks."

"A concession." Juuyu loosened his necktie and undid a few buttons. "I have always worked closely with humans, and I confess to appreciating the precision offered by clockwork. Punctuality has become something of a hobby."

"Wouldn't a phone be handier?" asked Akira.

"I prefer to leave such things to my partner. But here, Suuzu. This has become my nest." From around his neck, Juuyu unknotted a fine braided cord to which several items had been secured.

Suuzu scooted so close, his knees touched Juuyu's. Akira crowded in, saying, "That's almost like the sort of things wolves wear."

"One of my teammates came from the packs. He helped."

"May we?" Suuzu asked plaintively, ready to snatch back his hands.

Juuyu's low trill was almost like a purr. "That is our purpose, brother mine. Am I not your mentor in such things?"

Akira was about to ask for his own sake, but realized Suuzu actually had.

Soft as down, Juuyu added, "You would not be inside my wards if I did not trust you, Akira."

They explored the phoenix's necklace, and Suuzu finally ventured, "How does it work?"

Juuyu's lips took a wry twist. "This may seem little more than a flight of fancy, but I cannot deny that it calms the part of me that craves a nest."

"I get it. I think," said Akira. "These must be reminders of what's most important to you. Will you tell us what they mean?"

Juuyu began with a wooden bead, its milky blue paint showing signs of wear, as if it had been rubbed. "This is my piece of the sky." Touching the next item along the strand, he quietly said, "And this is for the star under which I was born."

Sharp facets glittered amidst the mooring strands.

"It's heavy." Akira held the stone up so it caught what remained of the daylight coming from above. He traded a glance with Suuzu before adding, "It sort of looks like a diamond."

"Naturally. And this is a pearl, to represent the tides that were once my only timepiece." Juuyu quietly admitted, "I have found that I miss the sound of the sea."

"Yes," breathed Suuzu. "Are these from Letik's tree?"

Juuyu hummed an affirmative and showed them how to open what looked like an ornamental test tube. "He refreshes the

72

petals whenever I visit."

Suuzu sniffed, and an expression of wonder crossed his face. "Home."

The fragrance had faded, but Akira recognized it right away. Both times he'd visited the Farroost colony, they'd slept in a kind of treehouse, high among the limbs of a massive tree that always seemed to be in bloom, no matter what the time of year.

A series of five crystals, each a different hue, glinted in their knotted settings. Akira couldn't tell if the items had any power anchored to them. He'd been tested more than once—and by the best—but it was no use. Akira didn't have a reaver's ability to detect stuff like that.

"These are tuned?" Suuzu asked.

"To the members of my team. They are a little like a flock." Juuyu's fingertip grazed the one with a greenish cast. "This one is for my partner."

His younger brother leaned forward. "You have a nestmate?"

Juuyu tweaked the end of Suuzu's nose. "Not so dear, but just as trusted. When our instincts interfere with our work, we help each other. As I will help you."

"With something like this?" Suuzu reverently returned the necklace to his brother.

"It may be some time before you need to rely on something so tenuous. I must go where I am sent with very little warning ... and with no idea of how long I might remain. But you are here, and this room will do very well." Juuyu tucked away his necklace and buttoned his shirt. "I only have tonight, but in the deep of winter, the night is long."

He was staying over? Akira was glad for Suuzu's sake. Although his best friend had more siblings than Akira could keep track of, he was obviously closest to Juuyu. An admired brother who was somehow also a mentor. Maybe because they had both left the island and worked closely with humans? More to the point, Akira asked, "You can help Suuzu?"

"I will do what can be done." Juuyu rose and paced the perimeter of the room. "I will do what Suuzu cannot do for himself—establish a nest."

"Why can't you...?" Akira asked.

His best friend didn't meet his gaze.

"Youth. The elders have given Suuzu an adult's status and responsibilities, and my brother has exceeded every expectation. But that which was given cannot replace that which grows." Juuyu came to crouch before them. Cupping Suuzu's face, he took a gentler tone. "You have not been sleeping, brother mine. Tonight, you two will be the chicks in my nest."

12

SHOW OF TRUST

Suuzu Farroost often wondered at the fleeting nature of humanity. He understood in part, for he remembered how quickly he'd fledged. Until the age of twelve, Amaranthine progressed much as humans did, but from there, maturation slowed. Days became decades, and the years became a gap that many Amaranthine preferred not to approach.

A phoenix's trust was barely gained before death crept in and a new generation rushed forward. Reavers in their enclave were like waves lapping the shore, barely cresting before sinking away, swift in their succession, an endless backdrop to a peaceful life. But Suuzu had spent enough years on quiet beaches to know that sometimes, a little wave would carry something precious onto the sand.

Akira was one such treasure.

It was a miracle Suuzu had found him. Given the swiftness with which humans escalated through adolescence to adulthood, a single delay, a year or two in either direction, and Suuzu's nestmate would have passed by, lost before he was ever found.

There were nights he trembled at the tenuous happenstance that had saved him from hopelessness and homesickness.

Circumstances had conspired—Twineshaft's call for support, a longstanding Farroost obligation, Juuyu's cautious recommendation—thrusting Suuzu into an integration experiment. He had thought himself prepared. Everyone had, or he wouldn't have been sent.

Three Amaranthine "students" transferred into a boys' middle school, accompanied by their reaver escorts. No one had been surprised when the two wolves had asked to room together, which left Suuzu. Would he consider a human roommate?

Yes. If the choosing was his.

Thus, the tour of classes took on a dual purpose. In each room, the reaver would talk about the Emergence while Suuzu and the two wolves stood to one side, very much on display. But the reavers were engaging, the wolves were gregarious, and the students were fascinated. A good beginning. Suuzu's escort would lead him up and down the rows of desks, dispensing interesting bits of lore and demonstrating the meeting of palms.

Suuzu's only real contribution was his presence, and his one task was proving more difficult than expected. Because fear and fascination made poor nestmates.

He'd begun subtle posturing when a student showed potential—flexing his claws, hardening his gaze, looming in general. The reavers didn't stop him because it *did* simplify the process.

On the third day, when his escort stopped beside Akira's desk, Suuzu peered down his nose at the boy in his best Juuyu imitation.

The boy immediately offered his palms.

With an unnecessary flourish of claws, Suuzu returned the greeting.

Rather than shrinking away, Akira grinned at him. "Hey, Suuzu! How's it going? Sure am glad you guys interrupted. This is *way* more interesting than a history lecture, you know?" He rolled his eyes expressively. "So didja pick a club yet?"

It was only the same sort of casual chatter he'd heard between classes and in the halls. Utterly guileless. Refreshingly casual. Shockingly hard to find. At that moment, hope fluttered in Suuzu's soul, and he whispered, "Please."

Akira glanced between him and the reaver. "What's up?"

The reaver must have prompted him, because the next thing Suuzu knew, sturdy hands were supporting his. Careless and carefree. Amiable and accepting. Exactly what he'd needed.   ✦

And they'd become inseparable.   ✦

Juuyu had worried, might *still* be worried. Because Suuzu's coping mechanism was more fleeting than diamonds or pearls … and rarer even than the petals of the rarest of trees.

A stage whisper cut across his musings. "You're gonna have to try again. He didn't hear you."

Juuyu warbled lightly from overhead, where he appeared to sit in midair.

"Brother?" Suuzu rose off the floor, fully prepared to lend whatever assistance he could in this next layering of wards.

But Juuyu waved him away. "Begin your evening patterns. I have more sigils to set—inside and out—and a ward at each window."

"So many?" asked Suuzu.

"As your kin and your closest, I regret that I cannot stay with

✦

you, but I *can* do this much." His brother's fingers flashed as he pulled another sigil into existence. "You would be surprised how much this will help."

Already, Suuzu could feel the difference. The walls fairly vibrated with Juuyu's care and concern. He'd been at it for hours, multiplying the strength of the protections that overlapped and interlocked, securing their dorm room. Suuzu hadn't realized his older brother was so accomplished with defensive barriers.

He frowned. Were these for peace of mind alone? Or should he be worried that some of the patterns looked suspiciously retaliatory? "Brother, are you certain this many safeguards are necessary?"

"Refresh yourselves and return here for preening." Juuyu curled his tenth finger, a private signal between them. One that meant he could say no more.

Which of course meant that there *was* more.

And that it posed a threat.

Akira yawned and stretched as he led the way back from the communal bathroom at the end of their floor. Reaching for the doorknob, he hesitated.

"Feel anything?" Suuzu asked softly.

"Never do." Akira sort of wished he'd inherited some little part of his sister's amazing abilities. Tsumiko's reaver ratings were top-level, but he didn't have the sort of soul that pulled at

Amaranthine. "Is it safe?"

"For you, certainly." The phoenix cocked his head, eyeing their door with obvious incredulity. "You and I may be the only ones who can safely pass through."

The door opened for them, and Juuyu spared a glance for the empty hall. "Were you expecting to entertain often?"

"Maybe," said Akira.

At the same time Suuzu said, "No."

"Okay, no." Akira shuffled inside, rubbing wearily at his damp hair. "If we want to hang out with anyone, we'll go down to the student center or meet up somewhere else."

Juuyu startled him by bending low enough to look him in the eye. "Thank you for the concessions you make for our comfort."

"It's no big deal."

"No?" Juuyu cut a sly look in his younger brother's direction. "If you give in to him every time, you may learn to resent a phoenix's preferences. And he will never learn to appreciate what can only be found by leaving one's nest."

"Yeah, we know." He and Suuzu had talked about it lots of times, and both of them had pushed past plenty of comfort zones already.

Juuyu's hum managed to sound skeptical, and Suuzu trilled a sulky retort as he pulled bedding from the closet. Akira tried to help, but as usual, his best friend came along right after him—smoothing, tucking, correcting. Which seemed a little silly since all they were going to do was mess it up the minute they laid down. But this sort of thing was important to Suuzu, and that was important to Akira.

"Into the nest, my chicks."

Juuyu's tone was taunting, but Akira liked that about him. Most Amaranthine worked so hard to not-scare the average human that they went out of their way to be nice and polite and passive. Not that Akira was against diplomacy. He was just more comfortable with people who were willing to get comfortable.

He sank to his knees on the bed, head bowed to accept the daily inevitability of preening. Back when they'd first met, he'd been embarrassed by the phoenix's touch. But they'd worked through stuff like boundaries and the appropriate time and place. This kind of thing was actually really nice. Relaxing. Soothing. And sort of revealing, because Akira could often catch a little of Suuzu's mood while he fussed. He could also tell when the one fussing *wasn't* Suuzu.

"Wrong brother," he mumbled.

"My nest, my prerogative." Juuyu worked his fingers through Akira's short hair. "Come closer, Suuzu. I can deal with two chicks at once."

Akira felt his friend settle at his side. Turning his head, he caught Suuzu's eye and smiled. Juuyu was subjecting them to a simultaneous preening, the very same sifting and kneading that Akira had found so flustering when he was fourteen. Now, it felt like family.

"You should let your hair grow," Juuyu murmured.

Suuzu chirped a crisp negative.

His brother chuckled. "A shocking rebellion. However, I cannot deny that you fit in better among humans with your hair shortened."

"Don't you work with humans?" asked Akira.

✦

80

"Reavers," clarified Juuyu. "And they don't look twice at my plumage. If they notice me at all."

"Because you're a stealthy super-spy?"

Juuyu made a sound that was new, so Akira didn't know how to interpret it. "Because my partner shines as you do, Akira. I yield to his greater enthusiasm for social interaction."

"Is your partner here in Keishi? Will we get to meet him?"

"Perhaps." Juuyu gave their heads a final caress. "More importantly, bedtime story or lullaby?"

Not the sort of question you'd expect from a person like Juuyu. But by moonlight or candlelight, the phoenix's sharp gaze mellowed along with his voice. This was a lilting, lulling time of day, when those closest were drawn closer, and secrets were safely shared.

Full-grown Amaranthine didn't need sleep in the same way as humans. They could go for weeks without, then crash for days on end. On balmy nights in the Farroost colony, Akira had fought his own weariness in order to experience what young phoenixes took for granted. They fell asleep to a mother's twittering lullabies or an uncle's wild story. There among the trees, under stars that seemed to pulse with every note and blush in rainbow hues, the colony fluted their piercingly beautiful songs.

"Why just one?" Akira flopped gratefully onto his pillow. "I vote for both."

"Hmm. There are things I need to say. To both of you." Juuyu motioned for his brother to lie back. "Suuzu, the elders have decided to accept your choice. In essence, you may keep Akira, with the Farroost clan's blessing."

Akira snorted. It wasn't like he and Suuzu needed permission to be friends.

But Suuzu seemed more favorably impressed. Propping himself up on his elbows, he asked, "Truly?"

"I added his name to the registry myself."

"Hold up." Akira wasn't quite so sleepy anymore. "Does this mean they *didn't* approve of me before?"

Juuyu clucked his tongue. "Be fair. Many humans outgrow the fascinations of their childhood. The elders wanted to see if your paths would diverge."

Suuzu grumbled, "He is mine."

His brother inclined his head. "Being fair to both sides, it does not hurt that your nestmate has lofty relations."

Incredulity added a note of injury to Suuzu's protest. "I did not choose Akira for his family."

"He didn't know about Sis when we started rooming together." Thinking back, Akira added, "We were friends before Sis even met Argent."

"Granted," Juuyu soothed. "But these are factors that worked in your favor. Akira Hajime, the Farroost clan considers you one of our own. If you choose, you may wear our clan's crest."

It was Akira's turn to prop himself up on elbows. "Seriously? That's ... major."

Clan crests were part of any Amaranthine family's identity. Juuyu wore his as a gold lapel pin. Akira sat up more fully and touched the small disk with its swirl of stylized feathers around a roughly triangular center.

"Suuzu would normally be discouraged from accepting a human nestmate, but they are willing to overlook the irregularity."

"Because of my connection to the Mettlebright foxes," murmured Akira.

"No." Juuyu quietly said, "Because Suuzu is a tribute."

"A what now?"

"It is ... a private family matter." Suuzu pulled Akira down so his head rested on his shoulder—their usual sleeping arrangement when Suuzu was in speaking form. Looking to his brother, Suuzu added, "We do not usually speak of such things."

"He is your nestmate. He will bear our crest." Juuyu's tone took on the edge of authority. "He can keep a secret."

"Yeah, of course!" Akira promised.

Suuzu turned his body so he could speak directly into Akira's ear. "Juuyu is a tenth child, and so am I. We are our clan's tributes."

"You have *nineteen* older siblings?"

With an affirmative hum, he shielded Akira as Juuyu transformed into a mythical bird—long neck, showy crest, and an extravagance of trailing tail feathers. It was nip and tuck, fitting into his newly-claimed nest, but Juuyu settled over them, as if further blanketing this conversation in secrecy.

Downy softness surrounded them as Suuzu told him what it meant to be a tribute. There were secret tasks and sacred roles that belonged to one child in ten. While he couldn't reveal everything that meant for *every* clan, he shared what it meant for the two brothers. "We had to leave the colony."

"Like ... ambassadors?"

"Yes and no." Suuzu sighed against Akira's ear. "That is more my role, for I was set apart for peace. Juuyu was set apart for war."

"And that's why he's a secret agent?"

He chuckled. "Juuyu is more investigator than spy, but he does carry many secrets. They are the birthright of every phoenix, but since the Founding, they were entrusted to our warriors."

"And Juuyu's one of these warriors?"

Admiration and conviction saturated Suuzu's simple answer. "He is."

The lateness of the hour was getting to Akira. Tucked as they were beneath Juuyu's chest, it was deliciously warm, although it was strange to share the scent and softness of feathers with Suuzu. Usually, Akira was the lone chick in this nest. "It's like you're both of you."

"Hmm?"

Akira shook his head. It was too silly to repeat. What had they been talking about? "Ambassador of peace ... sounds prestigious. It's almost like you're the Spokesperson for the phoenix clans."

"Yes."

"Huh?" Akira pushed feathers out of the way, but there was no hope of seeing his friend's face in the dark. "You're like ... one of the Five?"

"I cannot be one of the Five or there would be six."

"You know what I mean." He poked in the general vicinity of Suuzu's ribs.

"I do." Suuzu quietly admitted, "I am."

Akira finally snickered. "I'd like to go on record as having befriended you *before* I knew you were important."

Suuzu trembled with ill-contained laughter, and above them, Juuyu began the thrumming coo of a phoenix lullaby. Akira recognized the melody. It was the same one Suuzu sang over him most nights.

He nestled back down. "You've been holding out on me, Spokesperson Farroost."

"Few know." Suuzu had relaxed enough that his voice slurred with sleep. "This is my secret to carry."

"And mine."

Akira liked this part of being a nestmate. Hearing a song with your whole body. At times like this, at the edge of waking and sleeping, Akira could *almost* believe he was touching Suuzu's soul. Giddy peace enveloped him like a gentle fire, flickering around and through him without burning.

"What was Juuyu's again?" Akira asked.

"Hmm?"

"Is his secret as cool as yours?"

"Certainly. In the old lore, phoenixes have always fulfilled one role." Suuzu lapsed into the rhythmic patter of recitation. "Our warriors are keen of eye, swift in flight, alluring in song, and untouched by flames. We are hunters with one prey."

"Yeah?" Akira yawned. "Wassat?"

Suuzu's lips bumped his ear. "Dragons."

13

DOUBLE ESCORT

h, this was awkward. Kimiko's posture shifted to reinforce her words. "I'd like that. Really, I would."

"Good try, Kimi, but it sounds like you're leading up to an apology." Akira was on tiptoe. "We don't get enough time to talk in class. Hang out with us!"

She checked to see if Suuzu understood. The phoenix touched his best friend's shoulder. "If today is inconvenient, we could make alternative arrangements."

"Maybe," she said doubtfully. "I have family obligations. And sometimes I take part in these extra tutoring sessions with my younger sister. Long story short, I always have to go straight home."

Akira buried his hands in his pockets, the picture of dejection. "We noticed you're not in the dorm."

"That's right." Kimiko dropped soft boots onto the floor in front of the shoe lockers and stepped down into them, tugging them up over the dense weave of her winter breeches. "It's close enough, so I'm living at home."

Akira followed her out the front doors. "How far are we talking?"

Pointing north, she asked, "See the tree on that hill?"

Suuzu caught up, Akira's coat over his arm. He silently draped a scarf around the boy's shoulders while Akira gave the distant hilltops a considering look. "You walk that every day?"

"When the weather's good," she said. "It's a little over four kilometers, and I'm used to it. I spent the last couple years walking to Ingress Academy."

He caught Suuzu's eye, then asked, "Can we walk you home, Kimi?"

The polite thing would have been to protest—the time, the distance, the inconvenience. But Kimiko decided to be honest. "I'd like that. Really, I would."

Akira grinned. "This time, I believe you!"

"I could show you around a little—the prettiest spots, my favorite places." Kimiko checked the sky as she looped her scarf snugly around her neck. "If we're careful, we can avoid my mother."

"Why's that?" asked Akira.

"I do want you to meet my family eventually. I mean, it would be an honor to offer you hospitality, but...." Kimiko floundered for a way to explain. "Certain members of my family have been putting a lot of pressure on me. I'm used to ignoring their helpful advice, but if you fell into their clutches, things would get awkward."

"Pressure. Clutches?" Akira caught her arm. "Kimi, do you need our help?"

She laughed. "I'm not in need of rescue, but *you* will be if Mama finds out about your relationship to Lady Mettlebright."

"Sis?" Akira held up his hands. "Am I missing some kind of reaver joke here? Because I'm not actually a reaver."

"No, but your closest kin is a beacon, and that's excellent breeding potential." Kimiko shook her head. "You'd have a contract under your nose and a pen in your hand before the tea's poured."

Suuzu helpfully murmured, "Her relatives want an excellent prospect to improve their bloodlines."

"*Three* excellent prospects. And I'm really sorry." She tucked her chin, hiding most of her face behind her scarf. "I don't want our triad to be about making connections."

Akira patted her back. "I think I get it. And it sounds like I better find out about prospects and contracts and stuff, since I apparently have 'excellent breeding potential.'"

Suuzu made a low noise that was *not* happy.

Kimiko shot him a sympathetic look and begged for patience.

He gently rebuffed her apology, saying, "The matter will undoubtedly arise again. Akira should become informed."

Catching his eye, she expressed the depth of her feelings—abasement and reluctance to do harm, inner conflict and a sense of helplessness.

Akira caught her hand and stared at it. "What *is* that? You're always doing things like that. Little stuff. You move like an Amaranthine."

Kimiko smirked at him. "I'm a reaver. We learn things like this."

"No," countered Suuzu. "You are different."

She paused at the corner, waiting for the light to change. But she flicked him a quizzical look.

"There!" Akira mimicked the position of her feet and clumsily

88

adjusted his hips. "What's this supposed to mean?"

Suuzu said, "A mild protest, one that does not ask for confrontation. A plea for understanding. It would be more nuanced if she had a tail."

Akira tried again, and Suuzu's expression softened. "Not quite. Unless you were intending to proposition the nearest feline."

He tried again, and Suuzu's trill carried a note of amusement.

Kimiko chuckled. "You're either challenging a bear or apologizing to your herd, depending on the set of your shoulders."

"Hmm." Suuzu fell in step beside her. "Your fluency goes beyond the expected patterns. Are your people attached to an enclave?"

"Not at all. We're a shrine family." A convenience store caught her eye, and she pulled up short. "Say, do you mind if I make a quick stop?"

"Snacks!" was Akira's stamp of approval.

The boys followed her in, and Akira grabbed a basket, moving off toward a case of prepared lunches. She ducked down the aisle with crunchy snacks and immediately brightened. They had new flavors! Making a few choices, she moved to the candy aisle. It was a little too early for Junzi to have released their special edition wrappers for the upcoming Star Festival. But Kimiko was pleasantly surprised to find another chocolate bar in the plum blossom sleeve. She'd buy it for Mrs. Miura, since she was planning to drop in for her promised visit over the weekend.

Kimiko glanced around to check on the boys, and Suuzu met her gaze across the store. With casual grace, he made three distinct signals—rejoin us, trust me, and ... something she didn't know how to interpret. Hurrying to his side, she said, "I missed the last one."

"I know. It only holds meaning for the phoenix clans. Would you like to learn our ways?"

"Please!" Kimiko touched his sleeve. "What did you say?"

"At which point?" he asked solemnly.

She was used to this kind of thing from her Amaranthine tutors. They always favored hands-on lessons. Learn by doing. Emulating the tilt of his head, she flared her fingers before brushing her lips.

Suuzu's soft whistle was complimentary. "You are a fast learner."

Kimiko jiggled impatiently, and to her amazement, Suuzu smiled. "I asked for a bedtime story," he said. "And in returning the gesture, you have promised one."

That was new. Totally unique within her limited experience. She was still practicing the movement of fingers when Akira rejoined them then, swinging his bag of snacks, so she hastily moved to the counter to make her purchases.

They continued along the sidewalk, and she ripped open a bag of crisps. "Want some?"

Akira looked askance at the package. "A favorite of yours?"

"Never had it before," she admitted, popping one into her mouth.

"Any good?" he asked suspiciously.

"Not sure yet." She took another and smiled. "The flavor might grow on me."

He cautiously took one and sniffed.

Suuzu lifted a hand in polite refusal. "Returning to our earlier discussion," he said. "Who was your mentor at Ingress Academy?"

Kimiko shook her head. "Someone like me doesn't get singled out. I wasn't tapped for apprenticeship."

The phoenix's gaze sharpened. "I have seen you use a wide

range of expressions, representative of dozens of clans. Many of them so nuanced, you must have seen them firsthand."

"Oh! Well, yes. My sisters and I have had temporary tutors since we were little. From all over. None of them stayed for more than an afternoon or two, but my grandfather was good at finding more." Kimiko wasn't especially good at math, but two or three tutors a month over the course of a dozen or so years wasn't hard to tabulate. "There have been quite a few. Not so many lately, though."

Akira was counting on his fingers. "That's like ... almost four hundred teachers."

"It sounds more impressive than it was." Kimiko munched morosely. "When my older sister and I enrolled at Ingress, we were *so* far behind everyone else. There are huge gaps in our knowledge of the basics since we tended to follow our interests instead of a set curriculum."

Suuzu said, "Put another way, you have spent years refining an exceptionally narrow field of study across a surprisingly diverse cross-section of Amaranthine society."

"I guess." She scrubbed at the side of her face, which was feeling rather warm despite the winter winds. "It was the only way."

"Hmm?"

She didn't want to sound peevish, so she balanced her words with a hopeful posture. "Reavers of my rank hardly ever get close to an Amaranthine. We don't attract your interest or attention. It's not like we're banned from approaching you, but we're given no opportunity to do so. But I don't have to get close to offer a greeting." Kimiko offered signals for respect, gratitude, and a quirky tanuki blessing for a thick pelt in winter. "I never get to learn their names, but I can almost always win a smile. And that makes me happy."

"Reavers outnumber us a hundred-to-one, in every generation." Suuzu's hand found hers. "And most Amaranthine prefer the security of enclaves or seclusion."

"There aren't enough Amaranthine to go around." Akira seemed embarrassed. "Guess that makes me really lucky, huh?"

"To have a phoenix for a best friend?" Kimiko gave Suuzu's hand a small squeeze. "I can't even begin to compare. *My* best friend is a tree."

14

LOCAL LEGENDS

With no sign of anyone coming or going, Kimiko hightailed it up the shrine stairs. She was two-thirds of the way to the top—it was a matter of pride for all the Miyabe girls that they could climb the full length without stopping—when Akira called out.

"Wait up!" Akira gesticulated uselessly. She really needed to teach him some basics. "Suuzu's looking at something."

Kimiko moved to one side in order to see to the bottom, where the phoenix stood as still as the statue he was studying. Skipping back down, she stopped beside Akira. "Sorry, Suuzu," she said in a normal speaking voice. "I guess I should have started our tour with those."

He gestured for peace and patience as he circled the second crouching dragon.

Akira fidgeted on the edge of the step, but he also understood that Suuzu could hear them fine, despite the distance. "So ... *dragons*, huh? Is there a story behind those?"

"Of course! And it comes in two versions—one for the general public, one for members of the In-between."

Suuzu was beside them in a flicker of movement so fast, he seemed to step out of thin air. He said, "I would like to hear more. After you introduce me to your tree."

Kimiko couldn't imagine why he was so serious. She'd mostly been teasing. But she gestured for quiet and jogged upward, taking the last dozen steps two at a time.

Akira was puffing when he caught up, but his eyes were sparkling. "You *live* here?"

"Welcome to Kikusawa Shrine." And with a furtive scamper, she took a path shielded by an enormous rhododendron hedge that still clung to its leaves, a thicket of red-twigged maples, and a double row of burlap-wrapped lumps that would become showy hydrangeas come summer. "This way," she whispered, pointing upward.

They were already under the outermost edge of the vast canopy of the city's oldest living resident. Well, that had been its claim to fame before the Emergence. First and second generation Amaranthine were old enough, one of them might have actually planted the ancient tree.

Kikusawa's giant was as much a landmark of the Keishi skyline as the bell tower of Saint Midori's. All commemorative photographs taken by the Miyabe family—by most families in Kikusawa, for that matter—had a bark backdrop. It was considered lucky to mark milestones under the shelter of its limbs, as if all of them were including the tree in their celebrations. Birthdays,

94

graduations, weddings, reunions, festivals, and holidays. But Kimiko's attachment to the tree was more personal.

The tree was her hideaway. Tucked amidst its roots, she used to pretend that it was one of the fabled Amaranthine trees, sentient despite its long silence. She'd imagined her soul was a comfort, that her words could reach the person inside. So she'd tried to become the tree's steadiest companion; in return, it had become her confidante.

"*Wow*. What kind of tree gets this big?" asked Akira.

"No one's entirely sure. I mean, the official story is that it's an obscure variety of camphor tree."

"But it's not?" asked Akira.

"No," said Suuzu, peering up at its waxy, evergreen foliage. "It is not."

"Specialists from the reaver community come every once in a while, taking samples, running tests, and making a huge mess by scrounging through our archives." Kimiko led Akira and Suuzu to a spot on the quiet side of the tree, away from the path, out of view from the house. "Their best guess is that the tree is some kind of hybrid, a sort of halfway descendant of the trees of song."

Akira pressed a hand to the tree. "Why not ask the Amaranthine?"

"The reavers have. Lots of times. It's in the records, and they always give the same answer—Kusunoki is sleeping."

"What's *that* supposed to mean?" Akira flung his arms wide and sprawled against the trunk, but the tree was too big to hug. They'd have needed most of their class linking hands to surround it. "Anybody home?" he inquired softly.

Kimiko leaned into the tree, gazing up through limbs she knew how to reach—and still sometimes climbed. In summer, she liked to revisit the maze of limbs that cast shade over the shrine courtyard.

Settling into a familiar curve amidst the roots, she said, "I used to sit here for hours, especially when Grandma made me read. Sharing the drudgery with my tree made it easier to get through all the boring subjects I had to take at Kikusawa Middle. I wasn't very good in school, but trees are patient. We made it through somehow."

Akira groaned sympathetically and lowered himself to an adjacent twist of wood. "Same for me, only I had Suuzu and his tutoring to get me through."

Suuzu's soft trill was hard for Kimiko to interpret, but the accompanying posture was self-deprecating. That made sense. Especially when you added in Akira's small smile, which was all patience and fondness and *there you go again*.

After a scant week, Kimiko's accumulating impressions were settling into patterns. Suuzu was quick to notice but rarely spoke up. He was efficient and orderly, but in a quiet way, as if he didn't want to impose his preferences. She'd begun to think of him as passive, but that didn't jive with the enigmatic undercurrent she was picking up now. It was so … forceful.

Was he trying to wake her tree?

Shaking free of the fanciful notion, Kimiko said, "Kusunoki is my favorite part of home, but there are lots of other good places. Like the storehouse attic. The reliquerium. And the archive, of course." Kimiko had inherited care of the shrine's extensive literature collection after her grandfather's death. She might not like to read, but she excelled at organizing collections. "What would you like to see next?"

Suuzu shook his head. "You spoke of dragons. Tell us their story, and in return, I will sing you a song of trees."

"Okay, but not out here." Kimiko gave an exaggerated shudder. "Follow me to a warmer hiding place."

She led them on a roundabout path to the archive, which was located in one of the shrine's several detached buildings. Its key was hers, so their privacy was assured. Inside, she shed her boots and hung coat and scarf. While her partners did the same, she padded over to the clunky electric heater in the corner. She knew from long experience that it would pop and groan and wheeze in complaint, but it would soon be throwing off enough heat to set the battered gold kettle on top to steaming.

"A library? Wow, these look old." Akira jammed his hands in his pockets as if he'd been warned to look but not touch. "Do shrines have so much paperwork?"

"We *do* keep ordinary records, but most of our collection has to do with folk lore and fables. It's a Miyabe family tradition and entirely unique."

In truth, after her grandfather's death, there had been several carefully-worded invitations to move the contents of Kikusawa Shrine's archive to Ingress Academy's larger, more modern facility. But Grandmother had declined every offer in no uncertain terms. Their trove of stories, their handful of dusty relics, and the mysterious blade for which their shrine was named—all would remain in their trust and keeping. This was their whole purpose.

Kimiko said, "I'm in charge of them now."

"How many have you read?" asked Akira as he took a seat at the folding table in the center of the room.

"Hardly any, but I can *find* anything. I used to help my grandfather index these books and files." She quietly repeated, "I'm in charge of them now."

"How long?" Akira asked softly.

She didn't try not to understand. "Almost a year."

Suuzu's expression gentled, and his hands curved in an expression of sympathy.

Akira, who was paying closer attention to such things now, mimicked his best friend, adding a low, "Sorry."

"Thanks. It's okay, but ... thanks." Kimiko rummaged in the cupboard that held her chocolate stash and laid out the remainder of her convenience store snacks, opening two more bags of crisps. "We can make tea once the water's hot."

Akira wrinkled his nose. "Kimchi and Chives? Really?"

"It's a limited edition," she said coaxingly.

He peeked at the label on the other bag. "Why do you like such strange combinations?"

Kimiko beamed. "Don't shy away from the unknown! Risk can be *exciting*. And new experiences are hard to come by in a place that exists to uphold traditions." She nibbled thoughtfully at a chip dusted with green and purple flecks. "This may be as adventurous as my life will ever get."

Akira bit ... and gagged.

Suuzu considered her for a long moment, then gravely accepted her hospitality.

She chuckled at his pained expression. "I'll admit, I'm content to let Sardine Brulee remain a once-in-a-lifetime experience. Do you like sweets?"

"Not when they're mixed with fish sauce," grumbled Akira.

"I may dabble with daring flavors, but there's only *one* chocolate for me!" Kimiko placed the chocolate bars in the center of the table like a peace offering. "Junzi makes the finest in the world. You can help me eat these. All I ask is that you let me keep the labels. I collect them."

Suuzu's whole posture radiated welcome surprise and pleasure. "The renown of the Rindo clan is vast. My brother shares your fondness for their confections, though not your generosity."

Kimiko's eyes widened. "Junzi is an urban enclave?"

The phoenix ducked guiltily. "That … may yet be a secret."

"Rindo, huh?" Akira eased a chocolate bar out of a sleeve with a snowflake design. "I think I met one of them. Tried to use fudge to bribe Sis into letting one of their crossers come to us for schooling. Like she'd turn anyone away. Cute kid. Ringed tail."

Suuzu blinked. "And that was definitely a secret."

Akira crammed half a chocolate bar into his mouth, ostensibly to keep from spilling any more scandals. Suuzu was clearly flustered, and his posture begged for confidence. But he confirmed her suspicion. "Your favorite sweets are tanuki-made."

Kimiko cleared her throat. "How about I spill one of our shrine's secrets, and we'll all just … keep them."

They nodded, and she firmly changed the subject. "Have you heard of the Star Festival?"

"Of course," said Akira. "I've lived in Keishi all my life. It's coming up soon."

Suuzu inclined his head. "A city-wide street festival to celebrate a local saint."

"Saint Midori of the Heavenly Lights," said Akira. "She's supposed to have saved the city."

"How?" prompted Kimiko.

"By calling down the stars or something." Akira waved his hands around. "Everyone knows the song that goes with the bonfire dance. She came like an angel, and all that."

"Except Midori wasn't an angel," said Kimiko. "She was a reaver. More specifically, a beacon. And it's said that her radiance woke the stars, who flew to her aid. *Impressions*."

"Your story is ancient if there are imps at play," said Suuzu. "They were lost before the rise of the Kindred."

"Far from ancient," Kimiko said eagerly. "This story's only three-hundred years old, give or take, which means there may still be imps in the world."

Suuzu only hummed.

Kimiko said, "The Star Festival may be the only festival that's celebrated by humans *and* reavers."

"What do the Amaranthine have to say about it?" asked Akira.

She puffed out her cheeks. "Nothing. My grandfather once tried to get Harmonious Starmark to clarify some of the details. I mean, there's a *hound* in the story, and that hints at his clan's involvement. But Harmonious only said that he's always liked that story, then changed the subject. Grandfather was convinced he knows more—probably everything—but it's a big secret for some reason."

Akira held up a finger. "Hang on. If the legend actually happened, and Saint Midori was a reaver, what did she save the city *from*?"

Kimiko's smile widened. "Humans usually say it was a falling star. Although some think it was an earthquake, or even a volcanic

100

eruption. But every record at Kikusawa is very clear on that point. Our city was under attack."

"From ...?" demanded Akira.

"From those who are still depicted, cringing and cowering at the foot of Kikusawa and Kusunoki." Kimiko was delighted by how quickly they caught on.

"Oh, man. You're *kidding*, right?" Akira asked wonderingly.

Suuzu filled in the blank. "From dragons."

15

BRAVE FACE

All week long, Tenma held himself firmly in check. Watch and see—that was the way to get by. He would go with the flow, giving himself time to grow accustomed to the stranger parts of school life at New Saga. Quen was very kind, if in a distracted way. For all the importance of his connections, the young Starmark wasn't very ... industrious. It was already clear that they were counting on Isla to carry the group.

The girl was so poised. And unfailingly polite. Maybe he should be more embarrassed to be tutored by a girl of twelve, but she'd been quite happy to start him at square one. Her lunchtime lectures were easily his favorite part of the day.

He was getting by. And yet he was disappointed. And maybe that was unreasonable. What had he expected?

Tenma checked his empty mailbox. He kept his eyes on the floor as he crossed the student center. And when he saw others waiting for the elevator, he ducked into the stairwell. For the exercise, of course.

Sluggish steps eventually carried him to the dormitory's top floor, to the door of the room his parents had paid extra to secure for him. He knew it was their way of showing they cared, but it also showed how little they understood him.

Tenma had spent most of his life in an ultra-streamlined apartment that echoed slightly. His older brother was away at university, carrying their father's highest hopes. Their mother had been the secretary for a CEO for more than twenty years. Her boss considered her indispensable and paid her well, but he also monopolized most of her time. When Tenma's family came home after their chaotic days, they found respite in the hush and spare décor. For them, the restraint and stillness were soothing.

Leaving Tenma the only unhappy one.

He'd always stuck close to home, yet he'd felt homesick his whole life. As if he belonged somewhere else. He craved something that his family couldn't understand, and their contentment had left him lonesome.

Which is why their parting gift was in such poor taste. A room to himself.

They'd spared no expense to prolong his solitary existence—white walls, cool gray stone underfoot, and a distant skylight. His corner suite boasted views of Keishi to the south and east, an efficiency kitchen, and a tiny water closet. Father probably thought he'd want to avoid the dining hall and communal bathing facility. The furnishings Mother ordered in had all the warmth of an office lobby—icy grays, stark chrome, and glass.

The only spot of color was a flyer for the Star Festival, which he'd found tucked into a bag from the convenience store. Glossy and bright. Its array of starry pinwheels was so shockingly cheerful, tacking it up had felt like an act of rebellion.

Tenma dropped onto his bed and turned his head to watch a patch of sunlight creep across the wall. The pattern of panes stretched. Maybe he should read in the student center. He might still be alone, but he could watch the groups that gathered there. Read ahead a bit farther in his textbooks. And keep an eye out for Kith and Ephemera.

Now, *there* was an idea.

They'd been introduced to the school's Kith shelter earlier that week. Many of the Rivven beasts were intimidatingly large, but they were also gentle and intelligent. He'd been invited to stroke a wolf's shaggy pelt, and he'd had his hair lipped by a soft-eyed mare. Maybe the person in charge could use some help in the pens—freshening bedding or brushing coats.

Mind made up, Tenma hurried to change out of his uniform.

Eloquence knew every nook and knot of the New Saga campus. These lands had belonged to his father for centuries, but at Hisoka Twineshaft's suggestion, the Starmark clan had ceded a generous section for the needed buildings. And allowed the peaceful encroachment of many clans. Although theirs was an eclectic, changing mix, Quen wondered if this newest venture finally qualified their compound as an enclave.

He ran through the forest, keeping to a pace that was barely polite. Quen was missing dinner, but this was his only chance to get to the school's Kith shelter without Ever noticing his absence. Because Uncle Laud had oh, so casually announced that their dogs—the Starmark Kith—were disappointed in Eloquence.

What had he done?

His primary role in the Starmark clan was speaker for their Kith. Quen might not be the most hardworking soul, but he'd never once shirked his duty to his packmates, never once earned their censure. So he would track down the source of their complaint and tend to it. Quickly and quietly. Before word reached Dad. Quen wouldn't put it past his father to use it as an excuse to put off his attainment.

Unthinkable.

Slowing as he approached the entrance, he inclined his head to the pair of felines guarding the back gate. They sprawled languidly across the entrance, reminiscent of ginger housecats, but much, *much* larger. Whiskers quivered, and the female's eyes narrowed, but her attitude hinted at amusement.

More confused than before, Eloquence slipped into the courtyard.

New Saga's Kith shelter was a series of deep alcoves, shaded pens, and sheltered roosts lining a circular courtyard at the rear of the school grounds. Even though the center was open to the sky, overhangs and awnings kept the sun and rain out, and high walls checked the wind. He'd helped with the plans, and he'd shared in the labor alongside his brothers and sisters, aunts and uncles.

It was quiet. Not a whiff of trouble. Then why...?

Here he comes.

Flay's voice rang clearly in Eloquence's mind. He could hear their Kith; any member of the dog clans could. Wolves, too, given their close kinship.

My eyes may be dim, but my nose works.

That was Edge, bondmate to Flay. These Kith had been companions of Father's when he was a youth, and the centuries had turned their muzzles white.

Hurry along. You must see my new pup.

She sounded happy. Flay was the sort to dote on every little thing.

"Have you adopted another barn cat?" Eloquence ducked inside the alcove they'd claimed for their den.

Nestles like a lost kitten. Edge's tail thumped the straw. *About time you found him.*

For shame. But Flay's tone couldn't have been gentler. As if she didn't want to wake the figure huddled at her flank.

This one understands the need for pack, said Edge.

For shame, repeated Flay. *To place your seal upon him, then leave him so lonely.*

"You can tell the ward is mine?" Eloquence had realized Tenma was there as soon as he rounded the corner. His nose worked, too. But he was surprised the Kith had interpreted the simple barrier he'd created for the boy as a mark of belonging. That had never been his intention.

Yet his classmate curled tightly at his feet—glasses crooked, salt upon his cheeks, wholly unguarded. Now that he was paying attention, Eloquence decided that Tenma's scent had a wistful quality. "Has he spoken to you?"

Freely. Flay nosed the boy's hair. *He finds us good listeners.*

Meaning he'd been a poor one. Hadn't Tenma been running late and redolent of straw that morning? "How many times has he slept here?"

Last night. Tonight if you abandon him.

"I deserved that," Quen sighed. "Thank you for getting my attention."

Edge stuck to practical matters. *He needs a better den.*

And a better friend. Eloquence sank to his knees and gently shook his classmate's shoulder. "Tenma. Wake up, Tenma."

The boy rolled away from Flay's warmth and stared muzzily through off-kilter lenses. "Quen?" he mumbled. "Umm ... hi?"

"Why are you bedded down with my Kith?"

"Umm." Tenma snatched back the hand tangled in Flay's red-brown fur. "Yours?"

Eloquence sat beside him. "Edge and Flay are part of the Starmark clan. They're my packmates."

"Sorry." Color was creeping into the boy's face. "I didn't think anyone would mind."

Plucking straw from Tenma's hair, Quen promised, "They don't. They like you. In fact, you have their protection."

"Aren't they here to guard the school? They protect everyone."

He was fully awake now, but his guard was still down. Or maybe Quen's was. "They've decided you're special."

"I'm not." He seemed to shrink. "Not me."

Flay growled. Edge whined. And Eloquence was ashamed of himself. Choosing words that would leave them each a little pride, he asked, "Will you hear me out?"

Tenma nodded.

"I'm having trouble balancing the responsibilities I have at school with those of the den. Perhaps you could help me?" Quen brought his hands together, as if to capture an elusive midivar. "Bringing the two together might give me some peace."

"If I can help, I will." Tenma tentatively reinforced his words by cupping his hands under Quen's. "How?"

"Come home with me. Meet my brother."

16

COMPOUND

Tenma stumbled to a stop.

Quen turned. "Are you all right?"

"Tripped on something under the snow." He waved his hands, fending off his classmate's concern. "I'm fine."

Backtracking, Quen came to stand directly in front of him. "Can you see at all?"

"Not really," he mumbled. With nightfall, the world had been reduced to white and dark. It was enough to avoid walking into the trees in the forest behind the school, but he seemed to be stumbling over every clump and clod in between.

"Wait a moment. Help is on the way." Quen's soft grumble was disapproval. "Where are your gloves?"

"Not sure." Tenma started but quickly relaxed when large hands closed around his, warm and comforting. He definitely felt safer with Quen than any of the other Rivven he'd met. It wasn't that the others were frightening or anything, not since he'd begun carrying the sigil everywhere. But he'd looked up stuff about the dog clans. Promises of protection were serious. And now he'd been invited to Quen's den. Jittery and anxious not to botch things up, he mumbled, "Sorry."

A muffled gallop came from beyond them, deeper in the woods. At a low *wuff*, Quen turned to greet a dog as big as a horse, though stockier and shaggier. Tenma couldn't see much else in the dark.

"This is Rise. He'll give us a ride back."

Tenma hesitated. "Is that okay? Ms. Reeves said it was offensive to ask for rides."

"Asking Rise to carry us isn't a problem. Asking *me* ... well, that's another matter."

"You're a dog."

Quen chuckled. "Why do you keep going back to that? Yes, in my truest form, I look a whole lot like Rise. If a bit bigger."

"Can I see?"

"Rise is here because you *can't* see. Come on. You can sit in front."

Tenma had no clue how to board a dog without yanking fur or jabbing potentially sensitive areas with his boots. But before he could ask, Quen was lifting him, which made two things glaringly obvious. Quen was ridiculously strong. And Quen wasn't touching the ground.

"Allow me," he said, all composure.

Rise took off at a lope that drove Tenma back against Quen's chest. Why did everything end up so awkward? It was like ... the harder he tried not to offend, the worse things came out. "Sorry."

"Grab on with both hands and grip with your knees," said Quen. "And I would be pleased to show you my truest form sometime. But let's wait for daylight, shall we?"

"Makes sense." Tenma gingerly tangled his fingers in a thick ruff of fur. He mumbled, "Was it rude to ask?"

Quen hummed. "Not exactly rude, but neither is it something to spring on a passing acquaintance. But with someone you already know, they'd probably take it as a compliment."

"Really?"

"How can I put this delicately?" Amusement seeped into his tone. "You're inviting me to change into the form of a predator, presumably in close quarters. If my savagery matched my size and strength, nothing could save you. Yet you trust me. And I like that."

"I do trust you." It felt good to say it.

"Here we are."

The forest transitioned into a garden, beyond which stood several buildings. The style was old-fashioned—scalloped tiles and ornamental ridgepoles climbing by tiers, long porches, and covered breezeways. They passed through four different courtyards before Rise came to a halt before a modest pavilion.

Sliding off, Tenma paused to thank the Kith.

"No need for goodbyes. He lives with me," said Quen. "It'll be us and Rise and ..."

"Runt!"

Tenma turned at the barked call. Two figures strolled along the wide porch across the garden. Lantern light glinted on copper cloth, so he assumed this was one of Quen's relatives. A flash of movement behind his companion looked to be a tail. So they were both Amaranthine—dog and wolf.

Quen sighed. "Not the brother I *intended* to introduce you to, but he'll want a whiff. Merit's firstborn and exceedingly protective."

"Are you in trouble for bringing me here?" Tenma whispered.

"No. It's okay." Quen hooked his arm and guided him along. "But you know how it is. Greetings are an important part of being good hosts."

Tenma's hand stole into the pocket that held the sigil. His heart was hammering, but he was pretty sure his queasiness wasn't a recurrence. Just plain old nerves. When they mounted the stairs at the end of the porch, it became increasingly clear that Quen's brother was huge, and the wolf was even bigger. Without much in the way of dignity, he clung to his companion's arm with his free hand.

Quen made a soft little tutting noise, then lifted his voice. "Good evening, Brother. And to you, Boon. What brings you here?"

"What else? A trail." He offered his hands to Quen, but in a perfunctory way. Keen yellow eyes remained fixed on Tenma. "I've been hunting. But who's this?"

For the first time, Tenma could appreciate the fact that for all their impressive physique, Hanoo, Yoota, and Ploom were adolescents. Adult wolves carried more muscle, and this one radiated a more primal quality of wildness. Maybe because the Nightspangles were city boys, and this wolf had none of their ability to blend in.

The wolf's tail swayed the way Hanoo's did when pleased, which Tenma took for a good sign. He touched palms with the wolf, but words failed him.

Eloquence smoothly handled things. "Boon, this is my classmate from New Saga, Tenma Subaru. Tenma, this is Boonmar-fen Elderbough, a formidable tracker and a friend of our clan."

"M-may I ask about your name?"

"Sure, kid. That's real nice and proper of you. And I don't mind going through the formalities if Merit don't."

"Doesn't," sighed Merit. "Who taught you Japanese?"

The wolf reeled vaguely with his hands. "Island enclave. South Pacific. I'll admit he was sketchy, but it was all he had to trade."

"You traded language lessons for ...?" prompted Quen.

Boon crouched, arms outspread. "More like surfing lessons, but he liked to talk, so I picked things up pretty quick."

Quen huffed. "So you traded surfing lessons for ...?"

"Oooh, you know how it is." Boon waved off the question. "The less said about some things, the better."

Merit cleared his throat.

Boon grinned and elbowed him. "Wait your turn, Penny. He asked *me* first."

Quen's elder brother growled, but Tenma couldn't tell if it meant *get on with it* or *your doom is sure*. Either way, he got the impression that Merit and Boon got along all right.

The wolf thumped his bare chest—his fur vest hung open, revealing tanned skin, beaded accessories, and what looked suspiciously like the edge of a tattoo at his hip—and repeated, "I'm Boonmar-fen, third son of Adoona-soh Elderbough. My name means 'song circle,' because I was born during a festival."

Tenma searched for something to say. "What are you hunting?"

Boon's smile was no longer the happy sort. "Trouble. And the less said about that, the better."

A second set of palms was presented, and Tenma quickly touched hands with Quen's older brother. Again, Eloquence guided the introduction. "Merit is firstborn and heir to the Starmark clan."

Loose auburn waves, glinting copper eyes, stern gaze—this Starmark towered without actually looming. Oddly, Tenma's insides didn't dance skittishly because Merit was near. Only Boon made him nervous, as if his gadabout manner was simply a veneer.

"Subaru-kun, if Father was not occupied by urgent matters, he would bless your coming and bid you stay. Do not think less of us because the honor falls to me." Merit took him by the shoulders and bent to kiss his forehead. With a searching look, he said, "Friend of my brother, fear not."

So startled was he by the gentle treatment, Tenma lost his chance to ask Merit about his name, for the two adults were already moving along. Meetings to attend. Reports to discuss. He was a little fuzzy on the details.

But before they rounded the corner, Boon called back, "Fear not, but beware of dragons!"

Dragons. Tenma shook his head and looked to Quen. "He's exaggerating again, right?"

"I don't think he was lying." His classmate's brow furrowed. "But I think his words split onto two trails."

"Like a double meaning?"

Quen hummed and turned back toward the pavilion where Rise sat patiently. But he snapped to a halt and muttered something in a language Tenma didn't recognize. Even so, the tone was clear. He glanced around the snowy garden warily. What was bad enough to inspire rude words?

And all of the sudden, out of absolutely nowhere, Quen was tangled up with another person. Only it was more of a hug than an attack. Probably. Caught between needing to get away from this unknown source of oaths and trying to help a friend, Tenma stood frozen.

"El-o-quence," crooned the newcomer, his voice deep and rich. "Hide me. I cannot bear another question."

"Was there another inquiry?"

"Suspicions multiply, even though I am innocent as a breeze over open meadows." Winding slender arms more firmly around Quen's shoulders, he sagged disconsolately. "Have pity and offer us sanctuary."

Although Tenma wasn't clear on particulars, he felt certain that Quen was in no danger. But in the dim light, details were slow to come together. Male. Rivven. And ... drunk.

"You've had too much star wine, Lord Mossberne."

"I know." He exhaled on a fluttering note that definitely wasn't human. "It did not help. It never does."

Mossberne? As in Lapis Mossberne? Tenma stopped breathing. Could this person really be one of the Five? Catching Quen's eye, he pointed and mouthed *dragon*.

Rolled eyes and a nod.

But the exchange may have been a mistake, for the dragon lord's head turned, and light fell upon a lean face, putting fire into half-lidded sapphire eyes. "El-o-quence," he drawled. "Why is that boy sealed?"

He slithered out of Quen's grasp, and an instant later, Tenma was holding up a bleary Rivven who smelled strongly of flowers, spice, and liquor.

"Hello, sealed boy."

17

SEALED BOY

To Eloquence's relief, Tenma seemed more awed then scared by the clinging dragon. Unless Quen missed his guess, Lapis was playacting. Too much star wine certainly left him maudlin, but any actual inebriation never lingered for long. No. He was after what *any* dragon was after on a winter's night.

"He shouldn't be outside." Shifting into an apologetic posture, Quen added, "Help me bring him in."

Tenma's eyes were wide behind his glasses, but he radiated concern. "Lean on me, sir."

"Such generosity. Such hospitality." Lapis wilted against the high school boy. "I cannot care for this city of yours. There may be stars in your wine, but they are missing from your sky."

"We're a long way from the heights." Eloquence nudged Rise out of the way and opened his door. Inside was hushed and dim, meaning Ever was still with Mum. "Keishi's lights do muddle our view of the sky, but they cannot touch the stars in their intensity. Only distract from it."

"If you miss the stars so much, go and see them," suggested Tenma.

"Obligations confine me. It will be weeks before Twineshaft permits me to return to my home in the heights. Months, even. Whole *seasons* without jeweled nights and unfettered winds."

"But they're just above the clouds." Tenma staggered up the steps and fumbled out of his shoes. "I thought Rivven could fly."

Quen grimaced as Lapis shed his drunken pretense and turned Tenma's face. For a long moment, the dragon peered into his eyes. Voice deepening with shades of accusation, the dragon asked a question that wasn't one. "You are not a reaver?"

"No, sir."

Eloquence tried to intervene. "Tenma doesn't know anything about…"

Lapis lifted a hand to silence him. "I am a dragon."

"Yes, sir. I figured that out, sir. Lord Lapis Mossberne. You're one of the Five." He ducked his head and mumbled, "It's an honor."

The Spokesperson stroked Tenma cheek. "You know little of dragons?"

"Next to nothing. Sorry." As if wanting to be helpful, he added, "I do like all the colors."

Dragons were indeed showy. And they tended to *hold* the attention they received for all their gaudy coloration. Some felt they deserved the captivation, for the Maker had made them beautiful. Others were wary. Really, there were as many warnings about dragons as there were for trees. But Lapis was as good as pack, and Tenma could find no kinder teacher when it came to the dangers of dragons.

He was probably already being drawn in.

"Bring him into the inner room," Quen directed. "I'll get the fires going."

"Sure," said Tenma. "Do you need help with your shoes, sir?"

Eloquence, who had been speaking to Lapis, wondered if he looked half as surprised as the dragon. Tenma wasn't affected?

Lapis stepped out of bejeweled slippers with upturned tips, revealing azure painted claws and delicate rings on his toes. "Due to a tragic confluence of circumstances and consequences, I am unable to reach the sky. But my heart stirs at the promise of fire. January is such an inhospitable month."

"Close the screens behind you." Eloquence crossed to the first of two fireplaces. Uncle Laud must be back in town, for the firewood was already arranged on the hearth. All Quen had to do was strike a match and touch it to the kindling. Then he turned to a discreet wall panel and fiddled with temperature settings.

Tenma guided Lapis to a cushioned bench and peered around the room. The dragon pulled him down to sit at his side and continued his sly scrutiny, but Tenma hardly seemed to notice the predator at his side. Instead, he pointed to the control panel. "I thought Rivven were against technology and things."

"Usually, but an exception was made for this building." Quen knelt in front of their seat and touched the matting. "Radiant heating under the floor. For Ever. He's sensitive to cold in the same way humans are, so Dad had it installed."

Lapis stretched his feet toward the fire, wiggled his toes, and hummed appreciatively.

Eloquence huffed. "Certain clans—including the dragon clans—are picky about temperatures. They're good at finding hot spots, so

Lord Mossberne has been sneaking into our den every chance he gets. He usually attaches himself to Uncle Laud."

Tenma seemed to be having trouble reclaiming his hand from Lapis. "Oh. Umm. You live with your uncle?"

"Yes. He should return soon since we oversee Ever's bedtime together."

"Will he mind that I'm here?"

"Not at all." Quen reached out to touch Tenma's knee, then flicked Lapis, who finally let go. "Uncle Laud trusts my choices."

"May I beg a formal introduction to your sealed boy?" Lapis offered a tight little smile. "I am also interested in your choices."

Eloquence patiently observed the formalities, amused when the dragon curtailed his usual poetic effusion in favor of illumination. At the first opportunity, Lapis asked, "Why would our dear Eloquence seal away a star with no shine?"

Tenma flushed. "I was afraid. Quen rescued me."

"May I see this seal that banishes fear?" inquired the dragon lord. "I have made a detailed study of sigilcraft."

Tenma slipped a hand into his pocket but hesitated. "What will happen if I let it go?"

The dragon offered a sultry smile. "Let us find out."

Tenma trusted Quen, who was watching closely, so he relinquished the slip of paper that had given him so much peace of mind. Nothing much happened. At first.

Since he was expecting it this time, he wasn't surprised when a nagging uncertainty asserted itself. A little at a time, as if someone were turning up the volume on his anxiety. He was extremely conscious of both Quen and Lord Mossberne, and those impressions were clamoring for his attention. It was the strangest thing. Like an instinct. Or the sudden insight. A eureka moment of clarity. Only this time, there wasn't any push toward panic.

"Tenma?" prompted Quen. "Everything okay?"

He searched for a helpful answer. "I'm not exactly afraid, but … I feel strange."

Quen offered his hands, and Tenma grabbed hold.

"I have always envied the easy trust that dogs inspire. Such friendly relations. Quite cuddly." Lapis studied the slip of paper held between two upraised fingers. "El-o-quence. This is as inspired as it is impetuous. What possessed you to contain him?"

"I'm not sure what you mean. It's just a simple barrier."

Lapis responded with a whiffling vocalization that Tenma felt certain was patronizing. He had no idea why he'd gained that impression. Unless it was attached to this creeping awareness.

"The intent of most barriers is focused outward. Repelling notice, ingress, attack." The dragon's deep voice turned teasing. "This does not growl and snap at intruders. You have used a portion of your strength to hide him away. Even from himself. A unique—albeit effective—approach to the problem at hand."

"If it works, then no harm's done," grumbled Quen.

Tenma quickly said, "It *has* worked. I mean, I can barely tell you're here."

Lapis' jewel-like eyes swung back to Tenma—glittering in the firelight, smoldering with interest. "Me? Are you saying you have some sense of my soul? Impossible."

"S-sorry, sir. I don't understand these things very well yet." Tenma must have insulted him somehow. "Maybe it's only because you're holding Quen's sigil."

"Possible," murmured the dragon. "Remotely possible. What is it you think you can 'barely tell' about me, sealed boy?"

Tenma didn't like to say. Because if he put it into words, it would sound foolish.

Quen frowned. "Don't put it to him that way. You know it's not impossible for him to carry a bit of talent. Not *every* reaver bloodline is under my grandsire's watchful eye."

"Granted." Lapis made a gesture Tenma understood from class—*no offense intended*. Then he lifted both wrists. "The source of my skepticism lies in these, not with you."

The dragon wore two heavy bracelets that must have been carved from black stone. Each bangle had deep grooves carved into them, creating patterns similar to those Quen had drawn for him. Sigils. For a barrier? Curiosity prompted Tenma's touch. As his fingertips trailed along cool stone, his impressions grew even clearer. "I don't think I'm imagining things."

"Dragons like compliments." Quen nudged him and nodded. "Even if you find him frightening, it would probably please him."

He would rather have described Quen, whose presence curled around him with languid confidence, a sort of luminous warmth—settled, strong, reliable. Beside him, Lapis was all brittle edges, like shattered glass. "It's like you're broken." Tenma struggled for a more sensible description. "You're all blues and echoes and longing."

Quen sounded surprised. "You can see *color* in his darkness."

"How very impish of you," said Lapis. "If I am a lonely blue, what is your dear classmate? Copper I suppose?"

Tenma shook his head, not sure what to call the honeyed glow that flowed against him like syrup. But one thing was clear, and it took him by surprise. "Quen is lonely, too."

18

LAUD AND EVER

N ot at all," Eloquence said firmly. "And Lord Mossberne cannot be lonesome either, for we have come together, and our pack has found a good den for the night."

"Cozy and soon to be over-crowded, in the fashion of cuddling curs." Lapis rolled his eyes toward the door.

"Pack," murmured Tenma, his cheeks pink in the gaining light of the fire.

From the porch outside came the noise of a one-boy stampede and Rise's low *wuff* of welcome. For Tenma's benefit, Quen said, "My brother is home. Uncle Laud is bringing him."

A moment later, Ever tumbled into the room with a glad cry. "Bruvver!"

Quen scooped him up and nuzzled the three-year-old's hair, enjoying the mingled scents of baby shampoo and happiness. Cradling him close, he nodded to Uncle Laud, who urged Rise inside before shutting the inner door. A barely perceptible thrum assured Quen that the customary barriers were now in place. And for the first time, he realized that his uncle's shelter was the *containing* sort—more possessive than protective.

As was his right.

Laud was Dad's younger brother, born before the Waning. Harmonious was Glint Starmark's firstborn, a distinction that had led to his appointment as Spokesman for the dog clans. Laud was born twentieth.

There were enough resemblances to mark Laud as Harmonious' brother—the set of his jaw, the breadth of his shoulders, the pitch of his voice. But where the eldest son was charismatic and affable, the younger was serious and silent. And Laud had inherited his mother's coloring. Glint's bondmate was a famous beauty with pure white fur and copper eyes.

Quen had been in Laud's care from the time he was weaned, in the same way Dad had entrusted Quen with Ever. A fostered pup. Because the Starmark pack looked to their own. Even those who would never take a bondmate could treasure a child.

Lapis warbled a low welcome, which Laud answered by producing a drinking gourd, its wax seal still in place.

Tenma hung back, eyes darting. But then Lapis tucked the sigil into his front pocket, murmuring, "Adorable, is he not?"

Eloquence nearly laughed, for Tenma seemed confused over which person Lapis found adorable: Laud, Ever, or Rise. And in finding equal appeal in all of Quen's denmates—Kith, Kin, and crosser—Tenma earned a greater measure of trust on all sides.

"Ever," said Eloquence, tapping his brother's wriggling nose.

"I brought my friend from school to meet you. Will you greet him properly?"

Lisping an affirmative, Ever squirmed to be let down and ran trustingly to Tenma.

The little boy's chubby feet were bare, showing their clawed tips. And he was dressed in the same fashion Dad favored, with short-coat and sash over loose pants. By necessity, Ever's hakama had been notched at the back to make room for his tail, which wriggled with unguarded excitement. The boy was as fond of people as their father was. And he was equally good at winning them to his side.

"Hi, you!" Ever clambered right onto Tenma's lap. "You's *new*."

Uncle Laud growled softly, delivering the reprimand Quen hadn't wanted to voice. Ever's puppy ears drooped, and he settled back on his heels to present his hands. The form was good, but greetings were usually exchanged at a more polite distance. But Tenma wasn't bothered by the irregularity. Like everyone else who met Ever, he was charmed.

After a solemn exchange of names, the little boy asked, "Can I sniffen you?"

"Do you think that's a good idea?"

"Yeth."

"Will it hurt?" Tenma asked seriously.

"Nooo." Ever giggled. "I be gentle."

"Then you have my permission to ... sniffen."

Quen covered his smile as his baby brother wrapped his arms around Tenma's neck and rubbed his nose back and forth, snuffling noisily.

"He's learning your scent," Eloquence explained apologetically.

Tenma only smiled crookedly and asked, "May I sniffen you, too, Ever?"

"Course!"

Humans couldn't detect subtle nuances in scent, but Tenma took the boy's answer as permission to pull him close. He was awkward about it, as if he'd never held a child before, which was sad. But he did sniff Ever's hair and rest his cheek atop his head.

"I like your ears," Tenma announced.

"Pet 'em!"

"Is that allowed?"

"You 'lowed. But not tails." Ever shook one small finger under Tenma's nose. "Tails is purse-null."

"Yes, I know. My teacher told me on the very first day of school." He added, "There are wolves in our class."

"Wolfs has tails!" exclaimed Ever, his own a blur. "But dogs is best." Tenma asked, "Are *you* a dog?"

It was exactly the right thing to ask. "Yeth! Like Da. Him's mine."

Lapis interjected, "What of poor Eloquence?"

"Yeth." Ever belatedly acknowledged the dragon a wiggle-fingered wave and patiently explained, "Him's mine, too. My bruvver."

"And the silent lout over there?" inquired Lapis.

"Rise. Him's mine, too." In a loud whisper, Ever explained to Tenma, "Him's Kiff."

The dragon lord chuckled. "I was *referring* to the one with no ready excuse for his reticence." At Ever's obvious confusion, Lapis offered a broad hint. "The one with white hair."

"Uncle!" With that, Ever slid from Tenma's lap and trotted across to Laud, who sat on the floor beside the door.

126

Eloquence explained, "Laud Starmark raised me and remains my mentor. My den is his den." He tried to think of a way to explain their relationship so a human could understand. "I have two fathers."

Tenma offered a shy wave, which Uncle Laud answered with a casual flick of fingers. He'd never been one to stand on ceremony. Laud blandly countered, "Best to say *three* fathers, or Karoo-ren would feel slighted."

"An uncle from my first mother's pack," said Quen. "Though an ocean divides us, he returns when he can."

Quen noticed his uncle's deflection, but let it pass. That was simply his way. Watchful and quiet, attending to his duties without making a scene. Harmonious may have been Quen's sire, but Laud had raised him, and such loyalties ran deeper than blood, right into the bones. While Quen longed for Dad's attention and approval, he *had* Laud's.

This was the constancy Ever deserved.

Precious is the pup to his pack.

Lapis reclaimed the limelight, full of plans to provide Tenma with something more durable for sealing his soul. While he grew increasingly loquacious about the resonance of various crystals and the proper balance between a solid defense and tasteful design, Eloquence watched over Ever.

Up on tiptoe, the boy lifted both arms. Expression soft, Laud gave him the boost he needed to reach broad shoulders. Ever settled himself, then reached again, this time to touch their uncle's forehead.

Laud kept his unruly hair out of his eyes with an embroidered band tied across his forehead. It was his sole ornamentation, and it served another purpose. To hide his blaze. Laud had been born with a mark in the center of his forehead.

Pudgy fingers tapped, initiating a routine Quen had seen often. This was Ever's silent request, a plea for trust. In answer, their uncle wrapped one large hand around the boy's ankle. It covered most of his calf as well, but the ankle was the important part. Because a delicate scroll of pale green encircled it like a thread—Ever's blaze.

The boy gently slid the band from Uncle's forehead, wrapping both arms around and pressing his palms in its place. To cover one another's blazes was a solemn pledge, an unspoken promise to keep each other's secrets.

Laud's faint smile held pride and contentment. But Quen watched as the fingers of his free hand restlessly tapped hip, thigh, calf, and shoulder in repeated sequence. All the places he hid daggers.

Tenma stirred at the unfamiliar sound of birds. Were there birds in wintertime? His brain jumped through possibilities, trying to make sense of the cheery twitter. Bird feeder? Canary cage? Ring tone?

A moody growl vibrated against his back, and the noise cut short, along with the whispery retreat of wings. But now Tenma was more focused on the fact that he was not alone in bed. An arm under his ear. Fur against his feet. A small body curled into his chest. And an arm draped over them both—him and Ever.

And then he lined up more facts. Not *his* bed, because he was at Quen's place. Not alone, because dogs, especially young and unmatched males, preferred communal sleeping. Tenma couldn't believe how well he'd slept, given the warm press around him.

Tenma opened his eyes and squinted. Where had he set his glasses? He mostly needed them for reading, so he could make out enough of his surroundings to anchor himself, even with the pre-dawn gray and fuzzed edges.

Quen's uncle sprawled on his side along the far edge of the mounded furs and blankets. Judging by the nearby spill of indigo hair—and despite profuse criticisms regarding doggish practice—Lapis was cuddled against Laud. Probably borrowing body heat.

The encircling arm shifted, and a hand gripped Tenma's shoulder. Low and soft, someone spoke close to his ear. "Good morning, Tenma Subaru."

Not Quen.

Tenma's mind raced. He was sure he'd fallen asleep between Ever and Quen.

"I hope my sons acquitted themselves well in my absence, which was regrettable. I do prefer to greet our guests personally."

Tenma rolled enough to peer over his shoulder, straight into a face known the whole world over. Harmonious Starmark. He was between *Harmonious Starmark* and ... and his baby. Was that bad? Or was that only bears?

"S-spokesperson, sir!" he gasped, floundering for something to say. Gratitude? Apology? Introduction?

"Hush, boy, hush. No sense tucking your tail." He reclined on

129

his side, propped up on half a dozen pillows. Copper eyes were really quite mesmerizing at close quarters. "We're the ones imposing. Too many reports, too much wine, and too late an hour. It was suggested that we retire here, since Lapis' habits are long established, and Laud was good enough to let us in."

"I'm ... Tenma."

"Yes, you are. Hush, boy, hush," he repeated. The hand moved to gently tousle his hair. "I am only here to reinforce my sons' welcome. And to indulge my curiosity. I'll be up front. I saw your school application, read the essay and all that. You acquitted yourself well, but I am the sort of person who likes to get a good whiff of someone."

Harmonious Starmark had checked up on him. Like he was some kind of security threat. "I won't tell."

Shaggy brows lifted.

Tenma tried again. "If you're worried about gossip or anything, I'd never say things about your private life."

"Thank you for your loyalty to me and mine." Harmonious gave his head a final pat before returning his arm to its former place. "It's good you fell in among dogs. You hoped for a pack, didn't you?"

How ...? Oh, yes. He'd read the essay. Tenma squeezed his eyes shut, lapsing into mortified silence.

Harmonious jostled his youngest son. "Ever, help me with your new friend."

The toddler in Tenma's arms blinked once, twice, then exclaimed "Da!"

He flung himself at his father, who rolled onto his back,

holding his young son at arm's length and grinning indulgently while Ever wriggled and giggled.

Tenma sat up and found his glasses. He smoothed his hand over the unfamiliar cloth of his borrowed sleepwear, watching them tussle, feeling like an intruder. His gaze slid to Lapis, who slept on despite the ruckus. Laud offered Tenma a small nod, which he returned.

That's when he realized there was another person bundled up in the furs. He could see a bare shoulder, grayish hair, one pointed ear. Tenma leaned to one side, a little afraid of what he'd discover, only to start back when this Rivven gave a languorous stretch. It was just a peek before he turned away and tugged the blankets higher, but it was enough.

Nobody would believe it.

He didn't believe it.

Somehow, Tenma had rated a spot in a high-ranking sleepover. Because he'd woken up between Harmonious Starmark and Hisoka Twineshaft, with the world's first crosser snuggled under his chin.

And this counted for normal for Quen.

Tenma's gaze drifted to the Kith who'd been warming his feet all night and whispered, "Can you believe this?"

The big dog's mouth dropped open as if he was laughing.

"What's that?" Harmonious whispered something to Ever and set him down, then extended a hand to Tenma. "Don't be shy."

It was a big hand, and every claw curved to a neat tip. Just like Quen's hands. And the copper eyes with smiling crinkles at the edges are just like Quen's eyes. Because this is his father. And Ever's father. The kind of father who crashes sleepovers and wrestles on the floor and introduces himself to your friends. And a tiny part of Tenma—no, a *big* part—wished that he'd been born into Quen's and Ever's family.

So he crawled closer and met this fatherly person's palm.

A casual tug sent Tenma sprawling across a broad chest, and with a roll, he was trapped. Jaws snapped beside his ear, and he froze. Not until fingers tested the ticklishness of his ribs did he struggle. The ensuing battle could only be described as surreal—growling and dares, advice and laughter. When the tussle ended, Tenma was breathless and his glasses askew, and all he felt was ... elation.

Harmonious obeyed Ever's command to *sniffen* Tenma, and after an unnecessarily noisy perusal of his scent, the head of the Starmark clan declared, "He's warming to us. Shall we keep him?"

"Yeth!" Ever peered at Tenma over his dad's shoulder. "For Quen."

Tenma remained limp on the furs, by choice as much as necessity. Harmonious had him pinned and made no move to let him up. Something had changed, but Tenma wasn't exactly sure what. Only that his pulse was thready with anticipation, and that he wasn't even a little bit afraid.

"Quen brought you here, and that's trust," said his dad. "What do you say, Tenma Subaru? Would you be opposed to my treating you as pack?"

"I *must* protest," came a voice, low and lazy. "I saw him first."

How long had Lapis been watching?

Harmonious snorted. "Eloquence's claim is a matter of record. But if you crave kinship, I'll claim you next, dragonling."

Blue eyes widened, then narrowed. "Are you threatening me?"

"Let's call it a promise. But this one first."

Tenma's stomach flipped at the intensity of Harmonious' gaze. And the enormity of his offer. Dogs were reportedly friendly, Spokesperson Starmark more than most. So this probably wasn't as important to him as it was to Tenma. But even if this dog made offers of friendship and kinship to every person who strolled through his gates, Tenma wanted this.

"Please," he whispered.

"Good lad." Harmonious leaned down to kiss his forehead. "Welcome home."

The sob took Tenma by surprise.

Quen's dad mussed his hair and patted his cheek and quietly repeated, "Good lad. Come now, Ever. Sniffen your new packmate while I keep my promise to Lapis."

And in a flicker of movement too fast for Tenma to track, Harmonious was gone, leaving Ever with him. Propping up on an elbow, Tenma saw Lapis' futile attempt at escape. Laud had him by the elbow, and the hand on his shoulder must have belonged to Hisoka Twineshaft. Then Harmonious was on him—tickling and extolling the glories of pack.

Lapis' imperious demands dissolved into fluting laughter and growled oaths, but Tenma thought perhaps the dragon was enjoying the attention. Just as he had.

With a gentle tug at Ever's ear, Tenma whispered, "Your dad's nice."

Harmonious soundly kissed Lord Mossberne's forehead, then turned their way. "I almost forgot. Would you do me a favor, Tenma?"

"Yes, sir. Anything."

"Pass along a message to your teacher at school." Harmonious traded a glance with Uncle Laud. "I need to keep Eloquence home for a few days—a week at the most—on a matter of importance to the pack."

19
STAR FESTIVAL

Kimiko jumped a little when Akira brought his hand down with a *thwap* on the edge of their table. Hardly the most polite request for attention—even boars were more subtle—but effective. Setting aside her jumble of forms, lists, and reminders, she looked between her partner and the girl he had by the wrist.

Isla Ward wore an expression of strained politeness.

If Kimiko had to guess, she'd say Akira was about twelve seconds away from the end of diplomatic relations and the beginning of sisterly wrath.

She'd met the other reaver, of course, but in that fleeting way in which two people acknowledged one another's existence without any intention of learning more. Just like at Ingress. To be fair, *everyone* in class mostly stuck to their triad. This week was their first class-wide project, preparations for the Star Festival.

New Saga High School had been given a prime slot on the center stage. Classes 1-A, 2-A, and 3-A would be putting on a play, reenacting the story of Saint Midori. Kimiko would have loved to be one of the actors, but that was A-group's role. B-group had been assigned to costuming and set design. With the rest of C-group, Class 3-C was organizing a long line of booths, where festival-goers could buy traditional Star Festival treats and Amaranthine trinkets.

"Do that thing!" Akira's eyes were sparkling. "Please, Kimi. Isla won't listen, so you need to show her what you can do."

Isla tried to tug free. "Stop being a bother. Can't you see she's busy?"

"I'm telling you, she knows stuff you'll be interested in." He could be surprisingly stubborn. "Isla's decent, but a little superior. You've gotta make allowances for geniuses. But you don't mind, do you, Kimi?"

She might have fended off his pleading look, but Isla tipped the scales in his favor. Her expression was polite, but her posture betrayed her skepticism.

"I don't mind," Kimiko said blandly. "I need to check in with each team. Would that offer enough of a demonstration?"

"Do it!" Akira's hands fairly whirled with his excitement. "Watch her, Isla. You'll see."

The girl was tall for twelve, already a match for Akira, and a beauty. Fair as a fairy tale princess, with glossy curls and big green eyes. Kimiko wondered what kind of person she was under all the pedigree, power, and connections.

Pretty wrappers were no guarantee of quality chocolate.

"Sorry for Akira," Kimiko said, giving her partner's shoulder a cuff. "This won't take long."

Pulling out her chair, she used it to step onto their table, gaining the attention she'd need. And with the same orderliness with which she arranged her collections, she silently addressed herself to the Amaranthine members of each triad.

Casual greetings. Calls for reports. Compliments for those ahead of schedule. Assessing the needs of stragglers. And relaying requests for extra help so everything would be completed in time.

Maybe she was showing off just a little, tailoring her messages to each particular clan, adding the sorts of nuances that would please her classmates. All the while, keeping her gestures discreet, refined, subtle. To the untrained eye, it might look as if she was turning in a slow circle, surveying the room. And fidgeting a bit in the process.

Responses varied—amusement, relief, a spate of sly banter, gratitude, and more than one compliment. Kimiko brushed them off, consistently referring to her role as representative, serving the class.

Hanoo rolled his eyes and teased. Shouldn't a speaker for the reavers speak with reavers?

She laughed at herself. It was true, she was playing favorites.

While she had their attention, she made herself available in a general way, should any of them have questions or need clarification. And then she stepped down.

The whole process had taken less than a minute.

"That just leaves ... where *is* Eloquence Starmark? He's been gone all week."

Isla had been scanning the room, so her answer was a little distracted. "Quen had a family obligation and won't return to class until next week."

"But he'll miss the festival!" protested Kimiko.

"There will be other festivals."

Kimiko knew that her Amaranthine classmates might well see a thousand such festivals, should the tradition be carried forward through enough generations. But this was the only one Eloquence could experience with *this* class. Shouldn't he treasure these once-in-a-lifetime experiences more? Or ... maybe he did. And he was as disappointed as she would be in his place.

Isla turned around, and Kimiko noticed the change immediately. Excitement seemed ready to burst through her hefty wards. "You conferred with them all?"

"Except Eloquence." Kimiko tried not to look too smug. "Since he's currently out of visual range."

"Akira says you're teaching him." Isla slipped her arm through Kimiko's, leaning into her side. "Which is good, because he's awful."

"Hey!" he protested. "I didn't even know it was a thing before Suuzu pegged Kimi. She's genius, right? Admit it, Isla."

The girl pursed her lips, then huffed, then asked, "May I call you Kimi, too?"

"Please, do."

"And ... when you're giving Akira lessons, will you include me?"

"I'd love that," Kimiko whispered, then offered an earnest message. *You've made me glad our paths have crossed.*

After classes finished up for the day, Kimiko made the rounds with Hanoo and Sosuke, checking and double-checking their preparations. Once they were sure everything was as ready as it could be, she offered to report to Ms. Reeves in the faculty offices. Mostly so she could talk to her in private.

"Thank you, Kimiko." Her teacher smiled knowingly and asked, "Was there something else?"

Grateful for the opening, she blurted, "I'm wondering about Eloquence Starmark."

"He'll return to classes next week."

"*After* the festival."

"It *is* a shame." Ms. Reeves nodded, then nodded again. "Would you like to bring him some of the festival treats the class has prepared? I'm sure he'd appreciate the gesture."

"Shouldn't it be Isla? She's his partner."

The woman asked, "Who is the one who came to me because she wanted to make sure a classmate wasn't left out? And if you don't mind my saying so, I have an idea that you're especially fond of this festival."

"All of my memories of the Star Festival are good." Kimiko took a posture of acceptance.

Ms. Reeves nodded approvingly. "Fill some of those tiered boxes and wrap them up. Are you familiar with the Starmark compound?"

Kimiko laughed a little. It was a silly question. The whole world was familiar with the Starmark compound.

20

STARRY GIFTS

Kimiko didn't exactly gawk, but she felt a little like a tourist in her own city. The gates that appeared on television so often looked even bigger in person. Thick enough that knocking would be pointless. Heavy enough that opening them would be impossible.

Still, she wanted to get closer, to stand in the same place where so many press conferences had been held. The doors showed beautiful craftsmanship—carved wood, its fine grain so smooth, it looked oiled. Kimiko caressed the silken surface with her fingertips and immediately felt the trip and tickle of wards.

With the click of a latch, a door beside the gate opened a few centimeters. Was this an invitation to enter?

"Hello?"

Nothing.

Pushing the door wider, she peered inside. "Pardon my intrusion," she tentatively called, closing the door behind her. It was like stepping into a forest. She hadn't realized there were so many trees this close to the road. Then again, this had been the home of an Amaranthine clan for centuries, and they were famous for their nature preserves and wildlife habitats. She caught the faint and familiar rattle of leaves and followed the sound to a large camphor tree alongside the path. Perhaps a younger sibling to their shrine's grand specimen?

The wide road that began at the big front gates vanished into woods. It was clear of snow, which heaped up on either side, so she couldn't tell if there were trails or benches or garden beds. These woods must be lovely in summer. "Hello?" she called again.

Oh, well. She supposed they'd send someone after her eventually, and then she could explain her errand. But she'd barely taken two steps when she encountered a guard dog. A very small, chubby-cheeked guard dog. She recognized him, of course. Even without the ears, he was Harmonious Starmark in miniature.

Kimiko bowed and addressed him seriously. "Peace, young sir. Are you the gate guard?"

He looked between her and the door, which he must have opened. "Tenma coming?"

"Did you think I was him? I'm sorry to disappoint you." She showed her palms. "I know Tenma-kun since we're classmates. I was hoping to speak to Eloquence. Is he here?"

"Bruvver busy."

A large Kith stepped into the open. The dog's auburn fur had been brushed to the sort of high gloss one expected in show dogs. His ears drooped like a setter's or a spaniel's, and his eyes were the exact same copper as the little boy's.

Kimiko bowed again. "I go to school with Eloquence Starmark. He's been absent, so I brought him a gift for the upcoming festival."

The Kith sat, and the little boy trotted forward. "Who you?"

"I'm Kimiko." Setting down her bag, she knelt on the path so he could reach her palms. "May I ask your name?"

That put a bounce in his step. "Ever!" He made a very proper bow, then plucked at his sleeve, showing off his family crest. "Ever Starmark, cause I'm Da's boy!"

"You are a tribute to your den."

The boy's face scrunched adorably. "Nuh-uh. Bruvver's a triboot. I'm juss me."

Kimiko wasn't sure what he meant, but it hardly mattered. Ever was precious. And rather articulate for three years, though he lisped softly over his syllables.

"I should sniffen you," he announced.

"If you think that would be wise," she said with equal gravity.

And then she had her arms full of boyish curiosity.

"Short." He petted her hair. "Dun grow?"

"When my hair gets long, I cut it short." She whispered, "Sometimes people think I'm a boy."

He snuffled at her neck, then gave a small huff of disdain. "Smells like girl."

"What do girls smell like?" she asked.

Ever returned to sniffing as if investigating the matter and surprised her by adding a bit of a nibble.

She quietly asked, "What are you doing?"

He licked the spot in what was surely meant as an apology and leaned back. "You mind me of Mum."

"Is that good?"

"Like … dis." Ever held out a tight fist, then slowly opened it, as if releasing a butterfly. "Stars inside. I like dem, but she hides dem. Special for Da. Who are yours for?"

She skirted that question. "Your mother's a reaver?"

"She's Mum, but Da calls her Anna." Pointing to her bag, he asked, "What dose?"

Before she could answer, a male voice came from directly behind. "*Ever.*"

"Spect." The boy's ears drooped guiltily, but he clung more tightly to Kimiko.

She turned to look up—quite a ways up—into the face of a powerfully-built Amaranthine male dressed in Starmark colors. *Not* Eloquence. Carefully rising to her feet, she propped Ever on her hip and offered her free hand. "My name's Kimiko Miyabe of Kikusawa Shrine."

"Prospect Starmark," he replied curtly. "May I ask your purpose in coming here, reaver?"

It was awkward, relying on one-handed gestures, but she rather enjoyed the challenge. And the more she conveyed, the more Ever's older brother relaxed. She explained, "I came looking for Eloquence. He's my classmate." Bending to catch the handles of her bag, she asked, "Would you give this to him?"

"What do you think, Ever?" asked Prospect.

She felt something batting against her arm. His tail!

"Since you've come this far, Kimiko, I think you should see it through." Prospect beckoned for her to follow. "My runt of a brother won't be much longer. I'll show you where you can wait."

He guided her through a series of courtyards, sometimes on raised porches, sometimes along shoveled paths. Given how many buildings they passed, the Starmark clan was almost a city unto itself. Well, a neighborhood, anyhow. But she didn't see a single soul. Everything was quiet, as if the place had been evacuated.

"Where is everyone?" she asked. Maybe she shouldn't have. But her Starmark guide didn't seem to mind.

"Festival preparations, one way or another." He grinned at her. "Here's the den you need. Ever, be a good host until Quen returns. Kimiko, if you need anything, tell Rise."

The Kith leapt onto the pavilion's wide front porch and gave a welcoming *wuff*.

Prospect slid the front panel open, poking his head through to peer around. "You can duck inside if you need the shelter." He scanned the heavy clouds and hummed vaguely. "Shouldn't be much longer."

When he left, Kimiko gave in to curiosity, but there wasn't much in the pavilion's outer room—tatami mats on the floor, a single chest, and a low table with a neat stack of school books at its center. Sliding screens barred the view into inner rooms, and she refused to snoop any further. Mother would have. All the more reason not to, as far as Kimiko was concerned.

So she slid the door closed and rejoined Rise on the porch. "May I sit with you?"

With the Kith at her back and Ever in her lap, she'd be warm enough for a while.

The boy renewed his line of inquiry about her baggage. "What dose?"

"Do you know about the Star Festival?"

Ever's ears pricked forward, quavering. "Fessval?" he asked.

"Everyone in Keishi loves the story of the Star Festival." Encouraged by his eager expression, she offered a highly abridged version. "Reavers remember a long-ago day when a beautiful girl with the brightest soul called down the stars from the sky."

"Talk to stars?"

"That's how the story goes. Some say they were angels. Some say they must have been sky clansmen."

"Manthine?"

"Yes, from the clan of the sky." She knew these stories from her grandfather, and it was fun to share them. "Have you learned any stories about imps?"

"Dun know dem." He rubbed his nose against her chin. "Story?"

"Imps are the impressions of old." Kimiko adopted the sing-song tone that had been such a big part of her childhood. "The star clans belong to one of the four lost peoples—sky, sea, mountain, and tree."

Ever's wide eyes shifted to the surrounding woods. "Manthine trees?"

"They're my favorite in the stories, so I know lots of things about trees. But this is the Star Festival." Reaching for the bag, she explained, "Gifts are one of the traditions; we give starry gifts. And we wish upon the stars. Best of all, we share starry sweets. See?"

And she lifted the topmost box's lid, revealing an array of star-shaped fruit jellies and molded candies, some sparkling with sugar, others studded with nuts. The second box held chocolate wafers, and the third a honeyed cake, rich with butter and liberally flecked with orange zest.

"I brought these for Eloquence so he wouldn't miss out."

Ever tapped the edge of the box. "Trade wiff me?"

"I'm sure your brother would share," she ventured.

"Him dun like sweet stuffs."

Kimiko innocently asked, "But you do?"

The boy tangled his fingers together and shyly admitted, "I does."

"Then I'm sure we can work something out."

"Right back!" And the boy disappeared around the corner.

With a soft grunt, the Kith rose to follow.

"I don't want to get him into trouble," whispered Kimiko.

Rise turned back long enough to nose her chest and lick her cheek, then ambled away. Five minutes passed into seven before the boy came skulking back, carrying a bundle in both hands.

She asked, "What do you have there?"

"Better stars." Ever offered it very properly on both palms. "Stars for Bruvver. You make him happy?"

Kimiko wondered at his tone. "Is your brother unhappy?"

Ever frowned. He shook his head, then nodded, then shook again. "Bruvver's a big boy. Dis a big boy gift." He pressed it into Kimiko's chest, so that she had to take it or else it would fall.

With extreme care, she folded back the wrappings, revealing a lovely old comb. The fading light gleamed softly on its surface, which was indeed etched with delicate stars. "Ever, this looks valuable. You can't trade this for sweets." She refolded the cloth and extended it. "I can't take this."

"Not for you. For Bruvver."

Kimiko was willing to concede the point. Was there really any harm in indulging the little guy? He could have his sweets, and

146

when Eloquence arrived, she'd return what had to be a family heirloom. So she said, "Thank you very much, Ever. I'll make sure to give this to your brother."

21

HEIRLOOM

Ever munched happily on festival fare, kicking his feet over the edge of the porch. He'd brought a blanket out for Kimiko, who nibbled the point off a chocolate star while searching the overcast sky. The clouds sometimes whirled and spun in a wind that didn't reach the ground, and she could feel a kind of thundering. Not a noise, really. More like a rumble she could feel in her chest. "What *is* that?"

Her companion mumbled unconcernedly around a mouthful. "Uncle."

She wasn't necessarily surprised. There must be every kind of Kith and Kindred in and around—and above—the Starmark compound. Flight was a typical Amaranthine capability, so the clan must be romping around somewhere above the clouds. Maybe they had their own way of celebrating the Star Festival. Feats of strength or speed.

"He must be really strong," she said.

"Yeth."

"Is Eloquence up there?" she asked.

Ever didn't answer, but his ears were sinking fast. Had something happened? Only then did she register the cessation of airborne clamoring. And then something streaked across her field of vision ... and Ever vanished from her side.

The chocolate slipped from her fingers, and she scrambled to her knees. Standing a short distance away, Harmonious Starmark stood watching her, his young son in his arms.

By the time she'd extricated herself from the blanket, a second male stood by his side—massive, white-haired, and clad in copper armor. The unknown warrior gripped a bared sword, and he was riled enough that his presence pressed uncomfortably against Kimiko's quailing soul.

Harmonious wasn't much better. Stiff and stern. This was not the friendly face one usually saw on the news.

"Sorry," she whispered.

"Do you have reason to apologize?" inquired Spokesperson Starmark.

She shook her head, and her free hand offered a feeble plea for understanding. Where was Prospect to vouch for her? She glanced pleadingly at Rise, who was licking icing off his nose. The sneak had downed the last of the cake. "Mooch!" she whispered.

"My son is a little young to be entertaining a lady." Ever's father had mellowed, and it showed in his tone. "How did you happen to meet?"

She bowed. "I'm Kimiko Miyabe, a student at New Saga High School. I'm in Eloquence's class."

"Well met, Miyabe-chan." Harmonious' gaze shifted to a point past her shoulder. "Can you verify her claim?"

Kimiko turned to find Eloquence standing a little ways apart, looking very different than usual. He was breathing hard, and his hair was loose and wild. More shocking, he was also arrayed like a warrior—armed and armored, in a glory of copper and traditional silks.

"Reaver representative for Class 3-C," he confirmed in a rough voice.

He looked as if he needed a seat. And sounded as if he needed a pot of tea. And here she was, keeping him from creature comforts. "I'm sorry to have interrupted. I didn't want you to be totally left out of the fun of the Star Festival, so I brought a few things."

Nearly all of which had already been eaten.

Kimiko rubbed the back of her neck and sheepishly added, "Ever liked all the stars."

Eloquence seemed amused by something, but with a glance in his father's direction, he drew himself up and executed a gracious bow. "Thank you for your consideration. I will accept your generosity, and you'll be free to go."

Acceptance with a dismissive undercurrent. But Kimiko could almost feel the weariness rolling off him. So she didn't drag out her presentation with the explanation she probably owed. Extending the comb in its wrappings, she offered the traditional festival blessing. "May the stars grant the dearest wish of your heart."

A flicker of confusion crossed his face, but he accepted her gift. Lifting away the delicate folds of cloth, he went still.

Kimiko thought it best to explain, but Eloquence was suddenly much, *much* closer.

He quietly demanded, "Where did you get this?"

But his father's voice cut across her reply. "How fortuitous! And timely as well, since you are only now in a position to accept. I'll just go tell your mother the good news!"

Harmonious left, pulling the white-haired warrior along after him. Rise loped after Ever, who waved goodbye over his father's shoulder, leaving Kimiko alone with Eloquence.

"I don't understand what just happened," she said, easing into the most bewildered posture in her repertoire.

"Where did you get this?" Eloquence repeated.

"Your brother traded with me for the sweets I brought." She indicated the remnants of her original gift. "He seemed to think you'd like this better, and I didn't see the harm."

His expression, his posture—they gave nothing away. Yet she was sure she'd upset him.

"What's wrong?" she whispered.

"You don't know what this is?"

Kimiko's crisp movement roughly translated, *It is there before you*. Meaning it should be obvious to anyone. "It's a comb."

"This is the very comb that Glint Starmark gave to his bond-mate Radiance."

"Goodness! A family treasure, then," she murmured. Everyone had heard of Glint, First of Dogs. "No wonder you were concerned.

But I never would have kept it, I promise."

Eloquence shook his head and went on. "This comb came to my father, and it's been borrowed from time to time by my brothers. The giving of such a gift is highly traditional."

"I see," said Kimiko, but she really didn't.

"This is a traditional betrothal gift." Eloquence's voice tightened. "By giving this to me in the presence of my father, you've formally declared your intention to court me."

Kimiko needed a few moments to rally.

"*No wonder* you looked so stunned! Coming out of the blue. And we hardly know each other." She knew her words were empty. After all, *she'd* likely end up contracted to a relative stranger. But she could imagine Eloquence's dismay. "I take it I've made things awkward for you."

He seemed lost in thought.

"Please, don't blame Ever. The mistake was mine, and I apologize." she said. "Would it help if I explained ...?"

"No." He slowly drew the folds of silk around the comb. "No need."

"But your father thinks I *proposed*."

"Because you *did* propose."

"But it was an accident." Kimiko felt as if they were talking in circles.

"It *was* an accident," Eloquence quietly acknowledged. "But Dad didn't take issue."

Kimiko glanced in the direction Harmonious Starmark had gone. "Wasn't he just teasing us?"

Eloquence's fingers tightened around the gift, but then he held out his hand. "Are you taking back your offer?"

"I couldn't!" She waved her hands. "Not the comb, anyhow. It's obviously precious to your family."

"So your offer stands?"

The words came cautiously, with a nuance of body language that threw Kimiko for a loop. He wanted her to answer in the affirmative. But she couldn't fathom *why*. She asked, "You want it to stand?"

"Why wouldn't I?" he asked.

Kimiko edged closer and half-whispered, "You're not making any sense."

"No?" Eloquence tucked the comb into a pouch at his waist. "It's really very simple, Kimiko Miyabe. You may proceed with your courtship. I accept your suit."

22

SUITOR

Come inside where it's warm," Quen offered. Although he suspected the cold wasn't responsible for the sudden change in Kimiko's pallor. Her scent, her posture, her searching gaze—their underlying confusion was unanimous. At least there was no sign of fear or annoyance. She would hear him out.

But she hadn't lost the trail. "Why would you hold me to this?"

He hesitated. He hedged. "Am I unsuitable?"

Kimiko waved aside his attempt at distraction. "You're a *Starmark*. You're probably going to be one of the world's most eligible bachelors after graduation. It's *my* suitability at question."

"Because you're human?"

She seemed baffled. "Your Dad obviously doesn't have a problem with humans in a general sense. But *he* was in love."

"And you're not." Quen had a feeling this was going very

poorly. Was Kimiko the kind of girl who needed to be charmed ... or convinced ... or cornered?

"Most reavers don't have that luxury." She retreated, but only from the draft coming through the partially open door. "Isn't an emotional connection considered essential for Amaranthine bonding? Especially for canines. You mate for life."

The truth was not a terrible one, but it made him feel ungrateful. How to explain? "My role within the pack is ... unique. I will not take a bondmate. So *this* is the only den I will know."

Kimiko's brows furrowed. "I know dragons have celibate males, but ... not you guys. Then again, I thought the clans didn't go in for war. You'll make a lot of people nervous if they ever see you like this."

His armor. His sword. Quen winced. "Please, don't mention any of this to anyone."

"I won't," she said simply.

And perhaps because she didn't ask for more, he gave it. "Dogs have never made war against humans, but we have always defended our dens and our allies. My uncle put me in this for a special occasion."

She brightened. "Because of the Star Festival?"

"In a way." This week did hold significance for the pack. Doubly so, now. "Today marks my attainment."

"Congratulations!" Her hands fluttered through an eclectic series of compliments, some of which didn't actually apply. Especially the one about antlers. But each conveyed an appropriately celebratory note in keeping with one's rite of passage. "The Starmark pack is stronger for your place in it."

Her enthusiasm brought a flush of pleasure, but Quen needed to tell the rest. "I waited a long time for Dad's acknowledgement. I don't have my brothers' height or breadth. I'm … undergrown."

She looked him up and down, and his insides curled miserably. But he wanted her to know these things, because they were part of the reason he needed her agreement.

Kimiko said, "I never gave it much thought. You're still taller than the humans. Except Tenma."

He sighed. There was little use pointing out that members of his clan had some of the largest statures—in both speaking and true forms—and that her people tended to be small. If breeding held true, Ever would certainly outstrip him, for Anna's build and coloring showed she came from Scandinavian stock.

"And I'm older than you."

Kimiko actually looked insulted. "Hardly news."

Quen closed his eyes. "I have twice the years of any Amaranthine in our classroom."

"Oh. *Oh!* That's what Ever meant!" Kimiko's fingers settled lightly on his arm. "He seemed to think you were unhappy. And he wanted you to have a *big boy* gift."

"And you were his choice for me." He caught her hand but held it loosely. "Or rather, he wanted you to choose me."

She didn't resist when he threaded his fingers with hers. But her entire attitude was pointedly neutral. "Why won't you tell me why?"

"Will you keep a confidence?"

"Yes."

He wanted to pull her closer, but armor was far from welcoming. So he bowed until his forehead rested against hers. "My place in the family is traditional. I am set apart to serve the pack, not myself. And so I cannot seek a mate. But sometimes, people like me will attract the interest of another." Quen chose not to add that this exception usually applied to females of exceptional beauty. "I cannot court, but I can be courted."

Kimiko hummed softly. "Wouldn't it be better to wait for some nice lady dog to realize she could have a Starmark for her very own?"

"That won't happen, Kimiko Miyabe." He swallowed against the lump building in his throat. "Most see my role, not me. And even if they did see me, they would not give chase."

She didn't speak, but she seemed offended on his behalf.

"There's a reason my older brothers call me *runt*." Did he really have to say it? Quen muttered, "Females of breeding age are all taller than me."

Kimiko's eyes slid shut, and her other hand covered their linked ones. "Does that mean, that you think I'm your only chance? Because ... I'm not. One word from your father, and the heralds would be delivering marriage offers by the thousands. You'd have your pick of beauties and beacons."

"I'm already pitied in private; don't suggest public shaming." He rubbed his cheek against hers in silent plea. "Ever gave me to you. I need no other."

She was smiling, but not happily. "I need to tell you some things, too. For instance, my mother is the biggest gossip in Keishi, so publicity is practically guaranteed. And I *also* have a duty to my family. I'm supposed to improve the Miyabe bloodline by marrying a reaver of pedigree. And I can't leave Kikusawa because my people are shrinekeepers."

Quen didn't want to hear reasons, no matter how reasonable. She paused. "But ..."

His heart lurched.

"But if I understand your situation clearly, this chance is once-in-a-lifetime. I think I can convince my family that it's in their best interest for me to have a Starmark of my very own." Kimiko's previous calm grew increasingly flustered. "If you're actually serious."

He couldn't quite speak, but he knew a dozen ways to beg that required none. By the fifth, she was smiling. By the eighth, she caught his hands.

"Enough." Her face had flushed, and her heart had found a quicker pace. "If you'll help me settle matters with my family, I agree to become your suitor."

Eloquence didn't even care that she'd set conditions on her offer. He would fulfill every requirement. Gladly.

"And ... can we talk about this more? Another time, of course." She pulled free and eased toward the door, apology in her posture. "I have work. At the shrine. Festival stuff."

"I'll find you at school," he promised. "Only ... one more thing." She waited.

"It's traditional for a couple to signify their intent to proceed with a show of ... mutual satisfaction."

"Oh. Sure." And she thrust out her hand.

Eloquence guessed he'd put it too delicately. He accepted the handclasp with as much poise as he could muster, but his disappointment must have shown.

"Am I meant to kiss you?" The way her eyes were sparkling, she'd known all along.

"It would be traditional."

Kimiko's expression turned wry. "You know, I've been mistaken for a boy ever since I was small. I'm going to be teased *so much* for taking the manly role of suitor. But I won't mind if you don't." And to his amusement, she swept into a courtly bow over his hand. "Forgive my lack of eloquence; words fail in the presence of such beauty. Outshine the brightest stars and guide my way, for I cannot see the path ahead."

How she'd known the traditional form to use, he couldn't guess. Did reaver books include chapters on wolvish pledges? More intriguing was the playful use of his name and clan history and the teasing lilt to her delivery. For all her chivalrous posturing, she had a female's wiles.

Quen *really* wanted a taste, to see if his already-simmering interest would roll into full boil, but the only kiss he received was on the back of his hand.

And then she was gone.

23
UNSETTLING NEWS

Kimiko's steps lagged on her way to school the morning after the Star Festival. New Saga's play had drawn large crowds and thunderous applause, and curiosity-seekers remained thick around the school's booths even after they ran out of items to sell.

Following the launch of hundreds of starry lanterns, Suuzu had wanted a quieter view of the sky. So she'd invited him and Akira back to Kikusawa Shrine, which was on the city's fringe. Without her family ever realizing, they scaled the shrine roof and put Keishi's lights at their back. Long past curfew, she'd stared at the patterns made by winking stars without a thought in her head.

Only after Akira had dozed off, curled comfortably against his nestmate, did Suuzu remark on her quietness. But she had no words yet. Her betrothal to Eloquence was too new to believe, too strange to tell.

At her helpless gesture, he'd beckoned her close and drawn her down. Pillowed on Suuzu's other shoulder, she'd taken comfort from his calm. The boys spent the night locked away in the archive, and they'd stopped to buy piping hot croquettes and steamed sweet potatoes on the way in to school.

"Uh-oh," whispered Kimiko. Because Sentinel Skybellow was stationed at the gate, thick arms folded across his chest.

Akira ventured, "Are we in trouble?"

The burly, bluff head of security eyed them narrowly. "*Were* you in any trouble?"

"Not at all! But I guess we sorta slept off campus last night."

"I know."

Akira fidgeted. "Is there a rule against that?"

Sentinel blandly asked, "Are you acquainted with the student handbook?"

"I am," Suuzu said quietly. "The responsibility was mine."

"I know," repeated the dog clansman.

Kimiko didn't know exactly how Sentinel was attached to the Starmark compound. Probably not born to the Keishi pack, given his shock of silver-tipped brown hair and pale gray eyes. Married in, then? Or would that be *bonded* in. Like she would be.

Kimiko offered a weak apology. "Akira and Suuzu walked me home and stayed over."

"I gathered as much from your trail."

So he had tracked them to the shrine. "Sorry for the bother," she mumbled.

Sentinel brushed his shoulder. "You remained on good paths; you chose a safe den. All things considered, I have no complaints."

Kimiko was glad enough to be forgiven, but she couldn't decide why the dog sounded so ... glum.

The whole mood inside the school was off, but Kimiko couldn't put a label on the undercurrent running through the hallways. Except that the Amaranthine all seemed to know something the humans didn't.

In their classroom, Ms. Reeves' smile was fixed in place. Her measured tones betrayed very little, but Kimiko found signs of uneasiness in her posture. Yet her Amaranthine classmates betrayed nothing but respectful attentiveness.

She called the class to order. "This morning, we have some prestigious guests who've offered to visit our classes. A contingent of Elderboughs are currently in Keishi, along with several reavers who've trained with Kith companions."

An excited murmur went through the room.

The Elderbough pack was one of the oldest and perhaps the most famous of the wolf packs, in large part because Adoona-soh Elderbough, spokesperson for the wolves, was one of the Five.

Ms. Reeves continued. "Teams will be visiting each classroom in turn. As a few of you have already mentioned an interest in working closely with Kith, I've requested that Reaver Armstrong be the one to address our class."

Yoota and Ploom began signaling wildly to each other across the room, and the sway in Hanoo's tail increased to a swing.

Akira asked, "What sort of Kith does he belong to?"

"Isn't it the other way around?" asked Tenma.

Kimiko was glad that Isla's answering laugh held no trace of mockery.

The girl hooked her arm through Tenma's and, loud enough for everyone to hear, announced, "Our family is *owned* by a feline Kith. If Reaver Armstrong has a Kith companion, it's because the Kith chose him, *not* the other way around."

Only a few minutes passed before a light rap announced the arrival of a reaver and an Amaranthine at the door. The reaver was tall and blond, with an *aww, shucks* smile that made him look like the leading man in an American movie. His dark teal tunic designated him a battler, and the faint creases at the corners of his blue eyes suggested a genial sort of maturity. Kimiko guessed him to be about the same age as her father.

His Amaranthine companion—easily recognized as a wolf by the light brown tail flicking against the ragged cuffs of his jeans—strolled to the long row of windows and stood gazing out, as if he found the classroom claustrophobic. Leaning to one side, Kimiko managed a glimpse of the crest on his armband, and her heart gave a glad leap. Elderbough!

Kimiko studied his profile. While there was a certain resemblance, she knew this wasn't Adoona-soh's eldest son, the heir. But she wasn't familiar with the younger sons. Actually, this denim-clad wolf could just as easily be a grandson. Except she could feel his power like a low vibration—intense, impatient, irritated.

Yellow eyes locked with hers, as if he'd felt her gaze.

She surreptitiously offered him welcome and peace.

Thick brows lifted. His response was offhanded, but he wearily begged pardon, signaling distraction and directing her attention back to his partner in the simplest of terms. *Pay attention. This is important.*

After a brief consultation, Ms. Reeves raised her voice. "We're honored to have Christopher Armstrong with us today. Hanoo, if you'll unlatch the double-door, his Kith partner will also be joining us."

Hanoo, Yoota, and Ploom all leapt up, hurrying with the catches on the second classroom door, which usually remained shut. Their excitement made little sense until the Kith—an enormous black wolf—eased through the door.

Reaver Armstrong said something in English, then switched to Japanese with a broad American accent. "Cove is a wolf of the Nightspangle pack."

Ms. Reeves directed her three tail-wagging students to close up the doors and return to their seats, then yielded the floor to Reaver Armstrong.

"I apologize for the clumsiness of my words and for not having time to introduce ourselves properly. My name is Christopher Armstrong, and you are welcome to call me Chris. My Kith partner is Cove. And my other friend is Boonmar-fen Elderbough. Please, don't mind. He will move through the room while I am talking. Learning faces and scents. Okay?"

Kimiko glanced at Suuzu, whose expression had clouded considerably. Whatever it was, he knew. And it wasn't good. Akira seemed to be picking up on his best friend's mood. He'd moved his chair around and sat right beside Suuzu.

"I'm what the media usually calls a Kith handler," continued Chris. "But that's a misrepresentation. A misnomer."

He had clearly learned Japanese but didn't often use it, because he kept dropping English words into his sentences, then backing up to translate himself.

Isla raised her hand. "Would you like me to serve as translator?"

Chris shifted into a pleading posture. "That would be a big help, little lady."

Now that he wasn't working so hard to find the right words, the battler relaxed and included more nuances of posture, making it clear that he'd lived most of his life among wolves. Kimiko wondered if he belonged to the same enclave as Hanoo, Yoota, and Ploom.

"Cove has been my companion since I was twelve, and he was my grandmother's companion before me. I have seven siblings— three full, two half, and two step. The family joke is that I was both the runt and the pick of the litter."

Kimiko shook her head in wonderment. If this strapping blond man was the smallest in his family, his siblings must rival the Amaranthine in size.

"I'm enclave born and was raised to work in tandem with a Kith companion as a tracker. The role has been considered largely traditional for centuries, like many of the battler sub-classifications. But since the Emergence, both battlers and trackers are in high demand to work with law enforcement and criminal investigation. Or in the private sector as body guards, security guards, and even travel guides."

He spoke at length about the jobs available to reavers who aimed for battler classification and opportunities for humans in those same fields. Meanwhile, Boonmar-fen glided unobtrusively through the room. Those who spared him a glance had their attention firmly directed back to the front. More than once, he signaled for the students to listen to Chris.

Kimiko was impressed by Isla's poise. She and Chris quickly developed a pattern, taking turns speaking. Her polish not only put Reaver Armstrong at ease, it kept everyone in the classroom connected. Couldn't Ms. Reeves have done the same? But a glance in their homeroom teacher's direction made Kimiko sure that the idea hadn't occurred to her. Her attention was turned inward, and her downcast face was pinched and pale.

A knock preceded Sentinel Skybellow into the room, and Ms. Reeves leapt to her feet. She thanked and excused Isla, and Boonmar-fen returned to the front of the room.

This was it.

Ms. Reeves thanked Chris and encouraged young reavers interested in Kith-based careers or any of the battler specializations to speak up. "And now Sentinel needs to make an announcement."

Their head of security didn't drag it out any further. "Last night, during the height of the Star Festival, one of our students—Minami Li from Class 2-A—failed to return to the dormitories. Further investigation by experienced trackers has led to the regrettable conclusion that she was taken."

A murmur of dismay rippled through the room.

Sentinel grimly continued. "I will review the school's security measures with you, along with new guidelines to ensure the safety of every student. And Boon will want a word with anyone who may have noticed Minami any time after eight o'clock yesterday evening."

Rules were rehearsed. Restrictions added. Everyone could expect to see more Kith on campus. And Ms. Reeves went over simple statements they might use if questioned by friends and family ... or if cornered by the press.

Throughout, Kimiko had a hard time sitting still. She wanted to get home, to make sure her sisters were safe. Because she had seen the silent command issued by Boonmar-fen, watched it leap from one student to the next, galvanizing the Amaranthine to a single purpose.

Guard your reavers.

24

LADYS CHOICE

*S*entinel excused himself to speak with the next classroom, and Reaver Armstrong moved to the corner of the room with Cove to answer questions and allow students to interact with his Kith partner. Meanwhile, Boon circulated through the room, asking questions in low tones.

Suuzu touched Kimiko's hand. "You are wanted," he murmured.

She had no idea how long Eloquence had been trying to catch her attention.

His gesture was crisp, commanding. *Wait for me.*

Kimiko shook her head. "I can't. My sisters ...."

Eloquence's lips pressed into a thin line, but he inclined his head. His gaze shifted, and he said something she couldn't hear.

"He wishes you to meet him," Suuzu relayed. "After school. In the Kith shelter."

Akira was paying attention now. "What's up, Kimi?"

She could feel color creeping into her face. "I need to talk to Eloquence."

"How long?" asked Suuzu.

"Not long." She shifted into a consenting posture.

Suuzu's hand was warm around hers, and his declaration was just as crisp, commanding. "When you finish, Akira and I will walk you home."

Across the room, Eloquence inclined his head again.

In context, the gesture could indicate simple understanding ... or permission. With a sudden pang of uneasiness, she hoped it was the former. Calling Eloquence Starmark a beauty and kissing his hand had been a bit much. She'd wanted to win a smile, to give him a nice memory. But she hadn't stayed around, and she didn't know him well enough to guess if he'd been amused or insulted or ... or all the other little things she usually never worried about.

Flirting with schoolgirls was easy. A nonsense game with no consequences since she never saw them again. But there would be no avoiding Eloquence Starmark.

Did dogs understand games? Did Amaranthine even flirt? Did he think her behavior strange for a reaver? Middle school and movies had turned her into a bizarre hybrid, teetering on the borderline of acceptability as a reaver.

"You are worrying him." Suuzu left his chair to kneel beside her. "You are worrying me."

She caught a glimpse of taut concern before Akira came around and sat on the table, blocking Eloquence's view of her.

Akira asked, "What's his deal?"

Kimiko hadn't wanted to tell anyone until she felt more

confident, but maybe by confiding in Akira and Suuzu, she'd find the confidence she needed. Leaning to one side, she met Eloquence's waiting, worried gaze. And she proved that she, too, could be crisp, commanding. *All is well. No insult intended. Untuck your tail. May clear skies fill your eyes. Shake those antlers, you ruddy buck.*

Bemusement stole the tension from Eloquence's expression. The last chivvying encouragement even netted her an amused huff. And now that he was smiling, she quietly asked, "Can I tell them?"

The answer came without hesitation—*at your discretion.*

Akira and Suuzu readily agreed to wait until they reached the privacy of Kikusawa Shrine before Kimiko unburdened herself. They would be waiting at the gate. And she was hurrying toward the inner compound that the Kith called home.

Not many lingered in the mews and stalls. She supposed they must be patrolling the campus or helping search for Minami Li. Why would anyone kidnap a high school girl? And who would dare to do it here? Keishi was the informal headquarters of the Five, and more than any other clan, the Starmarks considered reavers their allies. Dogs and reavers—they were the In-between's founders and foundation.

Someone was going to *regret* taking that girl.

Given the number of trackers in town, Kimiko was rather surprised they still hadn't found her. Maybe Eloquence could tell her more?

A low bark from the back guided her to a straw-filled alcove partially sheltered from the wind by heavy curtains. Eloquence stepped into the open and quietly offered his palms. As soon as hers rested on his, his fingers tangled with hers.

"I apologize," he murmured. "For asking you to come when you would rather go to your family."

"My first impulse was to get home as fast as possible. My second was to text Sakiko. She's fine. So's Noriko." She felt foolish and let him see it. "I asked you for time to talk, then tried to rush off. I'm the one who owes an apology."

Backing up, he drew her into the shelter, which was large enough to accommodate a pair of russet-furred dogs with cloudy eyes and whitening muzzles. "This is Edge and his bondmate Flay. They belong to the Starmark pack. They've decided to ... conspire with us, I suppose." His gaze dropped and he gruffly added, "They offer their den for our trysting."

"I see," she said. Although once again, she didn't. "Thank you very much."

Eloquence seemed flustered. "They've always been matchmakers. As bad as my grandsire. And *full* of suggestions. To be perfectly honest, they'll make terrible chaperones."

Everyone knew Kith were sentient. But it was also universally understood that Kith couldn't speak. Unlike the so-called High Amaranthine, they couldn't take speaking form. Although Kimiko suspected she should be more concerned about his references to chaperones and trysting, she blurted, "What do you mean ... suggestions?"

His mouth moved, but no sound came. His hands spread, curled, and wavered without making any sense. Finally, he forced out one word. "Specifically?"

Kimiko studied the two dogs. "Kith communication is limited to rudimentary concepts and inferences gained from the inherent force of personality that comes with sentience."

Eloquence relaxed a little. "That is an excellent summation of Reaver Armstrong's lecture. That is the way of things between a reaver and the Kith."

"It's different for you?"

He said nothing, did nothing. Had she run up against some sort of clan secret?

This time, she made it a statement. "It's different for you."

"May I confide in you?"

She nodded, and he led her deeper into the shadowy alcove, behind the two lazing dogs. Eloquence sat in the rustling straw, using Edge as a backrest, and drew Kimiko down by his side. It was warmer here and well-guarded. A good place for sharing secrets.

"Kith have voices." Eloquence tapped his forehead. "We can hear those of our clan, our breed, and often of close kin."

"They speak in your thoughts."

"Yes. And I speak for them. That's my role in the pack." He edged closer so their arms touched. "That's why my father named me Eloquence. I speak for those who cannot."

"So you're in charge of the Kith?"

Edge grunted, and Flay reached over her mate's back to nose Eloquence's hair. He chuckled and said, "I'm theirs more than they are mine."

"And they know about the betrothal thing?" Kimiko responded

172

to his restlessness. As soon as she shifted forward, his arm slipped around her back.

"Rise was there, and he was pleased." Now that she was tucked up against his side, Eloquence seemed to relax. "Word spreads fast when Kith are involved."

"I see," she said. And this time, she thought she did. "Should we talk about what's supposed to happen next?"

"Yes. Because my father spoke with me on the matter." His voice was soft, calm, yet somehow cautious. "Dad has no objection to your choice, but he set conditions for me. The chase is yours. You must court me, not the other way around."

"I'm the suitor."

He hummed an affirmative. "I will not initiate contact."

Kimiko laughed. "Like now?"

Eloquence's eyes widened. "This is not courting behavior."

"I know." She turned into him, placing her hand on his chest. "But I haven't researched courting behavior, and books rarely go into nuances. If I'm going to take the lead, you'll still have to guide me."

"Ask anything." He smiled faintly. "I'm not an unfathomable mystery, unlike females."

Was he teasing? "Even Amaranthine have trouble under-standing girls?"

"Persons of your gender defy explanation. If you are uncomfortable asking me something, choose other confidants. One of the teachers, or I will gladly introduce you to my stepmother. Even though she will likely relay embarrassing tales of my childhood."

"She's human."

173

"Yes, and she's been part of the Starmark clan for many years. Her insights would surely inform you, although in her case, my father did the courting."

"Their betrothal *wasn't* an accident."

He smiled crookedly. "Everyone has seen the televised special detailing the two great loves of Harmonious Starmark."

"Well, yes," she conceded. "But there's usually a big difference between reality and publicity."

"There is more to the story than the people of this city remember. But theirs is not my story to tell." He lined up his words with great delicacy. "I can welcome your interest in me. If you have questions, ask them. If you want something, take it. Like tending with a trusted reaver, my answer will always be *yes*."

His tone and posture didn't match. He meant more than he was saying. And she thought she understood. "Are you asking me to ask for things?"

"Please."

"What do you need?" Kimiko signaled that she was listening, that she was willing. "What do you *want*?"

Eloquence elbowed Edge.

Apparently the Kith's suggestions were unwanted. In a way, it was too bad she couldn't hear Edge or Flay. Then she wouldn't be left guessing. All she could do was wait for Eloquence to find words ... or the courage to speak them.

He leaned down, once again resting his forehead against hers. Eyes firmly shut, he mumbled, "I do want a taste."

So she pressed her lips against his. Initiation accomplished.

Which seemed to be enough to fulfill the courting requirement, because Eloquence took charge, cupping Kimiko's cheek and slipping the tip of his tongue into her mouth. She parted her lips. He pressed soft kisses along her bottom lip, followed by a cautious swipe. Then a nibble and lick. She gasped for air, and he retreated.

"This is promising. And pleasant." He radiated excitement. "When the time comes, I know what to do."

She was *not* going to ask what he meant.

Eloquence nuzzled her hair and murmured, "Your blood is stirring as well. That's good."

Kimiko was pretty sure she nodded. And she was almost sure he was going to kiss her again, except he didn't.

Instead he asked, "Kimiko, have you told your parents?"

"N-no."

The restraint was back. "Dalliance without commitment would be an insult."

"I'm sorry." Yesterday had been so hectic, but that was a lame excuse. In truth, she hadn't known how to broach the subject. "I meant no insult."

"I would no more trifle with you than you would with me." Eloquence kissed her forehead. "We have my father's approval. Your father should have the opportunity to approve or oppose a match of this nature."

Kimiko suggested, "Come home with me? We can explain together."

"Gladly. Would tomorrow be acceptable?"

They quickly settled the details, and Kimiko made to leave. But Eloquence didn't release her. He didn't say anything, didn't start anything. But the silence begged her to ask for something, to start again.

She asked, "Was a taste all you needed to decide we're compatible?"

Eloquence grew suddenly solemn. "That is the sort of question males quail before, for any answer risks his lady's displeasure."

"It's not a trap." Kimiko decided to be blunt. "I'm not sure I care enough yet to take your answer personally."

He blinked.

She waited.

And he spoke. "I trust myself, and I have judged you to be trustworthy. Where trust abides, loyalty grows. And loyalty breeds affection, which dogs freely express." Eloquence waited for her nod before continuing. "In this, you are not alone. My parents, my brothers, my Kith, even Tenma and Isla have my trust, my loyalty, my affection."

"That's good."

"Very good." Again, he touched her face. His hand was warm, as was his gaze. "But I do not coax them into corners or linger over their lips in the manner of lovers. Nor could they ever cause my heart to race or my blood to rise. Because with one taste, you claimed such things as your due and yours alone. So yes, one taste was all I needed."

25
RALLY AROUND

Akira was actually pretty good with girls. Well, not in any sort of romantic sense. But brotherly experience made it obvious that Kimi needed the kind of support family could provide. Or maybe a couple of nestmates. "Talk to us, Kimi."

"I will." Her nose was buried in her scarf, and her gaze never lifted from the sidewalk. "I need to, but not here."

He'd have liked to pester, but Suuzu slid his arm around her shoulders and quietly said, "If you wish to register a complaint against Eloquence Starmark, I would willingly support and substantiate your claims."

Kimiko stopped and swayed. "Wh-what?"

"What's Quen done?" Akira demanded. He knew Suuzu was picking up on things he couldn't, like scents and maybe even the state of Kimi's soul. He could only guess at her mood and wait for her to confide in him. Plus, Suuzu's offer didn't make much sense. "I don't get it. Quen's a good guy."

Suuzu grabbed both their arms and hustled then around a corner. Pressing them against the dingy bricks in a cramped alleyway, he crowded close and murmured, "If there is a problem, tell me now, while enough scent lingers to satisfy the trackers."

Akira gawked at his best friend and repeated, "Quen's a *good guy*."

He tipped his head to one side, then the other. "Kimiko is distressed, and Eloquence is undoubtedly the cause."

"Kimi?" Akira grabbed her hand. "What's he talking about?"

She looked close to tears, but not sad tears or even angry ones. Akira's sister wasn't the weepy sort, so the only ones she'd shown him had always been tied to really strong, tangled-up emotions. And confusion. Not knowing what to do could be really scary for someone as confident as Kimiko always seemed to be.

"He *is* a good guy," she said firmly. "He was very ... gentle."

Akira was jumping to every kind of conclusion now, some wilder than others, and he really, *really* hoped they were off base. "Gentle, how?"

Kimi finally met his gaze then, and a laugh bubbled up—sad and silly. Then she shocked the socks off him by kissing his forehead. "Stop imagining the worst. And I promise to tell you everything, but not in the street."

Rubbing at his forehead, Akira mumbled, "You're worrying me. Seriously."

"And you're cheering me up." She hesitated. "Can you stay over again? Or would Sentinel have kittens?"

Suuzu hooked his arm through Kimi's, guiding her back onto the sidewalk. "We will stay."

Akira took her other arm. "Gonna stash us in that secret library again?"

"No, so gather your courage. I think it's time to introduce you to my family."

"Best manners," Akira promised.

Kimiko laughed again, sounding just as unhappy. "Wish I could guarantee the same courtesy. Just … I'm sorry in advance."

Akira finally put his finger on it. He'd walked into a sitcom.

The members of the Miyabe household were naturals—quirky, complicated, and likeable—delivering a whirlwind of well-rehearsed drama. They each *owned* their role. Doting father. Chatterbox mother. Kimi's older sister was all sweetness and soft smiles, and her younger sister was a cool beauty with a calculating gaze. The grandmother had all but demanded documentation of their respective pedigrees.

"Puny stock," she muttered. "What are your parents' classifications?"

Kimi jumped to his defense. "I'm the reaver in our group, Grandma. Akira's only human."

The old woman narrowed her eyes. "Their line of work, then. How have they distinguished themselves?"

"I'm an orphan, ma'am." Akira smiled apologetically. "I don't really remember my parents."

"How did you get into such a prestigious school?" The woman

seemed suspicious. "Academic excellence?"

"My grades are pretty average." Below average, if he was totally honest.

"I'm glad Akira was accepted," Kimi said, her voice slow and calm. "He and Suuzu have been wonderful partners."

"Better to pair you off with a nice reaver boy," grumbled the lady.

Kimi remained patient, but not apologetic. "That would defeat the purpose of integration, Grandma. Triads have one of each, and I'm the reaver."

At this point, Kimiko's mother saw an opening and seized control. "I'm sure we're honored! Aren't we?" A glance in her husband's direction seemed to confirm her suspicion, and her smile widened. Turning to Suuzu, she asked, "And what sort of creature might you be?"

"He's not a creature, Mama. Suuzu is a person."

"I never said he wasn't! But you're an animal-person, aren't you, dear?"

Kimiko's mom was all smiles as she blundered along, apparently ignorant of the oft-repeated guidelines of etiquette and courtesy toward Amaranthine citizens. Akira would have jumped in, but she didn't let anyone get a word in edgewise.

"You look exotic. *Are* you something exotic? A zebra, perhaps?"

Suuzu showed no sign of offense as he corrected her. Akira had always admired his patience when it came to some of the weirder questions people would ask. And now that he knew what to look for, he could see that all three of the Miyabe girls were fidgeting with purpose, probably apologizing to Suuzu even as they worked to interrupt and distract their mother.

Akira found himself liking the lady, if only because of the soft way Kimi's father had of looking at her. The rest of the family might worry about what she'd say next, but this guy was *listening* to her. And that mattered to Akira. It fit with the way he thought things should be.

Maybe that's why he wanted lessons in the signs and signals Kimi used. He hadn't realized he was missing out on part of a conversation.

"Hajime-kun?"

"Yes, sir?" Akira replied. Kimi looked a whole lot like her dad, who seemed a little old-fashioned, but that was probably because of his traditional clothes. He gave off a patient and wise vibe. Unfortunately, he was also pretty sharp.

"Are you perhaps kin to a certain unregistered bloodline recently recognized as producing potent reavers?"

Kimiko winced.

They'd all hoped no one would make the connection.

Maybe he wouldn't make a fuss. Akira said, "Yep."

"What?" demanded Mrs. Miyabe. "What can you mean, dear? I thought he was human."

"As human as you and I," he said fondly. "What I mean to say is that this young man's sister is Lady Mettlebright."

Kimi's mother might not know the ins and outs of Amaranthine etiquette, but she'd read the gossip columns. And Akira's brother-in-law was big news.

Her hands flew to her mouth. "You *are* a reaver!"

"I'm not. My sister is."

And he was surrounded, and everyone was talking at once. Akira was sort of relieved when Suuzu—very politely—extricated him from the excitable group.

Kimi had warned them, and she was pretty close on how everything would shake down. Except for the part about her mom and the contract. Her grandma was the one waving paperwork under his nose. And he was almost positive it was the younger sister who pressed a pen into his hand.

Akira dropped onto Kimiko's bed and stared at the ceiling. "That was intense."

She groaned. "I'm really sorry."

"Don't worry about it." There were more important things to consider. Like Suuzu, who stood staring out the window, stiff and straight. Akira asked, "Okay if we let in some air?"

"Please." She hurried to Suuzu's side and quietly urged, "Make yourselves comfortable."

He flicked the latch, slid the glass panel aside, and breathed deeply. Akira sat up and ruffled his hair. "Not that I'm complaining or anything, because it makes things a lot easier for us, but … wouldn't a mother normally discourage her daughter from spending the night with a couple of guys?"

"She's not a very clever schemer. I'm trying not to be insulted by her mercenary streak." Kimi's hands fluttered through a cycle of frustration and apology.

"Reavers are a little strange. No offense."

Suuzu murmured, "Her plan is ill-wrought. Even if an effort were made, Kimiko could not conceive."

She burst out laughing, and Akira covered his face with his hands. "Too much information."

Crossing to his side, Suuzu sat and began fiddling with Akira's hair. The calming effect was both immediate and mutual. Akira beckoned insistently until Kimi came to sit on the floor in front of them so Suuzu could reach her hair, too.

Long minutes passed, and the mood mellowed. And into the safe haven they'd created for themselves, Suuzu brought his first question. "Are you ready to confide in us?"

26

LONG INTO THE NIGHT

She probably should have been more organized, explaining things from the beginning, but Kimiko skipped to the matter weighing most urgently on her mind. "Suuzu, do you know anything about courtship?"

"A little." He searched her face, as if divining her reason for asking. "Enough to understand that each clan upholds its own traditions."

"What do phoenixes do?" She was only putting off the inevitable, but she really needed to work her way up to this particular secret.

"Hmm." Suuzu left off preening, his hands resting lightly on their heads. "In the old tradition, phoenixes make their hopes known through the singing of songs, the bringing of gifts, and the building of a nest."

"And how do you choose a nestmate?" Kimiko pressed. "I mean, do you just pick someone on impulse and hope it works out? Or do you flirt a little because you already like them and you want them to like you back?"

"Reasons would vary." Suuzu went back to stroking her hair. "What is it you really want to know?"

"You wouldn't trust to chance, would you?"

"I wonder." A faraway look entered his eyes, and there was a thoughtful mellowness to his voice. "A whole life can turn on the whim of a moment. And for all our years, even an Amaranthine cannot guess where the next moment might take him."

Kimiko nodded, then shook her head. Did it matter *why* she was betrothed? Or should she be focusing on fulfilling her responsibility to Eloquence? They were past explanations, yet she'd need a good one for her parents. Tomorrow.

Suuzu continued in soft tones. "I did not know Akira until the moment we met. I tremble to think what would be lost if that moment had slipped away."

Akira had been watching her with a solemn expression, but his gaze swung to Suuzu—dumbstruck, distressed.

With a trill that was more vibration than music, Suuzu pulled them all to seats on the floor, arranging everyone into close comfort. One under each wing, figuratively speaking. Leaning against the bed's side, Suuzu encouraged Akira to lay his head against his shoulder. Kimiko was similarly tucked, and snug quarters and hushed tones made it easier to believe her secrets would be safe.

Akira blurted, "Is Quen in love with you?"

"I don't think that's the right word," said Kimiko. "But he's relying on me to keep an accidental promise."

"What did you promise?" Suuzu prompted.

"To court him."

Eyebrows on the rise, Akira said, "I'm confused."

Kimiko's smile felt weak and wobbly. "That makes two of us. I'm still reeling."

Suuzu touched her chin and lifted her face, forcing her to meet his gaze. "Tell us what happened. All of it. Then I will know how to help you."

Akira nodded. "Tell us, Kimi."

So she picked a spot closer to the beginning and did her best to offer an orderly account. Akira only listened, eyes wide and eyebrows jumping, but Suuzu stopped her from time to time, asking for exact wording and nuances of body language.

"But why does it have to be you?" Akira asked. "Nothing against you—Quen's all kinds of lucky it *is* you—but why's he so set on your following through with this?"

"He mentioned something about his role in the pack. Due to certain circumstances he wouldn't normally choose a bondmate."

Suuzu's sudden whistle was the dawning of comprehension. "He is the Starmark tribute."

"Yes, that's the word he used."

"No wonder." Suuzu smiled softly. "If it seems right, you have my permission to tell your betrothed that I am a tribute of the Farroost clan."

"You, too?" Kimiko hardly believed her good fortune. "I'd never even heard of this custom, but it really is a thing?"

"A private matter, certainly." Suuzu frowned a little. "One shared in great trust."

Kimiko quickly signaled her intention to keep Suuzu's secret. "He knows I'm confiding in you."

Akira's face was oddly blank. When he realized she was looking at him, he dredged up a small smile. "Quen must be really glad. Aren't you glad for yourself?"

Was she? Again, the thing weighing most on her mind came tumbling out. "I told him I didn't care about him yet. This matters more than anything to him, and I should have considered his feelings, but ... that's what I told him. That I don't care."

"Yet," Suuzu echoed. "He will be counting on that *yet*."

"Isn't that what courting's for? Giving you guys time to figure stuff out?" asked Akira. "Don't you think you could sorta eventually get attached?"

She quietly admitted, "Reavers of my rank don't marry for love."

Akira looked ready to argue. But then a different expression overtook his face. "How's your mom gonna react when she finds out. Quen's a good guy, but he's got even less potential than me, assuming the goal is shiny reaver babies."

Kimiko giggled, then hid her face against Suuzu's shoulder when the laughter threatened to turn to tears. Instead of improving the Miyabe bloodline, she was going to muddle it completely. Would her grandmother see this as a betrayal? Or would the Starmark prestige and pedigree make up for producing children of mixed heritage?

"Oh, that's a strange idea," she whispered. "I'm going to have puppies."

"Pups," Suuzu mildly corrected.

Akira said, "I've met Ever, and his adorability is through the roof. Have Quen bring him along to the marriage meeting. He'll sweeten the deal."

She mumbled, "Good idea. Best yet."

"Would you like Akira and me to attend you in a more formal capacity?" Suuzu asked. "I am willing to serve as a go-between, to speak on your behalf and make necessary arrangements. And Akira's presence brings a certain balance to the proceedings, since he is kin to one of the Five."

Akira quickly added, "Fox *and* wolf. Because Adoona-soh's ties to my home den go way back."

Suuzu hummed. "Wolf-fox-phoenix is a strong alliance."

"You think we can swing Hisoka-sensei over to our side?" asked Akira.

"Spokesperson Twineshaft has many obligations." Suuzu's brows drew together. "I am unsure we can reach him for a private word. Not on such short notice."

"Isla!" exclaimed Akira. "She's Hisoka-sensei's apprentice."

Kimiko wasn't quite sure why they were trying to divvy up the Five. Or the rules by which teams were being decided. But she weighed in. "Isla is part of Eloquence's triad."

"I'm still asking her," said Akira. "We're practically family, and home trumps hearth."

Suuzu's focus returned to her. "Although I am young, I have been trained in matters of inter-clan etiquette and media relations. You may count on my support as a Farroost and my discretion as a friend."

Only then did Kimiko realize the position in which she'd placed herself. Breaking the news to her parents was nothing. This was breaking news, period. And on a worldwide scale.

"Puppies will be the least of my worries," she whispered.

"Pups," Suuzu gently corrected. "And press conferences."

"I'm not ready for either!"

"Amaranthine are patient," soothed the phoenix. "And we understand the importance of secrets."

Suuzu exercised his Amaranthine patience while Kimiko tossed and turned in her bed. Only after she dropped into an exhausted sleep did he murmur, "You are awake."

Akira sighed. "Wide awake."

While he was grateful for the Miyabe family's hospitality, Suuzu didn't expect to sleep. He was accustomed to watching over Akira's rest, usually in his truest form. But Kimiko's room was so small, the two futons she'd brought in for them barely fit in the available floor space.

Lifting the edge of his blanket, Akira offered to combine two beds into one nest.

Suuzu didn't hesitate. With the barest rustle, he rolled and slid, pulling Akira firmly into his chest. He would have liked to lull his nestmate with songs, but their swell would surely wake Kimiko ... if not the entire household. So with no stronger barrier than a borrowed blanket, the phoenix resorted to quieter means of comfort.

"You need sleep," he murmured against Akira's ear.

His friend only shrugged.

"What else do you need?" Suuzu pulled him closer, searching for the answers contact could bring. "Ask, and it is yours."

Akira squirmed a little, and their cheeks touched as he

whispered, "Just thinking about how we can help Kimi. And … about what you said earlier."

"Hmm?"

"Suuzu, you're a tribute like Quen."

"I am."

"Are you not allowed to choose a bondmate?" Akira's voice was small, sad.

"You are concerned for me?"

Akira nodded. "You said you were set apart, and that sounds lonely."

Suuzu searched for facts that would comfort his friend. "I have Juuyu, and he has me."

"But he can't always be nearby."

"You are here."

"Well, yeah. But …" Akira's hand fisted the front of Suuzu's borrowed night clothes. "Juuyu calls you his chick."

"He does."

"Will you have chicks?"

"I cannot guess what my future holds." He was content to hold this moment. And the one who shared it. "Better to tend to the day than worry for the next."

"It's night," Akira mumbled.

"I can tend by night as easily as day." Suuzu immediately regretted his words. They betrayed an impatience he couldn't fully master. Maybe Akira would let it pass.

But his friend lifted his head. "Is this about my hatching?"

Suuzu sighed. Akira might share a beacon's bloodline, but he was indistinguishable from an ordinary human. At first glance. Even a second or third glance. But as Suuzu's trust in Akira deepened, he'd noticed the glow of something unusual. Deep within. Tucked away. At the time, he'd compared it to a golden egg, warm and waiting.

Sliding his hand over a spot to one side of Akira's navel, Suuzu asked, "Are you curious?"

"Sometimes." He pressed a palm over Suuzu's hand, holding it in place. "What do you think will happen to me if we disobeyed?"

Over breaks and during holidays, they usually returned to Akira's sister's home, where they'd submitted to the gently intimate probing of Michael, the current generation's top-ranked ward. Suuzu had received his First Taste with Michael's careful tending, but the spark in Akira's soul had defied explanation. In the end, Michael had decided it was probably nothing, but it was probably best to do nothing.

Frustrating.

Suuzu could *see* the inner fire of reaver souls when he closed his eyes. And he wanted nothing more than to stir into flame the gleaming ember in Akira. And to feed the fire, tending it until it gained strength. Forging a trustworthy bond. One that would last.

"Suuzu?"

"Hmm?"

"You want to try, don't you?"

"Yes."

Akira whispered, "Can we?"

"Yes. But not until we are back behind my brother's wards." Suuzu was almost afraid to ask. "What are you hoping for?"

"Not sure." After several long moments, Akira softly added, "I guess because part of me is ... like you said, trembling because of what we might lose if we never try."

27

A PRIVATE WORD ON SHORT NOTICE

Dawn found Kimiko taking the shrine steps two at a time, weighed down with bags of fresh produce so they could treat Akira and Suuzu to an extra-nice breakfast. Mother had practically chased her out the door with a grocery list, and Kimiko had needed to knock at the back doors of the Nakamuras and the Satohs, to gather up all the ingredients on her grandmother's list.

Noriko met her at the door with murmured thanks. Sakiko swished past with a censorious eye roll. "You're even more of a mess than usual."

Kimiko couldn't deny it, but what else would she be, rousted from bed at four-thirty and running from door to door up and down Kikusawa's business district.

Her sister's voice dropped. "Signatures?"

"Nope."

192

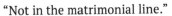

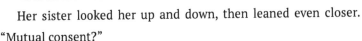

"Verbal agreements?"

"Not in the matrimonial line."

Her sister looked her up and down, then leaned even closer. "Mutual consent?"

Kimiko cuffed her sister's shoulder. "That only happens in cheap novels. I'll change, then help with the fruit plate."

But a light rap sounded at the front door. Odd, given the earliness of the hour. Kimiko was running through a mental list of neighbors who might make the trek up their hill this early, but a brief wash of power made her hair stand on end. Was Sentinel Skybellow here to scold her? But the fleeting impression hadn't been particularly canine.

She slid open the door and gaped.

"Good morning, Kimi!" chirped Isla, looking neat and fresh in her school uniform. "Please, pardon our dropping by unannounced."

Never in her life had Kimiko been more conscious of her shapeless tracksuit, her windblown hair, or her unwashed state.

"Miss Kimiko Miyabe." At Isla's side, Hisoka Twineshaft executed a small bow. "Would it be too much trouble if we were to beg entry?"

Suuzu was suddenly behind her, an arm sliding protectively around Kimiko's shoulders.

And then Akira was thudding downstairs, his hair a mess but his eyes alight. "Sensei! How did you know we needed you?"

"Do you?" inquired the cat, all innocence.

Akira's grin showed no trace of doubt. "You're here, aren't you?"

The implication was clear. And Kimiko was duly impressed by the staggering clarity of her classmate's conviction that Hisoka

Twineshaft would always be where he was needed. Akira beamed at their uninvited guest, as if they could rest assured that everything would be okay.

"I am undeniably present." The cat smiled pleasantly, patiently.

Isla lightly cleared her throat, eyebrows arching.

Kimiko recalled herself, for hospitality to the Amaranthine was every reaver's duty and delight. She set a light hand on Suuzu's encircling arm, silently confirming the phoenix's claim. He was her guide and go-between, and she needed him already.

With as much poise as she could muster, she said, "Kikusawa Shrine is my home, and the Miyabe family welcomes you. I can vouch for the width of our hearth, for the freshness of the fish, and for the loveliness of my sisters. Which my mother is sure to mention to you with an excess of hopeful enthusiasm. Please don't take offense?"

Right about then, Kimiko's mother poked her head out the kitchen door to see why her guests were congregating in the entry … and shrieked for her husband.

Hisoka didn't even flinch. With a gracious nod to Suuzu, he ushered Isla inside, ruffled Akira's hair in passing, and offered his palms to an astonished Akio Miyabe.

Kimiko darted upstairs to change, then joined her sisters in the kitchen. "What can I do?"

"You wash, I'll dry," said Sakiko. She was pulling out their nicest set of dishes from an antique cabinet—delicate nested bowls and dainty plates with gilt edges, all in shades of ruby and jade, with an elegant pattern of chrysanthemums. "They might be dusty, and that won't do for our esteemed guest."

"What did you *do*?" Noriko asked.

Kimiko busied herself filling a basin with soapy water. "I didn't know he was coming any more than you did."

"You must have done *something* if Hisoka Twineshaft took notice." Sakiko deposited a stack of plates on the counter. "Too bad his apprentice isn't a boy. Is she anybody important?"

"Well, she's Hisoka Twineshaft's apprentice." Kimiko wasn't in the mood for gossip. "Is Mama behaving?"

Sakiko tiptoed to the door and listened for several beats before scampering back to the sink. She whispered, "We're saved. Daddy's going to give them the grand tour until breakfast time."

A moment later, their mother whisked through the door. "You've done very well for us, Kimiko! If connections lead to contracts, you shall have the best husbands the world can provide!"

Kimiko could have pointed out that knowing the Spokesperson didn't actually improve their pedigree, but Noriko looked so hopeful.

"I wonder if I have time," Mama mused, already lifting her shawl from its hook beside the back door. "Ten minutes, girls. Twenty at most."

Kimiko turned from the sink. "Where are you going?"

"Just down the hill."

"But I bought everything on your list."

Her mother peeked in the little mirror on the wall, patting at her hair. "What's the point of having Mr. Twineshaft here if I cannot *tell* someone? The ladies of the Neighborhood Improvement Committee will have to agree this is a triumph!"

Not good. "Spokesperson Twineshaft is here *privately*. We need to be discreet, Mama."

"Nonsense!" Her mother added a touch of lipstick. "There was an Emergence. Everyone knows everything about everything now. I'll be back in no time, so don't start breakfast without me!"

"Wait, Mama!"

But her mother was already halfway out the door. Only to stumble backward with an alarmed squeak. An enormous Kith sprawled across the beaten path that was the woman's shortcut to the back gate. A sleek, long-limbed hound with black and tan markings.

"Please, don't be alarmed, ladies." A man in a Western-style suit had obviously been standing right outside the door. "I'm Dickon Denholme, and this is Rein. Added security. You understand."

Dickon was obviously foreign, but Kimiko couldn't guess his nationality. Long black hair showing threads of gray had been queued at the nape of his neck, and creases showed at the corners of eyes so dark, pupil and iris were indistinguishable. She couldn't place two of the lapel pins on his suit, but the third was the Starmark crest.

Mama drew herself up. "I have an errand to run."

The man extended a fine-boned brown hand. "If you provide a list, we'll handle the procurement."

"I don't want to trouble you." Mrs. Miyabe tried to edge around the escort.

"No one will cross the perimeter while Spokesperson Twineshaft is here." He barred the way with an apologetic smile, repeating,

"Added security. You understand."

Mama understood all right. And she was furious.

Kimiko was impressed with her father's composure. Daddy acted like it was the most natural thing in the world that the Spokesperson should be interested in the finer points of a shrinekeeper's duties. As they returned to the house for breakfast, Kimiko overheard her father exclaim, "You have? Do you remember the year?"

"A long while ago. Several generations back."

"Do you find Kikusawa much changed?"

Her father mentioned old photos in the archive, and Hisoka suggested a stroll along the boundaries after their meal.

"He's staying?" Kimiko whispered to Isla.

The girl made a small, secretive gesture to the affirmative.

Wary of eavesdropping felines, she silently begged for more information.

Isla was sparkling with happiness, but the only answer she offered was a quick peck to Kimiko's cheek. Not particularly informative, but sufficient to banish most of her worries. Whatever Hisoka Twineshaft's reasons for inviting himself over, they made Isla happy. And that had to be good.

Over breakfast, Kimiko was further impressed by Hisoka's diplomatic prowess. Poor Dickon Denholme was already the subject of several cutting remarks, but apparently, orchestrating the Emergence had provided Spokesperson Twineshaft with the necessary skills for dealing with a changeable woman.

Kimiko decided she should be taking notes. Because Mama was being handled by a pro.

"I will be borrowing your husband." Somehow, Hisoka sounded as if he was begging for favors, even though his words were a statement of fact. "My imposition upon your household will not outlast the morning."

"Imposition," scoffed Mrs. Miyabe. "You *must* stay! Won't our friends and neighbors be amazed to find a dignitary in our midst!"

Kimiko decided not to remind Mama that Dickon wasn't letting people in any more than he was letting her out. Without thinking, she made a sign that roughly translated, *the boundaries will hold*.

Across the table, Hisoka casually offered a return signal, *brighten the wards*.

She paused to think. When was the last time they'd brought in someone with a ward classification to do a bit of maintenance on their sigils? Was this why Hisoka wanted to walk the perimeter? Given recent events, she'd be glad of reinforcement. The next time his gaze met hers, she echoed him, making it a question. *Brighten the wards?*

His smile was serene. *The boundaries will hold.*

Noriko reminded everyone that it was a school day. "You don't want to be late."

Amidst the rush to gather up belongings and thank their hosts, Hisoka's calm voice carried a genial command. "A word, Kimiko Miyabe?"

He led her out the front door, where another canine Kith sat at attention, and out across the courtyard. She held her tongue, even though she was almost as curious as she was nervous, but an odd sight made her forgot her manners entirely. Grabbing Hisoka's sleeve, she whispered, "Who are they?"

A man and two women wearing the traditional attire of shrinekeepers were busy about the courtyard—sweeping the walkways, salting icy patches, polishing shop windows. All wonderfully helpful. Except the Miyabe family didn't employ extra workers.

"Two battlers and a trickster in training," Hisoka said easily. "Can you tell which of them is Amaranthine?"

Kimiko slowly shook her head. "Which of the trickster clans?"

"See if you can figure that out," he suggested. "I would be interested to know if they have any small habits that might betray their true nature. Because if they acquit themselves well here, one of our urban enclaves will benefit greatly."

She liked the riddle he'd posed, but she knew it was of secondary importance. "They're staying?"

"Indefinitely." Hisoka smoothly added, "Unless your family is opposed, of course."

And then Kimiko realized that she was putting a crease in Hisoka Twineshaft's sleeve, and she snatched back her hand, fluttering through apologies she was too tongue-tied to utter.

He caught her sleeve. "Relax, Miss Miyabe. Or I shall have an angry phoenix to contend with."

She followed his gaze to where Suuzu perched on the ridgepole of her house. She would have loved seeing her classmate blaze into his truest form, but she signaled reassurances. *All's well.*

"Firstly, I'd be pleased if you'd call me Sensei. It's friendlier without formalities."

Kimiko stared at the clawed fingers still holding her sleeve. "Why are you here, Sensei?"

"My purposes are twofold." But instead of listing them, he asked, "Is Suuzu Farroost acting as your go-between?"

"You know about Eloquence."

"I am one of very few who do. I have his father's trust." He repeated, "Suuzu?"

"Yes. He offered last night." She tried for a smile. "He thought I might need him."

"Very good. That makes this easier to explain." Hisoka released her sleeve to take her hand. "Harmonious made me *his* go-between. I will be acting on his son's behalf."

The weight of that statement took several moments to sink in. "Are you saying he sent you to see if I'm good enough?"

"Do not think it," chided Hisoka. "My old friend is *pleased* by your offer. He sent me to smooth the way ... and to secure your happiness. Can you trust me?"

Kimiko's words came slowly at first. "I want to, but I'm not really sure. I mean, I trust you on a grand scale, but that's not the same as letting someone make decisions for me. And my parents don't even know yet."

Hisoka gave her hand a small squeeze, then beckoned to Suuzu. The phoenix leapt from the rooftop, arriving at her side with a speed the Amaranthine never displayed in public.

Palms touched, and Hisoka continued, "With your permission, I will speak with your parents, relaying Harmonious' approval of the match and inviting them to the Starmark compound in a week's time to formalize the matter by making a declaration of your intentions."

"You'll tell my parents for me?"

He inclined his head. "While you're at school. Which brings

me to my second purpose. I'll be asking your family to take in my apprentice for the remainder of the year."

"Isla?" Kimiko was startled, but far from opposed. "That's actually really perfect. She wanted to learn more about the nuances of non-verbal communication used by various clans, and that will be so much easier if we're roommates."

Hisoka's whole expression warmed. "I'm sure she'll benefit from your guidance."

"But are you sure this won't be awkward? You've met my family. They're a little bit desperate to make the right kinds of connections." Kimiko grimaced. "Especially since I'll be disappointing them."

Flared eyebrows lifted. "Nearly everyone Isla meets is trying to use her."

Kimiko wanted to protest, but Suuzu interrupted with a light trill. Was he laughing?

Hisoka lifted the hand he still held, placing it against his chest and holding it there. His heart beat under her palm—sure and steady. "Isla is my precious apprentice, and you are not 'nearly everyone.' Isla likes you. Ever chose you. Harmonious wants you. Eloquence needs you. And I will trust you."

She understood that this was a vow.

And once again, she felt bad.

When Hisoka had asked if she could trust him, she'd said she wasn't sure she could. Just like when Eloquence had offered a lifetime of loyalty, even though she hadn't been able to say she cared. All her friendliness seemed flimsy compared with the commitments the Amaranthine were so ready to make. Why were they so quick to trust? Did they see something in her she couldn't see for herself?

She hoped she'd be able to figure it out.

Kimiko pressed her hand firmly to Hisoka Twineshaft's heart and told the truth. "I like Isla, too. I think we could be good friends—the best—and your trust is giving us that chance."

A purr vibrated through Hisoka's chest, and he tugged her into a gentle embrace. "May I make plain something you may have already realized?"

She nodded, lost for words.

"Harmonious is a dog."

Kimiko giggled. "Give me a little credit."

"As such, Harmonious has a strong desire to protect, but he cannot overstep traditional boundaries." Hisoka said, "A suitor might stand guard over their intended, but not the other way around."

Suuzu said, "And so Isla."

"I am indulging my apprentice, but I fear I am also using her." Hisoka's cheek rested against Kimiko's hair. "Because nothing will prevent those who love Isla from making Kikusawa Shrine safe."

With a little cry, she threw her arms around him and hugged him tight. Because even if there were machinations and ulterior motives in play, the end result was everything she'd needed to know. No matter what, her sisters would be safe.

28

INESTIMABLE VALUE

Usually, Eloquence relished these rare times when he had Dad to himself. But all he could do was stare into his father's face with ill-concealed dismay. "You did *what*?"

"Arranged everything." Dad cuffed his shoulder. "I'm taking care of you."

"I can take care of myself."

His father's indulgent smile wasn't very reassuring.

Quen tried reason. "Kimiko and I already came to an agreement. Surely you don't expect me to go back on my word."

"I expect no such thing. Don't worry so much. I sent a go-between."

"You ... wait. What?"

"I know my responsibilities!" His father beamed. "I did as much for every one of your sisters."

"Dad!" Could this be any worse? "I'm not a *female*."

His father snorted. "Gender isn't the issue. You have a suitor. No child of mine will go into the intricacies of a formal courtship without the support of a go-between."

The injustice stung. "Did you appoint a go-between when Merit or Prospect or Valor were pursuing their mates?"

"Of course not. They were quite capable of making their intentions clear."

"And I'm not?"

"You're not." His father was totally missing the point. "Kimiko is the suitor. The intent will be hers."

Eloquence conceded the point, but argued, "She probably isn't aware of our traditions, let alone your expectations."

"All the more reason to appoint a skilled go-between!" Dad countered heartily.

He was far too pleased with himself. Who would he have chosen? Any of his older brothers would be awful, since they'd tease. And Uncle Laud wouldn't be a good fit, since he rarely spoke. A horrifying idea crept into Quen's soul. "Please, please, *please* tell me it's not Grandad."

His father's eyes widened, and he actually swore and pulled him into a snug embrace. "Maker have mercy! This will be complicated enough without involving my sire. No, I chose Twineshaft."

Quen knew his father was within his rights to hold Kimiko to a high standard. Even so, there were so many expectations heaped on a suitor. "Kimiko is human. What if she decides that courtship is too complicated?"

Dad frowned. "Don't cheapen yourself simply because you're afraid of losing something that might not be worth having."

He was already growling over the implied insult to Kimiko.

But his father flicked his nose. "Watch your tone. All of your sisters know what I require in a suitor."

"I'm your *son*."

"And of inestimable value to me. So hear me out." Harmonious held him at arms' length and gravely said, "It's only natural to wonder if your suitor will care as much as you already do. Or to fear that they are your only chance at happiness."

Quen didn't appreciate being given a speech that was surely meant for a daughter of the pack, but he couldn't exactly deny that he'd entertained similar thoughts.

"Courtship raises questions so they may be answered. And a good suitor puts to rest every fear, making room for trust, affection, and commitment." Harmonious quietly added, "Your mother—my Aurora—used to say, 'Hold your suitor to the highest standard, and they will rise to meet you.' Kimiko must prove her worth without compromising yours."

Eloquence wasn't able to have a private word with Kimiko before class, but her gaze was steady, her posture confident, and her partners rallying close on either side. He tried a simple signal— *meet me later.*

Thankfully, she caught on. The tilt of her chin was favorable, and she murmured, "Yes, please. We *need* to talk."

Only the phoenix overheard. Suuzu's gaze slanted his way—

open, interested. Quen was quite sure he knew, and it was embarrassing how vulnerable he felt. But the young phoenix's head tilted in a birdish sort of acknowledgment. Almost deferential. His uncertainty must have been plain on his face, for Suuzu lifted his brows and repeated his earlier gesture—*meet me later*.

A sensible suggestion.

Kimiko looked between them, her eyes bright with understanding. "Suuzu's already proving himself a fine go-between. Where and when?"

The phoenix was her intermediary? "After classes, please. In the Kith shelter with Edge and Flay."

Suuzu bent to relay his message into Kimiko's ear, and she accepted with thanks.

All very promising, despite the cat having put in a paw. Kimiko's calm put Quen a little more at ease, but he couldn't really focus on Ms. Reeves, whose morning lecture began with the historical basis for the practice of tending. A much-abridged, Emergence-validating version that emphasized the beauty of trust and the strength found in cooperation.

Quen knew this version well enough, since it was part of his heritage. Glint Starmark, First of Dogs, had formed an alliance with early reavers—before they even came to be known by that name—becoming a co-founder of the In-between.

His grandsire had bucked the tradition of that earlier era, in which reavers were considered fair game. A piece of history that would have made for bad publicity, especially in places like America, where the peace process had a glossy enough coat, but the underfur was all snarls and burrs.

"Some clans are conscientious abstainers," Ms. Reeves was

saying. "And some introduce a reaver's tending as the final rite of passage into adulthood. Amaranthine living in cooperatives, where they come into casual contact with reavers, have benefited from the proximity."

"A sort of secondhand tending?" asked Sosuke.

Ms. Reeves hesitated. "How would you describe it, Hanoo?"

The wolf stood. "Tending is too intentional to splash around, affecting others. But having reavers at home definitely makes for a certain ... atmosphere."

"Heady," agreed Yoota.

Ploom nodded. "Homey."

Hanoo's tail swayed to a quicker tempo. "Some of it's the kids. Little reavers don't understand output, and they can send the whole pack into a whirl. Especially if they're stunners like Isla."

Attention flickered in Isla's direction, and she pushed back her chair. "That's one reason high-ranking children are transferred so quickly into academies like Ingress. Lessons in self-possession begin very early." She lifted her arms, showing off bangles etched with interlocking sigils. "These wards are as much for your protection as mine. While I don't exactly splash around, my emotions still mess with my control. Sometimes." At this, she wrinkled her nose. "Sensei and Papka are *strict*."

"For good reason," said Ms. Reeves. "All tending is regulated, for the protection of both parties. If a reaver were to have the whole of their essence drained during a tending, death would result. And the Amaranthine are similarly vulnerable when faced by those with potent souls."

Hanoo signaled his wish to speak, and Ms. Reeves seemed

pleased to hear his perspective.

"So it's definitely exciting when there's little ones underfoot, but some of it depends on the purpose of the enclave. Because some classes of reavers are seriously splashy. Their work areas have to be warded, but it changes the air. Like the scent of cinnamon stealing out of a closed oven or the tang of electricity that tells you there's a lightning bolt building in the clouds overhead."

Ms. Reeves nodded eagerly. "That's one reason why the Amaranthine equivalent to hospitals are often located in mining enclaves. The reavers who cut and tune the crystals find that their souls resonate over great distances. And healers have found that the augmentation and amplification is conducive to ...."

Eloquence slouched in his chair, his attention straying to Kimiko. She was wholly focused on the discussion; indeed, she looked ready to leap in with questions of her own. Somewhere deep down, he wanted to be the one to answer her questions, but he couldn't let his instincts rile over every little thing. Especially when he was supposed to sit back in the passive role of the pursued.

This was surprisingly frustrating. How did females endure it?

Maybe he should ask one of his sisters. Or Flay, since he'd be seeing her sooner.

When Ms. Reeves finally announced a break, Isla poked his shoulder. "You didn't raise your hand."

"Did I miss something?"

"An informal survey. About two-thirds of the Amaranthine in class have had their first taste. You haven't?"

"I have." Harmonious had arranged for his first taste early, probably in the hopes that it would lead to a growth spurt. "A long time ago."

"You don't like it...?"

Quen sighed. He liked the elation of touching a potent soul, but he didn't like the accompanying vulnerability. Trust was hard. And he immediately felt foolish, given how quickly he'd decided to trust Kimiko. "I liked it too well."

Her expression immediately wavered toward concern. "If this is too personal...."

"Nothing like that." He lightly touched her golden hair and smiled into eyes that reminded him of laughing green. "He was only a little older than you back then. And I haven't really wanted anyone since."

Isla's eyes had the same sparkle, her smile the same shape. "You and Papka?"

He nodded.

"Are you one of his special favorites?" She didn't wait for an answer. "Sensei still brings people to him for their first taste. Because he's a gentleman. And gentle. Was he your first taste?"

The question was intensely personal, but Quen answered with a shake of his head. "My last."

"Do you miss him?"

How to answer. "The person I remember was a boy. He has become someone else since the days when he tried to help me."

Isla pursed her lips. "Do people change that much?"

Eloquence sheepishly admitted, "I haven't mingled with humans enough to know."

"Well, if he tried to help you, he wouldn't forget." She had her phone out, tapping at the screen. "He gets attached."

AMARATHINE SAGA BY FORTHRIGHT

"What are you doing?"

"I may not have Papka's finesse, but I have his number. I'm texting him."

Before Quen could protest, she hit *send*.

Seconds passed as Quen's heart hammered, and his scalp prickled uncomfortably with sweat. He hadn't known he cared so much about Michael Ward, who had listened so seriously to Dad's gruff explanations before making two demands—privacy and time.

Unhurried and uninhibited, the First of Wards had won his trust. And for a few weeks, Quen felt as if he shared one soul with another person.

In the months that followed the young reaver's departure, the pack had written off Quen's dismal mood as disappointment that Michael hadn't been able to explain or cure his delayed development. But Uncle Laud understood. "You have grown."

Eloquence remembered demanding, "How?"

Laud had pulled him close, pressing their foreheads together. And for a moment, it was as if one of them were Kith, because Laud's voice found its way into Quen's mind, sharing words that were too private for utterance. *To love is to grow.*

Isla's phone offered a soft *ting*, and she leaned into his side, letting him see the screen while she tapped her way through a brief exchange.

> **Papka, I miss you.**
> **But my friend**
> **misses you more.**

210

KIMIKO AND THE ACCIDENTAL PROPOSAL

What's this, koshka?
A riddle to tease
your old man?
Who's there, please?

"He's always teasing." She talked as she tapped. "Koshka is *kitten* in Russian, and he started calling me that as soon as he found out Hisoka-sensei had elevated me to apprentice."

"Do you dislike felines?"

"Not at all." Her lip came out in a small pout. "But I don't want to be treated like a child."

Eloquence Starmark
He is in my triad
He seems lonesome for you

Teach him the way
to Stately House
The wards will accept him
Or bide a wee, and I'll
come to cheer him myself

You're coming?

Presently ... and in force.

Isla's smile widened. "That means he's bringing someone. Oh, I hope it's Gingko!"

Tell!!!

Shan't
All very hush-hush
Must dash
Shore up Quen until

I reach you both

Soon?

I promise
Is he close?

Hanging on your every word
And smiling

Eloquence realized she was right.

Just then, a chime signaled the end of their break, and the classroom door slid open with a snap. Quen had a fleeting impression of red-gold fur and round eyes before the wiry figure streaked into the room, springing across tabletops and setting off a stir of surprised exclamations. Papers scattered. The three members of the Nightspangle pack half-rose but held their ground, hands pointedly tucked behind their back.

Yes, their intruder was frightened. And … strange.

Sentinel Skybellow skidded into the room, looking harried. "Inti!"

The dizzying explosion of acrobatics came to a teetering halt on Ms. Reeves' podium, and without a sign of perturbation, their teacher raised her voice over the din. "Class, please join me in welcoming New Saga's first transfer student."

29

TRANSFER STUDENT

Tenma had been holding himself a little aloof, glad to see Isla slipping into what he thought of as her truest form. She was an amazing kid—poised with adults, brimming with facts, and serious about contributing to class. No doubt she was going places. An elite of the highest quality. But he was in a position to know that smart kids who outranked their peers were still kids. So he never interrupted when she forgot herself and acted all twelve.

He was really curious about her bracelets. Given her parentage and patronage, he wasn't surprised she needed the wards. Would she know how they worked? Probably. They seemed like the sort of thing Lapis had proposed to create for him. Much more durable than his little slip of paper, which was too easily lost or laundered out of existence.

The sudden *clack* of the opening door stirred him from his

thoughts, and he glanced toward the source of the noise. A boy. Or was he an animal? His unruly hair and the set of his mouth were decidedly simian, but the thin hands clutching the door frame were certainly human.

Before he'd fully made up his mind, the stranger sprang into the room.

Papers scattered, and some of the girls shrieked. Other than Hanoo, Yoota, and Ploom, nobody really moved. He glanced at Eloquence, trying to get a feel for the situation.

Quen's hand found his shoulder. "Stay still. He's frightened."

Another quick glance around the room showed the other Amaranthine similarly keeping their partners in place. Then Sentinel burst in, and the boy called Inti stopped, bare feet planted on Ms. Reeves' lecture notes.

Tenma leaned forward, adjusting his glasses. Was that a tail?

"Oh, how nice! A crosser," murmured Isla.

And the boy's strange features suddenly made sense, because such things were widely reported after the birth of Ever Starmark. Crossers often inherited animalistic features that hinted at their Amaranthine parent's nature. One of Inti's parents had clearly come from a monkey clan.

In a low, soothing voice, Ms. Reeves addressed the class. "Inti comes to us from an enclave based in a temple, where he's been under the oversight of monks for quite some time. With the Emergence, he's able to come out of hiding. Spokesperson Twineshaft decided that New Saga would be the best place for him to integrate into society. And in return, you'll all gain a greater understanding of the challenges faced by children of mixed heritage."

"A crosser?" exclaimed Sosuke.

"Yes," she confirmed. "Inti, would you like to say a few words?"

The boy ... *no*. Tenma knew that crossers shared an Amaranthine's lifespan, so Inti would have to be a young man by now. Or more properly, a male nearing adulthood. Inti's hunched posture slowly straightened so that he looked down on them. His wild hair was a light ginger. Thick sideburns bristled outward, following the curve of his jaw to his chin, framing a heart-shaped face. His lips compressed into a thin line, and small brows rose over unusually round eyes; they gave him an expression of perpetual surprise ... or worry.

"Three," he said softly. "Three, three, three."

Tenma felt bad. To be brought into their class, only to find a roomful of established groups. He must think there was no place for him. Without really thinking it through, Tenma lurched to his feet. Holding up three fingers, he raised a fourth and hoped his meaning was clear.

Isla bounced to her feet, up on tiptoe. "Miss Reeves, both Quen and I have experience with crossers."

"So you do. What do you say, Eloquence?"

Quen stood and signaled, and Isla added some sort of reaver sign. But Inti only looked more worried, and Tenma's heart went out to him. So he crooked his fingers in an entirely human way. "Four."

Inti crossed the room in two springs, flinging himself straight into Tenma.

He barely had time to set his feet when the monkey-boy collided and wrapped himself around Tenma—arms around his neck, legs around his waist. Grunting with surprise, he staggered backward into Quen's solid presence.

215

The crosser was trembling, and Tenma was reminded of his own first day of school. So he hugged him and murmured promises of help and belonging. Nothng like this had ever happened to him— hugging, holding. This wasn't how teenage boys typically behaved. New Saga was already changing him.

From across the room, Hanoo looked on with tail swaying. Ploom gave him two thumbs up.

"You're ours now, Inti," he murmured. "Welcome to Class 3-C."

At the sound of his name, the crosser leaned back to meet Tenma's gaze. His eyes were such a light brown, they were nearly golden, and his pupils were round. "Name?" he asked.

"I'm Tenma."

"Clan?" he pressed. "House?"

"I'm human, so I don't have those things. But my surname is Subaru." Turning a little, he said, "Here's Quen. He's from a fine house and clan. Will you greet him as well?"

Inti studied Eloquence's proffered palms and interpreted it as an invitation to transfer. Quen's superior strength came in handy as he swung their new partner up onto his shoulders.

"No wonder you like high places. You're related to one of the monkey clans," Quen remarked. "Have you met Goh-sensei yet?"

"Maybe, maybe, monkey," he answered softly, and proceeded to pull apart Quen's braid.

Tenma may have surrendered Inti, but the crosser hadn't fully released him. Inti's tail was quite long, and its end was loosely wrapped around his wrist.

"My turn," said Isla, hands outspread. "Although I won't be able to lift you."

Inti blinked down at her, then slid to the floor. When he fully straightened, it was possible to tell that he was a little taller than her.

With an impish smile, he echoed, "My turn," and swept her up.

"Gently," Tenma whispered.

"Like you," Inti said, giving him a thin-lipped smile. Then he solemnly addressed Isla. "You are bright as an angel. Are you descended from the sky or from trees?"

So he was capable of full sentences.

Isla giggled. "I am both the child of reavers and a reaver in my own right. Would you like to meet the rest of our class?"

"Please."

"Set me down first."

Inti obeyed. Returning to Tenma's side, he announced, "She is brightest, but you are best."

"Me? Why?"

Stealing the glasses off his face, Inti squinted through them, then peered over the frames, straight into Tenma's eyes. "Is a reason required?"

And in that instant, Tenma was absolutely positive that Inti was shamming. Not about his fear, since the Amaranthine had all picked up on that, but this monkey business. He was playing the fool, but he knew what he was about.

"No." Tenma hesitated. "I'm afraid I don't know much of anything about the customs of the monkey clans."

Inti's gaze skittered around the room before he sprang, flinging his arms around Tenma's neck as he clambered toward a perch on his shoulders. In the process, he spoke softly, his words tickling Tenma's ear. "That makes two of us."

30

SENSE

Dismissed early for the purpose, the entirety of Class 3-C escaped to the rooftop since Hanoo had declared that anyone who was continually—probably instinctually—seeking the highest point in any room would probably love the view.

Quen gently disentangled Inti from Tenma, perching the crosser on his own shoulders. Pointing across the treetops, he said, "That's Starmark land. I'll let our Kith know about you. If you need a place to run or climb, you're welcome. And if you need *me*, anyone you find inside—Kith or Kindred—will show you the way."

Inti locked his ankles together and wrapped his arms around Quen's forehead. Covered by the general chatter of their classmates, he simply said, "Good doggie."

"My brother's a crosser." Quen tipped his head, trying to see Inti's expression. "He'll love you on principle. He has an understandable fascination with anyone sporting a tail."

"Half?"

"Yes, Ever and I share a father—Harmonious Starmark." This was strange. Not many people hadn't heard of their clan, but Inti didn't seem to recognize Dad's name. "He's one of the Five."

"Ever is five?"

"Ever's three." Quen decided to let it go. It wasn't as if he was trying to trade on his father's fame to impress his classmate. "And next time Tenma stays over with us, you'll come, too."

"Show me."

Quen pointed to the spot where rooftops peeked above the forest. "My pavilion is near the Kith shelter. If your sense of smell is good, you can probably find it on your own."

"Good, good, good doggie."

Akira ambled over, a thoughtful expression on his face. "Hey, Quen. Say, Inti, can I ask you a potentially awkward question?"

The crosser flowed from Quen's shoulder and stood facing Akira. "Say it."

"How come you're here instead of Stately House?"

After a lengthy pause, Inti replied, "Reasons."

Interesting. The boy who claimed not to know about the Five had heard of Stately House?

But Akira accepted Inti's answer with a nod. "Good ones?"

Inti shrugged.

"Wanna visit sometime?" Akira described his sister's home with sweeping hand gestures, backing slowly toward the rest of the group and beckoning for Inti to follow. He did, taking Tenma with him, for his tail was still coiled firmly around his wrist.

Tenma offered a parting wave. "I'll make sure he gets safely to the dorms."

Quen signaled his gratitude, and then Suuzu was there, almost as if Akira had created the opening. Which he must have. With a wry smile, Quen offered a silent greeting.

Suuzu met his palms. "I will guide Kimiko to the Kith shelter at the appointed hour and remain close, but not too close. Your privacy is assured."

"Thank you."

"Afterward, Akira and I will escort Kimiko and Isla home."

"Isla?" She hadn't mentioned anything of the sort. Then again, Inti had rather monopolized their day.

"Isla is moving in with the Miyabe family," supplied Suuzu. "Hisoka Twineshaft arranged things so that his apprentice will be safe. He is your go-between."

"So I'm told." Quen stared at his feet for several moments. "I see the sense."

Suuzu touched his sleeve. "Those who are set apart see clearly."

His gaze jumped to Suuzu's. "You're a tribute?"

"The second of my clan. Peace, kindred." He slipped his hand under Quen's, then cautiously tangled their fingers together. "Those who do not choose for themselves understand the joy of being chosen."

"Yes. Perhaps that's what plagues me now. I haven't given Kimiko much of a choice."

Suuzu shook his head. "Stranger alliances have formed and flourish."

"Well, kindred?" He gave Suuzu's hand a gentle squeeze. "Whose part are you taking in this uncommon courtship?"

The hint of a smile appeared. "When it comes to nestmates,

the happiness of one is the satisfaction of the other. I cannot show favor without pleasing both."

"Thank you," he whispered.

Suuzu took a step closer, so they were toe to toe. "In the custom of my clan, it would be understood that I will carry twigs to the tree of your choosing, giving you time to sing."

"Meaning ...?"

"Leave any practical arrangements to your go-betweens. Focus on beguiling your future mate."

Eloquence snorted. "I cannot pursue her. Dad was clear on that."

The phoenix surprised him by snorting right back. "Even trees have flowers."

At a loss, Quen repeated, "Meaning ...?"

Suuzu's expression softened. "Kimiko needs you to lead the chase."

Eloquence arrived in the Kith shelter well before Kimiko. When his fidgeting turned to fretting, Flay took pity, in her own way. Quen was well-occupied with combing her luxuriant fur when his suitor finally ducked into the alcove.

"Sorry." She was breathless from running. "Made you wait."

"I don't mind waiting."

Ha! Flay's amusement carried clearly. *You pace and pine. If the moon was high, you'd be howling.*

Ignoring her aside, Quen steered Kimiko into the back corner and returned to combing. "Catch your breath while I finish."

Kimiko offered her hand to Edge, who scooted close enough that she could reach his ears. His tail was soon wagging.

As her pulse slowed, the whole atmosphere settled into calm. Quen supposed he should hold his peace until Kimiko was ready to speak, but Flay had other ideas.

Go to her. Flay's cloudy eye rolled toward Kimiko. *She is waiting.*

Rile her up and run for it. Edge's fond gaze was fixed on Flay. *Let her catch you.*

Before the suggestions could grow any more graphic, Quen slipped to Kimiko's side. "Warm enough?" he asked.

She hummed an affirmative while shaking her head. Her mind was elsewhere, and why shouldn't it wander off? He'd been inattentive. Taking her hand, he closed her fingers around the brush handle. "They've decided it's my turn."

Kimiko looked between him and the wide brush, matted with reddish fur. "You want me to brush you?"

Quen's skin prickled. "I'd let you."

She seemed unsure if he was teasing. "In your truest form, or this one?"

He hoped she couldn't tell that his heart was crashing around in his chest. "Either. Both."

"If combs are traditional courting gifts, would using one on you be considered courting behavior?"

"Definitely."

Her fingers touched his cheek. "You're blushing."

"Edge and Flay would have us rushing into all sorts of intimacies." He cleared his throat. "You wanted to talk?"

Kimiko nodded. "Things are getting confusing."

"Tell me." He made a coaxing motion, and to his delight, she nudged closer. Tugging and tucking, he didn't stop until he'd rid her of her bulky coat, which he draped around her shoulders once he'd pressed her head to his.

"This is really happening," she murmured.

"Not at all." At her baffled expression, he clarified. "Courtship is too intentional to be mistaken for happenstance. Nothing can happen without our consent."

Kimiko gaze softened. "That makes this a little less scary."

Quen's heart lurched. "You're scared?"

She slowly nodded. "Whenever I'm alone, I think about how many people I'm inconveniencing. And then I remember how much I don't know, and I'm sure that I'll embarrass you or hurt you or offend you or disappoint you."

He couldn't help smiling. "So you *do* care."

"I'm sorry for what I said last time." Kimiko pressed her lips to the underside of his jaw in a very proper apology. "I care, but not in the way I think I *should* care."

"Then we must be patient with each other." He kissed her forehead. "What has begun in haste can be completed at leisure."

"My parents will know by now." She curled against him. "I haven't dared turn on my phone."

"If Hisoka Twineshaft makes a pronouncement, the whole world finds it wise." He petted her hair. "And you will not face them alone. Trust Suuzu, Isla, and Akira."

"That's true." She wrapped the end of his braid around her finger. "What's next, then?"

"Next week, you'll make a formal declaration in front of both our families. They will approve of our betrothal once you let us know the shape it will take."

Kimiko stilled. "I don't know what that means."

"Am I not your guide in such things?" When she relaxed against him again, he explained, "Every clan has its own traditions where courtship is concerned. Some are showy, others secretive. Most are carried out over the course of months, even years, usually with some combination of gifts and vows. For instance, wolves must be courted according to the phases of the moon. Two of my brothers courted wolves, so they honored the traditions of their bondmates' packs."

"Will I be expected to court you like a dog?"

"I don't think that's possible. Since the majority of our traditions involve our truest form, too much would be lost in translation."

"Maybe I could adapt traditions from other clans? The ones that make sense for Amaranthine in speaking form."

He nuzzled her hair. "A solid strategy. And as a bonus, you'll drive Dad wild with curiosity over what you'll do next."

"Is that good?"

"Catching interest is the first step to keeping it."

Kimiko was quiet for a long time, lost in her own thoughts, but he hardly minded since he could hold her. Eventually, she stirred. "I'm not even sure where to start."

"I suggest confiding in Isla. She is a voracious researcher."

"I will. Thanks." She pulled away, clearly ready to leave. But she paused to ask, "What kinds of things count as courting behavior for dogs? Basic, pre-brushing stuff. For beginners like us."

To Eloquence's embarrassment, both Edge's and Flay's heads came up, and their tails beat the straw so fast, they raised dust.

Kimiko laughed softly. "I take it they're full of suggestions."

"Quite a few. Although most only make sense for those with four paws and a tail."

"Like what?"

"They're not anything humans would consider romantic." But since she seemed genuinely interested, he chose a few of the tamest pursuits. "Edge wants you to hunt for me, then feed me your prey morsel by morsel. Flay suggests the weaving of fur into a vest so that I will always have your scent upon my skin. And ... they both agree that the affectionate fondling of ears is the beginning of true love."

"Really?" Kimiko's eyes were sparkling, and her hands were reaching. "You do have pretty ears."

Quen was aware of the human fascination with Amaranthine ears. But it hadn't occurred to him that Kimiko might want to touch his.

Her fingers trailed along the upper edge to the tip, then the lower sweep to his earlobe. And again, slower, firmer. Pausing on her third circuit to knead the point.

He tilted his head to encourage her exploration. "You like my ears?" he asked huskily.

"Yes." She dropped a light kiss upon the tingling tip. "You like them touched?"

"Yes, Kimiko." Quen conceded to Edge and Flay that this was an entirely satisfying way for true love to begin. "Yes, I certainly do."

GOH SENSEI

Tenma started at the abrupt scrape and *criiik* coming from his ceiling and looked up just as a frigid flood of night air poured through the open skylight.

"Found you." Inti lowered himself through the gap, swinging from the edge for a few moments before dropping so the skylight fell shut with a sharp rattle of panes. He hit the floor and somersaulted, coming up at his side. "Your room. So high."

"The ceiling?"

"That, too." Inti bounced up to balance on the back of Tenma's chair. "Homework?"

"Personal study." Tenma showed the book he'd checked out from the school library. "This one's about bear clans. I want to learn about the Amaranthine in our class so I can understand them better."

"Bear." The tail that had been around his wrist all afternoon looped around Tenma's shoulders like a heavy scarf. "Tall, tall, Brev."

"Yes, I was curious about Brev." Tenma had to tip his head all the way back to see Inti's face. "I was going to look up monkeys, but I couldn't find any books. Maybe someone else checked them out."

"Maybe." From an upside down vantage, it was really hard to read the expression on Inti's face. "Maybe not."

Tenma thought it best to take a different topic. "So have you been racing around the rooftops?"

"A little."

"Is your room close by?" They'd parted in the student center, so he wasn't sure.

Inti's cheeks puffed out. "No. It's small and low and dark. Yours is bigger, better."

"Empty," muttered Tenma.

Quizzical eyebrows quirked. "Lonely?"

"I suppose." Tenma sighed. "Yes."

Fingers suddenly sifted through Tenma's hair, busily inspecting it by sections, gently scratching his scalp. He was being groomed. Which would have seemed odder if Tenma hadn't noticed how often Suuzu fussed with Akira's hair. "I just realized. You don't have claws?"

Inti hummed. "Mixed blood, mixed parts."

And all at once, the words came out. "Do you want to be my roommate?"

"Risky." But the tail around his shoulders tightened. "Tenma is kind."

He shook his head, because his motive was so much more selfish. "Tenma is lonely."

"Inti must race around the rooftops. Comings and goings,

227

but stayings. Good?"

"Good," Tenma agreed, reaching for the school directory. "I wonder who I need to speak to about room assignments."

As he flipped to the pages of contact information, a tuft of fur tickled Tenma under his chin. He automatically pushed it aside, then gasped, "Sorry!"

"Sorry?"

"I touched your tail!"

Inti blinked, then giggled. Soft and serious, he said, "My tail is touching you."

"But Ms. Reeves explained in class ... about tails."

"Wolves." He rolled his eyes. "My tail is not for decoration or for pride or for chasing. My tail is for balance and for hanging and for holding."

Tenma turned in his chair, and Inti's tail loosened to allow it. Searching the crosser's face, he asked, "Why do you pretend?"

Inti hunched forward until his nose nearly touched Tenma's. "Reasons."

Disappointment stung, but he only nodded.

With a soft sigh and a chittering of nonsense, Inti took Tenma's face in his hands and said, "Fools are harmless. Innocence is endearing. If Inti is sweet and silly, then Inti is simple."

He was talking about himself as if he were another person. "Why hide the truth?"

Inti shook his head. "Reasons."

Tenma let it go at that. "So ... may I touch your tail?"

The furred tip twitched under his chin. "My tail is touching you."

And since that seemed to be all the permission he needed,

Tenma lifted both hands to the tail that was as thick as Inti's arm and twice as long. It had weight and seemed to move with a mind of its own. Not wanting to intrude too far, Tenma confined himself to cautious patting.

Inti snickered. "My tail is not intimate territory."

"So you'll let anyone touch it?"

The crosser's fingers returned to grooming. "Would you take a stranger's hand and hold it."

"No." Tenma considered different social situations. "Not normally."

Inti nodded. "Like that."

Tenma remembered the casual intimacy he'd encountered while staying in the Starmark compound. Pack instincts. Family feelings. "What do monkeys call their friends?"

"Tenma."

He chuckled. "Okay, but wolves talk about pack and den. Some cats use hearth for home. And I've heard Akira refer to himself as Suuzu's nestmate. Are there simian equivalents?"

"Never asked."

He held up the directory. "Do you want to? Because Goh Impleer is one of the resident directors, and he's your sort. Let's go ask."

Inti stilled. "You ask. You tell."

"You don't want to go?"

"No."

"Aren't you curious?"

"I am free," Inti said softly. "That is enough."

"Will it bother you if *I* do some research?"

"You are also free." Inti gave Tenma's hair a final pat, then unwound himself. In one effortless spring, he reached the top of the kitchenette's cabinet and crouched. Making a playful flicking motion with his fingers, he said, "Go, go, Goh."

"Will you be here when I get back?"

"Tenma still wants Inti?"

"Why wouldn't I?"

With an impish smile, Inti answered, "Reasons."

The resident director lived one floor below Tenma's, on the building's opposite corner, so he hurried for the closest stairwell. Along one empty hallway, down another. The Amaranthine's door was clearly marked with a nameplate—GOH IMPLEER—and flanked by two precarious towers of clay pots glazed in shades of turquoise and orange. Very strange. Almost pretty. Probably intentional, like those artsy *installations* Tenma had seen in the lobbies of major hotels and corporate offices.

With a wary eye on the teetering arrangements, he tapped on the wide door.

A muffled voice hailed from inside. "It's open!"

Tenma turned the knob, and the door swung inward on silent hinges, leaving him gawking on the threshold. He wasn't sure if this was Goh-sensei's office, apartment, or both. The air was hot, thick, and smelled damp and green. Vines clung to the walls, climbing toward a darkened glass ceiling through which weak starlight showed. Tenma realized that while Goh-sensei's door was on the floor below his, this apartment soared to the roofline, creating a three-story column of tropics.

Lamps sparkled at intervals, many seemingly suspended in midair, their flames glowing through colored glass. More of those blues and oranges, which Tenma guessed might actually be the Rivven's clan colors.

"Goh-sensei?" he called softly.

"Up here. Dear me. My first guest, and me without a bookmark."

A baritone voice, playful, apologetic. Tenma caught a movement near the top, where sagging nets took up a portion of one lofty corner. A figure rolled out of the hammock, slowing a seemingly heedless descent with the help of tightropes and unnatural—or at least inhuman—grace. He landed a short distance away, and when he straightened to his full height, Tenma had to look up.

"Good evening, Tenma Subaru."

Goh Impleer might be a monkey, but that wasn't obvious at a glance. With the elfin ears, claws, and a fang-tipped smile, he looked like any other Rivven. No animal traits. Thick ropes of reddish hair hung well past Goh-sensei's shoulders, except for the parts framing his face. A ruddy shock stuck every which way, a cross between bedhead and the frizzled aftermath of a lightning strike.

Lamplight sparkled through a rakish collection of rings and dangling gems piercing Goh-sensei's ears. Maybe they did stuff, like warding or amplification. Of course, it was equally possible he liked to accessorize.

He was broad in the chest and long of limb, and he wore loose pants and a sleeveless shirt. Could these be his pajamas? That was an awkward thought. Tenma tried to remember the thing about

Rivven and sleep patterns. They did sleep, he was sure. Hadn't he woken up in the middle of the Five's slumber party?

Tenma was staring and stalling. And the Rivven was letting him get a good look. Suddenly self-conscious, he mumbled, "Hello, sir. Sorry, sir."

"Call me *Goh*." He strolled forward, beckoned for him to come all the way in, and closed the door. "You're a pleasant surprise. No need to be nervous, pup."

"Pup?" he ventured.

With a light touch at the elbow, Goh guided him to a cushioned bench and sat beside him. "Harmonious wouldn't take you in without letting it be known that you're under his protection."

"He *announced* it?"

"To the faculty," Goh-sensei confirmed. "Such are the dealings of dogs—more honesty than subtlety. But one always knows where one stands."

Tenma's face was heating. But he was also sort of ... *pleased* that Quen's dad had been serious about the whole packmate thing.

"What brings you to my door?" With a faint smile, he asked, "Trouble with our new student, perhaps?"

"Inti's no trouble, but ... this *is* about him. How did you know?"

"Oh, I have my ways."

Goh's evasiveness had a coaxing quality, as if trying to draw Tenma further into conversation. So he felt comfortable asking, "Like what?"

"I have an excellent sense of smell. And he's shed upon you. Groomed you, too, I'd wager." He lifted a few hairs from Tenma's sleeve. "But I'll confess to some curiosity about our newest student, whose lineage is unmistakable. As it happens, watching him meant watching you."

"We're in the same triad. Well, we're four now, so … quad?"

The teacher smoothed his finger over his lower lip, half-hiding a smile. "Is that your excuse for his sudden and persistent inseparability?"

Tenma answered slowly, unsure if he was being teased or misunderstood. "Inti was uneasy at first. He's fine though. Everyone in class likes him."

"But you are his favorite."

"Yes."

"Why?"

"I'm not really sure." Tenma thought back to what Inti had said earlier. "I don't think he needs a reason any more than I need an excuse. We get along. We're friends now. And we'd like to room together, please."

Goh bent closer, and Tenma could see the thin spike of his pupil showing against dark irises. Maybe brown. It was hard to tell in the shifting candlelight. But the Rivven's proximity was giving Tenma other impressions—colors and moods. Like the time when he was with Quen and Lapis. Was his sigil weakening?

"No need to be nervous, pup," he repeated softly.

Tenma took a deep breath and slowly reached for Goh-sensei. Fingers bumped cloth, hair, skin, rewarding him with a strengthening sense of an emerging personality. Mood and hue. Age and endurance. Wisdom and delight.

With a soft grunt, Goh caught his hand, enfolding it with both of his own in an oblique offer of support. "What do you see,

Tenma Subaru?"

"Brown, I think. But a cool brown. Earthy. Strong and pliant." He searched for the right word for the color of Goh-sensei's soul. "Clay?"

Head angled appraisingly, Goh said, "The potter's wheel is behind a screen in the corner, along with my store of clay. But scent is not sight."

Tenma frowned. Now that he was thinking about it, there *was* a clean, muddy smell to the room. Had he been listening to his nose instead of seeing with his soul? He wished he could express these impressions in a way that made sense. "I'm not sure how to explain. I'm not a reaver."

"Do not let lack of learning prevent you from choosing words. I will neither quibble nor correct."

So Tenma told him, haltingly at first, about his terror on the first day of school, about Quen's sigil, and about Lapis Mossberne's kindness.

Goh-sensei let him ramble, only murmuring encouragement and sympathy from time to time. And at last he said, "A good plan, which I'd willingly improve. Bring young Eloquence along someday soon, and I'll have him cut a sigil into clay for you. Once fired, it will give better protection than a slip of paper, and it will see you through until Lapis presents you with a gaudier ornament."

"Thank you." Tenma felt much better, though their conversation had drifted some distance from his intended purpose.

"Was there something more?" Goh-sensei beckoned encouragingly. "Information, perhaps. Or guidance?"

In a flash, Tenma remembered the question he'd been muddling earlier. "What do monkeys call their young?"

Goh's surprise melted into amusement. "I've been coached by the diplomatic division with regards to all manner of counsel, but I hardly expected curiosity about procreative processes."

"Oh!" Tenma waved his hands furiously. "It's not that at all, Sensei! I'm asking for Inti, since he doesn't seem to know much about his inhuman side."

"Wouldn't it be better if he came to me?"

Tenma nodded. "I think so, too. Maybe he will once I tell him what you're like. That you're nice and patient and ..."

" ... and *brown*?"

He nodded sheepishly. *Brown* fell so far short of the soul he could still sense—rich and real and right beside him.

"You're an interesting one." Goh gently mussed his hair, which seemed to be turning into another grooming session. Tenma bowed his head, accepting the touch. "Most of our human students struggle with the ordinary intimacies that are part of Amaranthine culture. But Harmonious claims you nestle like a pup."

Tenma couldn't decide if that was a compliment or more teasing. "Isn't that why we're here? To learn what we each consider ordinary?"

Goh laughed softly and continued his petting. "You're unusually accepting. It makes your tale of first-day fear difficult to picture."

Tenma's eyes had drifted shut. He hummed vaguely. "Probably because of Quen's sigil."

"What if I took it away?"

"Lapis tried that." He frowned, searching for words. "It's like alarm bells going off, warming me there's danger nearby."

"Interesting." Goh eased away, his expression thoughtful. "Far

235

be it from me to dabble with your distress. Trust Lapis. And if your new roommate is ready to learn about ordinary things, coax him to come to me as a tribemate."

Tenma was delighted by this new detail. "A tribe is like a pack?"

"Officially." Goh smirked. "Though many would argue that a more suitable collective noun would be *mischief*. We're one of the trickster clans, after all."

"A mischief of monkeys?"

"I'll order a hammock installed in your room. I do hope you're not afraid of heights."

Tenma's gaze drifted upward. "Not ... especially?"

"Good." Goh chucked him under the chin. "Packs nestle; tribes tangle."

✦

32
FOURTH ANNIVERSARY

Akira stuffed his hands deeper into his pockets and smiled. He didn't mind the bite in the air so much, seeing how Suuzu enjoyed getting out of doors. His friend might crave the safety and order of their dorm room, but he seemed equally attracted to the vast and changing sky. Peach and coral burned through clouds caught by the setting sun.

Kinda pretty.

Funny how he'd never given much thought to this stuff before. But Suuzu never seemed to get enough of two things—sky or sea. How long had it been since he went flying? Or trekked to a seaside place? Probably not since they were at Stately House—weeks ago.

"Say, everyone, is it okay if we stop in here?" asked Kimiko, hands pressed pleadingly. "I'll be quick!"

"Certainly," Suuzu murmured. "No need for haste."

A convenience store. Not one of the big-name chain stores, but

237

a pokey little place that looked like it had been in business since the granny behind the counter was their age. Kimi had a thing for little shops and seemed to know every single one in Keishi.

Akira rummaged through his pockets for change. "Want something, Isla? My treat."

She poked through the change in his palm. Slim pickings. But she matched his grin and suggested, "Split a steamed bun with me?"

"Pork or red bean?" he quizzed, even though he already knew the answer.

Isla simply winked.

Akira ambled over to the counter to order the sweet bun. Finding Suuzu at his elbow, he asked, "Want one?"

The phoenix passed him more coins than necessary, so Akira bought four to share out.

A soft squeal of delight came from two aisles over, where they found Kimi crouched before the candy section, stacks of chocolate bars teetering. Eyes alight, she exclaimed, "They're in! A whole line of designs to celebrate the Emergence!"

The fourth anniversary was next week, the weeklong holiday coinciding with the Lunar New Year.

Akira dropped down beside her, checking out her haul. "Clan crests are definitely a classy way to go. Is it just the Five?"

"No!" Kimi laughed softly. "I've found eleven different designs in this box, but I heard there will be forty all together. Not sure how I'm going to afford them all."

"That's a cinch," said Akira. "All you have to do is acquaint your betrothed with the Valentine's Day tradition. Then he can shower you with chocolates."

To Akira's amusement, she actually considered it. But only for a moment.

"I couldn't do that. Most of the fun is in finding them myself."

"That might be difficult." Isla pointed to the small print on a nearby sign. "Some designs are only available regionally."

Kimiko groaned. "Train fare, too?"

"Probably not," Akira cautioned. "The school is keeping close tabs on everyone, and Sensei is keeping even closer tabs on you. Or did you forget the security detail at your place?"

Her face fell.

Suuzu helped her gather up her stack, carrying them to the counter.

Akira nudged Isla with an elbow. "Think Quen knows about Valentine's Day?"

She shook her head. "You and Kimi grew up in human society, so it's familiar enough to you. But reavers don't share this particular custom, and there's no Amaranthine equivalent."

"Maybe someone should ask Ms. Reeves to add it to February's curriculum."

Isla poked his chest. "Talk to Sosuke. Since he represents your third of the class, he can speak to her on your behalf."

Not a bad idea.

Back out on the street, Akira fell in step with Kimi. "Any weird flavors today?"

"This one's new." She showed him a small bag with a bright green wrapper—HAPPY KAPPA CONFETTI CRISPS.

The character on the package was funny. Was there an Amaranthine equivalent to the kappa from folk lore? "So ... does Eloquence know about your strange taste in snacks?"

She shook her head. "We've barely talked, and it's usually about important things."

Akira snorted. "I coulda sworn this stuff was important to you."

"I'm not sure it counts as *important.*"

"But don't people who care about each other like knowing little things—even if they're as bizarre as your snack risks—*especially* the things that make them happy?"

Kimi opened the crinkling bag and popped a pale green crisp into her mouth. Akira wasn't sure if the resulting pucker was a good thing, but when she held out the bag, he took one. He sniffed and studied the odd hue before giving in to curiosity.

She asked, "Do you think knowing little things about someone is part of loving them?"

Akira considered that idea aloud. "Could be. I mean, the more you know about someone, the more reasons you may find to like them. Or maybe the more you like someone, the more you want to know the kinds of things nobody else does. Because that'd mean they trust you more than anyone."

She hummed. "Which was it for you and Suuzu?"

Akira hesitated. He hadn't been thinking about friendship kinds of love, but in essence, weren't they a lot alike? He shrugged. "Both, I guess. Plus a willingness to de-clutter. In *your* case, it'll probably be both, plus getting used to dog hair. You do realize it'll be everywhere, right?"

She laughed.

Even better, her posture shifted. Akira wasn't learning the nonverbal cues half as quickly as Isla, but he could tell Kimi was relaxed. Maybe even happier. He might not be a prodigy like Isla, but with Suuzu's coaching, he was keeping up with the basics.

He passed around the bag of steamed buns, and they meandered onward, always keeping the landmark tree in view.

Dickon welcomed them at the foot of the shrine's lengthy stairs. "Thank you, boys. I will see to the young mistresses' safety from here." His words held dismissal.

Figuring Suuzu would be only too glad to get home, Akira was already waving goodbye, turning toward home.

Suuzu put out an arm to stop him. "Are we unwelcome, Reaver Denholme?"

The man's dark eyes flashed. "Far from it, good phoenix. I apologize for any disappointment. By your next visit, the wards will be tuned to accept you."

"By what means?" asked Suuzu, pleasant but persistent.

Akira couldn't understand the challenge—if it even was a challenge. Then again, Suuzu was always careful about details. Maybe these were the kinds of questions a good friend should be asking.

✦ Dickon said, "By the most secure means admissible."

Suuzu's head cocked to one side. "Tuned crystals?"

"If you are willing."

Akira remembered something about tuned crystals from Juuyu's nest-necklace. He didn't really understand all the intricacies of crystal resonance and amplification. But he knew that wards could tattle on your movements and invisible barriers could feel like a brick wall if you weren't supposed to cross them.

Suuzu said, "Tuned crystals would be ideal, provided they are properly handled."

Dickon inclined his head. "Spokesperson Twineshaft arranged

for their installation."

Akira blinked. What were the chances?

"Far be it from me to question Hisoka Twineshaft's handling."

Suuzu's tone was stiff, yet polite. Akira grabbed his hand and rolled his eyes deliberately toward the girls. "Only the best for these two. Best of the best!"

Not as smooth or subtle as Kimi's posturing, but good enough to get by.

Recognition flickered, and Suuzu murmured, "Yes, of course. I am content."

"Take care on your return journey." Dickon's gaze swept the quiet lane. "It happened again."

"Another attack?" Kimi asked sharply. "Someone's been taken?"

Dread plunged in Akira's gut. "They didn't say anything at school."

Dickon's jaw tightened, and his shook his head once. "She is not a student at New Saga. The girl attends Ingress Academy."

33

THAT RADISH MAN

That Radish-man!" Mrs. Miyabe's knife beat a staccato across her cutting board, reducing a cabbage to vicious shreds. Dinner preparation was turning into a dangerous affair, and Kimiko wondered if she should try to separate Mama from her weapon.

She traded a look with Isla, whose eyes had taken on a definite sparkle. Kimiko was relieved that the girl didn't belittle or bemoan the circumstances in their household. On the contrary, Isla seemed to enjoy navigating Mrs. Miyabe's shifting moods.

"Which man?" Isla adopted an expression of innocent puzzlement. "Do you mean Reaver Denholme?"

Apparently, Dickon's name sounded enough like *daikon* to give rise to the insult. Mama clearly thought it a clever twist, but Kimiko thought her childish.

The woman took up a carrot and shook it. "Am I to be a prisoner in my own home?"

"Mama," Kimiko sighed. "He's here to keep us safe."

"From the Ladies Neighborhood Improvement Committee?" Her voice squeaked with her outrage. "They met *without* me because that Radish-man wouldn't let me through. Of all the audacity! I'm the chairwoman!"

It was difficult to say if that jibe was intended for their beleaguered security guard or the women who'd had the temerity to carry on without her.

"Spokesperson Twineshaft explained, and we all agreed it was for the best," soothed Kimiko. "It's too soon to let anyone know about my betrothal."

"Security. Secrets," Mama grumbled. "Can't a mother be excited over her daughter's good fortune?"

"You can." Kimiko was a little surprised. "I'm glad to know you're happy about the match."

But the woman rattled right on. "And that Nakamura woman, flaunting her sons-in-law and her oh-so-gifted grandchildren. This will put her back in a proper place."

"But Mama, you can't tell."

"I could *hint*!" Her smile was smug. "And even if she *were* to catch on, what's a secret or two between old friends?"

Kimiko chose not to point out that *this* was the reason Mama was confined to quarters. Temporarily. And Daddy's quiet support. Part of Hisoka Twineshaft's effort to stem the tide of gossip until the Starmarks were ready to go public about the bonding.

Preferably after graduation.

Noriko came in then, a patient smile on her face. "Don't you girls have homework?"

"Loads." Kimiko signaled her gratitude. "Isla and I will be in the archive until dinnertime."

Practically running, she led their escape.

Out of sight of the kitchen windows, Kimiko slowed and whispered, "Sorry."

"You have nothing to apologize for." Isla reached for her hand. "She'll come around eventually."

"Come around? To what?"

"Nope, *nein*, *nyet*." Isla's eyes fairly sparkled. "That's the only hint you're getting. Now where's this obscure reaver library you've been hiding from me?"

"I wasn't hiding it. Let's call it … saving the best for last." Unlocking the door, she slid it to one side and bowed Isla through. "Welcome to Kikusawa Shrine's least famous treasury. Not that any of them are particularly well known."

Isla swept through the door, swayed in place, executed a slow turn, then flung herself into Kimiko's arms.

"It's beautiful!" Isla rubbed their cheeks together in a great show of feline affection, raving nonsense in Russian and Old Amaranthine. "You're my new favorite person!"

"Because I hold the key to a roomful of books?"

Isla clung. "And because you're normal and nice and not jealous at all."

Kimiko swept up the slender girl and spun her around. "*And* I hold the key to a roomful of books."

"Okay, it's the books." Isla's kiss landed in the vicinity of Kimiko's chin. "I was nearly done with all the ones in New Saga's library."

"In a month?"

"Most of the books here are duplicates to Ingress Academy's collection. So I had a head start."

At the mention of Ingress, Kimiko's smile faded. "Do you think the kidnapped girl is someone you know?"

"Probably." Isla's expression grew solemn. "Sensei will do something."

It occurred to Kimiko that the cat might have multiple purposes in placing Isla at Kikusawa Shrine. For instance, if his apprentice was under guard and behind boundaries here, he would be freer. She whispered, "Is he out hunting?"

Isla lowered her voice, too. "Lately, he prowls more than he purrs. And I don't see him as often as I'd like, but I'm trying not to mind."

Kimiko gallantly settled the girl into the most comfortable chair. "While the cat's away, I'll keep you busy. Because I have a courtship to formalize and my knowledge of Amaranthine bonding is skimpy at best."

Isla hummed thoughtfully. "I know the most about fox customs. When I was little, I had the worst crush on one. Well, half of one."

Half a fox? She could only mean a crosser, and the only one Kimiko knew about was famous. "Do you mean Spokesperson Mettlebright's son?"

"Gingko." Good memories softened Isla's expression. "He's always lived with Papka and Mum, so he was always there whenever I'd go home."

Although Ever Starmark might be the first *official* crosser, unofficial ones had been stealing onto the scene. Just a few, here and there. Like Inti.

Isla went on. "I adored him, but he was never interested in me like that. When I was eight, Gingko did his best to let me down gently. I was heartbroken."

"He faced your feelings *because* he loved you."

"Yes, but that was harder to understand back then."

The twelve-year-old sounded so worldly-wise. Comparatively, she was. Kimiko had never given boys much thought. She'd always been Grandpa's girl.

"Papka explained to me that there are all kinds of love, and each is precious if you treasure it. And Mum reminded me that as a reaver, I have a responsibility to the next generation."

Kimiko murmured, "I've been worrying about that part myself."

"But you're not ...." Isla blinked, then blushed.

"It's all right to speak plainly, Isla. I know as well as you do that I have little to offer the In-between. My children would have been like me—raised in the human community, never rising above a middling rank." Kimiko really had put a lot of thought into the consequences of her choice. "The reaver community loses nothing of worth, but Eloquence gains something he never expected. To him, I'm unique, rare, and irreplaceable."

Isla's eyes sparkled. "Like a limited edition chocolate bar?"

"*That* is the finest compliment I've ever been paid!" Kimiko's laughter faltered, and she hid her face against Isla's knee. "This is all very flattering, but it's also intimidating. How can I show the Starmarks that I'm properly treasuring their son? Eloquence deserves more than I know how to give."

"Courtship can do that." Isla's hand smoothed over her hair. "I know traditions within all the major clans and most of the minor ones, but there are so many variations and nuances, depending on the message you want to convey."

She lifted her face. "Another form of non-verbal statement?"

"Exactly!"

Kimiko frowned. "I thought you said you only knew about foxes?"

"I know the *most* about foxes." The girl showed a dimple. "Sensei thought it best that I cover courting traditions before I hit puberty, since hormones make it difficult to stay objective about the intricacies of Amaranthine bonding. There are usually sexual overtones."

She was almost afraid to ask. "Hisoka Twineshaft taught you about Amaranthine mating behavior?"

"Don't look so shocked. He set my reading course, then handed me over to Mare Withershanks for a while. She explained everything, answered my questions, and took me along on her rounds. During that one summer, I attended seven births and two matings."

"M-matings?"

Isla's eyebrows arched. "Some clans fight for the right to claim a desirable female, so they bring in a healer to tend injuries. And some clans require someone in an official capacity to witness the mating."

Kimiko quailed. "Please, tell me that dogs like privacy."

"Yes. Dogs are both possessive and protective. The Starmarks will undoubtedly band together to ensure the sanctity of your den." Isla cheerfully added, "In the oldest traditions—which are naturally wolvish in nature—the bonded pair does not rejoin the pack until the coupling has met with success. But that was before the Waning."

"Let's not rush things," Kimiko mumbled. "As much as I'd like to leave Eloquence with a child, I'm not ready to think about kids."

Isla opened her mouth, and it snapped shut. "What do you mean, *leave him*?"

She said, "I'm human. Lifespan differences."

"Oooh, Kimi. I forget that not everyone knows. I can't believe nobody told you! That's so unfair, but typical of Sensei." The girl's babble cut off, and she drew herself up. "He's probably testing your motives."

Kimiko was getting worried. "A test?"

"One you've passed." The girl touched her cheek. "You really are doing this for Quen's sake."

That was obvious. "Isla, just tell me."

"Although it's not widely known, Sensei documented several cases which prove that a properly-tended bond between an Amaranthine and a human benefits both participants."

The girl slipped into full diplomat mode. Instead of talking to Kimiko as a friend, Isla subtly removed herself from the flow of information, which she delivered in a completely neutral tone. She sounded like a textbook.

"While ranking, intent, focus, and duration are variables that affect the degree of success, the results are similar in every case. The Amaranthine borrows the reaver's power, and their partner gains an Amaranthine's years."

Kimiko blinked. "You mean like ... like a tree-child?"

"Yes, just like in tree lore! Except you don't have to be born with a golden seed in your hand. Instead of a tree-sibling, you'll have Quen to prolong your life." Isla seemed puzzled. "But how did you know? Tales of the imps are hard to come by."

"Probably because most of them are archived here." Kimiko laughed and gestured to the surrounding books. "I grew up hearing stories about moon maidens, river guardians, and the four winds. But the stories about Amaranthine trees have always been my favorite."

Isla's second hug was even fiercer than the first. "I'm not leaving this shrine until I've read every one of them!"

"I'd love that." Kimiko held the girl close. "Grandpa would have been thrilled. If only ... if only *he* had been the one with a tree's years."

After a comforting hush, Isla's voice came softly. "Kimi, are trees truly your favorite?"

"Always have been."

"Then would you be interested in a courtship tradition from the Songs of Trees?"

Kimiko laughed. As a daughter of Kikusawa Shrine, nothing could be more appropriate. "Something to do with trees sounds *perfect*."

34

DYNAMIC ENTRY

Halfway between the shrine and the dorm, Akira suddenly asked, "Is it weird that dragons keep coming up?"

Suuzu studied his companion's face in the fading light. There was little mystery behind the seemingly random remark since Akira had a vested interest. His sister was fostering a dragon crosser, and there was a chance that the little one's biological father—a serial kidnapper and rapist—was behind the recent upheaval in Keishi.

Akira's expression was troubled. "You don't think it's *him*, do you?"

"No one has mentioned dragons in relation to the case."

"But your brother's in town. And phoenixes are experts in dragon-hunting."

"Juuyu is," he conceded.

Akira pressed his point. "Doesn't that mean there's a good chance he's tracking a dragon now?"

Suuzu thought back over his brother's visit and the care he'd taken in defending their nest. Would so many wards ordinarily be necessary? And had any of them been keyed specifically to dragons? Perhaps when they reached the dorm, he should take a closer look at the sigils.

"Don't you think?" prompted Akira.

"Yes," he conceded. "That is possible."

"How possible?"

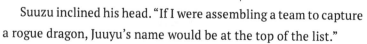

Suuzu inclined his head. "If I were assembling a team to capture a rogue dragon, Juuyu's name would be at the top of the list."

"So … it's probably him?"

"It is *possible*." Suuzu tugged at Akira's windblown hair. "Juuyu's skills are not limited to the tracking of our traditional prey."

Akira buried his nose in his scarf.

And in the succeeding lull, Suuzu sensed an unusual tension. Then a flicker of movement. Akira didn't react, for he couldn't sense the presence of Amaranthine, but Suuzu's awareness jangled with multiple alarms. Were they surrounded?

Suuzu closed ranks behind Akira, bending to speak in his ear. "Stay close."

"Something up?"

He clucked his tongue, his uneasiness mounting.

Akira fell silent, and when Suuzu slipped and arm around his shoulders, he went still. "Wolves," Suuzu reported. "Let us give them a moment to pass by."

"Trackers?"

Suuzu hummed an affirmative, scanning the darkening sky and deep shadows. A series of yips and a lone howl changed his opinion. "Pursuers."

"What are they chasing?"

"Something clever." Suuzu set his fingers over Akira's mouth, forestalling further questions. Because he could feel sigils in the air, illusions at play. Maybe they'd stumbled across one of Keishi's harmless enclaves, but ... maybe not. He pulled Akira against his chest, fully prepared to transform in the street and take to the sky, trusting his nestmate to forgive him later for the rough handling.

Akira felt the tension radiating through Suuzu's body, so he slowed his breathing and relaxed his muscles, ready to go limp if an airlift was imminent. They'd practiced all kinds of emergency maneuvers—partly because his best friend was a worrywart, but partly because Akira would never get enough of flying.

More difficult was holding his tongue. Suuzu needed to tell him what was going on!

He couldn't see anything or feel anything, but that was no surprise. Humans missed a heck of a lot, even when there weren't barriers or illusions in play. All he could do was trust Suuzu.

And pinch him.

"Hush." Suuzu curled more snugly against him, his talons lengthening discernibly.

When a figure stepped out of nowhere, the phoenix added a warning hiss, but the person lifted his hands in a plea for peace. "It's only us."

Us?

Then in scolding tones, raised to carry, "For pity's sake, old friend, stop pretending to be a threat. It's childish."

Tsk.

Tension burst like a bubble, and Akira wriggled free, barreling into the waiting embrace of Michael Ward. "You're here!"

"Well spotted. We only just arrived and are under strict orders to make sure you're doing as brilliantly as your texts imply." Michael made a show of looking him over. "Your sister misses you."

"I'm fine. We're fine." Akira eased away and presented himself to the aloof figure of his brother-in-law. "Hello, Argent."

A silver eyebrow arched. "Since when are you so reserved?"

Which Akira took as permission to step into the fox's arms. While his sister's mate was much more reserved than Michael, he was several times more protective. Argent checked him over, then gripped his chin. Pale blue eyes narrowed. "Why are you beyond safe boundaries?"

"We were seeing Kimi and Isla home."

He accepted that with a low hum, then switched his attention to Suuzu. Akira wanted to defend his friend, but Argent offered no criticism. "You noticed quickly and would have had him safely away. Well done."

Suuzu simply reclaimed Akira, who was getting rather used to being passed around. He said, "You didn't say anything about coming. Does Isla know?"

"In a general sense." Michael gestured vaguely. "I'm a bit ahead of schedule, due to this and that. Hints were dropped. I have a shrine to ward. Among other things."

Argent's attention remained fixed on some distant point, but his calm voice betrayed nothing. "We will be at the Starmark compound. Visit us there when your class schedule allows. Kyrie misses you."

"You brought him?" Akira glanced around, not liking the idea of his little nephew being at risk. Especially if tonight's skirmish was dragon-based.

"I sent him on ahead with Gingko."

Akira relaxed. "That's good then. We'll come as soon as we can. Tomorrow?"

Suuzu, who hadn't loosened his hold, promised, "Tomorrow."

Akira didn't have the senses to know exactly what was going on, but it didn't take a genius to tell *something* was happening in Keishi's neighborhoods. Dogs barked in every street, and he caught the distant howl of a wolf. "Trackers?" he whispered.

"Yes."

"They're still chasing something?"

"I do not think they would bring this much attention to themselves without cause." Suuzu steered him firmly along. "While there is no immediate danger, we should hurry."

"Yeah, okay." Akira broke into a jog before Suuzu could decide it would be more expedient to carry him.

At the dormitory entrance, they were cornered by Sentinel Skybellow. "Kimiko Miyabe and Isla Ward?"

"Safe," Suuzu assured.

The dog nodded. "All accounted for. We are closing the doors."

Suuzu led Akira by the hand across the student center, as if worried he'd run off. The resident Kith were riled up, and he was fairly certain he spotted Goh-sensei on the roost where the hawks usually perched.

"Tomorrow should be interesting," Akira said. "You think the school will tell us what's going on?"

"There will undoubtedly be a statement."

Akira pressed the elevator button. "Maybe we'll find out more when we go to the Starmark compound. Argent's bound to know."

Suuzu hummed a vague affirmative, but he was focused on reaching their nest.

Best course, really. Conversations could wait until they were safely behind Juuyu's extravagant barriers.

Inside, Akira moved through the familiar patterns that would give Suuzu peace of mind. Drop the keys, school bag, and shopping bag. Hang his coat. Empty his pockets. Plug in his phone.

Suuzu lined up their shoes, straightened their coats, then moved toward the closet where their bedding waited. Halfway there, he stopped short and crossed to one of the windows instead.

Hoping to calm his best friend further, Akira lit a candle and doused the lights. If Suuzu refused to leave the nest—which seemed likely—then dinner would be the few things he'd grabbed at the convenience store earlier. Good enough.

"See anything?" he asked softly.

"Hmm."

Akira dragged out their bedding and started arranging. Predictably, Suuzu came along behind him, smoothing and straightening the blankets. Now that it was just them, he was thinking about the previous night's promise. Curiosity knotted with little doubts. They weren't second thoughts, exactly. But the timing was terrible.

"It's kinda chancy, trying anything while Argent and Michael are here."

Suuzu looked up, all bewilderment.

"The … hatching thing," he mumbled. "If anything changes, they'd notice."

Sitting back on his heels, Suuzu faced him across the futon.

Akira waved his hands, babbling on even though there was nothing to say. "Not that I'm expecting anything to change. Michael said it was probably nothing. So I don't even know what I'm hoping for."

Confusion was shifting into concern. And here, he was supposed to be calming Suuzu down.

He let his hands fall limp to his sides.

"You are uneasy." Suuzu had migrated from concerned to distraught. "I make you uneasy?"

Akira shook his head. "Going against the advice of someone I trust kinda does. A little."

"Forgive me." Suuzu's posture shifted into a pose that meant *I'm no threat*, and he placed his hands behind his back.

"Stop that!" Akira crawled across their bed and grabbed Suuzu's shoulders. "I'm not afraid of you. I've *never* been afraid of you."

Suuzu warbled unhappily.

"Okay, I'm *uneasy*. What if something happens? What if this hatching thing means stuff has to change?" He lamely finished,

"I like how things are."

Suuzu carefully pulled him close. "I am content."

After their talk with Kimi, he was beginning to doubt that. He dared to counter, "Are you?"

"Yes. With you, yes."

And there was the actual problem. Akira was proud and happy that he'd always have Suuzu. A friend for life, but only a human's lifetime. How would his friend cope when his nestmate died? Akira felt guilty over this one-sided happiness ... and the empty nest that must follow.

Chest tight, eyes stinging, he asked, "What were you planning to do? I mean, do we have a plan?"

"No." Suuzu's hold tightened fractionally. "I do not know what to do."

"Is this why you agreed to Michael's offer? So you could learn about tending?"

"Hmm. Perhaps."

Akira had been there—at Suuzu's insistence—for the phoenix's first taste and subsequent tendings. The whole thing had seemed pretty uneventful. From Akira's perspective, all Michael had done was hold Suuzu's hand. Nothing much happened, except that afterward Suuzu was quieter than usual. And clingy.

"Could we start a nest?" Akira blurted.

Suuzu's quick intake of air came out in a funny little series of notes.

But Akira seized on the idea. "It can be one like Juuyu's. We can start collecting the things you'll need."

For when he was gone.

Still, Suuzu didn't answer.

"We'll find the perfect things. For stars and tides and everything that matters." Akira coaxed the only way he knew how, pushing his fingers through Suuzu's hair. Mussing and messing until the curls were loose enough to preen. "We'll collect everything, you and me together. That way, it'll be ours. Always ours. Do you want to?"

"I want to." Suuzu leaned into his touch. "Build with me."

Good. This was good. It felt all kinds of right, and it would give the phoenix something to hold onto. Smiling, Akira kept right on twisting his fingers through the dark tangle of Suuzu's hair. Peace. Finally.

Akira started at a sudden noise. A thud overhead that rattled the glass of their skylight. "Something's on the roof," he whispered.

Whatever it was struck with greater force.

"Juuyu's barrier." Suuzu narrowed his eyes at the darkened glass overhead. Then with a hiss, he scooped up Akira and dove for the corner. Just in time.

With a crash, the skylight shattered, and a bundled figure plunged through.

35

CLOAK AND DAGGER

Akira wasn't sure if he was shaking because of adrenalin or because of the cold air pouring into their room. Glass tinkled, and someone groaned. Peeking out past Suuzu's shoulder, he tried to see who'd invaded their supposedly impenetrable fortress.

"A little help here?"

He moved to assist, but Suuzu held him back.

"Sorry, sorry. Didn't mean to startle you boys."

Their intruder slowly eased to a hunched sitting position, tutting to himself as if he were in pain and favoring his left side. A hooded cloak hid his face, and the voice didn't sound familiar. But it was a nice voice. Akira's gut was telling him to trust this person.

"I swear, I have a good reason for bashing in like this." A pale hand with gold-tipped claws pushed away the hood. "I wish I could explain, but then I'd be breaking rules in addition to the window. Then again, some things are obvious. Help me, Suuzu?"

Akira asked, "You know him?"

"I do not."

The person pouted. "Only because *some* people are obnoxiously strict about rules and regulations."

Okay. Claws, fangs, and ears were the trademark features, but Akira could have pegged this guy as an Amaranthine on hair alone. Crazy-long hair had been woven into a complex braid that looked more like basket-weaving than a hairstyle. And it was a weird pale yellow-green, shot through with blond streaks.

"Really? Right." With a weary gesture, the guy said, "Will *you* help, Akira?"

He was halfway there when Suuzu jerked him back into his chest. The phoenix was furious. Akira could feel the emotion shaking, flaring. But the other person needed help. Why didn't Suuzu understand?

"Suuzu?" He tilted his head, trying to see his friend's face.

The gaze that met his flashed with emotions Akira rarely saw. But Suuzu answered calmly. "Look at your feet."

Akira's unprotected feet were a half-step away from the jagged remains of their skylight. Why hadn't he noticed? "Whoa. That would have hurt."

"Put on your shoes." Suuzu pointed him to the entry. "And call for Sentinel."

"Wait!" called the stranger.

So Akira stopped, turning to see what he wanted.

Suuzu stalked to Akira, lifted him bodily, and whisked to the door.

"Listen!" The green-haired Amaranthine raised his right hand and crooked his pinky. "I'm *sorry*, Suuzu. I wasn't trying to hurt your nestmate. And Sentinel's support would be welcome, but we need a healer more."

Awkwardly pushing aside his dark cloak, he revealed the huddled form of a dark-skinned girl—young, battered, and unconscious.

Akira whispered, "That's an Ingress Academy uniform."

"Put on your shoes," Suuzu repeated, setting Akira down and facing their intruder. "Is that the girl who was taken?"

"Yes."

"And you're a dragon."

Akira fumbled with his shoelaces. "He's a dragon?"

"Yes," said Suuzu.

That sent a little thrill down his spine—part fear, part fascination. "You're a dragon."

"I'm a dragon." Holding out a palm that pleaded for peace, he added, "Sinder Stonecairne, of the Icelandic Reach. It's nice to finally meet you both."

"How come you know our names?" Akira asked.

Suuzu added, "How did you break the barrier?"

"Your brother's barrier came in handy." Sinder gently eased his burden into a more comfortable position.

"This nest is warded against dragons."

"No. It's warded against *other* dragons." Sinder made the same kind of odd fluting sound that Lapis made when he was playing with Kyrie. "I'm almost hurt he never told you. Suuzu, I'm one of the good guys. Juuyu is my partner."

Sentinel Skybellow didn't seem to care about the wreckage in their room, the barriers that prevented him from entering, or the presence of a dragon. He only had eyes for the girl—soft and sad. "Mare Withershanks is at Ingress."

Before he could dash off, Akira asked, "What about this guy."

"Hide him here." With a delicate sniff, Sentinel added, "Tend his injuries."

And he was gone.

A few moments later, a voice hailed them from overhead. Goh-sensei placed a finger on the side of his nose. "I'll patch things up and add a little something extra. No one will notice the rough edges."

Sinder waved wearily. "Thanks, Goh."

"Not to worry, Sinder."

And a sheet of plywood banged into place, covering the gaping hole overhead. Suuzu cocked his head to one side, then remarked, "It is well-warded."

"Goh's top notch. No drafts." Sinder shivered dramatically. "Mind if we warm this icebox up a little?"

Akira turned toward the thermostat only to find Suuzu in the way.

The phoenix cupped his cheek and said, "You do not have to listen to him."

"He's cold."

"So are you. It is a reasonable request." Suuzu seemed to be pleading with him. "You are too easily swayed."

"The trusting ones usually are." Sinder made a gesture Akira recognized as an apology.

"Maybe you should explain," Akira said.

"Dragons are dangerous," said Suuzu.

Sinder begged to differ. "Dragons have the *potential* to be dangerous. We are captivating in our beauty."

"And they take captives with their words."

Again, Sinder countered, "Historically. Many clans have dark stories in their past that would make for bad press. But dragons have chosen peace. We are represented among the Five."

Suuzu's head dipped. "Granted. But your words are affecting Akira."

"Truly a problem." Sinder crooked his fingers encouragingly. "Come here."

Akira started forward, only to be stopped by Suuzu's hand at his wrist.

The dragon sighed. "Spokesperson Farroost, the people you trust most trust me. Bring him over, and I'll help him break the habit."

This was all very exciting and a little surreal, but Akira was pretty sure they'd gotten off track. Waving both hands, he stepped between them. "If our teachers trust him enough to leave him here, we're good. And Sentinel said he's injured. Shouldn't *that* be our first priority?"

Suuzu's attitude vanished. "Do you need a healer?"

"Not necessary. If you can manage the basic bandages and ointments." He grimaced. "And tweezers."

"And a broom," Suuzu murmured, already out the door.

Sinder chuckled. "He's so much like his brother, it's scary."

"Can you move?" Akira had noticed that the dragon hadn't budged, even when Suuzu took the rescued girl from him to give her to Sentinel. Injuries could be a problem for Amaranthine, since they were slow to heal. "Let's get you into a clean corner. By the heater."

"You're too kind."

Akira found the rips in Sinder's cloak, which he helped the dragon remove, exposing bruises, lacerations, and embedded glass. And six sheathed blades of various sizes. The shirt had to go, too, exposing lean muscles and milk-pale skin.

"So ... are you a super-spy?"

Sinder's pale eyebrows arched. "Two words. Elite taskforce."

"Are you all tributes?"

"Aren't *you* in the know!"

Which wasn't an answer. Akira tried the eyebrow thing.

Chuckling, Sinder answered, "Most of us, yes. But exceptions make us exceptional."

Before Akira could press for more information, Suuzu returned with cleaning supplies and a medical kit. Coming quickly to their side, he trilled his dismay. Passing Akira the kit, he set to work, gently extracting slivers of glass with the tips of his claws.

To distract their patient, Akira kept talking. "Are dragons one of the trickster clans?"

"No. The tricksters excel at visual deception."

"And dragons use words?"

"It's part of our charm," Sinder acknowledged.

"How does it work?"

He smiled. "Touch your nose."

Akira did.

"Touch your friend's nose."

Akira did that, too. Why wouldn't he? It was a simple request.

"Kiss your friend's nose."

Easy enough. Akira had a vague notion that he was behaving

foolishly. But the deed was already done, so why worry over it? Except Suuzu was looking rather harassed.

"You want me to keep going?" asked Sinder.

Akira was suddenly thinking clearly again, and he laughed. Sinder was *teasing* them. Really, he reminded Akira a little of Gingko, an incorrigible big brother who's actually pretty cool. Only sleeker. And greener. And part of an elite taskforce.

"Good thing you're a good guy." Akira shook his head. "I didn't even notice until the kiss."

"Not bad. Some people never realize they're being guided." Sinder shrugged. "Prolonged exposure weakens our hold. Play my game a little longer, and you'll be wise to serpents of any stripe."

He turned to Suuzu. "Is that true?"

"Yes."

While the phoenix seemed ruffled, he wasn't angry anymore. Permission enough to get on with it. "Okay. Keep going."

Sinder solemnly said, "Touch your nose."

Akira did.

The commands came again in sequence, as if the last round had been a rehearsal. Akira couldn't have been more relaxed, and could tell that Suuzu accepted the peck to his nose with more grace. But then Sinder said, "Kiss my nose."

Akira balked. Kissing Suuzu's nose had been enough out of character, but Sinder's nose was on Sinder's face. Did he really want to kiss Juuyu's partner?

"Good. You're trusting, but you have a highly developed sense of right and wrong. Living among foxes probably also works in your favor."

266

"This is so weird."

Suuzu was slowly applying ointment to Sinder's injuries with a knuckle. Akira thought the row of shallow gashes looked suspiciously like claw marks. "How'd you get *those*?"

Sinder said, "Touch your nose."

Akira did.

By the time Sinder released him from a lengthy round of harmless tasks, the dragon was neatly bandaged and Suuzu had all but finished the clean-up. Akira was a little fuzzy on how much time had passed. His roommate could move pretty fast, especially when something needed tidying.

"Are you even trying to resist?" Sinder asked.

He shook his head. "Everything you say just sorta makes sense."

Suuzu murmured, "Akira already trusts you."

"Normally, I'd be pleased." Sinder's faraway gaze suddenly snapped into focus. "Open the door."

Akira was halfway there when he collided with Suuzu. The phoenix took a firm tone. "I promised we would stay behind safe boundaries."

A light rap came, and Sinder offered a weary smile. "Open the door for Juuyu."

Suuzu got there first. Both boys were soon clasped against Juuyu's sides while he exclaimed over the mess and reassured himself that his chicks were unharmed. Sinder eased onto his knees and bowed until his forehead touched the floor, which brought Juuyu up short. "You are injured."

"Hardly worth mentioning."

And suddenly, Akira and Suuzu were standing alone by the door.

Juuyu grumbled as he fussed, thoroughly inspecting his partner's injuries as he quizzed him in undertones. Finally, he took a seat at Sinder's side, shoulders sinking to a disconsolate angle. "She will live," he quietly announced to the room.

"And ...?"

Juuyu shook his head. "He eluded us. Again."

Sinder whistled a series of notes that descended sorrowfully. "Poor Boon."

36

POOR BOON

The scent of blood had Eloquence on edge long before Lapis burst through his door, calling over his shoulder, "In here!"

"I do know my way around," grumbled his father's voice. Then Dad shouldered through the door with Uncle Laud, carrying the bloodied figure of Boonmar-fen between them.

Merit was at their side in an instant. "Boon, you idiot, stop struggling!"

"My quarry," snarled the wolf. "My *team*."

Quen had been closeted with his eldest brother all evening, listening, relaying information, and coordinating the movements of their Kith from the relative quiet of his pavilion. They had been the support for Boon's team, who had uncovered one of the kidnapper's hideaways.

"Your team sent for us," Dad soothed. "Come now, you're bleeding!"

"S'nothing." Boon's feet shuffled and dragged. Struggling free, he staggered, and both dogs were needed to keep the big tracker on his feet.

"*Nothing*," echoed Lapis, lavish with sarcasm. "I would prefer your recklessness not rob Adoona-soh of a well-loved son. Cooperate, whelp."

"I have more years," muttered Boon, his eyes rolling as they struggled to focus.

Lapis got into the wolf's face. "If you wish to *keep* your advantage, submit. You need a healer's touch."

"Do as you're told, for once!" begged Merit.

Eloquence had never seen his eldest brother lose his composure. Boon had been his best friend since weanling days.

"Shut it, Penny." But Boon's muscles went limp.

Merit helped haul his friend onto the sprawl of furs on the inner room's floor. Eloquence followed, and Dad signaled urgently. "Son, summon Courageous."

"No," Boon snapped. "Won't have her."

"I'm not matchmaking. Please, Boon. She's our healer, and you're in need."

Dad had a way of introducing unattached males to every potential female in the compound. Courageous was one of Quen's nieces, daughter to his sister Rampant and Sentinel Skybellow. How many other granddaughters and nieces had Boon *happened* to meet during his stay?

Eloquence had never really understood Boon's reluctance to establish a den. Or to run with his pack. Lone wolves were rare. Boon wasn't a tribute, but he lived like one. Maybe because the

◊

Elderbough tribute was still a child.

"*Not* her." Boon's growl could not be refused.

Merit said, "Rilka Withershanks is without rival, and she is close enough to collect."

"No females."

Quen's thoughts jumped through options. The only male healers close to hand were reavers. He was about to suggest names when Lapis knelt in the furs. He'd divested himself of several filmy layers and most of the jewels that usually sparkled at his fingers and throat.

"You will make do with me, you cagy beast." Lapis rattled off a list of herbs and oils, which Laud vanished to collect. Flashing Harmonious a look, he added, "He would have needed me anyhow. Or another dragon."

"Poison?" asked Dad.

Eloquence had been wondering at the strange scent hanging in the air—faint and almost floral. He hadn't been aware that dragons counted among the clans capable of releasing toxins. "You're poisonous?"

"Not personally." Lapis offered a brittle smile. "But the misfortune of my childhood is the fortune of your friend. I am the antidote he needs."

Dad begged for silence with a sad shake of his head, and Quen stowed his curiosity.

"You …?" Boon's sluggish question never made it any further.

"I was not always a lord." Lapis inspected the three ragged grooves cutting across the left side of Boon's face.

"You, a healer?" Boon managed to convey skepticism.

Lapis haughtily replied, "Nothing so prosaic. I am a scholar turned lord."

"*Honorary* lord."

The dragon graciously inclined his head. "And your attendant for the time being."

"Don't need it," muttered Boon.

"Oh, you do. It would seem your prey is as nasty as his proclivities." Lapis gestured an apology and bent low. "If you will pardon the necessity, friend wolf."

Quen didn't linger for long. It was unsettling to watch the dragon lapping up blood and gently probing Boon's wounds with his tongue. It was enough knowing Boon was safe, his hand tangled with Merit's, Dad standing guard.

Leaving the inner room, Quen let Laud pass through, his hands laden with items from their herbarium. His uncle quietly warned, "At the door."

Ever must be returning, since bathtime would have proceeded as usual. In Laud's absence, Prospect might bring him. Or Lyric or Lavish.

But no.

Gingko Mettlebright stood at the threshold, a rosy-cheeked, shampoo-scented youngster in each arm. Kyrie gazed about with wide red eyes, his hand fisted in his foster brother's tunic. Ever's tail thumped madly against the half-fox, whose silver tail had settled in a cautious curl around his bare feet.

"Hey, Quen." Ears pricked, nose twitching, Gingko asked, "This a bad time?"

"It's all right. Please, come in."

He'd played host to Gingko and Kyrie before, whenever Lord Mettlebright was in Keishi on business with the Five. Argent and Harmonious were encouraging friendship between their sons, who'd been born mere weeks apart.

"Boon?" asked Gingko, whose nose was sharp enough to mark a friend.

"In good hands." He waved toward the closed door to the inner room. "Lapis knows what he's doing."

Kyrie fluted softly, and Gingko bussed the dragon crosser's forehead. "Yeah, yeah. He'll be glad to see you, too, little bro." Dropping to one knee, he turned the boys loose. "Thanks for having us."

Quen's courteous response died on his lips.

Some part of his subconscious had been taking notice, ramping up his heartrate, adding a tremor to his soul. Even so, when Michael Ward stepped inside, Quen teetered inwardly.

Decades had passed and the adolescent he remembered was a grown man—settled, confident, and in his prime. Yet Michael was still Michael. Relief washed over Quen at finding the essence of his friend unchanged, quickly followed by a sudden bout of shyness.

It took him several moments to realize that Ever was tugging furiously at his pant leg. Bending to gather up his baby brother, Quen hid his burning face against Ever's hair.

"Who dis?" Ever asked.

Quen's voice broke on his answer. "Michael."

"Stars, so bright," his baby brother whispered.

He needed to rein in his rampaging emotions, or Ever would get the wrong impression entirely. With a smile that may have wobbled a little, Quen said, "Michael Ward is my friend. He is First of Wards, a very starry soul."

At least his voice was steady. If a bit high. Oh, this was mortifying.

"Hello, Eloquence." Michael's voice had deepened, but his smile was the same. "Would you introduce me to your newest brother?"

Quen managed a nod and gestured him closer. Palms were presented, courtesies exchanged, peace assured. Genial. Gentle. And not at all what Eloquence wanted.

Ever asked, "Should I sniffen him?"

He began to nod, then shook his head. "Me, first."

Michael expression brightened, and he enfolded them both in an embrace that granted the closeness and connection every dog craved.

37
PAPKA

Kimiko woke to a soft tap coming from the wrong end of the room. Predawn gray showed at the edges of closed curtains, but her alarm hadn't gone off. "Too early," she mumbled.

The tap came again, and this time, she oriented on the sound. Someone was at the second-floor window. Well, that certainly narrowed the possibilities.

A soft chime sent Isla fumbling for her phone, and she squinted at the display. Her scowl vanished, and she bolted from her covers.

"What is it?" Kimiko asked.

"They need me!"

"Who ...?" But the girl was already out the door with a bundle of clothing. A second later, Kimiko heard the bathroom door shut.

Another patient tap, and this time, Kimiko answered. Pulling aside the drape, she couldn't help laughing. Opening the slider, she signaled her delight. "Good morning, Sensei."

A formidable feline took up most of the lawn below, easily as tall as the house, despite his lazy slouch. Even in the dimness, she could detect the subtle sheen of pewter fur. Long whiskers swept outward, and intelligence gleamed in orange eyes.

Cold!

Hisoka's breath was steaming in chill air, and Kimiko stole a blanket from her bed to wrap around her shoulders. "I've never been this close to anyone in true form before," she eagerly confessed.

He blinked placidly.

It would have been easy to feel like prey trapped in a mouse hole, but fear was the farthest thing from Kimiko's mind. She had to wonder how often someone so respected was told the simple truth. "You're *beautiful*."

Hisoka loomed nearer, and his nose bumped her forehead.

Every feline seemed to understand that compliments were their due. Strange to think that Hisoka Twineshaft was no different. Tucking her hands behind her back to resist temptation, Kimiko risked rudeness. "May I touch?"

A barely audible purr began deep in his chest. Permission? Any doubt was banished when one large paw settled lightly below the sill, wider than the window, velveted against violence. Had he tapped with a claw, or changed after knocking?

She placed her hands over his paw, as if meeting palms, but her fingers pressed deep into dense fur, soft as his gaze. Her trust pleased him as much as his presence awed her. Hisoka Twineshaft was important to everyone, but he was here for her. All the things she'd ever wanted—even impossible, unspecified hopes—were coming to pass because of this Amaranthine's vision for the future. Hisoka's presence made the Emergence *personal*. Because her future was no longer bound by traditions, expectations, or years.

"What am I going to do?" she whispered.

Power swirled and condensed as Hisoka assumed his speaking form. Crouching on her sill, he touched her shoulder, then brushed her cheek. "About what, Miss Miyabe?"

"How do you choose what to do when you have all the time in the world?"

"Whatever seems best." He seemed utterly at ease on his narrow perch. "Short or long, lives brim with potential. What you choose is as important as what you refuse."

"Are you a bachelor by choice?" Kimiko winced at her own audacity, already signaling apologies for crossing into intensely personal territory.

Hisoka waved aside her embarrassment. "Your curiosity is natural, given your arrangement with Eloquence. And your considerable research ...?"

She followed his gaze to the stack of books on her desk—all borrowed from the archive, all containing annotated folk tales of a decidedly romantic nature. "Yes. Isla was up most of the night."

"If memory serves, many of the *Songs of the Amaranthine* involve the comingling of races." His eyebrows arched. "And as far as the old songs of the trees go, *Golden Lyric* is often, shall we say, *robust* in its descriptions."

Kimiko's face was burning. "Honestly, Sensei, it was research. For courting Eloquence."

He smiled serenely. "Did I not say your curiosity was natural? I'm sure I did."

"I wasn't looking for erotic stories."

"Yet I'm sure you found several."

Taking an apologetic posture, she mumbled, "You have to admit, it's a recurring theme whenever trees are concerned."

"For good reason."

Something about his inflection gave her pause. "Have you ever met a tree?"

Flared eyebrows lifted. "Only yours."

"You know Kusunoki?"

"As do you."

"Most everyone in Keishi knows about our tree."

"Naturally."

He was teasing her. Probably. Kimiko raked a hand through the morning mess of her hair and grumbled, "Isla's never mentioned how difficult you can be."

"She's as devoted as her father. Which brings us to my reason for interrupting your repose. Is my apprentice still lazing abed?"

His voice was modulated to carry, and Isla bustled in. "I'm here! I'm ready!"

"So you are."

To Kimiko's surprise, Isla bounded to her mentor and leapt into his waiting arms. She looked back, happiness shining along with the stars in her eyes. "Come with us, Kimi! Papka is here!"

Hisoka arranged the girl against his side and extended his hand. "Shall we?" he invited.

As eager as she was to meet Isla's famous father, it wouldn't be in her pajamas. "I'll be right there. Go on ahead."

It wasn't until they were gone that Kimiko realized how deftly

Hisoka had sidestepped her questions. No wonder none of the ladies of his clan had gotten their claws into him.

Michael Ward set aside a large chunk of amber crystal in order to offer Kimiko his hands. "Good morning, Miss Miyabe. It's a pleasure to finally meet you."

For someone whose ranking was so high, it was practically off the charts, the celebrated First of Wards was surprisingly unassuming. The father-daughter resemblance was very strong—blond curls, green eyes, and a genial brand of self-assurance.

"Thank you for welcoming Isla into your home." Abandoning the formal greeting, he gathered her hands between his, giving them a paternal pat. "She speaks highly of you."

He was easy to like, easy to trust. And maybe that was more important than titles and ranking. Leaning forward, she corrected him in conspiratorial tones. "She speaks highly of my archive."

Michael laughed. "Both. And having met the one, I hope to beg an introduction to the other."

"Does she get her love of books from you?"

"A fair accusation." He flung out an arm to pull his daughter to his side. "But she's more brilliant by far."

"*Papka*," Isla murmured in pleased protest.

"Then you shall both enjoy the riches of Kikusawa's archive," Kimiko promised. "It's a treasury beyond compare. At least, that's what my grandfather always claimed."

"He would be correct."

She turned at the new voice and fumbled for a greeting. In the end, all she managed was a respectful posture and a whispered acknowledgement. "Lord Mettlebright."

Spokesperson for the fox clans, Argent Mettlebright was numbered among the Five. The Mettlebrights were winter foxes, so he was pale, with silver hair and light blue eyes. He wasn't any taller than she, but his power and dignity were overwhelming. Argent Mettlebright towered.

"Oh, this is fortuitous! Argent's been eager to meet you." Michael's cheerfulness had a determined quality, as if trying to balance out the aloof fox. "I'm quite sure he tagged along for no other reason than to snoop."

"*Tsk.* Are you questioning my sigilcraft?"

Michael's smile didn't waver. "No, old friend. But I'll question your manners if you do not show Eloquence's suitor the courtesy she deserves."

This guy's diplomacy skills were rough-hewn, but effective.

Argent hummed, and Kimiko had never known a hum to communicate more skepticism.

However, he faced her and drawled, "So you are the suitor."

Which is exactly how he came across during newscasts and interviews. Prickly, but flawlessly polite. Haughty, but not particularly hostile. Especially with Michael smiling over the exchange like a beneficent angel.

So she signaled a crisp affirmative. "Yes. I'll be courting Eloquence Starmark."

"Why?" he asked.

"Because that's what he wants."

Argent pressed, "And you?"

Kimiko hoped she sounded more confident than she felt. "I am looking forward to tomorrow night's betrothal."

Michael said, "I've been invited to attend the festivities surrounding your formal declaration."

"We both have." Argent reached for her hands, sliding his own into a supportive position, gently cradling hers. "While I am certain Harmonious would speak freely and at great length, I do not think Eloquence wants another dog sniffing too close to his den. If either of you wish to come to me with awkward questions, I promise to embarrass you with detailed advice of an intimate nature."

She blinked. "You're too kind."

"On the contrary." Argent gently pressed a crumpled slip of paper into her palm. "But she is."

Kimiko clutched his gift to her heart. Lord Mettlebright had passed along his bondmate's contact information. Any reaver would be glad to make such a rare and valuable connection. There were only a dozen beacons born in any generation. But she was interested in Lady Tsumiko for a very different reason. "Akira's sister!"

This time, Argent's hum managed to convey amusement … and approval.

When Quen reached the classroom that morning, he was already in high spirits before Suuzu met him at the door.

The phoenix pulled him aside and placed a chocolate bar in his hands. "From your suitor, with her compliments and a request to meet in the usual place after school."

Quen flushed with pleasure at the token. Although he didn't often eat sweets, he knew there was none finer than those crafted by Junzi. And she'd chosen one that bore the Starmark crest—copper foil shining proudly against a wide sleeve of dark brown paper. An appropriate gift, surely intended to honor his clan.

His brows drew together, and he murmured, "Do you think she'll become a Starmark?"

Suuzu drew him further along the hall and traced a simple sigil upon their palms, guaranteeing their words stayed between them. Given how many sharp ears were nearby, Quen appreciated the phoenix's discretion.

He answered with bland diplomacy. "Joining *is* the usual intent of courtship."

"I mean our names. If she's courting me, would I be expected to take the Miyabe name?"

"Hmm. I see what you mean. There are few precedents, if any." Suuzu considered. "Taking into account both pack and public sentiments, I recommend she become a Starmark. For the press, for the peace, and for your pups. However, the decision is hers and yours."

Quen added it to his mental list of all the things he needed to discuss with Kimiko. "There is so much I don't know about her. So much she doesn't know about me. And a thousand ways in which our best intentions could be misunderstood."

"I know." Suuzu tapped the chocolate bar. "I can tell you something about your suitor."

Quen eased closer, signaling his interest.

"In the human culture of this area, a gift of chocolate has romantic overtones."

"A human courting tradition?"

Suuzu nodded. "In general, Kimi likes snacks—both salty and sweet. Akira often remarks upon her adventurous choices."

"Is that good?"

The phoenix pursed his lips. "I advise caution."

That bad? It had never occurred to Quen that he might learn things about his future bondmate that could be considered unpalatable.

"On a more personal level," continued Suuzu, "Kimi has a sentimental attachment to Junzi chocolate."

Quen's heart leapt, for Suuzu had doubled the value of his gift. While Quen didn't crave sweets, he longed for conversation with Kimiko. Here was a promising avenue of inquiry. "Thank you."

Suuzu led the way into the classroom. Eloquence immediately sought out his suitor. Kimiko was seated at her table, Isla perched on her knee. At the arch of his brows, the taller girl glibly signaled, *brighten the wards.*

Isla cheerfully added, *the boundaries will hold.*

Just then Tenma stooped to enter, Inti riding on his shoulders. Holding out both hands, Quen remarked, "You are redolent of monkey."

Inti slithered into Quen's embrace. "Inti is a monkey."

Tenma shrugged. "Dog's nestle. Monkeys tangle."

"Jealous?" Inti twitched his tail under Quen's nose.

"I do feel left out." The young crosser was certainly pleased with this recent turn of events. Quen wanted to encourage the sense of belonging. Including Tenma in his invitation, he asked,

"Will you stay in my den some night soon?"

"Not tonight," said the monkey, as if he had a full social calendar to consider.

Tenma seemed surprised. "Why not?"

Inti blinked innocently. "Reasons."

Ms. Reeves entered, calling the class to order and announcing, "We are extremely privileged to have a guest lecturer for the day. Isla, perhaps you'd like to handle his introduction?"

While the girl began the long list of her father's credentials, Michael Ward slipped into the room and scanned the class. Unassuming and amiable. And at the moment, overflowing with fondness for his daughter the diplomat.

Quen had spent the entire night watching over this man's sleep from the safety of his arms. For a while, his denmates allowed the monopoly, but as dawn approached, others stole in and settled close by—Father and Laud, Hisoka and Lapis, Argent and Gingko, Kyrie and Ever, Merit and Boon. Drawn to the gentle lure of a starry, sleepy soul, trusted and trusting, warded yet whispering. Perhaps this was another kind of magic, the way Michael effortlessly bound their souls to his, yet left them free.

Somehow, Quen wanted to have this kind of pull and push with Kimiko. To bind her soul to his own and to honor her choices. Maybe then, she would develop that special breed of loyalty known as love.

38

HER PURSUIT

After classes dismissed for the day, Quen wanted nothing more than to rush to the Kith shelter ahead of Kimiko. But Inti wrapped himself around his head and shoulders, seeking refuge from Michael, who advanced with palms upraised.

"Now, my young friend," coaxed Michael. "I'm not anyone to fear."

"This guy's like family to me!" Akira gestured broadly. "Our home's filled with crossers."

Isla crowded close on Quen's other side. "Come down, Inti. My Papka can be trusted."

Fingers drummed on a point between Eloquence's eyebrows.

He looked up into the impish crosser's wary face. "Yes, partner?"

"Dogs trust *carefully*?"

Quen patted the monkey's throttling tail. "We trust our noses more than words."

Inti's nostril's twitched.

Although he was skirting the question Inti actually wanted answered, Quen thought it best to make a few things clear. "Humans can't hide their scent any more than reavers can hide their souls."

"Wards!" Inti jabbed a finger at Michael.

The reaver lifted the wrist displaying a strand of heavy amethyst beads. "I'm not hiding anything, Inti. My wards are a courtesy. Otherwise I tend to become a distraction."

"And mine keep my soul in check." Isla wrinkled her nose. "Since I'm still in training, they're for your protection."

"Reasons," muttered Inti.

Eloquence squeezed his passenger's ankle. "My senses are keener than you might have realized. Humans can't hide anything, and half-humans can't hide much."

Inti's gaze dropped.

Point made. Quen asked, "Do you trust me?"

The monkey crosser's grip tightened, then slowly relaxed. "Yes, yes. But Tenma is best."

"Good." Quen reached up to muss Inti's hair. "Then trust me. Michael is *my* best."

"Lies!"

More amused than affronted, Quen said, "I'm not lying."

"No, no," agreed Inti. "You're late."

Had the brat had been delaying him this whole time? Growling and giving the monkey's hair an additional roughing, he lifted. This time, Inti let go. Dumping the snickering boy in Michael's arms, Quen strode for the door.

"Why are you in such a hurry?" Isla called sweetly.

Eloquence didn't hesitate, didn't look back, but he heard Inti answer for him.

"Reasons."

She was already there. He'd made her wait.

Dismissing his apologies, Kimiko announced, "I won't be in class tomorrow, so I need to explain everything now."

Quen sank to the straw between Edge and Flay, pulling her down to his side. "Is anything wrong?"

She shook her head. "Mama seems to think we need all day to fancy up. She'll probably attack my cuticles and smear mud on my face and pluck things. I swear, if she goes after my eyebrows, I will lock myself in the archive."

Eloquence considered Kimiko's face with careful neutrality. "Our courtship will involve ... eyebrows?"

"Not if I have any say in the matter. Never mind that part." She waved this aside—even though she'd brought up the entire matter—and frowned in concentration. "I wanted to talk about the courting tradition I chose, so you know what to expect."

"Please," he urged.

Kimiko rubbed at the side of her face, as if to discourage the color rising there. "I wanted something that made sense for *me*, but I also wanted something that would please you. And so far the only thing you've asked for is ...."

He had no trouble recalling his plea for a taste. "Kisses *are* traditional."

"Exactly. And for me, *trees* are traditional. In my family, special occasions have always taken place under our shrine's tree." With a shy glance, she said, "I'm going to borrow from the tale, 'The Wolf and the Moon Maiden,' a love story involving an Amaranthine and an Impression. To prove his devotion, they complete something called the Cycle of Moons."

Eloquence was already nodding. This was familiar territory for him, since Uncle Karoo-ren had faithfully taught him the wolf lore of the Ambervelte pack, his mother's people. "Twelve pledges sealed by twelve kisses."

Her hand found his. "Is it a good idea?"

"Certainly. You've found a way to combine your family's traditions with my people's lore. I'm willing, and Father will undoubtedly be pleased." Quen only saw one potential problem. "Do you wish to change locations, so that the feast takes place under your chosen tree?"

Kimiko grimaced. "Better not. Mama is both stir-crazy and starstruck. She's looking forward to visiting your home."

"Dinner for all at the Starmark compound, with your declaration of intent before a smaller group at Kikusawa Shrine afterward."

"Unless it's too much trouble ...?"

Quen smiled. "Make your wishes known to your go-between, and I'll do the same. Between them, Twineshaft and Farroost will take care of everything."

"Oh, of course. Yes. That's a good idea." She laughed a little, seemingly at herself, and said, "That just leaves one other detail."

"Can I help?" He was having trouble assigning a meaning to the shifts in her scent. They hadn't spent enough time together. Should he suggest more interaction, or would that create new problems in the form of public scrutiny?

Kimiko faced him squarely. "I have a question, and while everyone has been more than helpful, this is something I'd rather deal with in private."

"As you like, Kimiko."

She muttered, "This is embarrassing. And I'm nervous."

Quen's impulse was to get closer, but he kept still. "I appreciate your trust."

She gave in with a flurry of small gestures, mingling apologies with pleas for patience. "I know how to carry myself in *normal* conversations with Amaranthine from just about any clan. Which means I know enough to know that I don't know enough."

"About ...?"

Kimiko closed her eyes and continued. "When it comes to Amaranthine culture, a kiss can mean many different things—greeting, apology, gratitude, submission. Requests, pledges, claims. It's all in the nuance."

He could see where this was headed.

"And that nuance is all in the context, posture, delivery, duration." She was watching him through her lashes. "I'm going to kiss you in front of an audience, and most of them are going to be searching for meanings. Will you please help me? I don't want any trace of embarrassment or caution or fear to color what should be a glad moment."

Kimiko was right. This was important. Quen elbowed Edge,

✦

who liked her list and was cheerfully expounding on the themes of posture, delivery, and duration. "I'm willing."

"Thanks." Her shoulders squared. "So…will we both be standing?"

Rising, Quen helped her to her feet. She settled immediately into an attentive, expectant posture, and for the first time, he didn't take her stance for granted. Kimiko moved well—fluid, fluent. "You've been doing this all along."

The answering tilt of her chin was perfect.

"I didn't even notice," he admitted abashedly. Was *this* why the Nightspangle pack had singled her out? Was it why he'd felt he could trust her?

"I'll consider that a compliment." She offered him her palms. "Even so, a lesson in canine nuance would be much appreciated."

His pulse quickened. "May I touch?"

She acquiesced without a word.

Heart light, he coached her through three greetings that displayed varying degrees of affection, the chaste caress of contrition, and a grateful kiss that lost its way. Kimiko had taken inspiration from romance lore, and she'd come asking for courteous intimacies. His blood was already singing. His awareness blurred at the edges.

Edge's tail began a steady thump.

Flay sneezed. Pointedly. *Not the time for trysting, pup.*

Quen reluctantly pulled away, easing back a step.

Kimiko touched her lips. "Are you sure that was just *thank you*?"

"No." His voice cracked, and he cleared his throat. "Unless it was, 'Yes, thank you. More, please.'"

"Should I consider that a compliment, too?"

"Please do." It was better than he deserved. Here was willingness and trust, but he could feel her studious distraction. She wanted to understand the forms. He needed to teach without taking.

Kimiko asked, "What am I supposed to do with my hands?"

Eloquence brightened, for he craved her touch. Taking her wrists, he guided her hands through a variety of simple messages and cues. As he'd discovered with Tenma, it was difficult to put the subtle significances into words.

"*Another* kind of request?" Kimiko curved her fingers as he'd done.

"No, a reiteration, usually following a refusal. I call it the pudding please." Quen smiled at her bafflement. "Ever adores sweets, especially milk pudding. This is how he begs for a second serving."

Understanding dawned, and Kimiko's fingers glided along his jawline, sure as her meaning. "Is there a third level for cheeky beggars?"

"Although I cannot remember, Uncle Laud swears I perfected ten degrees of *please* when I was a pup."

Kimiko was smiling again, encouraging him with her interest. "What did you beg for?"

"A pet."

"Like a kitten?"

He huffed. "Nothing so easily acquired. I wanted a pet constellation. And to tame the north wind. And I begged a briner tank."

"Stories from Amaranthine lore." Her gaze turned inward as she stroked his cheek. "I used to want to go on quests—to find the hidden groves, to uncover a clutch of dragon eggs, to rescue a fallen star."

Quen leaned into her touch. "So you're an adventurer at heart?"

"No. Not really." Kimiko retreated, her hands dropping to her sides. "I loved my grandfather, and I loved his stories. It's my job to preserve them, not pursue them."

"Then it's a good thing that you've chosen to court me with kisses rather than gifts." His fingers wheedled lightly along her jaw, and he added a pudding plea. "Otherwise, I may have sent you chasing after Impressions to impress me."

"Is that how you refuse a suitor, by giving them an impossible task?"

"Perhaps. But that is not our situation." He reached for her hands, pulling her back into contact. "Kimiko, what is the underlying message you want to send during your declaration?"

"Something confident ... respectful ... and appropriately flattering. And specifically canine. I don't want to insult your clan by complimenting your plumage or purr."

The first two were simple enough. He guided her through postures, showing her the difference between his stance and hers. For this ceremony, it was his to await, hers to initiate. Which only left the flattery. Something he wasn't used to receiving. "Compliments can take any form. Did you have something in mind?"

"I could state the obvious—beauty and good breeding. But that's not very personal." Kimiko's eyes had taken on a sparkle. "But I probably shouldn't call you an amiable slacker with a soft spot for crossers."

He blinked. He blinked again. "*That's* what you think of me?"

"It's something I'm certain of, and it's something I like about you."

Quen had thought Kimiko was teasing, but she remained in

the stance he'd just demonstrated—confident, respectful. She was serious?

"You adore Ever. You're patient with Inti. And you want a family." Kimiko's gaze didn't waver. "Isn't fatherhood part of the reason you consider me suitable? Our children will be crossers. Ever won't be alone."

Astonishment rivaled with dismay. "I do want children. I *do*. I always have. But I've never thought of you as ... as breeding stock."

Kimiko's laugh had a wry twist. "Eloquence, I'm a reaver. My worth to the In-between is a matter of record, based almost entirely on my breeding potential."

He needed to correct her. He needed to be clear. But fear was boiling up inside, stealing his ability to speak. Devotion and fidelity were a mate's due. Yet she saw herself as a means to an end. Would Kimiko understand if he told her otherwise? Or should he show her?

She was retreating again, closing off.

"W-wait," he stammered. "Do you know how to tend?"

"I'm licensed, but my resources are minimal." Her body language shifted—caution, reluctance, wariness. "Reavers of my rank risk rapid depletion."

Eloquence sank to his knees, passive, submissive. "I don't want to take. I want to give."

"I don't understand."

"A human bondmate must be tended. You're a reaver, which means our souls can meet." He fumbled for better words. "Meet with me here."

After a lengthy silence, she asked, "How?"

"May I touch?"

"Yes."

Rising up on his knees, he slid his arms around her waist. "Nothing will happen at first. I'll leave myself open. Allow the connection and use it to find me."

"Where will you be?"

"Right here." Eloquence hid his face against her belly. Voice muffled, he promised, "I'll be waiting here."

Her hands settled lightly on his shoulders. "Like tending?"

Quen's attention had already turned inward, but he nodded. Her winter tunic was soft, and her warmth so close. It was all he could do to resist nuzzling.

She did not keep him waiting.

Kimiko's soul was neatly defined, a quality he'd come to associate with training. He teased at the edges of her awareness, alerting her to his presence and inviting more interaction. To his relief, she didn't shy away. Quen found her courage appealing.

Her soul didn't dazzle like the reavers who usually found their way into Harmonious Starmark's home. Her essence was taut and sweet, with the faint resonance, a single note, like the fading tone of a bell. The right crystal could amplify that power. With time and patience, he might be able to increase her modest reserves.

Would that please her? He wanted to please her.

As a sense of expectancy filtered through their tentative connection, he was startled to realize that nothing kept him at bay—no wards, no barriers. Were all reavers of her rank left to their own devices? Quen's protective instincts surged with the need to see her safe.

"What's wrong?" Kimiko whispered.

He lifted his face. "You're so vulnerable."

"Far from it. You should see the added security at our place."

"Personally," he clarified.

"It's not a problem." She smiled and touched his hair. "You'd be surprised how safe most of us are, living beneath the notice of peer and predator alike."

Quen wrapped his arms more securely around her. "I could give you a sigil to carry."

"Our Amaranthine classmates would notice. It would lead to questions."

"I'll ask Michael to create something."

"That would be easier to explain." Kimiko tugged his braid. "But I wish you'd explain what I'm supposed to be doing right now."

He hadn't meant to interrupt. "All you need to do is accept."

Kimiko shifted in his grasp, trying to communicate, but he had her by the hips. Like him, she had to resort to words. "Accept *what*?"

"Me." That came off sounding more profound than he intended. "Let me tend you, Kimiko."

Her brows drew together. "You're offering me my first taste?"

Quen hadn't considered this situation in those terms, but she was right. "Just a taste. With your permission."

Kimiko carefully pulled away, but then knelt with him. "Ready."

Their hands sought each other. Their eyes closed.

He liked this calm, this closeness. But they needed trust to run deeper, bringing her light into his darkness, spangling his soul. Eloquence slowly enveloped her, tuning the howl of his wilder instincts to the note he'd found earlier. Harmonizing at first, then locking into unison.

She gasped.

Recalling all the ways Michael had been gentle with him, Quen held back all but the barest hint of his hopes, woven with a whisper of the awe he'd felt at finding a star-strewn comb upon his palm. He would be hers. He had been chosen.

Kimiko murmured his name.

"Yes?"

"Is it always so …?"

Eloquence held her close, touched her hair, kissed her cheek, and waited. So much depended on her next word. Like the grades he received in his new school. Like the ranking assigned to every reaver. Someone else was about to determine his worth.

But she didn't pluck a word and pin it to him.

"I think," she began solemnly. "I think I underestimated you, Eloquence Starmark."

Something in her gaze thrilled him. It was as if she were seeing him for the first time, and it left him feeling exposed … yet hopeful.

"And I think," she continued, "that I may have underestimated myself."

"Oh?"

Kimiko hummed an affirmative. "As your suitor, I think I'd even tackle an impossible task in order to impress you."

"Because you like a challenge?"

"Because I like *you*." Her smile turned smug. "And because someone already did the hard part for me."

That threw him off. "What part?"

"Your pet. I can make your childhood dream come true."

Quen realized she must be joking. "You have a briner tank tucked away somewhere?"

"No. But we keep the north wind in a bottle."

A fanciful notion. Nuzzling her cheek, he murmured, "A fortuitous happenstance. I can only declare myself suitably impressed. Will you demand an impossible task in return?"

Kimiko hesitated, then shook her head.

"What?" He coaxed with a pudding please. "What is my lady's wish?"

"I think," she said slowly, still serious. "I think it would be wonderful if someone found a way to wake Kusunoki."

✦

39

STAR WINE SERENADES

nce Kimiko was safely away with Suuzu and Akira, Eloquence changed into his truest form and loped into the adjacent woodland on four paws. Dusk had settled into darkness, but he dodged confidently through the trees, lengthening his stride, picking up speed. Kimiko would formalize her claim tomorrow evening, but the connection they'd formed just now was a far sight more real.

Skidding to a halt and settling back on his haunches, he sang the note that still resonated through his core.

A chorus of Kith quickly joined him, their carrying howls echoing his joy.

Barking from closer quarters accompanied the bounding form of Rise. Quen turned to welcome him, setting off a grand game of tackle-and-chase through the snowy forest.

Are you happy, brother?

Quen returned to speaking form and leaned into the Kith's side. "Happier than I know how to express."

Because of Kimiko.

"Yes."

Do you love her?

He tugged at Rise's ear. "Yes."

Do you trust her?

"Yes."

Rise ducked his head, as if afraid Quen would lose patience with his questions. *Will you tell her about me?*

"Soon." Eloquence wrapped his arms around Rise's thick neck. "I'll have you trade places with Edge and Flay and introduce you properly."

I am Kith.

"She won't mind."

I cannot speak. Nervousness crept into his voice, making him sound younger than his years.

"Let me be your Eloquence."

Rise butted his head against Quen's chest. *Mine.*

"Yes, yours." Taking his usual seat astride his denmate, he said, "You and Ever will always be with me, just as I'll always be with Laud."

Home.

"Yes, let's go home." As the dog ambled toward the compound, Quen asked, "If you're here, where is Ever?"

Taken by foxes.

Quen laughed. "You make it sound so ominous."

Rise only grunted and picked up speed.

Before long, he could hear the noise of celebration—music and laughter and song. Typical for evenings when Dad had friends over. Quen was already picking up the telltale scents of wolf, cat, dragon, and fox. "All together?" he whispered.

The Five are assembled.

"And into the star wine." It was probably a good thing Tenma and Inti hadn't been able to stay over tonight. Knowing this lot, his pavilion would be full to bursting.

A thread of melody carried through the chill night, words slurring haphazardly. "What are they ...? Rise, stop here. What are they *singing*?"

They held still, ears tuned to a lusty ballad. Quen's mounting suspicions collapsed into utter mortification when he realized the song's subject matter. He hadn't been aware there was a translation from wolvish of "The Wolf and the Moon Maiden." Yet Dad was bellowing out the maiden's lines without a trace of shame. Adoona-soh had taken the hero's role, her deep voice rich with drama.

Their gender-swapped performance might have been amusing, but for the fact that he'd been similarly cast. At the chorus, more voices joined the song. Lapis' singing was lovely as ever. More surprising was Twineshaft's very passable baritone.

Quen was fully prepared to skulk home, but then Ever's voice broke through the rest. "Wiff naughty butt moon-beans for a dress!"

"*Tsk*. The line is 'naught but moonbeams,'" came Mettlebright's bland correction.

A husky laugh followed. "I dunno, Dad. I think little bro has her pegged."

That was Gingko.

"Moon-beans?" a child asked softly.

Definitely Kyrie. The little dragon crosser didn't talk half as much as Ever, but not because he couldn't.

"No, these are nuts, not beans." And then Argent's voice rose slightly. "Come along, Eloquence, or I fear they will never stop this caterwauling."

Caught out.

He was halfway to the door when Hisoka Twineshaft opened it for him. "Good day, Eloquence. Or good evening, if you like."

The rest had picked up the ballad again. Gingko seemed to be teaching it to them, translating off-the-cuff from wolvish. Quen had to wonder where a half-fox had picked up the knack, but he voiced a more pressing question. "Do I even want to know how you already know the form my suitor's declaration will take?"

"Isla submitted a proposed schedule to both me and Suuzu. All the necessary preparations are underway." Hisoka searched his face, then offered a palm. "Have I become an imposition?"

Quen guessed Twineshaft had been Dad's friend for much too long. How else could a cat have perfected a hangdog expression? "If you can prevent Dad from burying my dignity in the back garden, I'll welcome any meddling you deem appropriate."

Hisoka's usual poise slipped enough for Quen to tell he'd surprised him.

"You're usually more wary," Hisoka said.

"Less grateful, as well." Stepping into Twineshaft's personal space, he bestowed a pudding please. "I want to thank you for having me join the inaugural class at New Saga High School."

His expression softened. "Wasn't that my line?"

Quen tucked his chin. "Let's just say I've come around to your way of thinking."

"Most do." Hisoka pulled him into a loose embrace. "You may count on my continued meddling."

He snorted.

"Do you trust me, Eloquence?"

"You're a friend of this pack."

Hisoka inclined his head, but in the way a teacher does when granting partial credit. Close, but not quite.

Quen sighed. "What do you want?"

"More." The cat repeated his question with gentle emphasis. "Do *you* trust me, Eloquence?"

He'd always thought of Twineshaft as Dad's friend. Like all his brothers, Quen extended every courtesy, treating the Five as honorary packmates. But courtesy wasn't trust. Faith couldn't be forged secondhand. This was his choice.

Eloquence considered the weight and worth of his next words, for they would be binding.

Yet the answer was obvious, as if the moment of decision had come and gone long ago. All Hisoka was doing was calling the matter to his attention. A mere formality. A mutual acknowledgment.

"I do," he answered. "I have for a while now."

"Oooh, me next!" crooned the tipsy dragon who sauntered straight into Quen's arms. Draped and drooping, Lapis sighed boozily against his ear. "Say you love me, El-o-quence. Am I not better to you than cats and foxes and Icelandic interlopers?"

Hisoka smiled knowingly. "Come, Lord Mossberne. Sinder isn't a rival for your place in Eloquence's cozy den."

"You would not turn me out in the cold, would you El-o-quence?"

Quen tried to see past Hisoka into the brightly-lit room. "Who's Sinder?"

"An acquaintance from among the dragon clans." Hisoka stepped back and urged, "Come in out of the cold."

Lapis trilled his agreement, yet sagged more pitifully.

Having enough of delays, Quen all but carried him into the spacious chamber where Dad liked to entertain. For all the ruckus they were creating, the group was surprisingly small. Perhaps the noise level could be blamed on the star wine. Or on Gingko Mettlebright, who'd launched into yet another stanza.

Only Argent wasn't singing, nor had he been drinking, judging by the amount still sparkling in the glass he'd pushed away. The fox spokesperson offered Quen a polite nod, then returned to shelling gingko nuts for the children occupying his lap.

Ever vied with Kyrie for the treats, but at a murmured word from Argent, the little boy's gaze swung around. "Bruvver!"

"Having fun?" Quen scanned the room, but Lapis' Icelandic rival wasn't present.

"Yeth!"

"Help me get Lord Mossberne to a good, warm spot."

The boy quickly trotted to a pile of furs and dragged one over beside Argent. "Laps wiff us. I warm Laps."

The dragon's expression went all doting, and he murmured, "If you insist."

Argent helped drape the fur around Lapis' shoulders. Once Ever clambered into the dragon lord's lap, the fox deposited Kyrie there as well. For added warmth. Leaving the little ones to ply Lapis

✦

with gingko nuts and chatter, Argent gestured officiously to the cushion at his other side. "Sit."

Quen sat.

Argent was relatively new to his position among the Five. Quen rarely saw him, barely knew him, despite their common ground— fostering crossers.

"Here he is, my maiden son!" Dad boomed. "Suitably suitored, properly pursued!"

And then Hisoka was at his old friend's side, proposing a toast that granted Eloquence's upcoming claim some much needed dignity.

Argent raised his glass with the rest, took a polite sip, and arched a brow. "A human?"

"Yes."

✦

"Why her?"

✦

The line of questioning hardly seemed fair. Argent had chosen a human. "Why'd you take *your* bondmate?"

The fox smirked. "She is a beacon."

Eloquence waded through dismay and disappointment before reaching disbelief. Argent had to be lying. Or, at the very least, evading.

Argent seemed to be following his entire train of thought, for he gave a different answer. "I trust her."

"That's all?"

"Hardly," he scoffed. "But without first laying claim to my trust, she could not have taken hold of everything else."

Quen saw the sense. Argent's words rang true.

The fox asked, "How did your attachment come about?"

Had rumors begun to spread? He quietly admitted, "It was an accident."

"Serendipity or calamity?"

"What a thing to ask," Quen muttered.

"You have nothing to say? Ironic."

"I don't hear *you* waxing eloquent about the felicities of love."

"I could." Argent bluntly inquired, "Are your reasons for accepting Miss Miyabe personal or promotional?"

Quen grit his teeth. On the face of things, he shared enough common ground with the fox that they should have gotten along. Why was Argent goading him? Fists clenched, he asked, "Are you trying to insult me?"

"Already riled?" He tutted disapprovingly.

He mastered his irritation. Barely.

Argent went right on. "Many of the Kindred will infer that you are under pressure from your father. That you are following his lead, supporting his policies by echoing his actions."

Eloquence opened his mouth, a bitter protest ready to be flung. But he'd overheard so many of the conferences that had led to the Emergence. So he saw the trap in time. Argent was shading the truth, giving his own slant to the facts. The only way to set the record straight would betray clan secrets. And an ill-worded denial might imply that he didn't support Dad's policies.

"Some will believe that you are the perfect opportunity. Coming from the first clan to be tamed, you would grasp the need for close observation and careful documentation. To prove that your younger brother is no fluke, you and your human will agree to breed in captivity."

Fear and fury spiked in terrible tandem, and he drove his claws into the flooring to keep from lashing out.

"*Tsk*."

And then Dad was there, hugging him from behind, holding him back. "Easy, now. Stand down, son. Although I'd have throttled him myself for that last one."

Argent sniffed. "You would have *attempted* far worse."

"I daresay you've heard far worse," said Hisoka, who dropped into a crouch at Quen's side. "Forgive Argent's impudence. He is acting a part ... at my request."

Quen stilled and felt quite sick. Was this mockery? Or worse? He wouldn't have expected these people capable of so much ugliness. To his shame, tears flooded his eyes.

Someone swore. Probably Gingko. Someone began weeping. Poor, sweet Kyrie. Someone was railing against Dad. Definitely Adoona-soh. And someone gathered him up. At first, Quen thought it must be Laud, and he went limp with relief. But when his vision cleared, he realized he'd mistaken silver for white. He was in Argent's clutches, and the fox was *strong*.

"Leave him to me," ordered Argent, hand slicing through the air, which soon blazed with complex sigils.

A barrier, but not the kind Quen knew to make, for the world vanished. Fox magic. A mild voice alerted him to the presence of a third person within an otherwise empty space.

"Thank you for including me," said Hisoka.

Argent rolled his eyes. "The whelp feels betrayed. Make it right. *Now*."

The cat slunk into view, reached for Quen's limp hands, and bowed low so that his forehead touched them. "I am sorry for distressing you. I would much rather spare you everything—slights, slander, spurious assumptions, and scandalous speculation. As it is, we can only prepare you for their inevitability."

Quen's gaze swung to Argent's face. "You lied?"

"No. I told you what some will believe, what some will say."

Argent offered no apologies. Then again, he owed none. Eloquence eased out of the fox's arms, but he didn't make it far. Silvery tails fanned out and around. Propriety prevented Quen from touching them, which made them an effective prison. Even so, Quen felt more on equal terms, seated so close, all their knees were touching.

Hisoka said, "When your 'engagement' to Kimiko comes to light, the press will be no more gentle than Argent has been."

"Worse," muttered the fox. "You will face demands—not requests—for information every bondmate would consider intensely private. And that is just the public sector. The merry band of reaver researchers will ply you with questionnaires, schedule physical exams, and issue tactful pleas for genetic samples."

"Has Dad been dealing with this stuff?"

"Only since the announcement of Ever's birth," said Hisoka. "And Harmonious has been fierce in his protection of Anna. She's never been photographed or interviewed."

Quen touched Argent's arm. "What does Lady Mettlebright do?"

"Tsumiko is similarly elusive, by her choice and my enforcement." Argent's lips pressed into a thin line. "I am regularly approached by those who—for the good of the In-between—want access to the crossers who have found safe haven at Stately House. Our priority has always been their protection."

Hisoka said, "Argent is one of many sheltering those without clan or crest."

The cat probably also had a paw in. That would explain Inti's presence at New Saga.

"I understand that I need coaching." Quen had been so enamored of the future he'd imagined, he'd been blind to the accompanying battle he was ill-equipped to wage. "But why are you telling me this *now*?

Argent and Hisoka exchanged a long look.

"There is no hurry." Quen leaned forward, keeping his voice low. "Our courtship is meant to be conducted in secret. Over the course of *years*."

"*Tsk*. Tell him."

"There is a chance that I will need to *use* you and your 'engagement.'"

That creeping sense of betrayal was back.

Hisoka's smile was all sympathy, but no apologies were forthcoming from his quarter, either. "Recent events in Keishi are causing concern at the highest levels. Those most resistant to accommodating our existence are actively seeking proof that our intentions are less than honorable."

Hardly news. The debates had raged ever since the Emergence.

"The kidnappings?" asked Quen. They'd begun about the same time a large contingent of trackers had arrived, led by the Elderbough clan. "Boon trailed the culprit here and was injured trying to rescue one of the girls."

"Yes." Hisoka ran a hand over his hair. "Their presence here is part of an ongoing international investigation. The Elderbough pack has been in pursuit for nearly four years."

That was a long time to elude a pack famed for their skill in tracking.

"They've uncovered evidence of killings and kidnappings going back decades." He cut a look at Argent, who inclined his head. "Over the last several years, he has refined his technique. We know what he's after, but that hasn't helped us to stop him."

Quen was beginning to see the scale of this problem. "The kidnapper is Amaranthine."

"Yes."

Argent huffed impatiently. "He is a monster with discriminating tastes—only females, only reavers. Because they are the only ones who can give him what he wants."

Hisoka sighed. "That was an unexpected upshot to the investigation. I'm not sure anyone realized before."

Quen didn't ask them to hurry along. He could see the trail, and he wasn't eager to deal with what waited at its end.

"While humans and Amaranthine have always been compatible, not all couplings are the same. Just as a human bondmate must be a reaver in order to receive the tending necessary to extend their lifespan, a human woman must be a reaver in order for the coupling to result in offspring."

Argent put it bluntly. "He rapes the girls he takes in order to breed."

"Why haven't we stopped him?"

"Ah." Hisoka's smile was wan and weary. "Our trackers *have* succeeded. We're certain they've cornered our culprit more than once."

Quen finally wearied of waiting. "What aren't you telling me?"

"That part should be yours to tell, Argent."

The fox beckoned for Quen's hand, which he brought to his own heart. Holding it there, Argent touched his fingertips to Quen's chest. A request for secrecy and support.

Heart racing, Eloquence placed his hand over Argent's, pressing and promising.

"We are dealing with a rogue dragon," Argent said grimly. "And he is my son Kyrie's sire."

40

GUEST LIST

Kimiko overslept.

She swung her feet to the floor and considered the cluttered hush of her room, trying to remember why this was significant. Books were strewn everywhere. Oh, yes. Isla had been reading to her long into the night. Because Kimiko couldn't sleep. Recollection crashed into her, refreshing her half-forgotten jitters, just as a tap sounded on her window.

Was that what woke her?

Noting Isla's absence as she shuffled to the window, Kimiko drew aside the curtain, squinting into the midmorning brightness. Akira grinned and waved, gesturing for her to open the window. He looked totally at ease with both the height and the cradling hold of his nestmate.

Kimiko opened the window and was immediately assailed by noise.

Two vans were being unloaded near the base of Kusunoki, where a graceful canopy had been erected. Banners fluttered on stands—Kikusawa's red chrysanthemums alongside the celestial copper of the Starmark crest. Furs and heaters. Tea urns and tapestry rugs. Everything you'd expect for an extravagant human wedding. Only this ceremony would be Amaranthine. And it was hers.

"How did I sleep through this?" She pulled Suuzu and Akira in out of the cold.

"A barrier," said Suuzu.

Kimiko leaned out, trying to get a sense of what had changed. Something was definitely there, but it didn't feel like the crystal-based warding Isla's father had used along the boundaries. With a long last look at the box-laden people hurrying back and forth along their front walk, Kimiko shut out the cold. Immediately, the hubbub outside her room vanished. "Did Lord Mettlebright do something?"

Suuzu hummed. "No, this barrier has a wolvish feel to it. Several trackers arrived during the night. One of them must be responsible."

"Very considerate," she murmured. Maybe Dickon would know which of the wolves had gone above and beyond by protecting her sleep. "But why are you guys here? You're late for school."

Akira beamed. "Special permission to skip. Argent said so, and nobody argues with Lord Mettlebright."

Suuzu said, "I will remain by your side throughout the day, as your go-between."

With a sharp elbow to the phoenix's ribs, Akira added, "And as your friend."

"Hmm."

Any doubt on that score vanished when Suuzu frowned and

312

reached for Kimiko's hair. Glad of their presence, she bowed her head and submitted to a little friendly preening.

Akira spent the rest of the morning pitching in where he could, with regular pauses to take pictures with his phone. The shrine had plenty of interesting nooks and niches. He'd just zoomed in on a squat jar with a long neck that looked to have been carved from crystal when he received a heavy rap on the head.

"Security breech located," drawled a vaguely familiar wolf clansman with bandages everywhere. "No pictures, Akira."

This guy knew his name? Akira checked the three crests on his armband, the first of which designated him as an Elderbough. "Boon?"

"You know it!"

He'd only seen this son of Adoona-soh's once before, at a whelping feast for the child of her eldest, Naroo-soh. Gingko had introduced Akira to more wolves than he could hope to remember, but Boon stood out. Not so much because of his carefree manner, though he seemed like a friendly guy. But Suuzu had kept a wary eye on the wolf all through the festivities.

Boon bent until they were closer to the same level. "Seriously, kid. Today's doings need to stay under wraps. Let Eloquence and his lady have some scrap of privacy."

Akira extended his phone. "Sis was feeling left out."

The wolf snatched it out of his grasp, scanned the exchange, then pulled Akira into a headlock before taking a selfie. With surprising delicacy, he tapped out a message, adding a full range of emotes. "Not every day I get to scold a beacon."

"Not many to scold." Akira checked to see what Boon was saying to his sister. "So how'd *you* get hurt?"

Boon scratched absently at the edge of gauzy wrappings. "Nothing to worry about."

Akira guessed Boon had been part of the rescue effort. "Would you happen know anything about Suuzu's brother and … and his partner?"

The wolf's yellow eyes narrowed, and he delivered another smart knock to the top of Akira's head. "You really *are* a security breech."

"Not for *knowing* stuff," protested Akira. "Only if I tell what I know to someone I shouldn't."

Boon was back in his face. "And what makes you think I know Juuyu and Sinder?"

"I knew you knew! Is Sinder okay?"

"Patched up and perky as ever."

Jigsaw details slid neatly together. Sinder had said he was part of an elite taskforce, and Juuyu had mentioned in passing that a wolf had helped him create his necklace. "Are you one of Juuyu's teammates?"

"Here's the thing, kid. *I* am not a security breech." Boon deposited the phone in Akira's coat pocket. "The less said, the better. Savvy?"

With exaggerated solemnity, Akira said, "Your secret's safe with me."

That earned him another rap on the noggin, but it was light enough to count as affectionate.

Another possibility occurred to Akira. "Are you the one who added a barrier to Kimi's room?"

"What's it to you?"

Akira carefully adjusted his posture, trying for gratitude. "Kimi was glad. You did good."

"Look at you, flashing etiquette. Seems they teach something useful in that school." Boon gently adjusted the set of Akira's shoulders. "You totally have an avian accent, though."

Was that possible? He'd been living with a phoenix for a long time, but he'd never taken any notice of what Amaranthine *didn't* say until Kimi brought it to his attention.

Boon chuckled.

"You made that up!"

"Nah. That joke's older than tides."

An idea sparked, and Akira considered the impulse to trust. He needed a little help, a little advice, but he hadn't really decided who was close enough to trust, but distant enough to make secrets possible. He slowly reached out and touched the wolf's wrist. "Can I ask about something kind of personal?"

Boon immediately lowered himself to the floor. "Anything you need, little bro."

He laughed. "Gingko calls Kyrie that—*little bro*."

"Probably because I've been calling him that since he found his way into our pack." Boon's big hand closed around Akira's wrist. "He was as scrawny as you back then. And just as determined to be a security breech."

"Really?"

Boon made him sit and draped a companionable arm around his shoulders. "Haven't you ever seen him with Kel? Those two were close as two moonbeams. Couldn't train, tussle, or nestle the one without the other, so they got a double dose."

Best friends. "Like me and Suuzu?"

"Couldn't say for sure. Juuyu's not exactly chatty." Boon made a show of sniffing his hair. "But you smell enough of feathers and fraternity to convince me."

"Do you know about Juuyu's necklace?" he asked softly.

"His nest."

Akira was more than a little relieved. Boon knew, which meant he could help. "Did you help make it?"

"Not so much. My partner is the thoughtful one. It was his idea."

"Oh."

"That's not to say I don't know what's what." Boon pulled up the leg of his jeans, revealing his ankle accessories—colored cords, complex knots, and beads carved from different types of crystal. "Learning to make them is part of our lore. Comes standard for every whelp and weanling."

"Is it hard?"

"Want to learn?"

Akira nodded. "Suuzu needs one, and I wasn't sure where to start. I mean, how do you find nice enough things? And how do you make sure nothing falls off?"

"You're in luck, little bro. First step is confiding in a packmate of superior years and skills—me." Boon touched his bandages and grimaced. "Boss wants me in reserve until I heal up a bit, so I have time on my hands."

◊ ✦ ◊

"Are you sure?"

"*Better* than sure. I'm prepared." So saying, Boon slipped the tip of a claw into one of the complex knots and coaxed it loose. He unwound a glossy black cord that had been wrapped three times around his ankle. Its only ornamentation was a small chunk of orange crystal with a hole bored through its center, affixed at the midpoint by two ornamental knots. The wolf said, "It's braided from Juuyu's hair. That's why it's so long."

Akira took a longer look at Boon's ankle and easily picked out a looping braid that stood out from the rest. Springtime green against Boon's tanned skin.

With a snort, the wolf slid the cuff down to hide the rest.

"That'll do for the foundation of the nest you want to build with Suuzu. He'll like having a token of his brother. And the tuning means he'll always know what direction Juuyu's in."

Tuned crystals. Akira rubbed the pad of his thumb over the stone's rough edge, but all he could feel was its weight. To him, it was just a pretty rock.

Boon said, "Juuyu is important to Suuzu, which makes a gift like this the right kind of shiny. But before handing it over, you should add something of your own."

Akira smiled crookedly. "My hair's too short."

"Go with a crystal, then." Boon smirked. "Don't suppose you know anyone with a knack for tuning the things."

"Michael."

"High end. You have good taste. Wheedle a pretty rock out of him, and I'll make it secure."

"What about the other things?" Akira let the silky length of hair

317

slip between his fingers. "Juuyu had way more than two items."

"Probably took him years to collect them all." Boon shrugged. "You in a hurry?"

Akira wrestled with a sense of urgency. "I'm human."

"I noticed."

"Just an ordinary human."

Boon's gaze softened. "I get it kid. Okay. I never did get a good look at Juuyu's nest. Can you tell me anything about his treasures without getting too personal?"

"A nest is home, so they were reminders of home—stars, scents, seas, songs. And there was something blue to remind him of the sky."

The wolf smiled. "It *would* be blue skies. Rainy days put him in a mood. Right. There's your mission right there. Bring me either the tuned crystal or something blue, and you'll have yourself a good start."

Akira gave back the crystal on its cord.

Boon didn't keep it. Knotting the ends, he settled it around Akira's neck. "Wash this next time you bathe. Birds are less fussy about scent than wolves, but your nestmate won't like it if you seem to be treasuring something of mine. Wear it close to your skin. Make it yours before you give it to him."

Tucking the strand under his shirt, Akira said, "Thanks, Boon. Really. I owe you one."

"It's all good, Akira." Boon didn't quite meet his eyes. "We'll settle up some other time."

318

Kimiko eased away from Hisoka-sensei's entourage of experts and ducked into the kitchen, only to find Dickon Denholme already there, resplendent in traditional attire. "Very dashing!" she said approvingly. "Noriko, they're ready for you upstairs."

Her older sister set tea and a selection of snacks on the table. "That's an interesting choice, Kimiko. Has Mama seen you?"

She shook her head. "The Amaranthine in charge of wardrobe are keeping her occupied. She's eating up all their fuss and flattery." A veritable flock of avians had arrived earlier, toting boxes, chests, and trunks from which spilled a fortune in silk. "Don't you just love peacocks?"

"I thought they were pheasants," Noriko murmured, half to herself.

Dickon gazed at them over the rim of his tea cup. "I know the flamingo."

Kimiko shooed her sister toward the door. "Go and be preened, then come back down to show off for us. We'll repay you for your snacks with increasingly outrageous compliments."

"Don't be silly."

"I expect to see you in at least *three* empress-level designs," insisted Kimiko. "Indulge me!"

Noriko hung up her apron and departed with her head held high ... and cheeks pink.

Interesting.

Kimiko studied her companion, whose gaze was firmly fixed on his tea.

Doubly interesting.

She cheerfully said, "Hisoka-sensei thinks of *everything*."

"His attention to detail is … admirable."

"I'm not sure I like all the subtleties. Quen's straightforwardness is more to my taste."

He smiled faintly. "Then you have made a good match."

"May I ask an impertinent question?"

"Yes."

"Where do you rank?"

Dark eyes lifted. "Seventeenth."

She didn't even try to hide her astonishment. "In which class? Battler?"

"Overall." After a lengthy silence, he quietly added, "My father is the beacon of Wardenclave."

Kimiko gasped, "How are you *here*?"

"I have always been attached to the Starmark clan. Six months ago, when my debt to Glint was satisfied, Harmonious offered Rein and me a place. I wanted to settle down. Hisoka found out."

"Reaver Denholme, are you joining our family?" Kimiko playfully added, "For the ceremony, I mean?"

"Added security." He inclined his head. "You understand."

41

RELIQUARY

Eloquence lurked with Ever and Rise in the garden nearest the grand pavilion where Dad awaited their guests. Following some ancient protocol, Quen was being kept out of the way until he could make a grand entrance. So he'd been banned from the initial reception, leaving Dad to his fun—playing the host, with a side of paternal posturing.

"Yet?" whispered Ever.

"Soon," he promised. Quen's ears were tuned to the road beyond the heavy gates, which Valor and Prospect would swing wide at the Miyabe entourage's arrival.

His only real duty until his big moment was keeping Ever neat. But Akira, who had arrived ahead of the main group, had suggested leaving the parents to their own devices. While they handled all the formal introductions and fanfare, Quen could show his friends around.

"Yet?" Ever asked again.

Quen gave one puppy ear a tug and said, "Yes. Can you hear the car motor?"

His brother nodded eagerly.

"We must stay very quiet—you and me and Rise."

Ever pressed his face against Quen's neck to stifle a giggle. The pup adored games of all kinds, but especially when they were on the same team.

A line of black sedans rolled into view. Hardly subtle, but Quen was willing to bet that no one had noticed the cars wending their way through Keishi. Not with Argent Mettlebright as escort.

The fox emerged to open the door for Kimiko's kindred. The first to appear was undoubtedly her father. The man did a double-take when he saw who was holding the door for him. Had he not realized one of the Five was attending them?

Probably not. Foxes rarely brought attention to themselves except to distract.

Which was exactly the case. Quen nudged Ever and pointed.

While the shrinekeeper fumbled for words before Argent's haughty stare, Suuzu opened the opposite car door and calmly ushered out Kimiko. A murmured word, a quick hug, a grateful smile, and then his suitor's gaze was searching.

Quen deposited Ever on the snow-dusted path and commanded, "Quick and quiet, bring our lady here."

The mission was perfect. Even if Dad spotted Ever, he'd never interrupt a pup so convinced of his stealthiness. Where Eloquence would have been collared, Ever would be indulged.

Kimiko picked him up and followed the guidance of one

chubby finger.

Stepping into the open, Quen held out his hand to her. Nobody seemed to notice, with the exception of Argent, who'd glided to Suuzu's side. It would seem Akira's little scheme had serious backing. Assured of success, Quen turned his full attention to Kimiko.

This was the first time he'd seen her dressed in anything but the modest black and tan of her school uniform. Voluminous hakama swished softly with each step, the heavy red silk marked with a lavish chrysanthemum pattern. Far from the simple attire of a shrine maiden, but reminiscent in style. Here was a proud daughter of Kikusawa Shrine.

Wide pleats fell from a high waist, which was knotted over a wrapped shirt with full sleeves. He recognized Amaranthine craftsmanship, hand-painted flowers blooming across white silk. The vee of the neckline had been arranged to show additional layers beneath, colorful bands of silk creating a display of wealth and refinement.

More impressive than the quality of her clothing was the careless grace with which she wore it. No stiffness. No self-consciousness. In fact, he wondered if he should step in to keep *her* neat. Kimiko was doing nothing to discourage Ever's enthusiastic "sniffening."

"Mind your claws, Ever," Quen murmured.

"I mind." The boy settled his head on Kimiko's shoulder, tail swaying contentedly.

She sketched a casual greeting with her free hand. "Aren't you looking fine? Very coordinated. My sisters and I clash so much, nobody would guess we're related, but you three *belong* together."

He loved that she'd included Rise. Quen claimed her hand

and bent close, his head tilted invitingly. She rose up on tiptoe to bestow one of the greetings he'd taught her yesterday. The friendliest in her repertoire.

Mostly for Ever's benefit, he made a show of perusing her scent. To his surprise, he only found nuances of happiness and excitement. "You're not nervous?"

Kimiko rubbed noses with Ever. "Today is too special not to savor. I'm planning to enjoy every part of it." Her gaze was clear, and she seemed totally up to the challenge ahead. "Let's make a good beginning."

Kimiko found the Starmark compound both sumptuous and spare. Graceful lines. Serene views. Staggering scale. But there was very little in the way of accumulation or ornamentation. As if the buildings' only purpose was to provide the Starmark clan with a comfortable place to gather. The underlying attitude couldn't have been clearer. Dogs cherished Kith and Kindred above all else. Only when precious people filled these rooms did they become treasures.

"Akira is waiting for us." Eloquence's hand rested lightly on her lower back, guiding her along an inner corridor. "We have similar roles at the moment."

"Is he formalizing a betrothal?" she asked lightly.

Eloquence huffed. "He is—to use his term—babysitting."

He guided her into an inner room with low ceilings and

a sizable fireplace on each end. The space was noticeably warmer and furnished with low couches and tufted footstools. Embroidered curtains swathed the walls with color, and tasseled cushions mounded in corners. Books, papers, and crystals were strewn across a long worktable.

Akira sat sideways on one of the couches, facing a slim Amaranthine with pale green hair. They seemed to be deep in conversation. Kimiko gestured questioningly, not wanting to interrupt.

"I'll introduce you."

As Eloquence guided her closer, she could hear what was being said.

"Touch your nose."

Akira did.

"Touch my nose."

Akira obeyed. Was it some sort of children's game?

"Are you even trying?" sighed the stranger.

Kimiko took in the Amaranthine's showy coloring, sheer wardrobe, and excess of accessories and pegged him for a dragon. But not the one she'd been expecting, for Lord Mossberne was a blue.

He'd noticed them, but with a dramatic roll of his eyes, he continued his little game. "Touch Kyrie's nose."

This brought her attention to the child sitting on the dragon's lap. When Akira tapped the boy's nose, he giggled softly. The child's coloring was astonishing. Light brought out the faint iridescence of lavender scales along his hairline and on the backs of his hands. Wide eyes turned her way, showing the deep red of rose petals. Most astonishing were the four pale horns showing through his dark hair. A dragon crosser?

Kyrie offered a shy wave, which Ever returned enthusiastically.

The dragon offered the sign for peace, which he reinforced with a promise of protection. But then he went right on with his game, saying to Akira, "Kiss my nose."

This time, Akira hesitated. Then with great care, he reached up to grab the dragon's nose instead.

"That's the right idea!" he praised in nasal tones, thanks to Akira's pinch. "But who have we here?"

Akira gave himself a shake, then bounded up. "Kimi, you made it!"

But he swayed in place, and the dragon stood to steady him. "Easy now. Your good phoenix isn't here to prop you up."

"I'm fine. It's getting better, I think. But anyway ... Kimi, I want you to meet Kyrie!" He claimed the dragon crosser and brought him over. "I'm his uncle."

Eloquence said, "Our fathers decided early on that these two would need each other. Best friends, right Ever?"

"Best," agreed the pup, who'd claimed Kyrie's hand as soon as he was close enough.

"And Lilya," mumbled the half-dragon.

Akira mussed the boy's hair, which seemed to actually be purple. "Yep, you have Lilya at home." To Kimiko he explained, "She's Isla's baby sister. But this guy belongs to Sis. Meet my nephew, Kyrie Hajime-Mettlebright."

Kimiko offered her palms to the toddler, who met them with wide-eyed solemnity. She was more than a little confused. Everyone knew about Lord Mettlebright's crosser son, a fox-eared adult with a roguish grin. "How ...?"

"It's a long story, but it has a happy ending." Akira cuddled his nephew close. "We're blood related, me and Kyrie. For real."

"I had no idea," she murmured, offering her open arm to the boy.

Kyrie quickly made the change, clearly happy to be as close to Ever as possible.

Eloquence quietly explained, "Many crossers are fostered by a relative or by an enclave. Few are aware of Kyrie's presence in Argent's den, let alone his connection to Lady Mettlebright."

"What *handsome* young gentle-sirs," she gallantly declared. "I didn't know courting Eloquence would bring such treasures as you into my life!"

"Your lady has clear eyes." Sinder had been hanging back, but he joined their little knot. "Eloquence, may I meet your discerning suitor?"

Both Akira and Eloquence moved to reclaim the youngsters and free her hands.

"Sinder's pretty great," said Akira.

"He is here at Hisoka Twineshaft's behest," added Eloquence.

The dragon swept into a bow, but his formality had a teasing quality. "Sinder Stonecairne, a dragon of the Icelandic Reach, a person of little renown, more by design than by capabilities."

She liked his breezy braggadocio.

When his hands settled lightly over hers, Kimiko's gaze caught on the old rope chain wound across the back of his hand … and the item linked to it.

"Fascinating, isn't it? You'd consider it an antique." Sinder unwound the chain. "I was studying this before Akira and Kyrie found me. Bit of a mystery."

"Where did you find it?" she asked, cupping her hands in mute request.

"One of the trackers found it last night." Sinder let the heavy chain pool in her palm. "The catch is broken, so it was dropped."

Akira leaned closer. "So it's a clue?"

"It's a reliquary." At first glance, Kimiko thought someone had raided Kikusawa's treasury, but on closer inspection, the ornamentation was slightly different. Crafted from gold, the slender rod was no bigger than her little finger.

"You recognize this item?" asked Eloquence.

"We have something similar at home." She arranged her fingers along one edge, where she knew the catches to be. "May I?"

Sinder spread his hands wide, urging her to proceed.

Pushing one of the knobs, she pressed her fingernail into a grove and gave a careful twist. The end swung away, making it possible to slide a panel, revealing a hollow space. "Oh," she sighed. "This one's empty."

The dragon had her by the shoulders. "Tell me what you expected to find!"

"A seed." Kimiko was surprised at herself. That little detail was supposed to be a secret.

Eloquence growled, and Sinder snatched back his hands, fast sinking to his knees. Kimiko hadn't ever seen this posture before, but the abasement was clearly an apology, possibly unique to the dragon clans. Even so, he radiated urgency. "What kind of seed?"

She wavered between keeping the family secret and sharing what she knew. To her astonishment, Akira reached down and grabbed Sinder's nose. "Are you doing that thing? Why would you do that to Kimi?"

"Forgive me. The first time was unintended." Sinder lowered

his gaze. "I'm not plying, only prying. Perhaps it's better that she speak to someone she already trusts?"

Eloquence murmured, "Kimiko?"

Akira's friend. Hisoka's choice. Kimiko made up her mind to answer. "We don't know what kind of seeds they are, but they must be precious to be kept so carefully. Given the obvious similarities to the old stories, my grandfather always believed the reliquaries to be Kikusawa's greatest treasure."

Sinder's eyes widened. "Sweet zephyrs rising, you're talking in plurals."

"We have three." She sheepishly admitted, "I used to play with them when I was little."

"Three seeds?"

Kimiko shook her head. "One of ours was empty, too. But the other two are intact."

The dragon spoke slowly. "And when you say 'similarities to the old stories,' to which tales are you referring?"

She took a confiding posture, adding a signal for secrecy. "The Songs of Trees, of course. It's impossible not to think of Auriel when you're entrusted with two golden seeds."

Sinder snatched at Eloquence's sleeve and whispered, "Bring Hisoka."

42

EVERS MUM

Hisoka listened carefully.

Kimiko had expected more of a reaction, especially after Sinder's dramatics. She asked, "You don't think this is important?"

"It is. Undoubtedly. But there is a time and a place for everything, and this is neither." He took her elbow and guided her to the door. "Kimiko, you have people to meet and a betrothal to formalize. Eloquence, rejoin your father and brothers and await your suitor's pledge. Suuzu ... ah."

Suuzu stood just inside the door. More accurately, he leaned against the wall, looking dazed. He must have arrived close on Hisoka's heels, making him privy to the entire explanation. Here was the shock she'd anticipated, but why should Suuzu be so rattled? Automatically, she checked on Akira, who was already moving toward his best friend.

"Hey, Suuzu." Akira sounded worried. "You doing okay?"

The phoenix silently pulled his friend close, pinning Kyrie between them. The little crosser warbled a questioning note. Suuzu's low trill seemed to reassure him, but Kimiko was concerned by his posture. Suuzu radiated an inexplicable distress.

Hisoka said, "Sinder, I apologize for the inconvenience, but will you carry a message to Boonmar-fen Elderbough at Kikusawa Shrine, letting him know what's transpired. The two of you will protect the treasury. No access. From *any* quarter."

"Understood." Sinder left so quickly, he seemed to vanish into thin air.

Kimiko frowned at her companion. Suuzu held himself even more upright than usual as he escorted her toward her evening's obligations. "Are you worried about something?"

He seemed to haul himself into the present and managed a wan smile. "My role is minor. Better to ask if you are worried."

"Not really." She gestured broadly with her free hand—gratitude, anticipation, happiness. "I never once expected to have the full set."

"Of...?"

"The Five." Kimiko added a skip to her step. "Do you know the two I haven't met?"

"Yes."

"And you'll introduce me?"

"Gladly, should the need arise. But the spokespersons are quite forward when it comes to seeking human interaction." He gestured to the fore. "As you shall see."

Kimiko followed his gaze. The wolf watching their approach was quite tall, quite tanned, and quite beautiful. Hurrying her steps, Kimiko was already rattling off greetings and compliments. Adoona-soh Elderbough's surprise modulated into pleasure, and her posture shifted to a stance that was universally understood.

Shocked by her own boldness, Kimiko ran straight into her arms. She was pulled close, her cheek pressing a vest of thick golden fur. Warm and wild and a welcome surprise. Closing her eyes, Kimiko came to rest. This person was a stronghold, and she felt safe.

The she-wolf laughed, low and husky. "Not the least bit shy, this one."

Suuzu said, "At times like this, Kimi reminds me of Akira."

"That one," she scoffed in brusque affection. "Where is your nestmate?"

"With Gingko. Just there."

Kimiko drew back enough to see where Argent's famous son stood with Akira. She'd beg an introduction to the half-fox later, but she was more surprised by the quick change Akira had undergone. Isla's father was fussing with the folds of a formal ensemble the color of flames. "Suuzu, is he wearing your crest?"

"He is."

Guided by the phoenix's obvious pride, Kimiko decided that now was not the time for gossipy tidbits. Reaching for his hand, she gave it a quick squeeze. "He looks good in your colors."

Suuzu's soft trill was self-deprecating. "He looks embarrassed."

But just then, Akira spotted them and offered a small wave and a crooked grin.

"Don't be silly, Suuzu," Kimiko said. "He's as proud as you are."

"Hold your heads high," said Adoona-soh. "You especially, Kimiko Miyabe."

She eased out of the wolf's embrace, belatedly offering her palms.

Adoona went one better, her big hands settling around Kimiko's wrists. "I can see why Harmonious is so taken with you. I admire your resolve to tread a path less traveled." Leaning closer, the she-wolf confided, "The chase was mine, as well."

Now *that* was a story Kimiko wanted to hear.

"Your attention, please."

Hisoka's well-modulated voice carried across the buzz of conversation, which tapered off enough for Kimiko to catch the sound of her mother. Up on tiptoe, she spotted Mama near the center of the room, chattering at Lapis Mossberne. He acknowledged Hisoka's call with a lazy twirl that must have created a sigil, for Mama's voice was suddenly muted. Silenced by a barrier. With supreme poise, the attentive dragon guided Kikuko Miyabe to her husband's side. Kimiko was sure she was talking the whole way and cringed.

"You are like your mother," remarked Adoona-soh.

Kimiko was stung.

Adoona's expression betrayed amusement. "You do not care for the comparison."

"Mama is ...." There was no good way to finish that. Kimiko tried again. "I don't want to be like her."

"Resemblance takes many forms. Will you hear the favorable reports that have come back to me from Kith and Kindred alike?"

"Reports?" she echoed, uncomfortably aware that she was whispering instead of listening to Hisoka's welcoming remarks. Like Mama.

"Wolves often weave the day's surprises into their song, and many are glad to have crossed paths with you." Adoona's voice was low, sure. "A seeker of connections, an improviser of courtesies, a granter of smiles."

Kimiko had a hard time believing that those she met in passing actually remembered her. Surely a reaver of her rank wasn't worth noting. Here today, gone tomorrow. Then again, she cherished each happenstance. Weren't they wonderful *because* they were so fleeting and so rare?

"Others are brighter," she protested.

Adoona cupped her cheek. "Do not complain of lesser lights to one who cherishes the moon."

It took a moment for that to sink in.

The she-wolf wasn't finished. "Kikuko Miyabe entered this room as if it were her own, and by her courtesies made us welcome."

"Oh, I'm so sorry. She's very ... in charge."

Suuzu made a small sound. Was he hushing them? No, he was trying not to laugh.

Adoona said, "I know three Nightspangle whelps whose praises multiply. Hisoka purrs at the very mention of your name. Isla, who outshines whole constellations, looks up to you. And in a shocking turn of tricks, Argent approves of you." Her tail swung wide. "Eloquence may speak for the Kith, but *you* shall speak for your den. Much as I do."

Kimiko still wanted to protest. "I'm not anything like Mama. Everyone knows that's Noriko."

"The elder daughter?" scoffed Adoona. She certainly didn't shy away from confrontation. "She has your mother's form, but she has your sire's doting, deferential nature."

Just how much had transpired in the short time she'd been off with Eloquence and Ever?

Adoona searched her face and nodded. "Listen and consider. Kikuko is human, but she pursued a reaver and won his affection. Without her courage to defy tradition, you would not be here to pursue your own unlikely match."

Kimiko blinked, then blinked again as tears threatened. Never. Not once had it occurred to her that she was following in her mother's footsteps. Mama, who loved people and gossip and taking charge. Mama, who was hasty and stubborn and quick to befriend.

"Suuzu, am I like my mother?" she asked tragically.

The phoenix brushed her cheek with a hasty kiss. "I maintain my position—you are like Akira. Now take heed, for Harmonious has nearly finished building anticipation for Eloquence's grand entrance."

He and Adoona drew her into the center of the room and remained on either side. Kimiko faced her parents and Harmonious, who welcomed her belated arrival with a broad wink.

"The time has come to present my son," he boomed. "Eloquence is escorted by my dear Anna."

As every head turned, Kimiko went up on tiptoe, eager for a glimpse of the reclusive second wife of Harmonious Starmark. No one knew anything about Ever's human mother. Harmonious always laughed off questions, saying Anna preferred a quiet life and thanking the world at large for respecting her privacy.

Eloquence's questing gaze found Kimiko's, his face brightening enough to warm her cheeks. And then he bent to speak into his mother's ear. Not that he had to bend far. The woman at his side was quite tall and definitely not from their part of the world.

She was rosy-fair with hair the soft yellow of a sunrise sky, loose and straight as a mare's. As she came nearer, Kimiko could see that her eyes were blue. A striking beauty, like a storybook queen. Most startling was her age, for while Anna Starmark was clearly a woman grown, she looked no more than twenty.

Kimiko was grateful that Isla had told her that this woman's life was linked to her bondmate's. Anna probably looked exactly as she had the day Harmonious began to tend her. A sobering thought.

Would Kimiko's family grow old around her, while she remained unchanged, a living relic of the early days of the Emergence? Another thought came, more vexing than it should have been. Was she doomed to be mistaken for an adolescent boy for centuries to come? Perhaps Eloquence would agree to an extended courtship, giving her time to gain some semblance of maturity.

Figuring this was one of those times when she was meant to take the lead, Kimiko stepped forward and offered her palms to initiate the formalities. "Your son speaks of you with obvious affection."

Anna's smile was grave. "*Two* of my sons are utterly smitten, and I have no doubt you will rally the rest in support of your pursuit."

Her Japanese was perfect, if a bit formal. And it was a little difficult to tell if the lady thought Kimiko's pursuit was a good thing. She tried to get a read off Eloquence and found he'd adopted the receptive posture they'd practiced yesterday. She firmed her own stance, and his demure smile held approval.

"Your kin are shrinekeepers," Anna said.

"Kikusawa Shrine."

"When I first came to this area, Kikusawa gave me shelter."

Kimiko asked, "You lived at our shrine?"

"I considered it home." Again, that grave smile, and Anna's fingers tapped lightly upon the circlet of stones at her wrist.

Attention drawn, Kimiko saw that the bracelet was one of a matched pair. Each clear stone gleamed with an inner light, as if she'd captured starlight within the crystals. This woman wasn't just a reaver; she must be a beacon. Suddenly, Ever's fanciful description of his mother holding stars in her hands made sense. In the eyes of her child, she would shine.

"Kikusawa gave me shelter," Anna repeated. "But I repaid them poorly, for I brought nothing but trouble."

"I didn't realize. My grandfather was more familiar with the shrine records than I am. I don't remember any mention of a reaver named Anna."

The woman traded a long look with Eloquence, who dipped his head.

"Ever tells me that you love the Star Festival," said Anna. "Since your visit, he has been full of questions about angels and starfolk and saints."

"The Star Festival has always been an important celebration for my family."

"And for our pack," interjected Eloquence. He nudged his step-mother. "For good reason."

Kimiko was sort of relieved to see Anna's expression morph into fond exasperation. She was less stiff that way, more normal. Maybe even approachable, once they got over the awkwardness of beginnings.

337

Anna said, "It might interest you to know that once upon a time, I was Miss Anna Green."

"I see." But of course, she didn't. The English name stuck out, her accent somewhat different than Isla's. Kimiko wasn't sure if it signified a regional difference or indicated some earlier era.

Eloquence stepped in. "Before Anna met Dad, her family name was Green."

He gave subtle emphasis to the English surname, as if there was a connection he expected her to make. Her grasp of English was rudimentary at best, her worst subject. All she'd retained from middle school were a few basic phrases, numbers one to ten, the names of farm animals, some varieties of fruit, and colors.

Oh.

Kimiko quickly shifted into stammering, babbling, gesticulating comprehension. Green was *midori*. Midori was *green*.

The woman simply nodded.

With a warm chuckle, Eloquence banished any lingering doubt. "Kimiko, it is my distinct pleasure to introduce Reaver Anna Starmark, battler class, better known to history as Saint Midori."

43

TO SEE. TO HEAR. TO KNOW

Like most of Dad's gatherings, the evening proceeded casually, with music and mingling. Eloquence noted the opening of a second cask of celebratory star wine and caught wind of enough embarrassing childhood stories to heighten his color. Ever had flitted everywhere, glad to be included for once, but now nestled against Quen's shoulder.

As per custom, Suuzu never left Kimiko's side as he guided her through introductions with members of the Starmark pack. And Twineshaft remained at Quen's side, patient in his watchfulness.

Eventually, the cat leaned closer. "I don't think he'll find the courage, and time is short. Shall we?"

"I'd be grateful."

Taking Eloquence's elbow, Hisoka steered him toward the far corner where Akio Miyabe had taken refuge. Quen submitted quietly, for these were the roles they needed to play, the rules of a traditional courting game. He couldn't approach Kimiko's family without an escort.

"Good evening to you, Reaver Miyabe," Hisoka said easily. "I've coaxed Eloquence over. Will you welcome him?"

The man immediately offered his palms, which presented something of a ... situation. Not only were Eloquence's hands full with Ever, the little boy seized the chance to change partners. Mr. Miyabe found himself weighed down with a clingy cuddler.

"I should sniffen you."

A slow smile warmed the shrinekeeper's face, making Kimiko's resemblance to her father more apparent. "Hello, young sir. Should we be introduced first?"

"I dun know you." Ever frowned thoughtfully. "Does I?"

"Allow me, since introductions are one of my duties this evening." Hisoka gently tweaked Ever's ear. "Reaver Miyabe, the affectionate pup in your arms is Ever Starmark. Ever, the man you are preparing to *sniffen* is Kimiko's father. That's why he seems familiar."

Quen was proud that Ever had picked up on the similarities of scent. He and Laud had begun teaching him the basics of tracking, which required a discerning nose.

Ever's tail wagged so hard, he was wriggling. "Kimi's yours?"

"One of my precious daughters."

"She's mine too! Ours." At this, he reached back, and Quen eased forward so Ever's hand could rest possessively over his heart. "Bruvver's and mine!"

Mr. Miyabe asked, "May I meet your brother?"

"Yeth! Him's Quen."

Hisoka stepped in. "Eloquence is Harmonious Starmark's fourth

340

son and one of your daughter's classmates at New Saga High School. He is her choice, and the Starmark clan welcomes her pursuit."

The usual exchange of niceties was much interrupted by Ever's enthusiastic nuzzling, which put a shine in Mr. Miyabe's eyes.

"Ah," said Hisoka, as if just remembering something. "This seems as good a time as any to point out that you may well have grandchildren with similar features."

Akio Miyabe's astonishment ebbed away, and Quen was relieved to see acceptance, even anticipation on the man's face. Their pups would be welcome. He stole a glance toward Kimiko, who was talking animatedly with his sister Rampant. Even from here, he could feel her delight. Maybe because their connection was already forming?

Hisoka's hand settled on his back, and Quen brought his wandering attention back. Mr. Miyabe had been watching him watch his daughter.

Quen awkwardly asked, "Is there anything Spokesperson Twineshaft has not covered?"

"One thing, really." A searching look. A soft question. "Do you love my daughter?"

"Wholeheartedly." He slipped unthinkingly into a much more dominating stance than the occasion dictated. "She is my choice, as well."

"That's good, then. Yes, good." There was a tremulous edge to her father's smile. He caressed Ever's silky hair and touched his round cheek. "May I show this beautiful boy to Kikuko?"

"Soon," promised Hisoka. "The hour has come for Kimiko's declaration. Will you join Harmonious on the dais, please?"

Ever was sent trotting to his mother, and they wended their way to the low platform, reaching it at the same time as Suuzu, who guided Kimiko into position. Once again, Hisoka called for everyone's attention.

"Since the oldest of days, Amaranthine have gathered at the Song Circle to mark celebrations—rites of coming and going, the taking of apprentices, the binding of pacts, and the founding of houses. This night, the Starmark pack forms a circle to hear the pledge of Kimiko Miyabe, who claims suit and will pursue Eloquence Starmark."

Quen watched as his packmates quietly fanned out. Uncle Laud's white shock moved from door to door, sliding them open so their Kith could enter. He was theirs. Of course they wanted to be here— to see, to hear, to know the form Kimiko's promise would take.

Hisoka continued, adding dignity to the coming moment by his very presence. "Miss Miyabe, Harmonious Starmark wishes you to know that he will not yield his son to a half-hearted suitor. What do you have to say for yourself?"

Eloquence was grateful to have been spared the "maiden son" label.

On cue, she took her place in the center of the room, head high, posture radiating confidence. She took the time for a slow spin, meeting the gazes of those she'd only just met, taking in the strength of the Starmark pack. Last of all, she looked his way. The tilt of her chin, the lift of her brows—it was as if they were sharing a laugh or a secret. His blood began to sing, and the sweet note of her soul rang in his memory.

Then she addressed herself to the room in carrying tones. "My heart is as whole as it is his. Let courtship show my resolve, for I've resolved to have him."

A murmur ran around the circle, acknowledgement and approval, a few yips from the Kith contingent, and some elbowing among the adolescent males.

Harmonious grinned. "And what form will your courtship take?"

"A variation on the Cycle of Moons, which is found in the Amaranthine lore of trees. Twelve pledges sealed by twelve kisses." She waited out another murmur before adding, "I'm prepared to bestow the first kiss tonight, beneath Kusunoki, the tree at Kikusawa Shrine."

"Your purpose and your preparations are good." Harmonious cocked a brow in Quen's direction. "Well, son? What do *you* have to say for yourself?"

"I will be waiting in the appointed place."

Hisoka took charge again. "The Starmark clan has acknowledged Kimiko's suit. All that remains is the selection of representatives. Kimiko, Eloquence, name the member of your household who will bear witness to the twelve pledges, each in their turn.

Kimiko spoke without hesitation. "My father, Reaver Akio Miyabe."

The man took a small step forward, beaming proudly at his daughter.

Hisoka turned to Eloquence, eyebrows lifting.

Quen could *feel* his father drawing himself up, eager to be named, even as he felt Laud's presence withdraw, shrinking from a role that would bring so much attention his way.

"Eloquence," Hisoka prompted. "Who will you choose from among your packmates to watch over you and your lady?"

"This clan is strong, and there are many—Kith and Kindred alike— who could carry the honor. After much consideration, my choice became clear. I designate Ever Starmark as my representative."

Everyone's gaze swung to Anna Starmark, whose small son perched on her hip. The pup's ears pricked and swiveled. "Me? Is it my turn, Mum?"

"Yes, my child," said Anna. "Go to your brother. He needs you."

Ever crossed the room at full scamper, accomplishing the last meters in a gravity-defying leap. "Here I am, Bruvver!"

Quen swung him high, then cradled him close. "Will you be my representative?"

"Yeth." His face creased in confusion. "What dat?"

He crossed to Kimiko, guessing it would be easiest to explain his role if he understood Kimiko's place in their future. Quen said, "The pack needs you to do a very important job, Ever. As my representative, you'll listen to Kimiko say her words, then hear my answers."

Wide eyes blinked. "Why?"

"We are going to trade promises, and in keeping them, our den will be built."

"Where?"

"Our den?" Quen placed his hand over his heart. "Here first, then in the place Kimiko lives, high on a hill, with many stairs and a great tree."

Kimiko made a tiny noise. She seemed surprised. Hadn't anyone told her the terms Hisoka had negotiated on their behalves? In as soothing a voice as he could manage, he said, "Kimiko will take my name, and she will bring me into her home."

"Me, too?" asked Ever.

"Of course. You're mine."

"Uncle?"

"Yes, I think so." Quen couldn't imagine a den without Laud. "And Rise?"

"Yes, Rise is ours as well. But Kimiko will be especially mine, and I will be especially hers. That's what it means to have a bondmate. One for always."

Ever considered this with furrowed brows. "Not me?"

"You're my brother," said Quen. "Brothers can't be bondmates, but you can be my representative."

The little boy turned to Kimiko. "I Bruvver's res-sent-tive."

She smiled softly. "Eloquence must love you very much."

"Course!" He puffed out his chest. "We's bruvvers."

Eloquence thought it best to press the point, both for Ever's sake and so that the whole clan would know how matters stood. "Yes, we're brothers, and that will make Kimiko your sister."

Ever held out his arms, and Kimiko took him.

"And when we have pups," Quen continued, "you will be their uncle."

"Me?" he squeaked, but his tail lifted and began a tentative wag. "Pups?"

Eloquence felt the shift in Kimiko's posture—assertive, possessive. Without hesitation, he relaxed into an attentive pose, making it clear that the answer wasn't his to give. Ever picked up on the change because he nuzzled Kimiko's chin, whining as he worked up his very best "pudding please" to date.

"I hear you." Kimiko smiled crookedly. "But let's take things one step at a time, Ever. Promises first. Pups later."

✦

ЧЧ

TORN

Tenma was feeling very much out of his depth. Having never really had close friends before, he wasn't sure if he could be a good one to Inti. So far this evening, most of his impulses had been to correct and scold. Like a picky old lady. But he wasn't trying to tame or change Inti. He wanted to understand his new roommate. That's why they'd made plans to hang out together, from after classes until curfew.

"Aren't your feet cold?" asked Tenma.

Inti swarmed up Tenma's body like a squirrel up a tree. Claiming a seat on his shoulders, the crosser wriggled until his feet were stuffed down the front of Tenma's coat. Arms and tail settled snuggly. Tenma knew he looked a sight, strolling down the street with a furry tail for a muffler and a monkey-boy for a hat.

"Good?" he asked.

"Warm," agreed Inti.

"You *have* shoes, you know."

Inti gave the low rumble Tenma now recognized as the Inti equivalent of "ick." Even the slight glaze of ice on Keishi's sidewalks hadn't convinced his roommate to use the shoes New Saga provided.

Tenma decided not to mind all the staring, the smiles, and the shy nods. People needed to get used to seeing Amaranthine around town. The Emergence was about living openly. Integration needed to spread beyond the classroom.

Nice in theory. But Inti's unconventional behavior kept Tenma on his toes. He'd had to apologize a lot for his roommate, who was prone to touch, taste, or take things without invitation.

"How about a quick lesson," Tenma suggested.

"Again?"

"A little one. About sitting in public." Tenma pointed to a park bench. "It's quieter here, so this is a good spot."

"Inti will listen." He slid from his perch and bowed. "Teach me, sensei."

Tenma laughed and took a seat. "Humans have this thing called *polite distance*."

Inti cheerfully joined him, pressing snug against his side. "Inti is polite."

"Too close, Inti. Humans aren't always comfortable with direct contact. What feels most natural to you may be an imposition for them."

"You do not smell alarmed."

Tenma smiled. "We're friends. This lesson is about strangers. Shall I demonstrate?"

In a barefoot crouch on the bench, Inti watched with bright-eyed interest as Tenma backed up a few steps, then approached.

"May I sit here?"

"Sit, sit, sit."

Tenma left plenty of room between them. "Some people will place items beside them as barriers, like a shopping bag or a book. They're signaling a preference, but even if they don't, still give them room."

"Sitting with strangers." Inti studied the gap between them. "What about friends."

"That depends on how close you are."

Inti lifted a finger. "Classmate, but not Tenma or Quen or Isla."

Tenma stood, once more backing off and coming forward. "Here you are, Inti! May I join you?"

"Sit, sit, sit, friend." Inti was enjoying himself.

While Tenma still preserved a polite distance, he changed his body language, slouching back and leaning closer until their shoulders bumped. "How've you been?"

Inti grinned. "Hungry."

Lesson over. They were back to the main theme of their evening out. Tenma hadn't been able to think of a single form of entertainment that might appeal to Inti ... except food. So they'd been wandering through Keishi, stopping frequently to sample fast food and street food and the mysterious delights found in vending machines.

Inti leapt to his cozy perch on Tenma's shoulders. "You still have coins?"

"Plenty."

"Tenma is rich?"

"Beyond your wildest dreams."

Poking at Tenma's cheek, Inti asked, "Is Tenma teasing?"

"Yes, I'm teasing. But I won't run out of money for a while yet, even at the rate you eat."

They found a crepe shop, at which point Tenma learned that Inti was violently opposed to eating banana-anything. On principle.

"Defying stereotypes?" Tenma asked.

"I like what I like," he mumbled around a mouthful of strawberries and cream.

Tenma definitely appreciated moments like this, when Inti abandoned pretense enough to use personal pronouns. One thing he'd learned at school was how important nuances were to Amaranthine. Little things communicated big ideas—like caution, trust, and friendship.

"Where would you like to go?" Tenma didn't even try to hide his curiosity. "I mean, what do *you* usually do when you go out at night?"

Inti licked the last traces of cream from his fingertips and jumped onto Tenma's shoulders. Tapping the top of his head, he said, "Take me to trees. Someplace to run and climb."

At the next street corner, Tenma turned homeward, since the best place would be the forest behind their dormitory. Although it was Starmark land, there were no fences or barriers. Maybe some of the Kith in the shelter would like to join Inti in running wild.

Only they didn't quite make it to campus.

All of a sudden, Inti's tail whipped out from around Tenma's shoulders. Overbalanced, he staggered, then made a grab for his roommate's ankles. Inti was standing on his shoulders, peering off along a darkened side street. Tenma wanted to ask what was happening, but something in the crosser's attitude told him this wasn't a silly game.

Inti dropped to the ground and skittered off a short distance, then returned to dance in a circle around Tenma. "Too late, too late," he muttered. "Too slow."

Thinking it must be safe to speak since Inti was, Tenma nonetheless kept his voice low. "What's wrong?"

The only answer he received was more bouncing and fidgeting. Inti's eyes were perfectly round, and he'd begun gnawing on the end of his tail.

Hauling him close and caging him against his body, Tenma spoke into Inti's ear. "Tell me."

"A trigger. A trap. The hunter is coming."

"You mean the trackers?"

Inti's softly chanted negative was a like a desperate prayer.

A finger pressed to Tenma's mouth, begging for silence. Inti's other hand dove into Tenma's clothing, picking an inner pocket and coming up with a precious fold of paper. He shuffled back a step and, to Tenma's horror, ripped Quen's sigil in two, letting the halves flutter to the ground.

Awareness slammed into Tenma, clawing away his composure. Malicious, greedy, and closing fast—if the oncoming Amaranthine was a hunter, they'd be easy prey.

Inti's tail snaked around his arm, squeezing tight. Up on tiptoe, he whispered in Tenma's ear. "We need to run. We need to hide."

"Yes."

"You are too slow."

For a fleeting moment, Tenma thought Inti would leave him behind.

His fear must have shown on his face. Inti's hand brushed his cheek. "My turn, my friend. I'm stronger than I look."

A disorienting swoop sent Tenma's already-queasy stomach plunging, and he found himself clinging helplessly to Inti, who sprang recklessly along the rooftops.

45

TEMPTATION

Akira was pleased to be included in the much smaller group that made the trip to Kikusawa Shrine. It sounded like this pledge thingie was usually pretty private, with only the representatives necessary to make it official. But tonight's plan allowed the Miyabes to offer a return of hospitality to the Starmarks.

Argent had joined the group quizzing Akio Miyabe about the shrine's history and treasury. Sinder was among them, and it was pretty plain that they wanted a full tour once Kimi got around to kissing Quen.

Stuffing his hands deeper into his pockets, Akira shambled along toward the house, where Suuzu was overseeing some kind of last minute details. Probably preening.

He reached their front door just as it opened. Jumping aside, he let the Miyabe women pass in a soft rustle of fancy clothes, twinkling hair ornaments, and fur-trimmed capes. They chattered and giggled and wafted a heady blend of girly scents.

Must be almost time.

Suuzu stepped outside. The closing door cut off most of the light, leaving them in the dark. But the phoenix's eyes were as keen as ever, despite the lack of light. He closed in on Akira, straightening and fussing with a focus that betrayed his state of mind.

"What gives?" Akira asked. "You can't be nervous for Kimi. She's got this whole group handled, especially Quen."

"He yields gladly."

"And I'm happy for him, but I'm worried about you. Seriously, what gives?" Akira poked his best friend. "You've been weird ever since the thing about Kimi's family treasure."

"Yes." Suuzu lifted him and launched upward, rising high above the moonlit courtyard before coming to roost in Kusunoki's branches.

Akira didn't protest. Suuzu must need more privacy before answering. He wasn't surprised with the phoenix traced matching sigils on their palms. This conversation was for their ears only.

And still, Suuzu didn't speak.

From this vantage, mingling guests were hidden from view by leaves or the canopies where hot coals and warm drinks kept the cold night at bay. Akira could see Gingko playing with Kyrie and Ever, chasing along garden paths lit by stone lanterns. It was past their bedtime, and Kyrie wouldn't last much longer, even bundled as he was. The little guy didn't like cold weather.

Suuzu was back to arranging—his hair, his coat, his scarf. "Are you warm enough?"

"It's not so bad, but I gotta say, this Amaranthine cloth is kind of ... blowy."

"You are cold."

"It's fine. Honest." Akira said, "We should take a picture later to show Sis. And Juuyu."

"Hmm." Suuzu did his best to shelter Akira with his body. "You wear my colors well."

Akira was getting worried. "Is this something you can't talk about?"

He trilled softly. "My secrets are yours, but this one is ... embarrassing."

"We've gotten over a lot of embarrassing stuff." Akira smiled. "Remember the thing with the wool sweater?"

Suuzu covered his eyes with one hand. "This is a matter of understanding rather than misunderstanding. I fear Hisoka Twineshaft has found cause to question my integrity."

"Why would he do that? You're totally honorable."

"Temptation comes in many forms." Suuzu tugged and tutted, settling Akira against him so he could speak more quietly still. "He has seen my wavering will and moved accordingly."

"Sensei's our friend."

"Every traitor was once a friend."

Akira leaned into Suuzu's shoulder. "You're awfully serious about something, but you haven't really explained anything. Are you going to tell me or not?"

"Do you know the stories about Auriel of the Golden Seed?"

"Nope."

Suuzu spoke softly. "There is a forgotten lore, older than oceans, sung by the stars. These most ancient of tales recall a time when the waters parted and the heavens sent sowers over the emerging land. Some call this the first Emergence."

Akira chuckled. "If the stories are forgotten, how do you know them?"

"Because one of the ten tasks given to a tenth child is to remember what the other nine cannot." Suuzu continued, "One of the sowers was an angel called Auriel. To him were given the nuts, pods, and cones of every kind of singing tree, for they would be needed."

"Amaranthine trees?"

Suuzu nodded. "Hither and thither, he flew, seeking good soil in the world's secret places. And in his wake rose the elder orchards and ancient groves, gifts from the Maker for the good of all Creation."

"For real?"

A chiding trill. A wistful smile. "One age passed into the next, and Auriel's task neared an end. Only a handful of seeds remained in his pouch—burnished like gold, thrumming with promise. He searched for new ground, far from the places his efforts were already bearing fruit, and happened upon a group of women fleeing the harem of a cruel king. At Auriel's appearance, they wept for joy, saying, 'Guide us, for we have lost our way.'"

"I'm guessing he stuck around."

"Yes, and seeing that they were fainting from hunger, Auriel cast about for something they could eat. But the land was desolate, and all he had were the seeds he had yet to sow—twelve in all."

"How many ladies did he rescue?"

Suuzu nodded. "You are right, there were twelve."

"What happens when you eat a golden seed?"

"You are getting ahead of the story," grumbled the phoenix.

"Auriel fed the seeds to the women, who found strength enough for a great journey. He led them to a mountain where phoenixes made nests in the rocks, for in those days, wild phoenixes were plentiful."

Akira had met a few phoenix Kith, but he wasn't sure if there were any wild phoenixes left in the world. It had seemed rude to ask.

Suuzu said, "Two Amaranthine lived in the heights, nestmates watching over the wild birds that were their responsibility. They welcomed the weary travelers, making room for them and tending to their needs, which soon multiplied, for all twelve women were found to be with child."

"Oh, man."

"Before he left, Auriel handed down the first of the songs of trees, a prophecy which is still known by all Amaranthine children. It is one of our lullabies." Suuzu hummed a few bars. "The language is old, and much of the beauty is lost in translation. After a warning against the allure of trees, Auriel explains what happens to the heedless. For the consequences would be the same for them as for these twelve women."

Akira grumbled, "You're dragging this out on purpose."

Suuzu hung his head, then softly sang, "Take the golden seed from your child's hand, and plant it beside your front step. Teach your child to watch and water, to tend to their twin. In so doing, they will gain a tree's age and bring home many blessings."

"Wait, you skipped something. Where'd the kid get a seed?"

"They were born with a seed in their hand."

"All twelve of them?"

"Yes. And when the children were old enough, they obeyed the angel and planted the seed."

Akira's eyes widened. "And lived. Like Sis and Quen's mom, whose lives are tied to their bondmate's. Only the kids were matched up with their tree."

"We call them tree-kin."

"There's really such a thing?"

Suuzu hushed him, a finger to his lips. "The elder orchards and ancient groves fell long ago, ravaged by the human desire for immortality. But enough seeds survived. Few know about the groves. Fewer still know where they are hidden."

"Your island?"

Suuzu nodded once.

"Okay, that's pretty cool. But why does this make a problem between you and Hisoka-sensei?"

His friend laughed weakly and hugged him closer. "If those reliquaries hold golden seeds, then they hold Auriel's promise for the one who plants them."

"They'd still work."

"Yes. And Twineshaft clearly knows this, and he has set a guard so that I will not succumb to temptation."

"You'd steal a seed?"

His voice was thick with longing. "I do want one."

"But ... why?"

Suuzu made a broken little noise.

Hot tears splashed Akira's cheek, and his heart trembled. "For me?"

"*Yes*, for you. Even though I would break laws, break faith, break trust. Even so, I would take it and have you plant it beside the threshold of our home."

"I get it now." Akira leaned up to kiss his best friend's cheek. "That's a nice idea. I like it better than what I thought you were suggesting."

Suuzu hummed inquiringly.

"Well, with the story and all," Akira said. "I was sorta worried that you were going to try to get me pregnant."

With an exasperated groan, Suuzu gave in to a fresh wash of tears. But at least this time, he was laughing through them.

46
ROOFTOPS

enma had never been so scared in his life. Yes, his first day of school had shattered his courage, but this didn't begin to compare. It was one thing to be surrounded by passive, peaceful Amaranthine. Quite another to know with dread certainty that one of them moved like a predator, and you were its prey.

Were they to be the next kidnap victims? Would Ms. Reeves give Class 3-C the bad news tomorrow? No, wait. Beginning tomorrow, they were off for a week to observe the anniversary of the Emergence. But when their classmates returned, Sentinel Skybellow would grimly rehearse his safety protocols, reminding students to take extra care when leaving campus.

Because Tenma had been foolish. He might even die. This thing driving toward them, it felt merciless and manic. A soul-tearing terror he could never hope to outrun on his own.

Gradually, Tenma became aware that Inti was saying things,

patting his face, stroking his hair. He was less afraid of Inti than of the monster in the darkness. Of course, the crosser wasn't exactly Amaranthine. Tenma could see the split in Inti, two natures twining, both wild in their other-ness. Which made him curious if he could actually see the souls of reavers in the same palette of colors that filled his mind when he focused on a person. Maybe he should try it on Isla … if he survived the night.

"Ten-ma, Ten-ma."

The teasing sing-song pulled at his attention, but another wild leap left him dizzy. All he could do was lock his arms around his friend's slim shoulders and gasp for every breath. "I'm so scared, Inti," he confessed.

"Are you with me, Tenma? Can you hear my voice now?"

"I hear you."

"Good, good, good."

Inti changed directions so fast, Tenma groaned in protest.

"I know a place. I'm going to hide you there, then go for help. You'll need to stay quiet while I lead the threat away."

Tenma fumbled to straighten his glasses. "Inti, is that you?"

The crosser landed on the peak of a roof, slid down the opposite slope, and leapt over an alley. Coming to a halt, he met Tenma's gaze. A playful little smile warmed his expression. "Inti is here. Inti has always been here."

"I guess you have."

Inti let him down, but Tenma's legs quavered too much to hold him up. Even as he sagged to the ground, he caught Inti's pant leg, afraid of being left behind.

A warm tail wrapped around Tenma's chest, its tufted tip

tickling his nose. "Can you trust me?" asked Inti.

"I do trust you."

"This way." Inti levered Tenma onto his feet and guided him to the other end of the roof.

He wasn't sure exactly where they were in Keishi, but it was three stories above a busy street. Shops and restaurants were clogged with people already celebrating the international holiday.

Inti crouched before a dark metal box, some kind of ventilation unit, and pulled a louvered grate off the front. "In."

Tenma crawled into the tight space, pulling his knees up to his chest to fit. His roommate bumped his forehead with a hasty kiss, then snapped the cover into place. Through the downward angle of the metal shutters, Tenma could only see dim slices of the gravel and tar roof, but Inti's hand darted in and out of view, creating a pattern on the ground.

A sigil? Had Inti warded his hiding place? Or marked it somehow? Since when did their class clown know sigilcraft?

Further speculation was soon driven from Tenma's mind. Their pursuer had caught up.

Tremors rippled through his muscles, brought on by tension and by the cold. The monster was close enough, he was catching moods—gleeful, vindictive, triumphant. But he didn't want to be noticed, so he tamped down on the urge to explore further. Tenma wouldn't disremember this raw, reveling soul anytime soon.

A moment later, the predatory presence veered away, chasing after Inti. And instead of being afraid for himself, Tenma was wretchedly frightened for his friend. Was the crosser cunning enough to stay ahead of something older and wilier?

The panic vanished, which made sense. Without any Amaranthine in the vicinity, fear lost its hold over him. He slumped sideways in the chill space, queasy in the aftermath of all that adrenalin.

For a long while, nothing else happened. But then a howl bit through the darkness, jolting Tenma's heart back into overdrive. A second howl came, closer this time. Every hair seemed to stand on end, straining for any sign of a threat. Tenma went still, sure that something was coming for him.

Even though the reasonable part of Tenma's brain knew that Inti had promised to send help, its coming alarmed him. He was being hunted again. And he was trapped.

Something landed on his rooftop and came closer, snuffling. Padding steps, and a pair of large black paws appeared through the slats, their claws faintly scraping the roof's pebbled surface. A low whine sent ice down Tenma's spine.

It was stupid to be afraid. But he had to bite his lip to keep from sobbing.

A voice came, speaking in a foreign language. English. Then what he recognized as a muttered oath before he could understand. "Sorry, Subaru-kun. In Japanese this time. You okay?"

Familiarity did nothing to stave off the fear.

"Tenma Subaru?" The person outside crouched as if kowtowing in apology, keen eyes peering up through the metal slats. "Aw, man. He's so scared. Can you reach Hanoo?"

The howl poured through his heart like ice water, and he shivered.

"I'm opening the hatch, Tenma. Hang on, man. Nice and easy." He'd reverted to muttering in English, but he moved slowly. Setting aside the flimsy barricade that had kept Tenma hidden, he made the sign for peace. "You know who I am, buddy?"

"Ploom," he whispered.

"Yeah, it's Ploom." He gestured to the big wolf looming behind him. "And this is one of our Kith. You remember Cove? You met him in class, the Nightspangle wolf partnered to Reaver Armstrong."

He was babbling, just keeping up a soothing monologue, and he'd assumed such a submissive posture, he was almost groveling. Tenma closed his eyes. Ploom was his classmate, his friend. Easily as nice as Quen. Why couldn't he accept the closeness he craved?

A low call, the sound of running feet, and another voice. "Subaru-kun?"

Hanoo had come.

"Did something happen?" Hanoo frowned. "Hey, now. Where's your seal, huh?"

"Sorry," Tenma mumbled. "Lost it. Sorry, sorry, sorry."

"Nothing to apologize for." Hanoo sat on the ground, elbows on knees, hands hidden from view. "Bad news is … none of us knows beans about sigilcraft, so we can't give you any relief."

Tenma nodded.

Hanoo raked a hand through his hair. "Where is Quen in all this?"

Ploom said, "The entire Starmark pack is at circle tonight."

"Got it. Okay, then. Guess we're it." Hanoo said, "I know this isn't going to appeal, but the best way to get little reavers over their fear of us has always been touch. May I touch you, Tenma-kun?"

Anything, as long as it worked. Tenma struggled to move his numb limbs and scooted awkwardly forward, to be met partway. Hanoo lifted and pulled, and Tenma collapsed into the young wolf, who'd traded his usual school clothes for a fur vest. By this point,

Tenma was half-frozen, and some basic part of his nature had given up the fight. Limp and unresisting, he waited for Hanoo to put him out of his misery—one way or another.

"You're all jitters and jumps. Give your instincts time to catch up." Hanoo tucked Tenma under his chin and rubbed circles against his back. "Keep telling yourself I'm a friend. You're safe now."

Safe. Tenma withdrew into himself, trying not to think about anything beyond his next heartbeat. Little by little, Hanoo's presence took shape in his mind, heavy as a quilt, thick with comfort, a hushing darkness that rumbled like distant thunder.

"Did something happen?" Hanoo asked softly.   ◊

"Lost my sigil."   ✦

A hand stroked his hair, touched his back, and Tenma could tell it was Ploom, shining green-gold and shifting like sunlight through spring leaves. Tenma was sorry to have worried such a gentle, happy person.

Hanoo said, "Something else, though. We've been patrolling these streets since dusk, and none of us has seen anything. We were closest, so we got here first. More are on their way. Only I can't understand what you're doing, stranded on a roof, quaking like a slope full of aspens."

Was he serious? "We were chased. Me and Inti. He went for help."

"You smell anything?" asked Hanoo.

Ploom said, "Tenma always smells like Inti. Who was chasing you, Tenma-kun?"

"Something ... someone ... umm. Not a wolf." He was trying to sort out what he meant. Now that he was paying attention, he

✦

364

recognized an underlying similarity between Hanoo and Ploom. He noticed it because he was relying heavily on their resemblance to Quen. "Not a wolf or a dog. Not a bear or a horse. Nothing like our classmates."

"You can tell?" asked Hanoo.

"A little."

Ploom murmured, "Yoota's coming. He brought help."

"Surely, this is a false alarm."

The lilting voice had a peevish quality that sliced through Tenma's fears. He knew this person, trusted him, *wanted* him.

"The victims are always female. This one's clearly male."

The approaching steps faltered, and there was a harsh trill of displeasure. An instant later, Tenma smelled perfume, and rings sparkled on the hand that caught his chin. He couldn't help its quivering.

"Hello, sealed boy," crooned Lord Mossberne. "Or *un*sealed, it would seem."

"You know each other?" asked Hanoo.

"*Intimately.*" Lapis unfastened one of his earrings, whispered something to the stone, and pressed it into Tenma's palm. "There, now. Tell me you are impressed."

Oh, he was. He managed a noise. It wasn't a very dignified noise.

"Well, then." The dragon lord snatched him from Hanoo's grasp and assessed their surroundings with obvious distaste. "I do not care for the way the wind is blowing. Is there someplace *warmer* we can have this conversation?"

47

SHAMBLES

Kimiko took the time to greet each of the guests to Kikusawa Shrine, which is how she noticed Lord Mossberne's absence. "Are we missing a dragon?" she whispered to Hisoka.

His step checked. "Ah. Lapis volunteered to stand watch. He's perched on one of your stone dragons at the lower gate."

"Odd."

"Apt," countered the cat, his gaze taking in those gathered.

"Have you seen Suuzu?"

"Yes." Hisoka made an unobtrusive hand sign—*stay where you are*. "He and Akira have excellent seats for the proceedings. Which you may begin as soon as your representatives take their places."

Eloquence must have heard because he gathered up a sleepy Ever and invited her father to take his seat. An ornate bench flanked by heaters had been placed near Kusunoki's base. Ever squirmed happily on his cushion, then clambered onto Mr. Miyabe's lap. Eloquence tucked them both under one of the fur blankets provided by his pack, then moved into position.

Their place had been marked, and Kimiko had to wonder who was responsible for the red chrysanthemum newly painted onto the ancient paver at their feet.

She peered around, and conversations fell off. The balance between humans and Amaranthine was equal, thanks in part to the inclusion of Isla and her father. Dickon presided over the Miyabe women with the air of a bodyguard. Mama was beaming and dabbing at her eyes. Eloquence's brothers looked on with matching expressions of pride. Uncle Laud hang back from the rest, leaning against Rise's glossy bulk.

Kimiko's part didn't require anything drastic. In truth, she could have offered a few sentences, kissed the boy, and been done in under a minute. But this first pledge was for show, so she'd worked out a few things to say in order to prolong the moment.

Taking a slow, deep breath, she gazed up into the tangle of branches overhead. In this place, over the course of twelve kisses, her life would be changed. By chance and by choice. And by the one she needed to chase.

"Ready?" she whispered.

"As my lady pleases," he murmured, assuming a receptive pose.

She'd been fine throughout the evening, sticking to Suuzu's careful schedule. It was easy to be poised with him and Hisoka in charge of extraneous details. Their calm was catching. But she hadn't really thought about the fact that she'd need to look Eloquence in the eye while she said her piece.

He actually seemed flustered.

"Kith commentary?" she murmured.

Eloquence gave a tiny nod.

"Tell me later?"

"Ask me eleven pledges from tonight."

She reached for his hands and supported them. "Is that a promise?"

He was focused on her now, tuning out the other voices in favor of her flirting. And a smile teased at the corner of his mouth. He hummed an affirmative.

Aware that their onlookers were waiting, Kimiko adjusted her stance and changed the set of her hands over his. Without really meaning to, she reached for the connection they'd shared yesterday. Just a touch, but he reached back, a fleeting nudge that assured her that on some level, this was a private moment. Theirs alone.

Firelight glinted in his eyes, and Kimiko allowed a small, smug part of herself to admire his beauty.

Eloquence's eyes widened somewhat, then quickly lowered.

Kimiko began to speak. "In the Amaranthine folk tale known as 'The Wolf and the Moon Maiden,' a single encounter reshapes the hero's future. He never planned to meet the beauty who steals his heart. And he's equally awed that she would welcome his suit."

With a glance, she addressed herself to Harmonious and Anna. "Naturally, the moon is protective of her daughter and will not immediately entrust her to the wolf. She sets a series of tasks, requiring pledges and patience from the suitor. Beneath the branches of the tree where they met, he completes his courtship through a series of kisses, for in wolf tradition, a kiss cannot lie."

Murmurs of interest and approval made it feel as if she were in a dialogue with their guests.

Kimiko returned her attention to her intended. "Eloquence is no more a maiden than I am a hero, but I chose this story for the elements that hold true. Our encounter was unexpected, yet I've been warmly welcomed. I am pleased by his kindness and calmed by his strength. Eloquence has my trust. Here, I will prove my devotion, beneath the branches of the tree that … watched over … my childhood."

She trailed off, for the crowd was stirring, distracted.

Eloquence's head turned. Kimiko shaped her fingers into a plea for information, which he answered with a similar hand signal—*hold*.

"Someone is at the gate," he said. "And they are very loud."

"I don't hear anything."

Eloquence answered distractedly. "The barrier has noise dampening properties. I had not realized … the city is full of noise. Elderbough's trackers are on a scent."

Kimiko watched his gaze turn fully inward, and she assumed he was listening to the distant voices of Kith. Off to one side, Rise had begun to growl. Eloquence's face suddenly shifted into alarm, just as a lone figure dashed into the courtyard.

Even at speed, she recognized him. "Inti?"

The crosser hurled himself at Hisoka, who caught him without a fuss and strolled over to Harmonious. Eloquence's brothers joined them, and soon, Inti was standing on Hisoka's shoulders, gesturing broadly while he talked.

"What's happened?" asked Kimiko.

Eloquence said, "I'm not sure, but Tenma needs me."

Two trackers—Elderboughs by their coloring—hurried over to Adoona-soh, whose face betrayed nothing of her thoughts.

Kimiko whispered, "Do you need to go?"

He didn't budge. "My place is usually with Merit. My eldest brother and I help to coordinate the movements of our pack as they patrol the city. This is especially important when they are tracking something."

"So you need to go," she surmised, loosening her hold.

Eloquence firmly declared, "I will not rebuff my suitor on the very night of our betrothal."

"But it's an emergency."

"Then kiss me quick, Kimiko."

Formalities. Her pledge wouldn't be complete without the requisite kiss, and if he left without one, his clan could consider her spurned. Up on tiptoe, she brushed her lips quickly across his. Only when she tried to back away, he caught her wrists and pulled her back.

"I was in a hurry to begin the kiss, not to end it," he chided. "Besides, I don't think Ever was watching."

At the sound of his name, the little boy's ears pricked.

With both representatives looking on, Kimiko kissed Eloquence again, soft and slow.

He hummed against her mouth and even stole a tiny taste. Boots began stomping, coming from the direction of his brothers. And Rise broke into a howl that set off every other canine in the vicinity.

Pulling back, Eloquence whispered, "Do not make me wait too long for your next pledge."

"In a hurry?" she teased.

He stole a quick kiss, then hurried over to Merit, Prospect, and Valor, who welcomed him with much back-slapping and roughing up of hair.

Kimiko was about to go see if she could help Isla calm down Inti when she realized that Anna Starmark was striding her way, talking over her shoulder at Harmonious, whose whole posture was placating.

He was saying, "... to the boys and me. There's no need for you to ...."

"Is it *that* dragon?" Anna asked sharply.

"Not specifically, my love." Harmonious offered a slow, reluctant nod. "But he is of the same bloodline."

Her lips thinned and she moved past Kimiko to stand before Mr. Miyabe, who still sat with Ever on his lap. She said, "If you would be so kind as to watch over my son while I take care of an unfortunate matter, I would be grateful."

"*Anna*," groaned Harmonious.

"I am a Starmark. I will protect my pack and the city we call home."

"As is your right," he reluctantly acknowledged.

Spinning to face Kimiko, Anna asked, "May I enter your treasury?"

It was really more of a command than a request, but it baffled Kimiko. The question must have shown on her face, for Anna Starmark wasted no time in answering.

"I must reclaim my sword."

48

POCKET ENCLAVE

Tenma attempted a protest. "I can walk."

"You cannot." Lapis addressed the three Nightspangle wolves. "Have you been granted a secure den somewhere?"

"Yessir," said Hanoo.

"Lead on," the dragon implored, with a sharp chirrup for emphasis.

Yoota and Ploom ran ahead in lanky tandem, making for New Saga's campus. They bypassed the dormitory, circling around to one of the class building's back doors. Either it wasn't locked, or they had a key. Then again, from what Tenma had learned, any number of wards or barriers could be involved.

Tenma couldn't see much in the darkened halls, but the Amaranthine carried him along passages and up three flights of stairs before stopping at a blank stretch of wall. When Hanoo pressed his hand to it, a sigil appeared, and part of the wall vanished.

Pushing aside a heavy drape, he gravely said, "The Nightspangle pack welcomes its friends."

"You have your own room in the school building?" Tenma asked.

"Den," Hanoo corrected. "And yes. We're far from home, as are many of the clans who've agreed to help with Twineshaft's venture. Clans who sent five or more representatives were guaranteed a safe space to retreat."

Yoota said, "Hisoka-sensei calls them pocket enclaves."

"Come and see," urged Ploom, who eased Tenma out of his shoes.

Hanoo lit a lantern, filling the air with the scent of struck matches and burnt wood. A brave candle glowed behind amber glass, revealing a space about the size of a club room. When Lapis set him down, Tenma sank into the coarse rug, which was either incredibly thick or spread over heavy matting. It was like a wall-to-wall futon. "This is nice," he mumbled, dropping to his knees. "What *is* this?"

"Fur," said Yoota.

"Nightspangle fur," Hanoo added proudly.

That was hard to process. "Like ... pelts?" Tenma asked warily.

"We use shed fur," said Ploom. "Before we left, our families had a good long brushing, and our weavers used everything that was collected. That's why this room smells like home."

Hanoo added, "It makes it easier to be so far away for so long."

Tenma absently petted the carpet, glad to know no Kith or Kindred had died in its making. "I didn't think a year would seem long to you guys."

"We committed for the first decade." Hanoo grinned. "Hisoka-sensei has us repeating your grade ten times over."

The grin reminded Tenma of little things like fangs, and he

gripped the crystal in his hand a little tighter. Whatever Lapis had ordered it to do, it had worked. No qualms. No quakes. His classmates no longer scared him silly. He said, "A minimum of five clan members. I didn't realize there were other Nightspangles here."

Yoota said, "My younger sister is with the first years, and an aunt is a teaching assistant. She also helps out in the Kith shelter, since we brought eight of our wolves over."

"It's better for them here," said Ploom. "What with the confusion back home."

Hanoo rolled his eyes. "Werewolf scares, if you can believe it."

Tenma couldn't. "Sounds like the sort of thing Sosuke and his Cryptid Club would be interested in."

Lapis cut in. "Are you calmer, unsealed boy?"

"Yes. Sorry. Yes."

The dragon lord held out his hand. "Excellent. Give back my bauble."

Tenma curled protectively around the stone. "But I need it."

"More than you need us?" Lapis arched his brows. "You require taming, so I am throwing you to the wolves. They clearly understand the process."

Hanoo said, "We do. It was our job back home. Although it's been a few years since we had to deal with a strong aversion."

"Not since Jiminy." Yoota rolled his eyes. "What a handful he was."

Ploom knelt before Tenma, putting them closer to the same level. "Little ones can't understand why they're scared, but you do. And you trust us, right?"

"Taming." He still wasn't ready to let go of Lapis' earring. "You mean I'd be cured? No more panic attacks?"

"It's why young reavers are exposed to Amaranthine early." Ploom eased a little closer, his voice coaxing. "So they can master their instincts and get a shutter on their shine."

"Sort of like potty training," Yoota offered.

Tenma laughed nervously. "I'm already housebroken."

Lapis held out an imperious hand. "*I* am the only Broken here. If it puts your mind at ease, unsealed boy, I will monitor your progress."

"Join us," offered Hanoo.

A dismissive trill. "Focus on this one. He is more rare than you realize."

And Tenma found himself the focus of three wolves. With what scraps of dignity remained, he sucked in a final breath and surrendered his stone to Lapis. Just as quickly, the three wolves leapt into sharp focus, his senses registering the threat they presented to him—body and soul.

They held very still.

He gulped for air.

Softly, gently, Hanoo said, "You did good to trust us, Tenma. You still okay with my touching you?"

This was so much easier when the starting line wasn't a state of blind panic. Tenma's hands weren't even shaking when he met Hanoo's waiting palms. But he didn't quite trust his voice.

"Let's get you settled. You must be tired." Hanoo took his coat.

Yoota pressed a warm washcloth to his cheek. "Need the restroom?"

"R-really?" Tenma's gaze roved the room, found the door.

"All the conveniences of a modern den," said Ploom. "We have a mini-fridge, too. Nice, huh?"

"It is," he managed.

When he returned from washing up, Yoota and Ploom had arranged blankets and cushions in the corner. Hanoo waved him over. "Settle in. It's the easiest way to stay in contact."

Tenma smiled weakly. "I slept over at Quen's once. Like this."

Tails began to wag. "Pack style?" asked Yoota.

"Yes. Lord Mossberne was there."

Lapis glanced up from studying his claws, which were tipped in blue. "Harmonious claimed the boy as pack. All very touching."

"Cool. This is like that." Hanoo indicated the heaped furs. "Kind of a relief to be welcomed, honestly. Not a fan of polite distances."

Tenma sank to his knees with a shaky laugh. "You and Inti both. Is he okay? Do you know?"

"He's good," Yoota promised, stretching out on his side. "He's at that shrine they put on lockdown last week. Safe behind a barrier."

Lapis touched an earlobe. "I gave him a tuned crystal to get him past that barrier. I hope he realizes it was a loan. That particular shade is rarer than beacons."

Tenma had barely stretched out when Hanoo muttered, "Closer's better. Come right on in. Use my shoulder."

"Make room for me." Ploom crowded into the scant space between Tenma and Yoota.

It probably should have been unsettling, but Tenma paid little attention to the jumble of bodies and limbs. This close, he was aware of them in less tangible ways.

"You're doing good." Hanoo removed Tenma's glasses, stroked his hair. "You probably won't be able to feel this, but bear with me for a while."

But Tenma *definitely* felt the gentle pressure, an unfamiliar intrusion that lit up his mind.

"Breathe," Hanoo ordered. "Relax and breathe. It's only me, and I won't hurt you."

"Doesn't hurt," he mumbled.

From behind, Ploom nuzzled Tenma's hair. "Gently, Hanoo. He's barely more than a glimmer."

"That's all I need." Hanoo pulled Tenma snug against his larger frame. "Work with me here."

Tenma hummed an affirmative.

Lapis' voice came sharply. "What are you boys messing with?"

"Best way we've found to settle a new denmate," said Yoota.

The dragon's voice came closer. "Who taught you?"

"Nobody," said Yoota. "We made it up. Ploom figured out how to do it, but Hanoo's best at it. Kids get their nestle on real quick when he's the one gentling them."

"You will *not* meddle without proper supervision." Lapis tossed aside furs, wading in. "This boy is mine."

"I thought you said Harmonious claimed him," Yoota dared to point out.

"I saw him first." Lapis pointed to the spot he intended to take. "Starmark made him an honorary packmate, which is fine in its way. Harmonious excels at fathering. That is not a role I have ever expected to play."

Hanoo gave way with grace. "You're welcome, of course, Lord Mossberne."

Lapis insinuated himself between Tenma and Hanoo, and after much grumbling and shifting, the dragon settled with his back

✦

against Hanoo's chest, his face hidden in the vicinity of Tenma's ribcage. Blue hair was absolutely everywhere.

"Never nestled with a dragon before," Ploom said, sounding awed.

With a low hum, Lapis remarked, "Shared body heat is blissful in winter."

"Why didn't you *say* you were cold," Hanoo exclaimed, chaffing solicitously at the dragon's shoulder.

Yoota pulled another thick blanket over them, burying them deeper in fur.

Lapis gave a happy little squirm, and Tenma grunted. "Your hands are cold."

"Hospitality to the Amaranthine is every reaver's duty and delight," he intoned.

"I'm not a reaver."

"You are not registered." And with the magnanimity of a benevolent conqueror, Lapis said, "Proceed, young Nightspangles. With *extreme* care."

378

49
RETURN OF THE SAINT

Kimiko led the way to a discreet side door in the largest of Kikusawa's storehouses, an ancient two-story stone building with a deep basement. Packed with the clutter of decades past, she and her sisters slyly referred to this as the shrine's closet. Never within her grandmother's hearing, though. To her, this was the Treasury.

A glance confirmed Kimiko's suspicion. Hisoka, Argent, Sinder, and Boonmar-fen had fallen into step behind the Starmarks, probably eager for a peek at the promised reliquaries. She hoped they wouldn't confiscate them. Grandmother would definitely consider that theft.

"Lady Starmark, I should check. We have quite a few weapons, so I don't want to assume." Kimiko lifted the bar that secured the door and paused on the threshold. "Is it the Chrysanthemum Blaze?"

"You know where it rests?"

Kimiko laughed. "In a place of honor. There is some debate as to whether the shrine is named for the blade or the blade for the shine. I had no idea it was yours."

Anna Starmark's tone was brisk, but she answered patiently. "The sword is much older than I, and this has been its hiding place for more than a millennia. Rumors of its existence brought me here, and it became mine by virtue of necessity. In defending myself, I defended this place and its people." With a pointed look at Harmonious, she amended, "*We* did."

"You're the hound in the legend?" Kimiko asked.

Harmonious grinned and bounced on the balls of his feet. Not an answer, but certainly confirmation.

For the first time in her life, Kimiko was grateful that her grandmother was so strict about year-end cleaning. Thanks to the annual banishment of dust and dishevelment from *every* corner of their shrine, the treasury still smelled faintly of soaps, oils, and waxes. Although the shelves were crowded, everything was in its proper place.

Stacks of lanterns. A festival float. Mask and drums. Cloth-wrapped bundles secured by knotted cords. Trunks with faded labels, some with sigils faintly gleaming. And scores of lacquered and inlaid boxes, each a work of art. These last were the building blocks of Kimiko's childhood, for she'd treated the Treasury as a playhouse since her earliest days.

Hisoka scanned the room. Kimiko had to wonder if he'd been here before. The cat seemed to know everything about everything, yet he gazed around with nothing more than polite interest. Was this a matter of feigned ignorance, or was he keeping the intensity of his curiosity under careful wraps?

She leaned toward the latter. Sinder had been so urgent to inform Hisoka about the presence of golden seeds at Kikusawa.

"Do you know what's in all of these?" asked Sinder.

"Oh, yes. I was *such* a snoop when I was little." Her grandmother and her father had passed down the stories of the most prominent treasures in their care. But she and Noriko had nosed through every box, memorizing the pretty patterns on each lid and handling the items inside. Later, when Sakiko showed the knack, it was decided that she would walk Grandmother's path. Sakiko could recite the history of every item, rattling off names, dates, and facts with impressive poise.

Kimiko supposed that made Sakiko the realist. Given Noriko's temperament, she was easily cast as the romantic. But where did that leave Kimiko?

"There," said Anna Starmark, pointing to the cabinet that dominated the far wall. "The blade is there."

"Yes." Aware of their close scrutiny, Kimiko took extra care, shielding their view with her body. The deep cabinet was as intricate as a puzzle box, with clever catches and hidden panels hiding its contents. A casual perusal would uncover a wealth in painted scrolls, jade carvings, and precious artifacts. But treasures of the In-between were more closely kept.

"That cupboard is embedded with sigils, then overlaid again," remarked Sinder.

"Amaranthine workmanship?" asked Boon.

"Silverprong craftsmanship," said Kimiko, adding gentle pressure to a carved chrysanthemum as she lifted the catch. Members of the deer clan were responsible for several of their most beautiful cupboards and screens. And the carved wooden panels over their doorways, which were *such* a hassle to dust and oil.

When she opened the double doors, Boon grunted.

Hisoka sidled closer. "How unusual."

Understatement. Red crystals created a lavish floral pattern on the naked blade resting in its holder. While beautiful, the gleaming stones made the blade quite heavy for its size. The edge was certainly keen, but a sword so heavy wouldn't be practical in battle. An Amaranthine could have lifted it, but the weapon was reinforced with a dazzling array of sigils to fend them off. Their mysterious sword was intended for reavers' use.

"Are you kidding me?" Sinder was backing away. "That thing actually exists?"

"It's been hidden here for quite some time." Harmonious moved to the dragon's side. "Kept in reserve for emergencies."

"The Chrysanthemum Blaze is our most valuable and most enigmatic treasure. Our records offer little more than the name and an order to keep its presence here a secret." Kimiko gestured for Anna to reclaim the blade. "We're only supposed to yield it to someone who already knows it's here."

Anna hefted the sword. "Until today, Harmonious and I may have been the only ones to know."

Kimiko really wanted more information. "My grandfather speculated that the craftsmanship is Amaranthine, but the blade somehow fell into reavers' hands."

"You could say that." Sinder was actually hiding behind Harmonious now. "That thing's one of the Junzi."

While Kimiko's mind leapt immediately to her favorite brand of chocolate, she guessed he was making reference to classical art.

"Are you saying this sword is part of Amaranthine lore?"

"It's certainly part of *dragon* lore," said Sinder. "Every hatchling knows about the danger represented by the Junzi. They're the stuff of nightmares."

"The Four Gentlemen—chrysanthemum, plum, orchid, and bamboo," said Hisoka. "They have long represented the seasons."

"How well-mannered and tame." Sinder remained on edge. "*We* call them the Four Storms."

Kimiko had assumed the sword must be ornamental, a work of art in the form of a weapon. She liked to think it might have been used as an anchor for a vast barrier or illusion. But thanks to Michael's recent lessons in crystals as amplifiers of sigilcraft, she knew that wasn't possible. Crystals of this color were a lure, useful in the construction of traps. She was almost afraid to ask. "I don't know much dragon lore. What's this sword meant to do?"

The dragon closed his mouth and shook his head.

Anna answered for him. "In a reaver's hands, the Chrysanthemum Blaze has two uses. The first is to trap dragons."

Tension rippled around the room, and Kimiko tried to break it. "That's oddly specific."

"Aptly specific," murmured Hisoka.

Boonmar-fen eyed the blade with interest. "Funnel a beacon's blaze through that much red crystal, and she'll out-ply any dragon."

"Only if they're fool enough to stay within range," said Harmonious. "Last time we used the Blaze, the dragons fled, and Keishi was spared any further destruction."

Hisoka hummed. "You mentioned *two* uses, Lady Starmark?"

"Yes." She angled the sword with a practiced air, studying

its edge. "A terrible one."

"Oh, just *say* it, already! That weapon was designed to slay dragons." Sinder's fluting trill had a hysterical edge. "She's holding an executioner's blade."

Boonmar-fen grabbed the dragon's arm and said, "How about you *not* be in the room when she drops her wards."

Sinder made a choking sound. "No offense, Anna."

She inclined her head. "You have a quarter of an hour. Get as far as you can."

His companion's tail puffed. "Won't a barrier suffice?"

With a grim shake of his head, Harmonious said, "Not against a beacon."

"Ah. In that case ...." Hisoka held up a finger and backed toward the door. "I'll just verify Lapis' location. Argent, you should see to Kyrie."

Argent looked vaguely insulted. "Gingko is already moving him."

The Starmarks followed them out the door, leaving Kimiko to close up.

Alone again, she delayed long enough to trail her fingers along the smooth surface of one of four tall bottles on a recessed shelf, half-hidden behind the empty sword bracket. She touched the first with a twinge of regret. She'd smuggled it out to Kusunoki when she was much younger, breaking the seal to release its captive, sure that it held the Amaranthine equivalent of a genie.

Kimiko had been disappointed when no magical being appeared. Even the fleeting gust of wind that rustled Kusunoki's leaves was probably a product of her fable-steeped imagination. But she'd never told anyone what she'd done.

Grandfather would have been disappointed in her.

Grandmother would consider it a betrayal of trust. Which it was. Which was probably why she was so protective of the remaining three bottles. She touched them each in turn—north, east, and west.

Maybe one day, she'd show them to Eloquence. One of their shrine's little novelties. "It's not as if anyone could *actually* seal away the wind."

Kimiko returned to the courtyard, thinking to catch up to Anna Starmark. The woman held out her wrists to Harmonious, who kissed her palms, then set about releasing the clasps on her bracelets. His expression made Kimiko hung back.

At her side, Argent Mettlebright casually remarked, "I have them inside a barrier, but you may pass through."

She jumped, for she hadn't noticed him there. "I don't want to intrude."

"A daughter is always welcome."

"I'm not a daughter yet."

"*Tsk.* I have seen that same look on young Eloquence's face." He indicated Harmonious. "Others will notice, and many will say it—like father, like son."

"A fine compliment." She smiled slyly at the aloof fox. "Even if it does betray a certain lack of imagination."

A smile curled Argent's lips. "You will do well."

Kimiko dared to correct him. "I could not do better."

Harmonious pocketed his bondmate's bracelets, then knelt on the paving stones. Anna lifted the heavy fabric of her formal silks, revealing standard breeches underneath and low slippers that allowed for the heavy bracelets around her ankles.

More wards.

"How strong *is* she?" Kimiko whispered.

"As it happens, I have some small experience when it comes to the shuttering of beacons." Argent's eyebrows lifted. "While it would be ungentlemanly to compare, I cannot deny my curiosity. This is the first time I will see Lady Anna unfettered."

The last of Anna Starmark's personal wards came away, and Harmonious stood to his full height, heavy-lidded and swaying. Kimiko was certain that his bondmate was the only thing he could see.

"What does she look like to you?"

Argent tipped his head to one side, then answered, "Fury."

Anna certainly didn't look angry to Kimiko. Only poised, very likely for battle. She asked, "Does she compare to your lady?"

"Who can say? There are advantages on either side." His gaze softened slightly. "Both are suited to their place and happy in it."

"I can hope for that much, at least."

"You cannot compare with our beacons." With a subtle flick of his fingers, he robbed his words of their sting. "Rather, you will surpass them."

She dismissed his suggestion.

Argent studied her face and simply repeated, "You will do well."

Kimiko looked back in time to see Harmonious shift into his truest form. The dog bore a striking resemblance to Rise, although he had upright ears, like a wolf's. Harmonious towered above every tree except Kusunoki. Nosing around in its branches, he barked playfully, tail wagging.

Suuzu dropped into view, gliding toward Kimiko with Akira in his arms. Both boys looked sheepish at being flushed out. On closer inspection, she thought Suuzu had been crying. As soon as he'd set down his best friend, she hurried to her go-between and hugged him tightly. "Stay over," she urged. "You guys can wait in my room if you like."

"Akira and I gladly accept." Suuzu's gaze flitted to the storehouse behind her, then slid guiltily aside. In subdued tones, he said, "Thank you for your hospitality."

"And *congratulations*," interjected Akira. "You were so pro! You know, with Sis and Mrs. Anna always hiding away, you could totally become the Five's spokeswife."

She shook her head, more interested in Harmonious, who'd eased down, belly to the ground. In theory, he was humbling himself, but Kimiko could read only pride and pleasure in his manner. He'd lowered himself so his bondmate could more easily scale his bulk. Anna Starmark secured her blade in a twist of copper sashes and climbed with surprising ease to a seat upon his back. Not until Harmonious leapt into the night sky did Argent's hold slip.

Barrier gone, power reverberated, and everywhere around the shrine, the Starmark pack bayed their approval. Their leader and his mate had joined the hunt. High overhead, Harmonious bounded in ever-widening circles. Upon her colossal steed, the battler took up her former role, pale hair streaming. Keishi's saint had returned, and the stars seemed to change course in order to follow her.

"What are those sparks?" asked Kimiko.

"Hey, yeah," said Akira. "Can you see them, Suuzu?"

"They are Ephemera." Suuzu quietly explained, "A rare variety that develops a symbiotic relationship with certain trees. They must have been hibernating inside, but the presence of so many potent souls brought them out."

"Lady Anna's blade is an effective lure," said Argent. "She is like springtime to them."

Suuzu touched Kimiko's shoulder. "If they remain active, I would not be surprised if your friend bloomed this year."

"How fortunate we sealed your boundaries." Argent darted upward and returned with a small creature caged between his fingers. It looked like a winged monkey, no bigger than a sparrow, with pale fur glowing softly in the darkness. Round eyes blinked drowsily at them as it clung to Argent's fingers. He said, "I should bring one home to show Tsumiko."

Akira rolled his eyes. "Like you don't want it for your collection." To Kimiko, he added, "Argent's a repeat offender when it comes to smuggling Ephemera across borders."

Suuzu scanned the lights darting through Kusunoki's branches. "Cull three pairs, and you could easily establish a colony. They make excellent pollinators and good pets, so long as they have ready access to a reaver of sufficient prowess."

"Which would explain why we've never seen them before," Kimiko said wryly. "Not for three hundred years."

Argent tutted. "I am certain you can secure a reaver of 'sufficient prowess.'"

"What level are we talking?" she asked, thinking he might mean Isla.

"Ideally, seventeenth."

Kimiko nodded sagely. "Then our future is both bright and brightening."

The fox eyed her with what could only be called respect. "I believe I shall second Akira's nomination."

She drew a blank. "I've been nominated for something?"

He hummed a coy affirmative. "Spokeswife."

50

GLIMMER

Hanoo said, "Let's try this again."

Tenma had all but forgotten his fear. Either this whole taming thing worked fast, or Lapis was acting as some kind of counteragent. A wave of calm settled around him, and he could tell Hanoo was the source. Cocky. Carefree. Then came a gentle shower of golden happiness. Tenma smiled and reached for Ploom's hand, which rested on his shoulder.

Ploom had gotten closer, but not physically. Tenma could discern him as an individual—steady, loyal, and loving. He treasured his parents, his packmates, but especially Yoota. It was as if he and Ploom were two parts of the same person.

What had it been like for these wolves, leaving behind their packmates and crossing an ocean, only to be divided further? Had it been hard for Ploom and Yoota to be in different triads? Such courage.

Tenma's gratitude welled up, and Ploom uttered a low sound. Then he really *did* get closer.

"You guys ever meet Ever?" Tenma asked.

"Quen's kid brother? Nope," said Hanoo. "Haven't had the privilege."

"Fair warning. He likes to 'sniffen' people."

"Same." Ploom sighed contentedly against the nape of Tenma's neck.

He was curious what his classmate was looking for. "Can you smell fear?"

"Not at the moment," said Ploom, whose mood set off another golden cascade. "You're doing great."

Could wolves catch the scent of a soul in the same way he could detect colors and feelings? If so, he hoped these wolves found his presence pleasant.

Fear had faded, and weariness dragged at his senses. Tenma felt safe and warm and liked. Maybe even a little bit needed. A small, insignificant part ... but still a part. Turning his thoughts further inward, the next time Tenma felt Ploom's surge of happiness, he responded with gratitude and affection.

Ploom made another soft noise.

Surprise?

Tenma could tell he'd startled his friend, and he could feel an accompanying uncertainty. Not wanting to worry him, Tenma searched for a better way to express himself to the kindhearted wolf. But his thoughts were drifting now.

Fingers drummed on his chest. Lapis inquired, "What was that, unsealed boy?"

Tenma stirred enough to mumble, "What?"

"Are you conscious of what you just did?"

"Sorry, I was mostly asleep."

The dragon asked, "May I?"

"Huh?"

"My turn, little glimmer," said Lapis. "I want you to show me what you showed Ploom."

Tenma asked, "Is that safe?"

"Are you threatening me?"

He fumbled until he located one of the heavy stone bracelets around the dragon's wrist. I thought these were to keep reavers at a safe distance."

Lapis' low trill carried a note of impatience. "You are not a reaver."

"I'm not registered," he said, not sure how he'd ended up on the other side of their earlier argument. "More importantly, I don't want to hurt you."

"Then I have nothing to fear."

The three wolves had a rushed exchange in English before Hanoo spoke carefully. "Frankly, Tenma, Lord Mossberne is more a danger to you than you are to him. I'm not sure what would happen if your little bit of shine got snuffed."

Lapis frowned. "I cannot deny my former excesses, but I have never harmed a soul."

Tenma tentatively asked, "What does it mean to be Broken?"

"He's an addict," said Yoota.

Ploom's voice held sympathy. "Were you mishandled?"

The dragon's low chuckle had frayed edges. "Nobody likes a

sad story. Better to delve into the mystery in our midst. What do you say, unsealed boy? Can you trust a tattered and tainted soul like mine?"

"Sure. As long as it can't hurt you."

Lapis said, "Our trust is mutual, as is consent. Now, show me what you showed Ploom."

Tenma nodded even though he had no idea what he was doing. He wasn't even sure he'd actually *done* anything. But maybe if he began the same way he had with Ploom, Lapis would gain some clue to the source of his ... glimmer.

So he closed his eyes and turned his attention inward, searching for the brittle blue that defined the dragon. Lapis held very still, but that wasn't right. Ploom had reached for him, found his hand, welcomed their connection. "Mutual trust," Tenma mumbled.

Lapis didn't move.

"Lord Mossberne. *Lapis*." Tenma wasn't sure how else to ask. "Are you afraid of me?"

"Preposterous." But the dragon curled in more tightly on himself. "I am afraid that you will prove me wrong."

Tenma had no idea what he meant. "What happens if you're right?"

"A miracle."

"I don't understand what you expect from me," he said, touching the dragon's shoulder, then tugging him closer. "But I'll try."

Lapis found his hand, threaded their fingers together, and took a more optimistic tone. "I am often right."

Tenma laughed. Back on the roof, he'd wanted Lapis more than Hanoo, but he hadn't been in any fit state to wonder why. Now, he weighed that impulse. Was it instinct? Had some mysterious part of his soul decided that he needed more than a dog and a monkey in his life? Cracking a smile, he asked, "Are there pheasant clans?"

Hanoo said, "Sure there are. Why?"

"Never mind." Tenma redirected his wandering thoughts. Lapis had been friendly, interested, curious ... but remote. Harmonious was the one who'd confronted Tenma's loneliness and banished it. Hadn't the leader of the Starmark pack done the same for Lapis?

Well, he had *tried*, but it must not have been enough.

So what did Lapis need?

And in a moment of mind-boggling clarity, Tenma's perspective flipped. He really had no business thinking so highly of himself, but he was sure he was right. He was drawn to Lapis because the dragon needed him. Desperately.

So while Yoota made comforting noises and Ploom murmured encouragement, Tenma reached for Lapis in intangible ways and was met partway. This was trust, and he tried to reciprocate. Not in words, but in impressions. Like adopting a helpful posture or extending an upraised palm.

Lapis made an odd little hiccupping sound.

Hanoo threw an arm around both of them, humming deep in his chest.

And Tenma found little ways to keep Lapis close. Awash in blue, he did his best to warm what was cold, to soften what was brittle, to mend each fracture and tear. The dragon's soul whispered to him of regret and respect. Here was devotion and damage, hesitation and hope. Tenma found the shreds and gave them shape, soothing away the sorrows and bolstering what was brave.

The dragon exhaled on a fluttering note that breezed straight through Tenma, like breath across embers, kindling fresh flames.

"Is he taming him?" asked Yoota.

"Who's taming whom?" whispered Ploom. "I can't tell."

Hanoo cautiously asked, "Is that taming or *tending*? Because I think they're both gaining."

Yoota ventured, "Does it matter? Seems to be doing them both some good."

"Of course it matters," said Ploom, whose happiness shone in Tenma's periphery. "Now hush. I don't want to miss the miracle."

Tenma jolted awake with a yelp of fear.

"Shh, shh, shh," soothed Hanoo. "It's just us, remember?"

But Tenma's alarm was ramping up.

Low voices came from the direction of the door. " … personal wards must have spared you. A mercy. She is not one for delicacy."

"How did that Icelandic waif fare?"

"Ask him yourself. Harmonious wants everyone back at the compound."

Tenma twisted around to see who had come. Lapis and Yoota stood at the door, talking to a newcomer. Recognition made him feel foolish. Lord Mettlebright, one of the Five, was gazing at him with so much skepticism, Tenma lowered his gaze.

"Bad dream?" asked the fox in patronizing tones.

Hanoo took up his defense. "You spooked him. Ease up."

"Fox," said Tenma, swallowing hard. "I haven't been close to a fox before now. Not to know it, anyway."

Argent Mettlebright held up a finger to forestall whatever Lapis was about to say. Moving to the edge of the heap of furs, he crouched. "Subaru-kun, why are you afraid of foxes?"

"Because one tried to kill us tonight. Or was it last night?" He couldn't tell how long he'd been asleep. "Inti and I barely escaped."

"Really? Because nobody else has been able to confirm the presence of a pursuer—no scent, no sound, no trail to follow."

Argent's casual tone didn't match the outrage Tenma was picking up on.

"Most are dismissing the whole story as a foolish monkey's prank."

"It was real," Tenma insisted. "It happened."

Argent shook his head. "You enrolled at New Saga from the human community. How would you know?"

"I can tell."

"You claim to be an unregistered reaver?"

"Not exactly. Well, maybe. I don't know!"

"Even if I were to acknowledge that unregistered reavers might be at risk, you do not fit the profile of the kidnapper's usual prey."

Tenma sat up a little straighter, wanting to be taken seriously "The fox wasn't after me. She wanted Inti."

In the sudden silence, Argent's voice was dangerously soft. "*She*?"

51
A TRUE SON

T he following morning, Michael Ward arrived at the Miyabe's front door in time for breakfast. Kimiko assumed—quite naturally—that he'd come in order to spend time with his daughter before a return trip to Stately House. But a secondary purpose presented itself mere minutes later, when someone else knocked at the front door.

"Amaranthine," said Michael.

"Dove clan," chimed in Isla.

Michael innocently remarked, "Small world! Our usual herald is also a dove."

A significant look passed between Mama and Grandma, and Sakiko flew to answer. That's when a knowing smile flitted across Michael's face. Noticing Kimiko's gaze, he favored her with a wink and a single hand sign—*wait*.

"One came!" Kimiko's younger sister returned, cheeks flushed, waving a thick packet with an official seal.

Daddy went to her, but only to retrieve the reaver communique under her arm. His bland smile gave Kimiko the distinct impression that he *also* knew what was coming.

Mama bustled forward, wringing her apron. "A contract? Is it a contract for Noriko?"

"We were promised one." Grandma's calm was *almost* convincing. "Well, then? Is the offer worth the paper it's written on?"

Kimiko poked Suuzu's leg under the table.

His eyebrows lifted, and he pleaded ignorance.

Akira leaned across him to whisper, "Kinda like requesting a marriage meeting."

She nodded.

Meanwhile, Mama had seized the envelope and broken its seal. Even from across the table, Kimiko could see the difference between this set of papers and those they'd received up until now. Handmade paper. Elegant brushwork. Multiple crests.

"What does this mean?" Mama exclaimed, confusion snarling her brows. "This part here. Son of a what, now? Is it a foreigner?"

"Let me see, Mama," Sakiko wheedled.

Kimiko was impressed that Noriko showed no particular interest in the contract. She walked right past the others to fetch the rest of the breakfast things from the kitchen. Kimiko left the table to help serve their guests, eavesdropping the whole while.

"Where is the six-digit number?" Mama asked peevishly. "Is this the wrong form? How are we to know if his numbers are good?"

Kimiko blushed and glanced sheepishly in Michael's direction. That they usually entertained six-digit offers betrayed the depths to which they'd sunk.

But his gaze spoke only kindness, and his tone was a study in casual interest. "Has a contract arrived for Noriko? How felicitous!"

Reminded of their audience, Grandmother waved an impatient hand. "Give it to me, Kikuko. How many of these have we received, and still you cannot make sense of them? I will tell you if this boy has a chance with our Noriko."

Grumbling the whole while, she perched a pair of reading glasses on the end of her nose and scanned the initial page. And stopped. And began again from the top.

"Well?" Mama demanded. "Is he any good?"

The old woman set aside the papers and her glasses and stood, then moved down to Kimiko's place at the table.

"Grandma?" she asked.

A soft, wrinkled hand cupped her cheek for several moments, her eyes shining. Then the old woman moved along to Noriko and kissed her forehead. Without a single word, she left the room.

Michael took charge. "Perhaps I can be of assistance? I have daughters, you know. I'm familiar with the whole process."

No one protested, and the man declared, "Miss Noriko has indeed received a fine offer. The supplicant is a son of Waaseyaa."

Suuzu asked, "True son or descendent?"

"True son." For the benefit of the rest, Michael explained, "By old reaver custom, it's permissible to claim sonship for up to three generations. However, this man is a true son. Waaseyaa is his biological father."

Mama asked, "Who is this man with the unpronounceable name? You speak as if he's famous, but I've never heard of such a person."

"Ah, he's something of a recluse. Never makes the news these days." Glossing over her other questions, Michael pointed to the top corner of the page. "I believe I've solved your little mystery. The reason there's no six-digit number is because of the applicant's level. See this copper ribbon? That's Glint's mark, which is necessary to confirm a double-digit rank."

Kimiko glanced at her sisters, then looked to Daddy, who had an odd little smile on his face. Michael was downplaying everything even as he dropped names of vast historical significance. Glint and Waaseyaa had *founded* the In-between.

Michael continued to explain the form. "Here is his overall rank. Sometimes, there will also be a class rating as well, but this particular symbol indicates ... ah." And turning to the corner where their silent security guard stood, he said, "Thank you for your service to the community. Are you looking forward to settling down, Reaver Denholme?"

Every eye swung to Dickon.

He inclined his head. "This is a good place."

Every eye swung to Noriko, only to find she'd set another place at the table. With a patient smile, she said, "Come and sit. You must be hungry."

Dickon accepted, sitting right across from Mama.

No one could fault that Radish-man's courage.

Into the stunned silence, Michael nattered on. "I can't say I'm surprised to find such excellent references and highest recommendations. After all, Dickon is the son of a beacon."

Mama shot her husband a pleading look. "Isn't that really very good?"

"Yes, my dear." Daddy smiled softly and promised, "Only the best for our girls."

After breakfast, Daddy and Mr. Ward spread the local paper and the newly arrived reaver communique on the cleared table. Their expressions brought Kimiko closer. Head tilted to read sideways, she scanned the headlines. Keishi's top story was cause for concern—RUNNING OF THE WOLVES.

"Is it because of the trackers?" asked Mr. Miyabe. "Looking for those missing girls?"

"Their movements have been attracting more attention." Michael touched the communique, which was open to a terse report under a bold heading—UNREGISTERED RISK. "The most recent victim was from a bloodline that lapsed four generations back. The case has crossed over into the public sector."

Kimiko asked, "Why is that a problem?"

"The suspect isn't human." Michael grimaced. "Allegedly."

Both she and her father made the sign for silence. Kimiko added one for support.

Michael's gaze turned inward for a moment. "There go the wards. You have company."

Kimiko hurried to open the door and quickly stepped back to

admit Hisoka Twineshaft. Storm clouds had crept in overnight, slicking the city in icy rain. "Come in!"

He signaled for a compromise. "Get your coat?" he suggested.

She joined him under his umbrella, and he escorted her to one of their house's few blind spots. No matter which window someone might be snooping through, they wouldn't catch sight of the esteemed personage in their garden and insist he come in for tea.

Speaking above the rattle of rain on their umbrella, Hisoka said, "Your betrothed asked me to carry a message. He cannot come in person, since he must abide by his father's wishes. But every courting couple is expected to pass messages. Harmonious cannot criticize."

Kimiko blinked. "Is that your way of telling me I should be sending messages?"

"You're quick." He inclined his head. "The Starmark pack would consider the regular comings and goings of assorted couriers a sure sign of increasing attachment."

"I'll work on that." She adopted a quizzical air. "But you can't have come over just to offer courting tips."

"A go-between's duties may be small and sundry." Hisoka took an offhand tone. "However, I might mention in passing that it's a fine day for a stroll through the azalea garden."

Kimiko flatly stated, "The weather is *terrible*."

He took her hand, pressed the curved handle of the umbrella against her palm, and smiled benignly. "Then I suggest taking shelter with someone willing to keep you warm."

"Matchmaking games and passing notes and having secrets. I think you're enjoying your role a little too much," she accused.

"May the same be said of your role."

He was practically purring, and that made her suspicious.

"The azalea garden," he repeated, giving her a gentle push in the right direction.

When she turned to give back his umbrella, he was already gone.

Kimiko passed between two stone lanterns onto the narrow path that was an alternative route to the azalea garden. It was her habit to take the back ways, leaving the wider paths with their serene views for guests. Not that she needed to bother. Kikusawa had been effectively cut off from the neighborhood while the In-between secured the site.

But this was a neighborhood shrine. The Miyabe family was united in their insistence that they were a necessary part of their community. All Hisoka would say, though, was *soon*.

In the shelter of a gazebo, Eloquence waited beside the Kith who lived with him and Ever. Rise's tail, which had been swaying contentedly, went still. Was that a bad sign? She motioned welcome and peace, joking, "What a strange coincidence, finding you here."

Quen beckoned her into the covered seating area. "Thank you for coming. I wanted you to meet Rise."

"But we've met," she reminded, looking between them.

"Not properly." Eloquence moved to the drooping Kith's side, reaching his arms as far as they'd go around his neck. The big dog's tail gave a tentative wag, then went still again. "Sorry. He's nervous. I guess we both are."

Kimiko gave them a moment by shaking off the umbrella and propping it against a pillar.

Eloquence spoke in low tones. "I count Rise as my brother. We were rarely apart until I started classes at New Saga. If it weren't for Ever, he'd probably have followed me to school every morning."

To her surprise, Rise butted Eloquence with his broad forehead, knocking him flat on his back before flopping on top of him, his broad muzzle covering most of Eloquence's midriff.

He submitted with a low chuckle. "See how he treats me?"

"It's clear who's boss." Kimiko sat on the closest bench. "After all, you belong to the Kith."

"Yes. He says I'm telling things all out of order. And that it's debatable which of us needs minding more—Ever or me." Eloquence stroked Rise's fur. "I'm older than you, you know."

Rise huffed.

"He says, 'Not in dog years.' Which I'll concede is a valid point." Eloquence tipped his head back to search Kimiko's face. "Kith do not go through a lengthy adolescent phase."

"Does Rise have a family, then?"

Eloquence's expression wavered. "No. He could, but he's made a pact to never leave my side."

"Because you and Ever need him," she guessed.

"Because we three are brothers." Eloquence and Rise were both watching her closely.

She was missing something. "Packmates, pactmates ... and denmates, for that matter."

"Kimiko, Rise and I are true brothers."

True brothers. Like a true son. But how did *that* work?

Eloquence's hands formed a rarely-seen sign, one that asked for a pledge of secrecy.

She crossed to him and linked their hands, completing the vow.

"I am my father's son. My parents were both High Amaranthine, and so am I. Ever is my father's son. His mother is human, making him a crosser."

Kimiko's mind was leaping ahead, but she forced herself to listen quietly.

"Rise is my father's son. His mother was a dog." Eloquence gave her a moment to process that before continuing. "This was before I can remember, but Uncle Laud explained that we were part of the Starmark pack at Wardenclave then. Glint Starmark, my grandsire, gave her to my father to keep him from succumbing to grief after my mother's death. Dad kept her close, and in the course of things, she bore him a son."

"You ... you're compatible with animals?"

"In truest form, yes. We don't talk about it with outsiders." Again, he signaled for secrecy. "Reavers have always assumed our Kith to be lesser cousins, somewhere between the High Amaranthine and the Ephemera. But in truth, they are crossers."

Kimiko tried to think how many Kith were attached to the Starmark compound. Dozens? Scores? And all of them had an Amaranthine father ... or mother. "That's a lot of mixed-species couples."

"Not at all. Kith form breeding pairs, and their children are also Kith."

She laughed at herself.

His gaze held sympathy. "In the early days, the first of our kind mingled more with the animals under their protection. My grandsire, First of Dogs, coupled with domesticated canines before settling down. His children by those bitches are the oldest Kith in the dog clans."

"But that doesn't happen anymore?"

Eloquence hesitated. "One of the ten duties given to a tribute is the care and continuance of strong Kith bloodlines. From time to time, a clan may decide to add Kith to their pack or fold. Directly."

"Have you ever …?"

He quickly shook his head. "I'm not a Kith-sire, but some of my uncles are. Since I'll have a bondmate, that particular duty will not fall to me. Honestly, it never would have, for fear I would sire other runts."

"I'm not sure if I should be offended or relieved."

Eloquence smiled. "Either of those are better reactions than we feared."

"Oh, I'm astonished. And trying not to think about how a dog the size of a house could manage to …" She held up a hand and shook her head. "Nope. Not thinking."

Rise barked.

"I am *not* translating that." To Kimiko he said, "I was ten when Dad gave Rise to me. He was just a puppy, and he was my responsibility. That was also the year I began training with my uncles, learning my responsibilities as a tenth child."

"So you've been together almost your whole lives." Kimiko nodded to herself. "And we'll always be together from now on."

Rise's tail thumped the ground.

Still pinned beneath his half-brother, Eloquence said, "He thinks you should kiss me."

She arched her brows at Rise. "Is he putting words in your mouth?"

The tail doubled its speed, and he *wuff*ed.

"Let him up so I can kiss him properly," Kimiko ordered. "We'll call it practice for the next formal declaration."

Rise heaved up and settled on his haunches, freeing Eloquence.

She stood, dusting absently at her breeches. "Do we need to schedule the official kisses according to the moon?"

"I think not. Dogs don't reverence the moon." He slipped into the neutral posture for which diplomats were famous. "Did Hisoka speak with you about recent events?"

"No, but I saw this morning's paper. And he hinted that there was a role I'd need to play."

Eloquence stepped closer, took her hand. "Hisoka Twineshaft is my go-between, and he will always act in our best interest. However, he carries a great responsibility to our people—yours and mine. As Spokesperson and a member of the Five, he's making two requests of us."

"The first?" she prompted.

"In order to distract the media from less savory events … and to appeal to the recent craving for inter-species romances, he would like to make our courtship public."

"*How* public?"

"Very." He smiled faintly. "The next time you kiss me, it would be in front of hundreds of cameras."

Kimiko rolled her eyes toward Rise. "No, the next time I kiss you, it will be in front of your brother."

The dog nosed their joined hands, adding a small lick.

"I'm not opposed to practice kisses," Eloquence said, adopting his demure pose of the night before.

But when she went up on tiptoe to kiss him, he leaned away. "What's this?" he inquired.

"A kiss ...?"

"You have already kissed my lips."

"Once," she said, confused by his teasing tone. "One down, eleven to go."

"My dear suitor, you have declared your intention to fulfill the famed Cycle of Moons, also known as the Lover's Circuit or the Tour of Devotion. Each implies movement."

"Of the moon."

Eloquence shook his head. "I can understand your confusion, but you have misinterpreted the song. The moon bears witness, as does the tree—both are constants. It is the *kisses* that move. Twelve kisses in twelve places, presumably bestowed in increasingly intimate territory."

Kimiko did a quick reconnoiter, adding up places she'd be willing to kiss during what might well be a live, worldwide broadcast. Quite the challenge. And getting the placement and pledge to match up would take a little extra creativity.

She was still tallying on her fingers when Eloquence eased closer. "Rise would like to point out that it's not forbidden for you to touch my lips again. Unofficially."

"Your brother is really looking out for you."

"Pack does." He asked, "Are you willing?"

Kimiko asked, "To kiss you, or to help Hisoka-sensei?"

"Both. Either. Anything."

"Close your eyes," she directed. "And bend a little, so I can reach."

He acquiesced, tipping his head slightly to one side, as if listening for her movements. Perhaps even for the race of her blood or the song of her soul. She rose slowly, hoping to surprise him, and caught the flash of copper under his lashes.

"Peeker," she chided.

When she pressed her lips to his forehead, he hummed encouragement. When she tried to step back, he slid his arms around her and blithely returned the gesture. As his lips lingered, then wandered, it occurred to Kimiko that Hisoka-sensei had been right about Eloquence's willingness to keep her warm.

"Oh." She stopped Eloquence with a finger to his lips. "All right. I can be persuaded to court you in front of cameras, but you didn't say yet. What was Sensei's second request?"

He kissed her finger, her wrist. She placed her hand against his cheek to stop him, and he leaned into her touch, his expression peaceful, then puzzled.

"Something about a ... spokeswife?"

52
REASONS

Tenma woke enough to register brightness against his eyelids. Morning already? Where ...?

Flexing his hands, he met fur instead of bedsheets, a helpful clue. The events of last night filtered back with increasing clarity—his Nightspangle rescuers, Lapis' trust, Argent's arrival, and the urgent command to decamp.

This was the Starmark compound.

Sometime in the darkest hours of the night, he'd been put to bed between two toddlers by Quen's white-haired uncle. Tenma could even remember waking twice. The first time to find Eloquence there, stroking his hair.

"I hear you had an adventurous night."

Taking in his classmate's elaborate costume, Tenma had asked, "Where've *you* been?"

"With my brothers." Plucking at his embroidered finery, he'd huffed. "Oh, and I'm betrothed."

"You're getting married?"

"The Amaranthine equivalent."

Tenma had almost asked about the fiancée, but he didn't really know any other dogs. Quen was the only one in 3-C. Knowing Isla would wheedle all the details out of their partner, he just murmured, "Congratulations."

The second time Tenma woke, a green-haired stranger was shaking his shoulder. "Touch my nose," he'd said.

Odd request. Maybe he was drunk? But then Tenma realized what sort of Amaranthine he was dealing with. Patting the space at his side, he'd mumbled, "Room here if you're cold, dragon-san." And he'd rolled over, pulling his blankets over his head, wishing that dens were quieter, but grateful they weren't ever lonely.

Now, it was hushed, and Tenma knew he was alone. But then the door slid open, and food smells wafted thought. Turning to check, he rolled right into a tackling hug and gladly returned Inti's frantic embrace. "I was so worried about you!"

"Inti is safe."

"That's what the wolves said, but knowing firsthand is better."

"Tenma is wise."

He grumbled, "Tenma is *tired*."

Inti poked his cheek. "Tenma is awake."

"Not yet."

"When?"

Tenma repeated, "Not yet."

Inti quietly fussed with Tenma's hair.

He went limp and let his mind drift back toward sleep, but

411

his stomach growled.

Inti snickered. "Time to get up, Tenma."

And he opened his eyes, mostly because that had sounded like lucid Inti. So that part of the night hadn't been a fear-drenched figment of his imagination?

Sitting up, Tenma surveyed the otherwise empty room while Inti sprang lightly to the door. The crosser swept up the waiting tray and sprang back without rattling so much as a spoon. Tenma uncovered the dishes and started in. Inti joined him, eating with his fingers in the absence of a second pair of chopsticks.

"Did they catch her?" Tenma asked.

"Her?"

"The fox who was chasing us. Well, she was after *you*."

Inti was back to playing dumb. "Why would a fox want a monkey?"

A bland voice came from the direction of the door. "Because he is very clever and very sly. Yet also quite trustworthy."

Tenma gulped and coughed, then wheezed, "Lord Mettlebright."

"I understand you have been a friend to Inti."

"And he's been a friend to me."

"*Such* fast friends, you went so far as to invite him to live with you."

Was there a problem he was missing? All Tenma could do was confirm, "Yes, we're roommates."

"Why?"

"Why not?"

Lord Mettlebright held up a finger. "If you were the usual sort of student, with the perception of pavement, I might accept your answer. But you are an unregistered oddity who reduced a dragon lord to a quivering mess of tears and reckless vows. So I ask again … why Inti?"

Tenma fidgeted. "Is Lapis all right?"

"On a first name basis, are you?"

He blushed and backtracked. "Is Lord Mossberne all right?"

"He is surprisingly well, a state he attributes entirely to you. The mares and Michael are cautiously optimistic." Argent came closer and dropped into a crouch. "And beginning to suspect that Lapis is correct."

"He often is."

Argent's gaze was cool. "I will ask it again, Tenma Subaru. Why did you choose this irascible and incorrigible ingrate?"

"Hey." Tenma didn't like name-calling. "Should a member of the Five be bullying crossers?"

The fox smirked. "Protective of him, are you?"

"He's my friend."

"So you keep saying."

"Because it's true." Tenma knew he was glaring. "What's it to you?"

Argent's tone lost some of its prickle. "I can be protective, too. Which is why I would like to know the reason you are tangling with my apprentice."

Tenma frowned. "Because monkeys tangle. How does it work for foxes? W-wait." His gaze swiveled to Inti. "Apprentice?"

His roommate waved to Argent with both hands, as if making an introduction, and intoned, "Reasons."

For the next several minutes, Tenma listened to a tale so clipped around the edges, he could tell Argent was abridging and censoring. But the basics were enough to communicate the urgency of the situation.

"A rogue dragon." Tenma pushed at his glasses, then removed them to polish the lenses. He put them back and stared at his hands. "That's why Sentinel and the battlers asked us to keep quiet about the kidnappings. Because people might panic if they found out your people aren't all peaceful."

"*Might* panic?" echoed the fox.

Tenma grimaced. "Yeah, they would. Not all of them, but enough to ruin it for the rest of us."

"We are cooperating with criminal investigation teams worldwide. Many of their agents are here in Keishi, working alongside our trackers and the reavers. But the ongoing investigation has been kept from the public."

"Why tell me?"

Argent indicated Inti, whose tail was a firm and familiar presence around Tenma's middle. "We are conducting an independent investigation. One I *expected* to be an exercise in patience, but I did not account for you."

"I didn't do anything."

"It is far too late for denial." Argent frowned. "And thanks to Lapis, I cannot have everything my way."

Tenma looked to Inti. "What did I do?"

"You looked. You listened. You like me."

"We're friends. Why is that so hard for people to imagine?"

Inti's tail tightened. "Tenma, you knew there was a fox."

"So did you."

"That's why we make such a good team." Inti leaned his head against Tenma's shoulder. "I wanted to keep you."

"I'm not going anywhere." Tenma hesitated, then amended, "That I know of. How come you're *not* keeping me?"

"Different reasons." Inti smiled up at him. "You fixed Lord Mossberne last night."

Is that what Argent had meant?

Lord Mettlebright nodded once. "He is no longer one of the Broken."

Tenma remembered the fear, the hope, and the tears. And holding Lapis together when the sobs threatened to shake him apart.

"He is grateful." Argent's eyebrows rose. "And I sincerely doubt you are prepared to deal with a grateful dragon. I recommend appointing a go-between."

"You?"

"Alas, he named me as *his* go-between." He sounded bored. "I cannot recommend Harmonious, who is too trusting. And Twineshaft is currently preoccupied by his responsibilities as Eloquence's go-between."

Tenma glanced at Inti, who quickly hid his eyes. "Not here. Not me."

"Is there someone you trust?" asked the fox.

"Quen."

"Someone *not* currently in the throes of romantic entanglement?"

"Why do I need a go-between?" Tenma asked. "Can't I forgo their services and represent myself?"

"Ignorance is a poor ally." Argent's eyes glittered. "Unless you *want* to be added to Lord Mossberne's harem as the East Bride."

"Wh-what?"

"There are only so many ways a dragon can add an outsider to his household."

Tenma held up both hands and shouted, "Isla! I want to be represented by Isla Ward!"

Argent pondered him for a moment, then nodded. "She would serve you well. If any complications arise, she has Twineshaft's ear. And as an added bonus, my affection for her will curb any temptation to resort to … bullying."

"You and Isla are both from Stately House." Tenma nudged his roommate. "If you're his apprentice, why didn't Isla or Akira know you?"

"Never been. Never seen. Never knew." More plainly, he added, "I came straight to New Saga."

Tenma thought back. "From a temple?"

Inti's expression closed.

Argent sighed. "It was more of a lab."

53

FLASHBULBS

As the single peal of the shrine's bell began to fade, Eloquence took a deep breath and stepped out from behind a shimmering privacy screen, doing his best not to flinch at the sudden explosion of flashbulbs. With quiet deliberation, he moved along the petal-strewn path that curved along the edge of the audience before eventually returning him to the relative privacy of the silken tent at Kusunoki's base.

The ceremony hadn't truly begun yet, and the gathered crowd kept up a steady buzz. He'd made this circuit twice already. Not until the fourth would Kimiko appear to "catch" him and lead him to the low dais prepared for the pledge.

At the point nearest the main gate, broadcast booths lined the central walkway, where festival booths were normally arranged. Quen could hear interviews underway in several languages.

" ... switching over to Reaver Lin Waller, who can explain for us the distinctions between the wolf and dog ..."

" ... delighted to be speaking with Merit Starmark, another of Harmonious' sons ..."

" ... that the bridal circuit is a wolvish tradition, meant to emulate the moon's path ..."

" ... understandable comparisons to a royal wedding. But the Amaranthine don't have ..."

"... to be cast in the role of suitor, which has endeared Kimiko to ..."

" ... not a wedding, per se. Her spokesperson Suuzu Farroost confirms a three-year courtship, culminating ..."

Three years. Eloquence lifted his face into the gentle drift of petals. Kusunoki had indeed bloomed, shocking them all with a profusion of tiny red flowers.

Shutters clicked on every side, and Eloquence realized he'd been smiling. Fodder for the surprising number of fans Kimiko's courtship had already gained. Her popularity was on the rise, and Hisoka couldn't have been more pleased.

The howl of trackers had been recast as the celebration of dogs.

The rogue had fled before the saint's fury, an unsolved mystery.

The shrine now served as an international stage, with Kimiko in the lead role.

Quen knew she could handle herself, but he would feel better once he could see her again. Kimiko was off with Laud and Ever, who'd wanted to see the dragons at the front gate. Surely they'd return soon. He hadn't seen her since changing into today's costume, and he was ... self-conscious.

Kimiko's intentions for her next pledge—and the placement of its attendant kiss—had come by messenger, setting off an excited din in the Starmark compound. At Hisoka Twineshaft's suggestion, Harmonious had opened up an entire wing of one pavilion to a team of designers, seamstresses, and tailors so that his maiden son could carry the pride of his clan in fine style.

The cut of today's ensemble was unusual for a dog. Clothing was one of the small ways in which they'd set themselves apart from their wolvish relations. Where the wolf packs ran barefoot, the dog clans wore boots. And while wolves thought nothing of showing skin, dogs held to a tradition of modesty.

Over gathered pants, patterned scarves bound Quen from hip to midriff, and an open vest left his chest bare. To give Kimiko access.

He completed his circuit and hid in the warded tent. His future bondmate might flourish in the limelight, but he liked nothing better than to steal away with her and coax for time and talk and casual touches.

Rise greeted him with a soft whine. *You are anxious.*

"I want to make a good impression."

She will be pleased.

Eloquence leaned into Rise and mumbled, "That would make me happy."

Be happy.

The Kith's head swiveled, ears lifting. Moments later, Kimiko burst into the tent, all smiles. "This worked perfectly!" she exclaimed, showing off one of the clay seals Goh-sensei had fired for them. "No one even noticed us. We probably could have tickled Sinder's whiskers and gotten away with it!"

Whether it was meant as a show of strength, a sign of good

fortune, or a plain old publicity stunt, Lapis and Sinder had taken up positions on either side of Kikusawa's stairs. In true form.

"Bruvver, hims a *green* dragon. Not like Laps."

Quen went to pick up his little representative, but Uncle Laud intervened, settling the boy on his broad shoulders. They were all under orders not to besmirch their finery. Laud quietly said, "You two should practice."

Kimiko's lips twitched. "That's usually Rise's line."

Rise *wuff*ed.

Laud wrapped his hands around Ever's ankles. "What do you think, pup?"

"Bruvver likes kisses."

Eloquence wasn't about to pass up a chance to kiss Kimiko. "I am willing."

Her expression softened. "So am I."

He awaited her touch, trying not to think too hard about where this kiss would land. He was learning Kimiko's ways—fond and flirtatious, always coaxing for a smile. She took hold of his braid, wrapping it around her hand in order to draw him close enough to deliver a small peck on the tip of his nose.

This gambit earned the pup's appreciative applause.

Quen asked, "What do you think, Ever? Was that a good kiss?"

"Silly!"

"You don't think courtship can be silly?" asked Kimiko.

The little boy shook his head. "Bruvver's growed up."

Eloquence said, "I think I should be allowed to have fun, even when I'm grown."

"Bruvver's growed up," insisted Ever. "Tained and troved."

"But I'm still your Quen."

Ever took interest in the decoration on the front of his tunic. In a small voice, he said, "Quen is for Kimi."

This time, when he reached for his little brother, Laud yielded.

Quen lifted him high, swung him low, and tickled the pup until he gasped and squirmed. Only when the wag was back in Ever's tail did Eloquence firmly state, "I have reached my attainment, and I am betrothed. *And* I am still your Quen."

"My bruvver." And more cautiously, "My Quen?"

It was the first time the boy had called him by name, and it seemed both a gift and a promise. His pup would always need him, even if the ways changed. "Always and ever," Eloquence promised.

Ever took hold of Eloquence's braid with both hands and pulled. When Quen leaned in, his brother kissed his nose. "Luff you, Quen."

Just before Eloquence was to leave the tent for his final circuit of the courtyard, he stood with Kimiko, shoulder to shoulder, hands clasped. All his senses told him she was pleased and present, embracing the noise and the excitement. "What are you thinking?" he asked.

"Savoring the moment." Kimiko rubbed the side of her face. "And wondering if Junzi will release a special line of chocolate bars to celebrate our wedding."

He chuckled.

"And another thing." Her sidelong look had a speculative quality. Crooking her fingers to bring him nearer, she whispered in his ear. "I've been wanting to ask, and I seem to have you to myself for the moment."

"For the moment," he agreed.

"If my pledges are supposed to lead into increasingly intimate territory, where is my final kiss supposed to land?"

Quen managed to answer evenly. "My blaze."

Kimiko's fingers settled on his bare chest. "And where do you keep that?"

His heart had begun to hammer. "I'm sure you'll find it if you look hard enough."

"Would the uncovering of blazes count as courting behavior?"

"Definitely." And while they were near enough to the matter, he said, "I have also been wondering. The placement of today's kiss ... who chose it?"

"I did."

Kimiko's message had asked him to prepare for a kiss upon his chest, right over his heart.

Eloquence chose his words with care, not wanting to presume. "Traditionally, that placement carries a certain significance."

Her whole posture was confident confirmation. "Like a pudding please."

That wasn't quite what he expected. "In what sense."

"With a kiss *here*." Once again, her fingers rested lightly on his skin. "The suitor makes a rather brazen request. Not for concessions or connections, peace or promises. But for a place in their beloved's affections."

422

Quen covered her hand. "Are you quoting lore when you call me beloved?"

Kimiko turned the question around on him. "Is it true, what the fables say about wolves and kisses?"

"I'm not a wolf."

"I still think we could put tradition to the test." Her posture relaxed into one of easy camaraderie. "In a few more minutes, you'll go, and I'll follow. And once I catch you, the whole world will hear my pledge. But you are the only one who'll feel my touch."

Anticipation stirred him into a more dominant stance.

"And according to wolvish tradition, a kiss can't lie." Kimiko reached up to pluck tiny red petals from his hair. "So when I do, you'll know the truth."

With an impatient growl, he pressed his forehead to hers. "Don't make me wait, Kimiko."

Her lips were light and didn't linger, but they told the truth. And finding himself cherished, Eloquence Starmark found he couldn't speak. So he bandied about some of the gestures she dearly loved, ones used by courting canines—*may the stars find us trysting, a kiss for every flower, rise and I will follow*, and a subtle cue that simply meant, *more, yes, more.*

Kimiko not only followed his little demonstration, she responded in a similar vein—*share my flight, your beauty rivals the dawning, my heart is at full gallop*, and a return of his own plea, *more, yes, more.*

He chuckled.

She beamed.

The bell tolled, and as its note reverberated, Kimiko caught his sleeve. "Go, so I can follow."

Quen bowed over her hand, brushing his lips across her knuckles. "Come and claim your place."

54

SOMETHING BLUE

Akira's feet dragged along the dormitory hall. "*How many more times do we have to do this?*" he groaned.

"Ten pledges remain." Suuzu frowned and evicted a red flower petal from his nestmate's hair. "The next phase of their courtship is not scheduled until summer's end."

Akira had spent the whole day alongside Argent and Gingko, standing in for his sister. That's why he was garbed from head to toe in Mettlebright colors—icy blue edged in frostlike embroidery—and marked by the crests of both Argent Mettlebright and Stately House.

Suuzu waited patiently as Akira patted through unfamiliar pockets for his set of keys.

Even though he radiated weariness, Akira smiled softly. "Quen and Kimi seemed happy."

"Yes." Because Suuzu was watching, he saw the sudden change in Akira's expression. "Hmm?"

"Nothing. Well, it's *something*, but ... sort of a secret."

Keeping secrets? That was a first. Whatever was in Akira's pocket, it had wiped away his weariness. Suuzu was puzzled by the sudden hurrying of his nestmate's pulse and the warming of his cheeks.

"Found the keys," Akira mumbled, opening the door.

Suuzu merely hummed again and followed him inside.

Once behind wards, Akira raised his hand, as if asking to address a classroom. "I have something for you. It's usually really hard to hide things from you, but you didn't notice I was up to anything."

He felt the need to apologize. "I have been preoccupied with Kimi's needs and the demands of the ...."

Akira shook his head. "No big deal. It worked out because it'll be fun to surprise you. I hope."

Suuzu searched his memory for any hint of scheming, but he truly had not noticed anything out of the ordinary. He was ashamed to have been so inattentive.

"Hey." Akira touched his arm and offered a tired smile. "Let's clean up. I want to be preened for this."

"You need sleep."

"No kidding. But I won't be able to sleep until I do this." Akira was already pulling off the fancy outer tunic. "Most of the gift has been ready for a while, but I was waiting for one last thing. Got it today from Argent. He was cool about it, promised not to tell anyone."

Suuzu obediently kept his gaze averted while Akira hid the contents of his pocket under the discarded tunic, even resisting the urge to tidy the rumpled garment. Their evening patterns were perfunctory at best, with Akira nearly falling asleep in the bath.

Back in their room, Suuzu pulled out their futons and bedding, swiftly assembling their usual nest. "I can be patient. You should rest."

Akira only shook his head and sat cross-legged atop their blankets.

With a soft trill of concern, Suuzu joined him.

"For you." Akira held out an empty palm.

Suuzu cocked his head to one side, unsure how to interpret the gesture.

"Oh, sorry. Hang on." Akira poked and prodded, and with a soft pop, a ward vanished, revealing a small wooden box that still bore a tracery of seals. "Boon did that part. Pretty neat, huh? You never knew it was here."

"I did not." This gift was becoming more elaborate and more mysterious by the moment.

Suuzu accepted the box, teasing away an additional seal and lifting the catch. A neat braid coiled within, and he was picking up the faint presence of tuned crystals. Recognition pulled a soft warble of surprise from him.

Akira pushed up onto his knees. "I went ahead and started on our nest."

The box's contents mostly smelled like Akira, but there were hints of others' handiwork. He lifted the slender black cord and whispered, "Juuyu?"

"His hair." Pointing to a russet crystal, Akira added, "This one's tuned to him. I got it from one of his teammates. Can you really tell where he is?"

Suuzu immediately pointed to the west.

"Nice!" He scooted closer, their knees touching. "Tuning one to me was trickier, since I'm not a reaver. But Michael worked it out. See?" From the bottom of the box, Akira brought a second black cord, which he quickly looped around his ankle, settling a smooth, milky blue stone against his skin. "This cord's made from Sis' hair, and your crystal's tuned to mine."

Suuzu caressed the blue stone knotted into his necklace.

Akira bounded up and crossed to the closet, ducking inside. He called, "Does it work?"

"I know where you are."

He leaned out. "I know, but does it work?"

Suuzu smiled and waved for him to come back. Belatedly fussing with Akira's half-dry hair, he said, "I always know where you are."

"You do?"

"Hmm."

Akira narrowed his eyes skeptically. "How's that possible?"

Suuzu brushed his knuckles along Akira's cheek. "Homing instinct."

His nestmate's eyes softened.

Taking a formal tone, Suuzu said, "I will wear your tokens. We will build our nest. My songs will all and always be for you."

Akira lowered his gaze and fidgeted.

For a moment, Suuzu feared he had crossed a line. His nestmate was not looking for pledges.

But Akira shyly said, "I have one other thing to add, but I held it back since it would have been the bad kind of surprise." He slipped his hand into the pocket of his pajama pants and brought out a folded blue envelope that glittered with sigils. "I really wanted you to have this, but ... just ... it's *empty*, okay?"

Suuzu accepted the second gift. At his touch, the seals vanished, proof of Argent's skill. Slitting the paper with a claw, Suuzu tipped the contents into his palm. Etched leaves twined around the slender rod of metal, which was capped with a green stone.

"It's a reliquary, just like the one Sinder had, just like the ones in Kikusawa's treasury." Akira took it from his palm and showed him the trick to opening its tiny panel. "I was thinking it would be good to add this to our nest. I mean, I know it's empty, but it *exists*."

Suuzu didn't trust his voice.

Akira quietly said, "And since it exists, we can hope."

With a fluttering exhale and a broken sob, Suuzu pulled Akira close and hid his face against his shoulder. His nestmate's fingers were in his hair, making a mess as surely as he disarranged his composure.

"Hey, it's okay. I'm not going anywhere."

Suuzu's voice came out muffled. "You are mine."

"I know."

He lifted his face, needing Akira to understand. "I want to find a way."

"I know."

His eyes slammed shut. "Akira ...."

"I know." He pulled the phoenix's head back onto his shoulder and held on tight. "Suuzu, I get it, okay? I know."

And that had to be enough. For now.

THE END

never more than
FORTHRIGHT

a teller of tales who began as a fandom ficcer. (Which basically means that no one in RL knows about her anime habit, her manga collection, or her penchant for serial storytelling.) Kinda sorta almost famous for gently-paced, WAFFy adventures that might inadvertently overturn your OTP, forthy will forever adore drabble challenges, surprise fanart, and twinkles (which are rumored to keep well in jars). As always... be nice, play fair, have fun! ::twinkle::

FORTHWRITES.COM

In doing her part for world peace, she puts one crosser's whole world at risk.

Conspiracy theories, werewolf scares, and protest rallies have hampered the peace process in America, where social and political unrest keep most Amaranthine from declaring themselves. Those not in seclusion rely heavily on illusion to mask their true nature.

As the newly appointed principal of a small elementary school, Tamiko Reaverson is doing her part for world peace. She rallies her community's support and applies for Hisoka Twineshaft's school revitalization project, which will bring Amaranthine to her hometown. Little does Tami realize that Fletching was founded by one of the oldest and largest urban enclaves in the United States. And two of her staunchest supporters—janitors at her school—share a secret neither wants exposed.